THE UNRAVELING

BENJAMIN ROSENBAUM

EREWHON

THE UNRAVELING
Copyright © 2021 by Benjamin Rosenbaum

First published in North America and Canada by Erewhon Books, LLC in 2021

Edited by Liz Gorinsky

Erewhon Books
2 W. 29th Street, Suite 3S
New York, NY 10001
www.erewhonbooks.com

Erewhon books are available at special discounts when purchased in bulk for premiums and sales promotions as well as for fund-raising or educational use. Special editions or book excerpts can also be created to specification. For details, send an email to specialmarkets@workman.com.

Library of Congress Control Number: 2019956226

ISBN 978-1-64566-001-9 (hardcover)
ISBN 978-1-64566-006-4 (ebook)

Cover art by Minah Kim
Cover text design by Dana Li
Interior design by Liz Gorinsky
Chapter header icon adapted from Molecule by Kylie Hana and Carbon rings by Ben Davis from the Noun Project
Dispersal of humanity chart by Cassandra Farrin

Printed in the United States of America

First US Edition: May 2021
10 9 8 7 6 5 4 3 2 1

To Aviva and Noah: the spoon is in your hand!

To Esther, my delight and my Sheltering.

*And to the former denizens of the Maelstrom,
our own little Unraveling.*

BEGIN DOCUMENT

TRANSMISSION

DOCUMENT CONTENTS

Document prepared, translated, and transmit-
ted during the year 467,341 After Dispersal
(standard origin coordinate time)

Extent of the Dispersal of Humanity

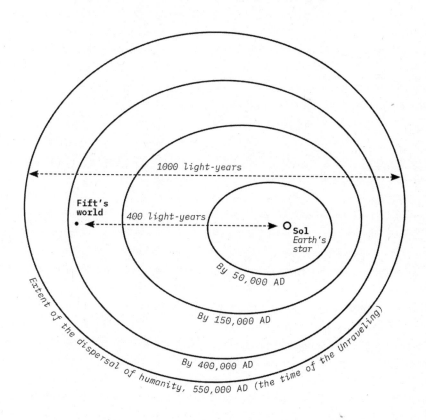

1000 light-years

Fift's world

400 light-years

O Sol
Earth's star

By 50,000 AD

By 150,000 AD

By 400,000 AD

Extent of the dispersal of humanity, 550,000 AD (the time of the Unraveling)

The world runs on pride.

The heart of the world is its economy, and its economy is an economy of the heart. Every encounter is a transaction: a tiny battle, in which something is seized, and something is lost.

The one who loses, who is cast out, we call: Older Sibling.

The one who wins, who nestles in, we call: Younger Sibling.

Across genders (it is so for every Staid, as ze sits quietly at the center of things, composing zirself . . . for every Vail, as ve sallies forth, vir heart full of rage or joy!); across nations; across name registries, social clusters, professions, religions (Kumruist, Tricksterian, Unfeeling, Groon, Ascensionist, Diversionist . . .); though some revile it, some deny it, some seek to evade it, or at least clothe it in a decorous subtlety, the fact remains: the heartbeat of the world is the heartbeat of struggle.

The heart is the heart of the Sibling. And every contest hearkens back to that first contest, over the love of the Parent, when Younger displaced Older.

—Omolo, student of Melihor, in the second excursus of the ninth work of the third cycle of the Long Conversation

BOOK ONE

FIRST CHILDHOOD

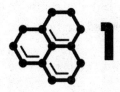 1

Fift was almost five, and it wasn't like zir to be asleep in all of zir bodies. Ze wasn't a baby anymore; ze was old enough for school, old enough to walk all alone across the habitation, down the spoke to the great and buzzing center of Foo. But ze had been wound up with excitement for days, practically dancing around the house. (Father Miskisk had laughed; Father Smistria had shooed zir out of the supper garden; Father Frill had taken zir to the bathing room to swim back and forth, back and forth, "to calm zir down!") Just before supper ze'd finally collapsed, twice: in the atrium, and curled up on the tiered balcony. Father Arevio and Father Squell had carried zir, in those two bodies, back to zir room. Ze'd managed to stay awake in zir third body through most of supper, blinking hugely, breathing in through zir nose, and trying to sit up straight as waves of deep blue slumber from zir two sleeping brains washed through zir. By supper's end, ze couldn't stand up any longer, and Father Squell carried zir last body to bed.

Muddy dreams: of sitting on a wooden floor in a long hall . . . of zir name being called . . . of realizing ze hadn't worn zir gowns after all, but was somehow—humiliatingly—dressed in Father Frill's golden bells instead. The other children laughing at zir, and dizziness, and suddenly, surreally, the hall being full of flutterbyes, their translucent wings fluttering, their projection surfaces glittering . . .

Then someone was stroking Fift's eyebrow, gently. Ze tried to nestle further down into the blankets, but the someone started gently pulling on zir earlobe. Ze opened zir eyes, and it was Father Squell.

"Good morning, little cubblehedge," ve said. "You have a big day today."

Father Squell was slim and rosy-skinned and smelled like soap and flowers. Fift crawled into Squell's lap and flung zir arms around vem and pressed zir nose between vir bosoms. Ve was dressed in glittery red fabric, soft and slippery under Fift's fingers.

Squell was bald, with coppery metal spikes extruding from the skin of vir scalp. Sometimes Father Frill teased vir about the spikes, which weren't fashionable anymore; and sometimes that made Father Squell storm out of the room, because ve was a little vain. Father Squell had never been much of a fighter, the other Fathers said. But ve had a body in the asteroids, and that was something amazing.

Squell reached over, Fift still in vir lap, and started stroking the eyebrow of another of Fift's bodies. Fift sneezed in that body, and then sneezed in the other two. That was funny, and ze started to giggle. Now ze was all awake.

"Up, little cubblehedge," Squell said. "Up!"

Fift crawled out of bed, careful not to crawl over zirself. It always made zir a little restless to be all together, all three bodies in the same room. That wasn't good; it was because zir somatic integration wasn't totally successful, which is why ze kept having to see Pedagogical Expert Pnim Moralasic Foundelly of name registry Pneumatic Lance 12. Pedagogical Expert Pnim Moralasic Foundelly had put an awful nag agent in Fift's mind, to tell zir to look zirself in the eye, and play in a coordinated manner, and do the exercises. It was nagging now, but Fift ignored it.

Ze looked under the bed for zir gowns. They weren't there.

Fift closed zir eyes—ze wasn't so good at using the feed with them open yet—and looked all over the house. The gowns weren't in the balcony or the atrium or the small mat room or the breakfast room.

Fathers Arevio, Smistria, Frill, and another of Father Squell's bodies were in the breakfast room, already eating. Father Miskisk was arguing with the kitchen.

{Where are my gowns?} Fift asked zir agents . . . but the agents didn't say anything. Maybe ze was doing it wrong somehow.

"Father Squell," ze said, opening zir eyes, "I can't find my gowns, and my agents can't either."

"I composted your gowns. They were old," Squell said. "Go down to the bathing room and get washed. I'll make you some new clothes."

Fift's hearts began to pound. The gowns weren't old; they only came out of the oven a week ago. "But I want *those* gowns," ze said.

Squell opened the door. "You can't have those gowns. Those gowns are compost. Bathing!" Ve snatched Fift up, one of zir bodies under vir arm, the wrist of another caught in vir other hand.

Fift was up in the air, wriggling, and was held by the arm, pulling against Squell's grip, and was on zir hands and knees by the bed, looking desperately under it for zir gowns. "They weren't old," ze said, zir voice wavering.

"Fift," Squell said, exasperated. "That's enough. For Kumru's sake, today of all days!" Ve dragged Fift, or as much of Fift as ve'd managed to get ahold of, out the door. Another of

Squell's bodies—this one with silvery spikes on its head—came hurrying down the hall.

"I want them back," Fift said. Ze wouldn't cry. Ze wasn't a baby anymore; ze was a big staidchild, and Staids don't cry. Ze wouldn't cry. Ze wouldn't even shout or emphasize. Today of all days, ze would stay calm and clear. Ze was still struggling a little in Squell's arms, so Squell handed the struggling body off to vemself as ve came in the door.

"They are *compost*," Squell said, reddening, in the body with the silver spikes, while the one with the copper spikes came into the room. "They have gone down the sluice and *dissolved*. Your gowns are now part of the nutrient flow. They could be anywhere in Fullbelly. They will probably be part of your *breakfast* next week!"

Fift gasped. Ze didn't want to eat zir gowns. There was a cold lump in zir stomach.

Squell caught zir third body.

Father Miskisk came down the corridor doublebodied. Ve was bigger than Squell, broad-chested and square-jawed, with a mane of blood-red hair and sunset-orange skin traced all over with white squiggles. Miskisk was wearing dancing pants. Vir voice was deep and rumbly, and ve smelled warm, roasty, and oily. "Fift, little Fift," ve said, "Come on, let's zoom around. I'll zoom you to the bathing room. Come jump up. Give zir here, Squell."

"I want my gowns," Fift said, in zir third body, as Squell dragged zir through the doorway.

"Here," Squell said, trying to hand Fift's other bodies to Miskisk. But Fift clung to Squell. Ze didn't want to zoom right now. Zooming was fun, but too wild for this day, and too wild for someone who had lost zir gowns. The gowns were a pale blue, soft as clouds. They'd whispered around Fift's legs when ze ran.

"Oh, Fift, *please!*" Squell said. "You *must* bathe, and you will *not* be late today! Today of all—"

"Is ze really ready for this, do you think?" Miskisk said, trying to pry Fift away from Squell, but flinching back from prying hard enough.

"Oh please, Misk," Squell said. "Let's not start that. Or not with *me*. Pip says—"

Father Smistria stuck vir head out the door of the studio. "Why are you two winding the child up?" ve barked. Ve was tall and haggard looking and had brilliant blue skin and a white beard worn in hundreds of tiny braids woven with little glittering mirrors and jewels. Ve was wearing a slick swirling combat suit that clung to vir skinny flat chest. Vir voice was higher than Father Miskisk's, squeaky and gravelly at the same time. "This is going to be a *disaster*, if you give zir the impression that this is a day for racing about! Fift, you will stop this *now!*"

"Come on, Fift," Miskisk said coaxingly.

"Put zir *down*," Smistria said. "I cannot believe you are wrestling and flying about with a staidchild who in less than three hours—"

"Oh, give it a rest, Smi," Miskisk said, sort of threateny. Ve turned away from Fift and Squell and towards Smistria. Smistria stepped fully out into the corridor, putting vir face next to Miskisk's. It got like thunder between them, but Fift knew they wouldn't hit each other. Grown-up Vails only hit each other on the mats. Still, ze hugged Squell closer—one body squished against vir soft chest, one body hugging Squell's leg, one body pulling back through the doorway—squeezed all zir eyes shut, and dimmed the house feed so ze couldn't see that way either.

Behind zir eyes Fift could only see the pale blue gowns. It was just like in zir dream! Ze'd lost zir gowns, and would have to go wearing bells like Father Frill! Ze shuddered. "I don't want my gowns to be in the compost," ze said, as reasonably as ze could manage.

"Oh, will you shut up about the gowns!" Squell said. "No one cares about your gowns!"

"That's not true," Miskisk boomed, shocked.

"It *is* true," Smistria said, "and—"

Fift could feel a sob ballooning inside. Ze tried to hold it in, but it grew and grew and—

"Beloveds," said Father Grobbard.

Fift opened zir eyes. Father Grobbard had come silently, singlebodied, up the corridor, to stand behind Squell. Ze was shorter than Miskisk and Smistria, the same height as Squell, but more solid: broad and flat like a stone. When Father Grobbard stood still, it looked like ze would never move again. Zir shift was plain and simple and white. Zir skin was a mottled creamy brown with the same fine golden fuzz of hair everywhere, even on top of zir head.

"Grobby!" Squell said. "We are *trying* to get zir ready, but it's quite—"

"Well, it's Grobbard's show," Smistria said. "It's up to you and Pip today, Grobbard, isn't it? So why don't *you* get zir ready!?"

Grobbard held out zir hand. Fift swallowed, then slid down from Squell's arms and went to take it.

"Grobbard," Miskisk said, "are you sure Fift is ready for this? Is it really—"

"Yes," Grobbard said. Then ze looked at Miskisk, zir face as calm as ever. Ze raised one eyebrow, just a little, then looked back at Fift's other bodies. Ze held out zir other hand. Squell let go and Fift gathered zirself, holding one of Father Grobbard's hands on one side, one on the other, and catching hold of the back of Grobbard's shift. They went down to the bathing room.

"My gowns weren't old," Fift said, on the stairs. "They came out of the oven a week ago."

"No, they weren't old," Grobbard said. "But they were blue. Blue is a Vail color, the color of the crashing, restless sea. You are a Staid, and today you will enter the First Gate of Logic. You couldn't do that wearing blue gowns."

"Oh," Fift said.

Grobbard sat by the side of the bathing pool, zir hands in zir lap, zir legs in the water, while Fift scrubbed zirself soapy.

"Father Grobbard," Fift said, "why are you a Father?"

"What do you mean?" Father Grobbard asked. "I am your Father, Fift. You are my child."

"But why aren't you a Mother? Mother Pip is a Mother, and ze's—um, you're both—"

Grobbard's forehead wrinkled briefly, then it smoothed, and zir lips quirked in a tiny suggestion of a smile. "Aha, I see. Because you have only one Staid Father and the rest are Vails, you think that being a Father is a vailish thing to be? You think Fathers should be 've's and Mothers should be 'ze's?"

Fift stopped mid-scrub and frowned.

"What about your friends? Are all of your friends' Mothers Staids? Are they all 'ze'? Or are some of them 've'?" Grobbard paused a moment; then, gently: "What about your friend Umlish Mnemu, of Mnathis cohort? Isn't zir Mother a Vail?"

"Oh," Fift said, and frowned again. "Well, what makes someone a Mother?"

"Your Mother carried you in zir womb, Fift. You grew inside zir belly, and you were born out of zir vagina, into the world. Some families don't have children that way, so in some families all the parents are Fathers. But we are quite traditional. Indeed, we are all Kumruists, except for Father Thurm . . . and Kumruists believe that biological birth is sacred. So you have a Mother."

Fift knew that, though it still seemed strange. Ze'd been *inside* Mother Pip for ten months. Singlebodied, because zir other two bodies hadn't been fashioned yet. That was an eerie thought. Tiny, helpless, one-bodied, unbreathing, zir nut-sized heart drawing nutrients from Pip's blood. "Why did Pip get to be my Mother?"

Now Grobbard was clearly smiling. "Have you ever tried to refuse your Mother Pip anything?"

Fift shook zir heads solemnly. "It doesn't work. Ze's always the Younger Sibling." That meant the one who won the argument. But it also meant the littlest child, if there was more than one in a family. Fift wasn't sure why it meant both those things.

Grobbard chuckled. "Yes. There was a little bit of debate, but I think we all knew Pip would prevail. Ze had a uterus and vagina enabled and made sure we all had penises for the impregnation. It was an exciting time."

Fift pulled up the feed and looked up penises. They were for squirting sperm, which helped decide what the baby would be like. The egg could sort through all the sperm and pick the genes it wanted, but the parents had to publish something or other to get the genome approved, and after that it got too complicated. If someone got a penis they'd have one on each body, dangling between their legs. "Do you still have penises? One . . . on each body?"

"Yes, I kept mine," Grobbard said. "They went well with the rest of me, and I don't like too many changes."

"Can I have penises?" ze said.

"I suppose, if you like," Grobbard said. "But not today. Today you have something more important to do. And now I see that your Father has baked you new clothes. So rinse off, and let's go upstairs."

"Obviously I'm not talking about the *details* of the . . . process," Father Smistria said, flinging vir arms wide.

"I should hope *not*," Father Squell said. "Hold still, Fift!" Ve gripped Fift's head firmly between one pair of hands and stooped over zir in another body to gently scrape away the last of zir hairs with the depilator. "It's *completely* inappropriate to discuss it at all, Smistria. It's a Staid matter, and that's all there is—"

"I'm not *discussing* it," Smistria said. Ve squirted oil onto vir palm and rubbed it into another of Fift's scalps. "I certainly don't want to know anything about what goes *on* in that room, for Kumru's sake."

"I should *hope* not!" Father Squell said.

Fift was in bright white shifts, like Father Grobbard always wore, and Mother Pip mostly did. All of zir was scrubbed and polished, one of zir heads was already shaved and oiled, and zir fingernails and toenails were trimmed. In the body that was already done, ze got up from the wiggly seating dome and wandered across the moss of the little atrium.

"Fift, don't go anywhere, and don't get dirty," Father Squell said.

"But what *does* matter is the *outcome*," Smistria said. "The *outcome* affects our entire cohort!"

Father Frill—lithe and dusky-skinned with a shock of stiff copper-colored hair sweeping up from vir broad forehead, wide gray eyes, a full mouth, and a sharp chin—swept into the room. "Kumru's whiskers, Smi," Frill said, "is that really what you're wearing?"

"What's wrong with it?" Father Smistria snapped, looking down at vemself. Ve'd changed out of vir combat suit into a tight sheath made of silvery blobs that flowed and split and swelled and shivered when ve moved.

As ze passed Fift's waiting body, Father Frill bent down and ran a hand over zir bare oiled scalp (which felt nice, but also strange, like a layer had been stripped away and there was nothing between zir and the world). Frill wore cascades of gold, silver, and crimson bells that tinkled as ve moved. Vir martial shoulder sash hung with tiny, intricately worked ceremonial knives and grenades. "For one thing, Smi, it makes your potbelly look like a newly discovered high-albedo moon," Frill said. "For another, it's basically *gray*."

"It's *silver*!" Smistria shouted.

"Oh, please, you two," Squell said, straightening up. Now all Fift's heads were shaved. Squell closed the depilator. "Smistria, come on, just one more scalp to oil . . ."

"You take that back about the *moon*," Smistria said, "or you'll answer for it on the mats!"

"No doubt," Frill said, "but not *this* morning, because we have somewhere to be. Seriously, Smi, are you thinking at *all* of what's at stake here? I'll do the oil, you go change. Into something colorful!"

Smistria stormed out and Fift followed vem in the two bodies that were ready. In zir third body, ze was still stuck in the atrium with Frill and Squell. Frill was massaging oil into zir scalp; vir hands were smaller and smoother than Smistria's, and ve smelled like a sharp-toothed wild hunting animal from some forest far above them, up on the surface of the world.

"I'll give vem a high-albedo moon," Smistria muttered as they passed the supper garden. "Arevio! Do you know what time it is? Are you planning to attend this affair with your hands covered in dirt?"

Father Arevio, doublebodied, started guiltily up from vir plants. "Well, in fact, Smistria Ishteni, I was thinking of going singlebodied . . . I'm already dressed upstairs, and . . ."

"Oh no. Oh no. If *I* am going doublebodied to this . . . this void-blessed *sit-about*," Smistria growled, "then by *Kumru's sainted balls* you are doing the same." Father Smistria only had two bodies, like Father Nupolo—all Fift's other parents had three or four—and Smistria hated going anywhere in both of them.

Fift lingered by Smistria's side in one body and went ahead down the hall in another. Back on the wiggly seating dome, ze dug zir toes in the moss, and Frill said, "Almost done, Fift. Don't fidget."

Father Arevio sighed, brushing off vir hands. "All right. I'll change. I must admit, I am not terribly fond of these affairs."

Smistria snorted. "Who is? *We* have to sit outside in the gallery, cooped up, gawking at each other's outfits and taking offense—I swear, more mat challenges are issued at First Gates of Logic than any other time!—while *they* pass spoons and . . . well, *whatever* it is that they do in there . . ."

"It's easy, Father Smistria," Fift said. "All you have to do is . . ."

"Fift Brulio Iraxis!" Arevio said, coming forward.

"You stop right there, Fift!" Father Smistria said. "Do not say *one word* to us about the . . . about that."

Fift swallowed. Ze must have looked scared because Father Arevio said gently, "it's all right, Fift Brulio."

"But it's nothing bad," Fift said.

"Of course it's not bad," Father Arevio said.

"Obviously!" Father Smistria said. "But you don't talk about it with *us*."

"Don't let your Father Smistria worry you, Fiftling," Father Frill said, in the little atrium, rubbing Fift's head. "There's nothing at all wrong with *the Long Conversation*." Ve said the words with emphasis, like ve was showing that ve wasn't embarrassed to say it out loud. "It's very important. It's at the heart of everything. And you're going to be just fine. It's just that Staid things are Staid things and Vail things are Vail things. You wouldn't want to watch us fight on the mats, would you?"

"No." Fift didn't like the idea of zir parents angry and hitting. The mats sounded scary and strange. On the other hand . . . what if ze could sneak in and watch, with no one knowing? Just to see. Ze probably would. Still, 'no' was definitely the right answer.

"Well there you are," Frill said. "It's the same sort of thing."

Arevio and Smistria went upstairs. Fift stood in the supper garden watching a golden cloud of spice-gnats hover around the vines and smelling their warm, cozy, tingly smell.

All it was going to be, this time, was sitting still and waiting to be passed a spoon, and saying "the spoon is in my hand," and passing it on at the right moment, and telling the names of the twelve cycles, the twenty modes, and the eight corpuses. The Long Conversation. You couldn't use agents to help with anything, but that was okay, because Pip and Grobbard never let zir practice with agents anyway.

In the body down the hall, ze poked zir head into the main anteroom.

Mother Pip was there, singlebodied, in a white shift like Fift's, zir skin a deep forest green. Ze had stubby fingers that were usually relaxed, but right now they were tugging on zir thumb: tug, tug, tug. Ze had powerful, searching eyes that looked deep into you, white and gold and black. They were blazing. Fift wasn't sure, but ze thought maybe Mother Pip was furious.

Fathers Miskisk and Nupolo and Frill and Squell were there, too. Nupolo was glaring. Squell was holding vir hands over vir mouth. Frill was throwing up vir hands in exasperation.

Father Miskisk was shouting. And pointing at Mother Pip.

"It's always Pip! Ze's the Mother, ze guards our ratings, ze decides where we'll live and when little Fift has to—has to—"

"Will you calm down, Misky?" Frill said. "Pip's not going to be Mother twice over—even ze knows that would be too much! It will be Nupolo or Arevio, or Thurm if ve'd agree to it, or—well—" Ve tugged at one of the knives on vir sash as if waiting for someone to say "or Frill," but no one did.

"If I may—" Pip began.

"*Why* are we talking about this?" Nupolo said. "On Fift's big day? There's no rush here. Ze's not even five—"

Squell looked up, then, and saw Fift in the doorway. In the little atrium, where Frill had finished oiling zir last scalp and was rubbing vir hands with a towel, Squell said, "Come away from there, Fift. Come back in here, please."

"This is the age when it matters!" Miskisk roared, tears streaming down vir face. "And what makes you think it will ever change? *None* of you will ever dare struggle with Pip over the maternity, and *none* of you have the strength to watch Fift be supplanted!"

Pip's mouth tightened into a line.

"Fift," Squell said, in the little atrium.

"Oh, for Kumru's sake, Squell," Frill said, in the little atrium, "just get zir out of there. Do *I* have to do it?"

Fift came out of the supper garden and into the hallway. Ze hesitated. Father Squell wanted zir to come back to the atrium, but ze looked down the hall at zirself, standing at the door to the main anteroom . . .

Miskisk was crying. Zir Vail Fathers cried all the time, but this was different. Vir limbs had loosened with sorrow and hopelessness; ve looked as if ve were going to collapse.

A chill raced down from Fift's necks and settled in zir stomachs. Ze headed down the hall towards zir body watching Father Miskisk.

"It's true!" Miskisk cried. "You're too cowardly and too comfortable! You'd rather ze end up *sisterless* than endure the discomfort of zir supplanting!"

Sisterless was a bad word; Fift knew that much.

Fift caught up with zirself and came doublebodied into the anteroom. "Father Miskisk," ze said, "do you want to zoom? We could zoom."

Miskisk wailed, and Father Squell hurried across the room, picked up one of Fift's bodies, and held out vir hand to the other. "No more zooming, cubblehedge. Come with me."

Fift didn't budge.

Squell picked up Fift in the little atrium, too, and said, "A little help, please, Frill?"

In the little atrium, Frill sighed. In the main anteroom, ve sighed again, crossed the floor, and scooped up Fift's third body.

Father Smistria, dressed in an explosion of bladelike crimson and orange feathers, pushed past vem, going in.

"Smi, tell them!" Miskisk sobbed. "*You* agree with me! It's too *early* for this—Pip can't just—Fift deserves a little more time at home, to run and play and wear more colors than white, before—"

Smistria crossed vir arms. "Do I agree that Pip is *bossy?*" ve said. "And that everyone here is all too eager to postpone *any* argument, *especially* in the matter of Sibling Number Two? Certainly I do! But do I think you should be allowed to keep Fift here as a *baby*—dressed up in bangles and 'zooming about'—to satisfy your *selfish* wish for a vailchild . . . ?"

Fift's Fathers bustled zir up the stairs, doubly cuddled up against Squell's soft soap-smelling skin and squashed into Frill's bells, which tinkled around zir.

"Why is Father Miskisk upset?" Fift asked.

"Don't worry about that, Fiftling," Frill said. "You focus on what *you* need to do today."

"Today of all days!" Squell said. "I can't *believe* vem!"

"Am I going to be an Older Sibling?" Older Siblings were poor and pushed aside. Younger Siblings nestled in. But having a Younger Sibling also meant not being alone, having someone to protect and support, someone to share a childhood with. Fift had only ever been an Only Child. But there was something wrong, somehow, with being an Only Child.

Frill and Squell looked at each other over the tops of Fift's heads and Fift could feel their bodies tighten.

"That's enough of *that* topic, cubblehedge," Squell said. "There are far too many thoughts jumping around in those heads of yours. We're all just going to focus on what *you* have to do today, all right?"

{Why is it bad to be an Only Child?} Fift asked zir agents.

{That is not the polite term.} sent Fift's social nuance agent. {You should say "an individual with an abundant-concentration-of-familial-resources childhood."}

{What about *sisterless*?} Fift sent. Ze knew that word was bad, and ze shouldn't say it, or even send it. But ze also knew it described zir. *You'd rather ze end up sisterless . . .*

{That is not a word we say.} sent the social nuance agent primly.

{*Sister* is an archaic word for *sibling*.} added the context advisory agent.

Fift closed all zir eyes and rummaged around among zir agents. The feed-navigational one could help zir find the main anteroom . . . and there it was. Ze could see it.

Miskisk had fallen to vir knees. "You are crushing my heart," ve said, tears dripping from vir chin. "I have no voice here at all. It's all *zir* cold dominion . . ." Ve gestured at Mother Pip.

"If I may," Pip said, in a voice like ice.

"I cannot *do* this anymore," Miskisk roared. "I cannot—"

"We have a *pledge*," Nupolo said, in horror.

And then Frill and Squell and Fift were out of the apartment, through the front door, and up onto the surface of Foo. The inside of the house was swallowed into its privacy area, and Fift couldn't see it anymore. Frill put Fift down, but Squell, doublebodied, held onto zir.

Above them was the glistening underside of Sisterine habitation: docking-spires and garden globes and flow-sluices arcing away. In front of them was the edge of Foo. Their neighborhood, Slow-as-Molasses, was at the end of one spoke of Foo's great, slowly rotating wheel, and beyond it, this time of year, was a great empty vault of air . . . and then fluffy Ozinth and the below and beyond strewn with glittering bauble-habitations . . . and beyond that, habitation after habitation, bright and dim, smooth and spiky, shifting and still, all stretching away toward the curve of Fullbelly's ceiling.

Father Grobbard was waiting for them on the path ahead where it meandered past a flowgarden.

{What's a pledge?} Fift asked zir agents.

{A pledge is a promise that people make.} began the context advisory agent.

{But what do they mean?} Fift sent. {What pledge did my parents make?}

There was a lag, and when the context advisory agent replied, it sounded almost reluctant. {Your parents pledged to stay together for all twenty-two years of your First Childhood. To all sleep in the same apartment, once a month at the least; to attend family meetings; various such requirements. They had to. The neighborhood approval ratings for your birth weren't high enough otherwise.}

{But this is not at all unusual.} the social nuance agent sent. {You shouldn't worry.}

"Let's get started walking, shall we?" Grobbard said. "You

have a big day ahead; we might as well be early. The others will catch up."

"But what about Father Miskisk?" Fift said. "Father Miskisk is sad—"

Grobbard laid a gentle hand on Fift's shoulder, and Fift remembered that outside their apartment, they weren't on the house feed. They were on the world's feed, and anyone in the world could see and hear them.

"They'll catch up, Fift," Father Grobbard said again. "Clear your mind, please, and get ready." They started walking, following the path among the gardens and gazebos of Slow-as-Molasses: Frill striding ahead, Grobbard looking off into the vault of Fullbelly, and Squell, doublebodied, holding hands with all three of Fift's bodies.

{Father Miskisk!} Fift sent. {I'll do my best, Father Miskisk!}

All it was was sitting still and waiting to be passed a spoon, and saying "the spoon is in my hand," and passing it on at the right moment. Saying the names of the twelve cycles, the twenty modes, and the eight corpuses of the Long Conversation. Sitting still in white shifts on a wood floor, zir heads shaved and oiled. Zir Vail parents waiting in the gallery outside. Ze'd do it well, and everyone would be proud, and there would be umbcake and sweetlace afterwards. And Father Miskisk would smile.

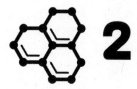 **2**

"So you're latterborn again," Umlish said. Ze smirked. "I guess we should congratulate you."

Umlish was talking to Shria, a skinny nine-year-old Vail who had joined their class a year ago.

Fift was a little way down the trail from them in the woods, beyond the clearing where they stood. Ze could hear them with zir ears, and see them through the branches and bracken, though the view was clearer over the feed. Fift was nine, too. At ten, Umlish was one of the older kids on this excursion to the surface.

Shria's hand paused a fingerlength from a tangle of silver-barked sticks, some of them furry with greenish lichen. Ve didn't look up. Vir eyes were red from crying already.

Shria: lavender skin and fiery red hair, orange eyebrows that curled like flames. Bony bare knees and elbows poked between the red and blue strips of cloth of vir suit. Vir clothes were a bit too big and too skimpy for the surface, as if whoever had cooked them up had been distracted. It was misting up here—tiny droplets of water sparkling in the air, the strange wild atmosphere hesitating between fog and rain. Shria crouched down, doublebodied, one body's arms already loaded up with sticks, the other gathering.

Umlish didn't look cold. And ze wasn't carrying any wood. Ze stood, singlebodied, half a bodylength from Shria, zir hands lost in the folds of zir white robes. Hair, eyes, skin the same sheer gray—zir parents had probably decided to match them like that. It was show-offy, in a staidish way. Kimi and Puson, two other Staids, stood behind Umlish, both double-bodied. Puson was also nine. Kimi, who was only eight, was carrying all the sticks. They were watching Umlish, doing their best to look calm and expressionless, but they couldn't help looking excited by what Umlish was talking about.

Because Umlish was talking about what happened to Shria's sibling.

Shria's hand moved again, picking up the next stick.

"That's not going to burn," Puson said. "Lichen means it's too wet. Especially in this weather."

Umlish smiled primly. "You do *have* an environmental context agent, don't you?"

Fift's own arms were full of sticks, some of which had lichen on them, or small fungi.

Ze shouldn't have split up after arriving in the forest. Ze was here in one body gathering sticks; in another, ze was over past the ridge, dragging a large log back to the campsite. Ze would have to drop all the sticks if ze wanted to sort through them.

Ze didn't like being together in the same place. Zir parents were still sending zir to somatic integration experts.

Umlish had found out about the experts at one point. Umlish had written a poem about it.

Umlish could be merciless.

Fift shouldn't have muted all zir automated agents, which would have warned zir about the lichen. But the agents distracted zir: from the tall trunks of trees, some of them as thick around as elevator shafts, others thin as a child's wrist; from the crunch and crackle of moss and leaves underfoot; from the roiling pale-green clouds in the roofless emptiness above zir.

"Your parents should have made sure you had the appropriate agents for a trip to the surface," Umlish said. "They do seem very distracted, don't they?"

{Why did the Midwives take Shria's younger sibling away?} Fift asked zir agents.

Shria dropped the stick ve'd just picked up, and stood up in both bodies. Ve clutched vir pile of kindling. Ve was quivering, vir faces pale. Ve looked around.

{In cases where there is insufficient consensus among neighbors and the parent-monitoring reactants of Fullbelly in favor of an additional child}, Fift's social context agent explained, {sometimes the Midwives refuse to gender the child unless the birthing cohort yields custody. Either another cohort is found, or the Midwives adopt the child into their order.}

There were a couple of other Vails—Perjes and Tomlest—across the clearing. They looked amused, and unsympathetic. Shria glared at them.

Fift could tell Shria was yearning for the other Vails to get involved, to say something, even to laugh out loud at what Umlish was saying. Them, ve could fight.

{But they didn't take vir sibling away the first day.} Fift sent zir agents. {Wasn't it . . . three weeks?}

{You are correct.} the social context agent said. {There was a period of negotiation regarding the child's status.}

Shria would get in trouble for another unauthorized fight—there had already been two scuffles on this trip, and ve had been warned.

At home, in zir third body, Fift rolled over. Ze hadn't really been sleeping anyway, just wallowing under the blankets, zir eyes closed, zir attention on the surface. The house feed showed Fathers Frill and Grobbard and Smistria in the breakfast room. Fift rolled out of bed, scratched zir feet, and went downstairs.

Zir Fathers looked up as ze came in.

"Hello, smoothling," Frill said. Vc raised vir head, and a swarm of bright cosmetic midges launched themselves from vir gilded eyebrows to dance in the air. "How is it going with your—ah, yes," vir eyes shone. "Out in the wilds! Looks damp." Ve grinned, goldenly.

"I never go to the surface," Smistria said, leaning back—vir other body leaned forward, messily chewing a crusty broibel, which flaked into vir braided beard—"if I can avoid it. We had this nonsense when I was your age, too. It's *perverse* up there. The sky can just dump water on you or electrify you any time it takes the notion. Horrible place."

Under that dangerous sky, Umlish took a step closer to Shria. "I wonder if they might still be a bit overburdened? Your parents."

Across the clearing, Perjes turned to Tomlest. You could tell they were sending messages. Tomlest's eyes screwed up in amusement, and ve laughed.

Shria's bodies both twitched. Vir empty pair of hands came up, almost to a guard position. But Tomlest didn't look over.

"Oh you," Frill said, swatting Smistria. "You have no sense of romance! The wild sky, our ancient origins!"

"Our ancient origins, for that matter, were under an entirely different—"

"Oh, don't be such a *pedant*! I know as well as you—"

"Um," Fift interrupted. "Um, I have a question."

Perjes and Tomlest ran off into the woods. Shria exhaled a shaky breath. Ve turned abruptly and started to walk away. Not run; ve moved slowly, like an animal preserving its energy. Ve kept vir eyes focused on vir feet. Umlish, Puson, and Kimi trailed after vem.

"Yes, little stalwart?" Frill said. "What is it?"

"There's this Vail in my class, Shria"—in the forest, still watching Shria, ze checked lookup—"um, Shria Qualia Fnax, of name registry Digger Chameleon 2?"

Smistria looked at Frill and bared vir teeth. "Oh yes. That one."

"What, what happened? They took away vir sibling, but why—why did they wait so long? And why did vir parents have the baby if they didn't—"

"Because they're slackwits," Smistria said.

Fift frowned.

Grobbard spread zir hands. "It was a gamble, Fift. Fnax cohort thought that once the baby was here, opinions would change."

Shria trudged through the underbrush, crushing dawnflowers and gemmon underfoot. Ve reached the trail, a ragged strip of bare dirt traced by surface animals, and headed toward Fift.

"A *slackwitted* gamble," Smistria said. "If people didn't trust you to raise another child in the first place, why would they trust you after *that* behavior? Provoking a standoff with the Midwives? Letting your child just . . . *hang about* for three weeks—"

"Ungendered," Frill added, shaking vir head, "not entered into lookup, not enrolled in a name registry, like—like a surface animal, or—"

"Or someone who doesn't exist at all!" Smistria cried.

Grobbard sighed. "Yes. As if lingering still unborn, outside its Mother's body."

"But why would they do that?" Fift asked.

"Because," Smistria snapped, "they thought they could *coerce* the rest of Slow-as-Molasses and every parent-monitoring reactant in Fullbelly!" Ve drew vemself up in vir seating harness, still chewing vigorously with vir other mouth. "They were so arrogant, they didn't even invite adjudication!" Smistria was a well-rated adjudication reactant.

"They would have *lost* adjudication," Frill said.

"Exactly!" Smistria said through a mouthful of broibel, forgetting vemself.

Umlish, Kimi, and Puson trailed behind Shria like a parade. Their eyes darted back and forth—you could tell from their small, prim grins that they were amused by the messages they were sending one another. Puson started chuckling, but Umlish frowned at zir and ze composed zir face more sedately.

"And think of the poor older siblings," Frill said. "Especially your classmate. From latterborn to middleborn to latterborn again in three weeks!"

"Well," said Grobbard quietly, "at least ve was briefly middleborn." Grobbard was, it occurred to Fift, also an Only Child. It wasn't something ze talked about, but you could see it right there in lookup: **Grobbard Erevulios Iraxis of name registry Amenable Perambulation 2, 4-bodied Staid, 230 years old, education topology mediator, Only Child.**

It wasn't a great thing to be an Only Child. It kind of meant you were less of a person. Maybe Grobbard had always dreamed about being middleborn, too.

"*Briefly* middleborn! But come on, Grobby," said Frill (who was latterborn). "Not like *that*."

Umlish looked up the trail and saw Fift standing there, as if frozen. Umlish's eyes narrowed. {Oh, hello Fift.} ze sent. {Are you finding what you need? Don't you think you have enough sticks?} Zir eyes flicked to the left, feed-searching. {Oh my. Look at you dragging that thing.} Ze had found Fift's other body, hauling the log. Zir eyes shifted back to Fift's. {That's so . . . robust of you. "Mighty was Threnis in zir time," eh?}

Fift flushed. Umlish was farther along in the Long Conversation than ze was—already learning the sixth mode. Was

Threnis mentioned in the third corpus? Ze couldn't remember, and Pip and Grobbard never let zir use search agents for the Conversation. ("It's a corrupting habit, Fift," Grobbard had said, with starker disapproval than Fift had ever seen on zir solemn face. "Once you begin using them, you'll never stop. You must know the Conversation yourself. Unaided.")

Umlish's eyes widened in triumph; ze could tell that Fift had no idea who Threnis was.

Shria looked up nervously, saw Fift, and frowned. The tips of vir ears were bluish with cold. Vir mouth was trembling, but vir jaw was clamped tight, almost as if ve was trying *not* to cry—like Fift when ze was six or seven, when ze'd begun doing zir horrible somatic integration exercises in front of the whole world. It had taken all zir strength not to humiliate zirself by bursting into tears.

But of course no one would mind if *Shria* cried. If anything, it was strange—even slightly ridiculous—for a Vail to be so rigid with the effort *not* to.

Fift cleared zir throat. It was thick somehow, and the morning dew was clammy on the back of zir neck. "Shria," ze said, "can you, um, help me?" Ze hefted zir pile of sticks. "Some of these aren't going to burn. They've got lichen on them."

Shria stopped, in both bodies, and glared at Fift. Ve hunched vir shoulders in a little further. Ve thought ze was making fun of vem, too, and so did Kimi and Puson, whose grins escaped their prim confinement. Umlish wasn't so sure; ze raised an eyebrow.

"I guess I should have checked with my agents," Fift said, zir voice a little unsteady, "but I turned them off. Who wants to have agents chattering at you up here? It's sort of missing the point, isn't it?"

Puson's face froze; Kimi looked back and forth from Puson to Umlish. Shria blinked.

Umlish's mouth soured. "You *like* it up here?"

Fift didn't, exactly; it was cold and strange and mostly pretty boring, though there was also something fascinating about being under this strange sky which, as Father Smistria had said, could do anything it decided to. Ze didn't *like* it, but ze wanted to experience it. But ze wasn't about to explain that to Umlish.

"Oh, Umlish . . . are you having trouble with this?" Fift said. "I guess it can be a little scary if you've never been on the surface before. But don't worry—"

Umlish recoiled. "I'm not *scared*, you sluiceblocking toad-clown. It's just *disgusting*." Ze waved a hand at the forest.

A small grin crept across one of Shria's faces.

Fift swallowed. Ze wasn't sure what else to say.

Father Grobbard's eyes had been closed. Ze often meditated at the breakfast table. Now ze opened them and glanced at Fift. {Threnis}, ze sent Fift, {appears in the sixth and seventh odes of the first additional corpus. Would you like to study them this afternoon?}

Fift gulped. It was easy to forget that zir parents could read zir private messages: they didn't often bother to. At least, ze didn't *think* they did. Grobbard didn't seem angry, though. Ze placed zir hands together, resting them on the table. Peaceful as a stone worn smooth by a river.

"Well, if you like it so much," Umlish snarled, "why don't you live up here? Maybe you could get permission to build a little hut out of sticks and the two of you could *play cohort.*"

"Okay," Shria said, coming forward up the trail. "Yeah, I'll help." Ve stopped in front of Fift, wiped a streak of snot from vir nose with the back of vir wrist, and then reached in, holding the good sticks back with one hand, and pulling the mossy ones out with the other. Ve kept those eyes on the task, but the other two—in the body ve was holding vir pile of sticks with—searched Fift's face, sizing zir up.

Fift swallowed. Ze kept zir face still, expressionless, but ze could feel the blood rising into zir ears.

"Will they take away the other children, do you think?" Father Frill asked.

"What?" Fift asked. "What other children?"

"Of Fnax cohort," Smistria said.

The cold dug into Fift's chests, and not just the ones on the surface. "Like Shria? Why?"

Frill shrugged and smoothed the bright blue-and-orange braids of vir hair with vir hands, releasing another swarm of midges into the air. "It can happen. If their ratings fall enough. If people think they're doing an inadequate job, that your friend would be better off elsewhere."

"Ve's not . . ." Fift began. Ze didn't really have any Vail friends. It had gotten hard to tell who zir friends were.

Two years ago, ze would have said Umlish was zir friend; they'd played together when they were little. But Umlish was the kind of person who was your friend as long as you did exactly what ze said. When Umlish wrote that poem about Fift's somatic integration, ze'd tried to laugh along. But after today . . . Umlish would never forgive Fift now.

"They're starting the campfire, Umlish," Kimi said. "Should we go back?"

"Or are you playing siblings?" Umlish snapped, ignoring Kimi. "How exciting for you, Fift! A sibling of your own!"

Father Frill cocked vir head to one side and narrowed vir eyes, searching the feed. "Hmm. Ve's been fighting—your friend. Ve's a little old for that. By that age, Vails should be learning to keep their fights on the practice mats." Ve shook vir head. "That's not good for ratings."

The hairs on the backs of Fift's necks stood up. "What would happen if they took Shria away? Away to where?"

Frill shrugged. "Well, the Midwives live at the Pole. If ve's lucky, perhaps ve'd be trained there . . . as one of them . . ." Ve gestured vaguely. "It's a great honor."

Fift could see zir own faces over the feed. Ze looked horrified: one day ze'd come to class and Shria would be gone, taken from vir cohort, forbidden to talk to vir parents, off to the Pole to become a Midwife forever. How many more fights would it take? Could Umlish cause this all by zirself, with zir words? Fift struggled to compose zir expressions into mildness, like Grobbard's.

The closed and skeptical look on Shria's face softened as ve stared at Fift. Ve yanked the last of the mossy sticks from the pile (in zir other body, Fift yanked the log free from a knot of underbrush; there, ze could hear the sounds of the campsite through the trees. They were building the bonfire). Shria raised one of vir thick, curling eyebrows.

"You'd better plan on being the Older Sibling, though," Umlish said, "because Shria doesn't want any Younger Siblings. Ve was glad to get rid of that little baby—weren't you, Shria?"

Shria blinked. Vir nostrils flared with a long indrawn breath. Vir eyes were still locked on Fift's—drawing strength? Then ve turned to Umlish. "Don't spit all your poison today, Umlish," ve said. "You might run out, and then what are you going to do tomorrow?"

Umlish drew zirself up, scowling. "You sluiceblocking—"

"You used 'sluiceblocking' already," Shria said. "See? You're running out."

"Let's go back, Umlish," Kimi said. "We don't want to miss them lighting the fire . . ."

Fift cleared zir throat. Zir hearts were pulsing, unstaidishly fast.

"Don't tell me what—" Umlish snapped.

"You could try 'flowblocking,'" Fift said.

Shria's eyes lit up. "That's kind of the same thing, though," ve said, chewing vir lip.

"Corpsemunching?" Fift said.

Shria giggled. "That's good! What's that from? Yes, call me a 'corpsemunching sisterloser,' Umlish."

"'Sisterloser!'" Fift's eyes widened. "Wow!"

Shria grinned, a glimpse of white teeth between pale lavender lips. "You like that one?"

Fift dragged zir log into the clearing. Perjes and Tomlest ran up to take it from zir and toss it onto the pile.

Umlish's face was a mask of anger.

Puson cleared zir throat.

"See there, Umlish?" Shria said, clapping zir on the shoulder. "You don't need to worry. If you run out, we'll help you."

"Get your hands away from me!" Umlish cried. "You're disgusting!" Ze turned and swept up the path, followed by Puson. Kimi, released from the agony of waiting, darted ahead towards the campsite, zir bodies caroming off each other, running a few bodylengths before remembering to slow down to a more sedate and proper pace.

Fathers Frill and Smistria had finished breakfast and wandered off. Father Grobbard was waiting, still, watching Fift with zir immovable serenity. It seemed like ze was waiting for something.

It was turning colder. When Umlish, Puson, and Kimi were gone, Shria exhaled, a brief exhausted sigh: it came out as a plume of white fog. Vir shoulders slumped.

They were lighting the fire. Brushing bits of bark from zir hands, Fift found a place on a rock, not too far and not too near, and settled onto it. The expedition director, a fussy two-hundred-year-old middleborn Staid, was anxiously directing the two Vails holding the lighted torch. Kimi rushed up the path, walking just slower than a run, eyes wide with expectation.

Alone on the path with Shria, Fift was at a loss. Were people watching them? There was a way to check audience numbers on the feed, they'd gone over it once in interface class . . .

After a moment, ze found it.

No one was watching them as they stood in the forest; no one at all. Not even Grobbard.

Grobbard raised an eyebrow. As if waiting for Fift to answer a question.

"Oh," Fift said. "Yes, I—" Ze switched to sending. Ze shouldn't speak aloud about the Long Conversation in the breakfast room, where zir Vail Fathers might hear and get annoyed. {Yes, Father Grobbard, I would be interested in studying the sixth and seventh odes of the first additional corpus. Thank you.}

Fift's arms were getting tired from holding the pile of sticks. Ze took a step up the path, and Shria matched it. They headed back towards the campsite.

Shria watched the darkening sky, sunk in vir own thoughts. At the edge of the circle of firelight—red shadows dancing on the trunks, every body wreathed in a streamer of exhaled cloud as the children began to sing, ve looked at Fift once and sent: {Thanks.}

They dumped their kindling on the pile and Shria went off somewhere. Fift sat down with zirself, body against body, huddled up against the cold.

 **INTERLUDE**

Please answer the following questions to help us counsel you in possible new career opportunities.

What is your gender?
◉ **STAID**   ◎ Vail

How many bodies do you have?
　3

Are any of those bodies off-planet, undersea, in polar regions, or in long-term residency on the surface?
◎ yes   ◉ **NO**

What is your birth order?
◎ elderborn   ◎ middleborn   ◎ latterborn
◉ **WITHOUT BENEFIT OF SIBLING RELATIONSHIPS**

What nation do you live in?
◉ **FULLBELLY**   ◎ Hardwon   ◎ Tearless   ◎ Spoon
◎ the Manysmall   ◎ other   ◎ multinational

Are you currently undergoing an ontological collapse?
◉ **NO**   ◎ yes, and in an Idyll   ◎ yes, but awaiting a spot in an Idyll   ◎ yes, but short-term/at-large

How many times have you undergone an ontological collapse?
◉ 0 ◎ 1–5 ◎ 6–20 ◎ 21+

Would you prefer to experience ontological collapse more frequently or less frequently?
◎ More Frequently   ◎ Less Frequently
◉ **CURRENT FREQUENCY IS FINE**

Have adjudicators ever issued a ruling against you on fraud, theft, unreliability, unlicensed dueling, cowardice, sloth, or gender nonconformance?
◉ **NO** ◎ Yes ◎ Yes, but overturned on appeal

Which best describes your current economic status?
◎ Dejected/apathetic/peripheral
◎ Subservient/cheerful   ◎ Defiant/engaged
◎ Satiated/joyful ◉ **UNRESOLVED/UNCERTAIN**

Are you a parent?
◉ **NO** ◎ yes, a Father   ◎ yes, a Mother
◎ yes, both a Mother and a Father

On an average day, what is the peak audience viewing your actions?
◉ **0–99** ◎ 100–999 ◎ 1000–99,999 ◎ 100,000–9,999,999 ◎ 10,000,000–999,999,999
◎ 1,000,000,000–999,999,999,999

Would you prefer to be viewed by more or fewer people?
◎ More   ◎ Fewer   ◉ **CURRENT AUDIENCE IS FINE**

What is your cohort status?
◉ **CHILD/STUDENT** ◎ courtship/seeker ◎ pair, triad, or quaternad proto-cohort ◎ semi-cohort ◎ full cohort ◎ large or mega-cohort ◎ fragment or dissolution ◎ not in, and not seeking, a cohort ◎ it's complicated

How old are you?
<u>15</u>

Our apologies: this survey is designed for career-seekers between 100 and 800 years of age. Please employ a reputable childhood advisory *[—SURVEY TERMINATED BY USER—]*

 **3**

"Fift," Father Frill said, pulling vir battle gloves off, "I think you should consider unraveling."

Fift was fifteen, and Father Arevio was showing zir how to score the vines in the supper garden, cutting long, shallow gashes along each to let the spice-gnats feed on the sap. Father Frill had just swept in: singlebodied, wearing a crimson leotard, covered in a sheen of sweat, vir coppery hair in disarray. Straight from sparring in the large mat room, in other words.

Father Smistria, following Frill at a leisurely pace—ve was sweaty too, and still wearing battle gloves—stopped to lean against the wall at the entrance of the supper garden. Ve crossed vir arms.

"In ancient times," Frill said, "you would nearly be considered an adult by now, do you realize that?" Ve dropped vir gloves—Arevio frowned at this—and ran vir fingers through vir hair to untangle it. "We have this *idea* of First Childhood being some kind of peaceful *oasis*, but it's not! It's a stressful time! It was for me. Of course, it's simpler for a staidchild, I suppose—but still. You seem glum. It might help if you just, well, lose it entirely. You know . . . collapse."

Arevio meditatively flipped the short-bladed knife ve was

holding, caught it by the hilt, then turned back to scoring the vines.

Glum? Fift thought. Ze seemed glum? Ze felt . . . how did ze feel?

Frozen. A chunk of ice tugged along in a stream. In the wake of Mother Pip.

In another body, ze sat next to Pip, looking through the porthole of a robot bat, wheeling through the space between the habitations. The rotating spoke-wheel of Foo, home to Fift and a million others, fell away behind them.

They were on their way to see a client.

Fift forced zirself not to fidget in zir seat.

Pip should have had a more worthy apprentice than a fifteen-year-old Only Child with no real triumphs to zir name. Fift should have been working for one of the one-stop-shop banker-historian/bookie/clown/logician booths at a walka-round market, or doing menial work of the most peripheral kind at some big institutional-memory conglomerate.

But Pip (who was the *third* of *four* siblings) bulldozed through such considerations. Zir clients admired zir habit of flaunting conventions; zir eccentricities worked to zir advantage.

Whether Fift could afford eccentricities . . . that was another question. The wrongness of zir position clung to zir like an itch.

Father Smistria snorted. "Glum? Glum? How should ze *seem*? Should ze be dancing and singing around the house?"

Frill ignored vem. "I unraveled several times as a young person," ve said, "and I think it did me a great deal of good."

"And you think," said Father Smistria, stepping forward into the supper garden, tugging on vir beard, "that our fifteen-year-old staidchild checking into an Idyll would do our *ratings* a great deal of good?"

Frill flung out vir hands. "Irrational prejudice!" ve snapped. "The idea that unraveling is vailish! Unraveling isn't vailish, it's just *human*. It's a basic human right. And in fact . . ."

Ve paused and turned vir head towards one wall of the garden. So did Smistria, and so did Arevio. It took Fift a moment to realize why: Father Miskisk had gotten up.

One night every month, Miskisk came to sleep in their apartment, as the birthing pledge required.

Over the house feed, Fift saw Miskisk stalk through the corridor. Vir shoulders were hunched, vir gait stiff and hurried. Ve hesitated at the door of the supper garden—Fift's hand tightened on the vine ze was holding—but kept going.

Father Frill sighed.

In the bat, Mother Pip sent: {You have not adequately studied Pom Politigus's career.}

{I studied the weave you gave me.} Fift sent. It had been slow going: Pom Politigus, proprietor of Stiffwaddle Somatic Fashions, the most prestigious body-design emporium in a billion cubic bodylengths, had been Mother Pip's client for two hundred years.

{Fift, I can see perfectly well from the access trail which strands of the weave you've haphazardly blundered along. A banker-historian must know zir client intimately, more intimately than the client knows zirself. To study—to absorb—the life, the career, the public emotional history of the client, is the merest preliminary.}

Fift pressed zir nose against the porthole, as far as ze could get from zir Mother in the cramped space. They were almost at Stiffwaddle Somatic Fashions, which occupied the second of a cascade of angular translucent baubles, arranged in a glittering helical chain. The chain hung luxuriously in a great swathe of empty space that residents of Foo called "the below and beyond."

Fift pulled the weave back up, fumbled through it again.

Pom's emporium was large enough for hundreds of bodies to be serviced, remodeled, and remapped simultaneously by zir elite staff of two dozen. It was a middlebrow establishment in the wider scheme of things; but for ten million people in the immediately surrounding cubic volume, it was a marvel. Stylish and confident younger siblings from Foo would save up a year's worth of daring for a chance to impress their friends with some minor bodily enhancement from Stiffwaddle. Certain of Fullbelly's ultrarich—virtuoso logistics coordinators, major attention brokers, celebrity statistician-poets—dropped by weekly.

A low-level pattern-recognition agent called Fift's attention to the apprentices at the bottom of the staff list. And there ve was: `Shria Qualia Fnax of name registry Digger Chameleon 2, 3-bodied Vail, 15 years old, genital design specialist.`

Shria! Fift's heart gave a pulse. It had been months, maybe a year, since ze'd seen vem. There had been a time—years ago—when they'd seen each other every week: in class, or meeting somewhere around Foo. Sometimes ve'd come over to the Iraxis cohort's apartment; a few times, Fift had gone over to Fnax cohort's. Fift's parents liked vem. In class, the ten-year-old Shria had been guarded and sullen, but in the supper garden with Frill and Squell and Arevio, sheltered from the broad world's feed by Iraxis cohort's privacy regime, ve'd been self-confident, alert, funny.

The last few years it had gotten harder. There were fewer things Vails and Staids their age could do together. Less of their homework overlapped as their curricula diverged. Fift was spending more time on the Long Conversation, and that wasn't something ze could talk to Shria about. And Shria was doing Vail things now. Ve had a gang of Vails who sparred together and swaggered around the byways, trying to find quarrels legitimate enough to justify a real fight on the mats. And there were other things—sexual escapades—that Fift wasn't supposed to know about. Even if Shria had wanted to tell zir, it wasn't like there was anywhere ve could; their parents could still read their send logs, and hear them over the house feed.

{The career of the *client*, Fift.} Pip sent. {Not of the client's youngest apprentice, no matter how impressive vir debut.}

Get out of my head! Fift thought, but didn't send. Ze hurriedly flipped away from the staff list to browse the annual growth of Stiffwaddle Somatic Fashions' audience and ratings. There was an ache in zir chest when ze thought of Shria.

"Anyway," Father Frill said, pacing across the garden, "unraveling can be *so* rewarding for those Staids who *do* allow themselves to collapse. I mean, part of the whole *gift* of a collapse is to let go of worrying about what other people think!"

Smistria snorted.

"Frill Evementis," Father Arevio said, "could you pick up your gloves? They are lying on the gladblooms."

They disembarked on the swaying lip of Politigus's bauble. Fift admired the sparkling translucent blue of the surface beneath zir feet and concentrated on keeping zir balance as the bat shoved off; it would not do to stumble. When ze looked up, Shria was standing doublebodied in front of zir.

Ve'd grown. Ve was taller than Fift now, broad-shouldered, vir bright red hair styled back in looping curves, vir smokily translucent Stiffwaddle Somatic Fashions uniform stretched tight across a row of four small breasts.

Ve grinned. For an instant Fift had the startling sense that Shria was going to launch vemself onto zir in a ballistic embrace, right in front of Mother Pip. But they weren't ten

anymore. Instead, ve turned, saying nothing, and helped Pip
from the robot bat.

Pom Politigus was crowded near the main entrance in six
strikingly, unnervingly, stylishly heterogenous bodies. All the
bodies had the same face, but there were two tall, curvaceous
heavy-bosomed bodies (one ruddy, one sallow); two short,
smooth, roundish midnight-blue bodies; a tawny, gaunt angular body; and a thick, well-muscled body with iridescent
dark purple skin. Fift was amazed—Politgus's proprioceptive
integration must be brutal, not to mention zir self-concept.
Indeed, most of Politigus was swaying slightly, zir hands poised,
occasionally grabbing one of zir own shoulders for support.

"Welcome!" said Pom Politigus, speaking from one of the
short blue bodies. "How kind of you, Pip! To travel out here to
my little campsite."

"'Out' indeed!" roared Pip. "You know this bauble of yours is
becoming the heart of Fullbelly! What haven't I heard about
you in the past months, Pom Politigus? You burrow to the
heart of not only fashion but design—and somatic technology,
too! Aren't the likes of Frundle and Kwonk and that body rent-
ing fellow . . . why, aren't they all falling over themselves to woo
you as their showcase? You don't need a banker-historian but
an inflagrist-poet, to burn the rest of Fullbelly as an ode to
your name!"

"Oh, enough, enough, you scoundrel," laughed Politigus.

"And yet you don't forget your old friends," said Pip.

"Oh come, come," Politigus said, looking very pleased. Two
bodies stumbled into an exuberant hug.

"May I introduce my child and apprentice, Fift Brulio
Iraxis of name registry Yellow Peninsula Sugarbubble 5," Pip
said, turning to Fift so sharply ze barely managed to suppress
a yelp of surprise. "Ze is learning the trade."

Shria winked.

"Very good, very good," said Politigus. "This, by the way, is Shria Qualia Fnax, of name registry, ah"—Fift could tell ze was having to do the lookup zirself, which rather spoiled the effect—"Digger Chameleon 2—"

"We know Young Expressive Fnax, as it happens," Pip said. "Ve is another child of Foo . . ."

"Indeed, indeed," said Politigus. "Pip, I'm dying to tell you about the work we did for the local chapter of the Cirque. Shria here was the principal designer of the erotics and sensuals. At vir age! Oh, it was so well received. You'll have to see what you make of it, of course, but I think, speaking frankly, that it was quite a coup. There's some talk of other chapters adopting the design! I mean, the Cirque Fantabulous, Pip! Now, I would argue that the Cirque is at the aesthetic-thematic *crux* of Fullbelly, if not the world! Midwives and feedgardeners and adjudicators may hold things together, but to whom do we look to stir things up?"

"To be sure, to be sure," murmured Pip.

"—and, oh, I don't want to presume, it's up to you of course, but when you see the recordings, I really think we came out as— pardon my vulgarity—the Younger Sibling! Don't you think so, Shria? Be honest."

"We kicked military clown butt," Shria said.

"They were so impressed!" Politigus's two curvaceous bodies said in chorus.

"All right, all right," said Pip, chuckling. "We shall see. Plenty of time for that. Let's sit down, have a drink, and take a look."

"Certainly," said Pom Politigus. "This way!"

"Boss," Shria said, "while they're here, remember the other transactions you wanted them to take a look at?"

"Oh, that can wait," Politigus said, flicking three hands as if dismissing three buzzing flygrams.

"But since there are two of them—"

"Oh, I see." One of the hands closed into a fist. "Pip, is your apprentice up to clearing out some of the more routine transactions while we get started on the Cirque business? Shria is always very anxious to get the practical details tidied up. Unusually diligent for a Vail!"

"Gee, thanks, boss," Shria said drily.

Pip inclined zir head, willing, as always, to throw Fift into deeper waters. "Certainly," ze said. "If anything is unclear, Fift, make a list of questions for me. But I expect your training should be more than adequate to run up an accounting of a few months of routine work. Routine for this bauble, that is— which is to say, unprecedented brilliance by anyone else's standards . . ."

"Oh, you!" said Politigus, zir six slightly weaving bodies herding Pip off to the salon as fast as ze could manage.

Shria stood to either side of Fift, bouncing on the balls of vir feet. "Wow," ve said from Fift's left, and then from zir right. "Did you see Pom? Ze's so excited ze's practically giving birth." Ve bounced toward Fift, almost as if ve were about to collide with zir, then swiveled away and put vir hands in vir sleeves. "Come on," ve said, and started off in one body.

The other body lingered next to Fift, still rocking slightly from foot to foot. Shria seemed to be full of nervous energy. Without thinking about it, Fift put out a hand to still vem, touching vem lightly on the elbow. Shria settled a little. Ve looped vir arm in Fift's, and they followed vir other body down a long corridor.

"In here," ve said.

The door before them was a stylized representation of a womb-passage. Shria pushed aside the labia and they squeezed through the antechamber and stepped through the dilated cervix to a large womb room full of the tools of Shria's trade:

vats, couches, tubs, racks of smooth shiny implements, blobs of haptic goop and meshgloves on shafts dangling from the ceiling. The passage squeezed shut behind them.

Shria scooted up to sit on a table in one body. In the other, ve stood in the center of the lab, spreading vir arms. "Here it is!" ve said. "Welcome to my domain!"

Everything looked mildly dangerous to Fift. Ze sat on a couch. "It's terrific," ze said. "Your boss is really impressed with you. And so is—mine, I guess. Impressed with you, I mean."

Shria grinned. "Of course, the agents do a lot of the hard stuff," ve said. "I just do the fun part: the ideas . . ."

Fift had no idea what that meant in the context of genital design. "So the whole Cirque has . . . or, that chapter, I mean . . . they have, um, identical . . ."

"Ugh, no." Shria's faces had identical looks of horror. "Are you kidding? This isn't Uncle Foolu's One-Stop Body Shop, you know. Genitals are not hats! Our experience of the world is deeply rooted in our genitals! You have to do the matchup very carefully. The wrong set of genitals can make a person *miserable*."

"Oh," Fift said.

"But they do, you know, sort of *work* together," ve added. "They're not identical, but they are *coordinated*. That was . . . the fun part." Ve grinned mischievously.

Fift felt zir face flushing. *The fun part?*

"Anyway," Shria said, "we don't need to talk about my work. You're finally here!"

"Finally?" It was an odd thought, Shria waiting for zir . . .

"Yeah! I've known you were coming for a week! I shifted my schedule around so we . . . I planned this!" Ve grinned. In the center of the room, standing, ve put vir hands on vir hips.

"Oh," Fift said, a little perplexed. What was so special about meeting Shria at work? Ve could have just come over to the apartment . . .

Shria cocked one of vir fiery red eyebrows, crossed both sets of vir arms. Ve was waiting for zir to notice something . . .

{What's going on here?} Fift asked zir agents. {What am I missing?}

But zir agents were silent, plunged into a dreamless slumber by the total privacy regime of Stiffwaddle Somatic Fashions.

Of course! The bauble's elite patrons valued their privacy. Fift remembered the praise in the weave ze'd stumbled through for the extreme measures Pom Politigus took to preserve the secrets, protect the surprises, planned by those who had themselves altered here . . .

"So no one outside the bauble can see us?" Fift said, frowning. "Even our agents are . . ."

"Outside the *bauble*? No, Fift, outside the *room*! *Pom and Pip* can't hear a word we're saying. No agents can record or remember a thing—I mean, our parents could still read our send logs later; but if we speak aloud, no one will know a thing we . . . We can talk about *anything we want!*" Ve was practically dancing with excitement.

In the supper garden, Fift stood shoulder to shoulder with Arevio, scoring the vines. Spice-gnats swarmed around the knife blades. Fift paused in zir slicing, glanced over at Arevio. Zir Father showed no horror at vir staidchild's disappearance into an abyss of privacy. Arevio chewed vir lip, deciding whether to remove a low-hanging loop of vine.

The house feed showed Smistria and Frill lounging in the bathing pool. Miskisk, singlebodied, was awkwardly saying goodbye to Squell in the anteroom, holding vir overnight bag. Thurm and Grobbard had no public locations listed; Nupolo and Pip and Frill had bodies walking through public spaces— but they, too, showed no reaction. But then, why would they react? Pip was busy with Pom Politigus; and to zir other parents, unless they explicitly queried zir agents, this wouldn't look any different than if Fift was visiting any private home . . .

Fift's heart hammered there in Shria's secret room—and zir other hearts sped up, too, fast enough to wake zir sleeping body.

For a moment ze didn't know if it was terror or excitement. But Shria hadn't said *We could do anything*—of course not. Ve'd said, *We could talk about anything.*

(Fift was now awake in zir bed. Arms and legs splayed among pillowcloths, zir skin hot. Ze shivered anyway, rolled over, kept zir eyes squeezed shut.)

"Wow," Fift said. "Okay then, um, what . . . should we talk about?"

In vir standing body, Shria put vir hands together, cracked vir knuckles. "Well, um, we could . . ." It seemed to Fift that ve was on the verge of saying something specific, but lost vir nerve. "Want to see my new genitals?" ve said brightly.

Fift almost choked. "Your—new—"

Shria slid off the table, lifting vir hands, and said, in that body, "Yeah! You were asking about the Cirque design? These are sort of . . . well, not exactly *related*, but 'inspired by,' let's say? I just had them done. I'm really proud of them, and I haven't gotten to show them off much! My parents don't care, and it's not like I can show them to other Vails, because, you know"—ve raised vir eyebrows—"that would be kind of forward? If I show them to another Vail, it means we're going to, ah, *employ* them . . ." Ve grinned. "But no danger of that with you, so . . ."

"Ah," Fift said, "but what about those, um, transactions I was supposed to look at . . . ?"

Shria stopped, shrugged. Vir hands fell back to vir sides. "Oh, well . . . okay, sure, of course—"

"I mean," Fift said, "just to get them out of the way. You know, because . . . they *will* ask; at least, Pip is going to—"

"Sure," Shria said, sending the transactions.

Fift closed zir eyes and scrolled through the history; the transactions were well-organized, and most of the accounting was done already, with highlights clearly marking where zir professional attention was required to specify the exact outcome.

"Here," Shria said, poking zir with a thin, translucent folding screen. "Here's a physical instantiation. So you can at least look at me while you do that."

Fift took the screen, spread it open. In one body, Shria sat down next to zir, watching; in the other, ve walked over to the tool rack and started pulling down tools, one by one, and rehanging them in a different order. "Hurry up, okay?" ve said.

Fift poked at a couple of zir agents, the specialized ones for evaluating banking-history, and they sluggishly stumbled out of privacy-sleep. There was nothing particularly complicated here. A few cases with disgruntled customers needed zir resolution, though nothing came close to requiring formal adjudication. A staff member who'd been depressed had ultimately unraveled completely, requiring two months' worth of revisions to the emotional valences of certain transactions (mostly in Politigus's favor). In a couple of places, Fift could drop exotic algorithms in for standard ones, benefiting the shop. It was easy work: Mother Pip had heuristics, rules, and practices for all these cases, and had required Fift to unaugmentedly memorize them zirself. Fift had chafed at that, but it helped now, when zir agents kept drowsing off.

It was good that the work was easy, because ze couldn't help being aware of Shria next to zir on the couch, looking at zir, then away, vir long, muscled body loose and tense at the same time.

"Done yet?" Shria said.

Fift swallowed. "I'm done." Ze put the screen aside and

turned to Shria. Fift took a deep breath. "Look, you . . . went to a lot of trouble to arrange this, right? You wanted to tell me something. You . . . you've got a secret."

In the body next to Fift, vir hands entwined, vir legs swinging back and forth, Shria shrugged. In the standing body, a tool in each hand, ve said. "Well . . . yes. Sure. More than one! Don't you have any secrets, Fift?"

Fift flushed. "Of course."

"Everybody does!" Shria said. "A trillion people walking around on the feed, acting their parts for the whole world to watch . . . and every one of them is stuffed full of secrets! Did you ever think about that?"

"No," Fift said, "not really."

"Well, I do!" Ve hung up the pair of tools and started pacing across the floor.

"So now," Fift said, zir heart beating, "we get to tell those secrets?"

In the drowsy warmth of the bed, Fift was safe, nestled in blankets, restless, alone, lonely. In the dappled green light of the garden, blades cut into the green flesh of the vines: slow and thorough work, almost dreamlike. Here, though, in the lab, everything was new and gleaming, and Fift was acutely awake.

Shria cracked a grin. "If you want to! We'll start small and work up. I mean, I won't grill you about the Long Conversation *right away . . .*"

Fift's gut tightened. "You'd . . . you'd want to know about . . . I mean . . ."

Shria laughed. "Sweet Kumru," ve said in the body sitting next to zir, "look at your face. I was *kidding.*" In both bodies, ve grinned wickedly, but then vir faces sobered. "Kumru's tits, though, Fift . . . would I *want* to know? Seriously? Don't you think every Vail in the world is *curious? Especially* the ones who act all disgusted if you even allude to it?"

Even in total privacy, it felt wrong to talk about this. Every Vail in the world? The idea of Fift's Vail Fathers wanting to know about ... no, they would never. "But you wouldn't—"

"I wouldn't, huh?" Shria's eyes flashed, hovering somewhere between mischief and anger. "You know there's supposed to have been a time in history when, when they even let Vails *watch*?"

The Compromise of the Spoons, the Permissive Compact ... how did Shria even *know* about that? It was part of the Long Conversation, so it wasn't talked about in general history. "That was, it was a long time ago ..." Fift said. "And there was a war ..." Ze stopped, unsure of what ze should tell Shria. The privacy and silence around them, the deep hidden womb. *We can talk about anything.*

"It's okay, Fift." In the body next to Fift's on the couch, Shria looked away. "You don't have to tell me. It's just how things are set up. *You've* got this whole huge millennia-long tradition, this whole hidden intellectual *world* that helps shape *everything* about *our* world—every decision that Staids make about anything—and we're not allowed to even glimpse it!"

Fift swallowed. "But, I mean, you've got, well ..."

Shria snorted. "What have *we* got? Hitting each other and sex. There's not much mystery there. You can go look up mammal behavior on any science flow on the feed and see all you need to know. And Staids get around to sex eventually, anyway."

Fift felt zirself flushing. Sometimes ze thought ze ought to get zir skin tone darkened. It was a muddy brown, too light to conceal blushing.

"Hmm," Shria said, looking at Fift quizzically. "I guess I can imagine you *might* get curious about sex ..."

Fift's throat was dry. "I'm not—I can't—I mean—"

Shria shrugged. "I think it's perfectly natural. I don't really believe Vails and Staids are that different! There, that's a pretty big secret for you! Because, get this: I've shaped the same genitals for Vails and Staids, and guess what: at the level of the body, it's the same. Getting aroused is the same, feeling pleasure or pain is the same! Maybe the difference is willpower—okay, it's got to be . . . but you can *learn* willpower! You can *learn* concentration! I mean, if I'd been trained since age five to . . . to do whatever you do in the Long Conversation . . . I'd have plenty of willpower, too . . ."

In the body sitting next to Fift, Shria looked heartbroken. Ve stared down at vir hands, folded in vir lap. In vir standing body, ve looked angry, vir eyes flashing beneath vir red eyebrows, and then ve turned away, controlling vemself.

"Whatever," ve said, in vir standing body. "Anyway, it's not all it's cracked up to be."

"It's"—Fift cleared zir throat—"not? What do you mean?"

Shria shrugged. "I mean, it's fun. Sex is fun, if you—if you're not scared or upset or thinking about the wrong thing, if you can focus on what you're doing. I mean, I wouldn't be a genital designer if I didn't . . . you know . . ." Ve paused, and frowned, and began again. "So, Vails my age, the sex is supposed to be, like, this sudden explosion, like more of the same energy and wildness as the fighting, right?"

In vir standing body, ve darted a glance at Fift. Ze nodded.

"You do it," ve said, "and then either you laugh about it, or you get pissed off and fight about it, or you cry. Whatever. *Release.* But if you get too attached to one person—if you get, like, *caught* and carried along in their wake . . ." Ve looked away again, vir expression obscure, like the clouded sky they'd seen years ago, up on the surface of the world. "And you want *vem*, and not just *it* . . . then you get made fun of. Because that's staidish, right? Mooning after someone, longing for their love . . . it's ridiculous. Sometimes I wish *I* was a Staid."

"You *do*?"

Shria shrugged. "Yes. No. I don't know. Maybe that wouldn't be any better. I just want . . . I just want it all, you know? Instead of feeling like half of life is cut off by this wall of what's not allowed." Ve shrugged. "It's a stupid way to even think. It's dangerous."

"It doesn't sound . . ." Fift said. "It doesn't sound stupid . . ."

"It is. You can't fight ratings," Shria said. The jaw of vir sitting body clenched tight. In vir standing body, ve said, "My parents found that out the hard way."

Vir shoulder was a fingerbreadth from Fift's. Ze could put zir arm around vir broad, powerful back. Ze'd done it any number of times; why was ze afraid to now? What would it be like, ze wondered, if they were a hundred years older, if their Courting Century had begun? Then there wouldn't be anything wrong with Fift having the thoughts ze was having now. Even then, Staids were supposed to be shy, to care about the emotional connection and not the physical . . . but you could see plenty of grown-up Staids and Vails kissing, and Fift had lingered at times, careful to just seem to stumble on them in the background of something else ze was looking for . . .

"What . . . person?" Fift said.

In the body sitting next to zir, Shria turned, cocked one eyebrow in question.

"You said, 'if you get too attached to one person,' instead of just . . . fun explosions. So . . . who?"

Shria ran vir fingers through the long red loops of vir hair, swept it from vir foreheads—the same gesture, in both bodies—snapping it together in a clip mounted behind each left ear. A tracing of silver glittered at vir temples, against vir lavender skin. It looked applied, not grown. "Hmm," ve said. "No. I've been telling all the secrets so far. I think it's your turn."

Fift swallowed. "Don't you think maybe Pom and Pip will be—"

"Ha. Stop stalling." Standing, ve put vir hands on vir hips. "Pom will never shut up about zir glorious coup with the Cirque Fantabulous until someone shuts zir up. And your Mom won't be in any hurry to conclude such a profitable transaction. We have plenty of time. No. You. Secret. Now!" In the body beside Fift, ve gave zir a playful shove, vir long-fingered hand clapping on zir shoulder, a gentle, electrifying pressure.

"Okay," Fift said. Ze took a deep breath. If not Shria, then who? If not now, then when? At zir center, deep in, where there should be peace and stillness, there was an unruly sea. "Sometimes I . . . you know what you were saying about sometimes wishing you were . . . not what you are? Sometimes I wonder, well . . . they can make mistakes, can't they?"

"Who?"

"The—the Midwives. When they . . . I mean, they come when you're a baby and they . . ." Fift had watched the house-feed footage of zir gendering a hundred times. It had taken the pair of Midwives, a dour Staid and a bubbly, talkative Vail in matching robes, maybe half an hour—ringing small bells in zir ears, stroking zir tiny hands with feathers, probing and measuring zir reactions—to decide ze was a Staid.

Shria whistled. "I guess. I mean, all those old epics have heroes who get regendered. And people apply today sometimes, too, right? Claim there was a mistake, try to get an adjudicator to declare them *mis*gendered? But I think it hardly ever *works* anymore; they just get postponed and postponed. But Fift, um . . . I mean . . ."

Fift scowled. "I know what you're thinking. I'm not very vailish. I'm not brave or strong or wild, I don't care about dressing up or showing off. I'm not even like Mother Pip, who people used to make fun of because ze's so decisive and loud . . ."

"Right," Shria said. "Or Pom Politigus—I mean, ze gets away with it somehow. I guess people expect a somatic styling impresario to be weird—but all those wacky bodies—!"

"I know," Fift said. "I'm not saying I'd be a better Vail than I am a Staid. I'd be a lousy Vail. You'd probably be better at both—"

"Oh, quit it!" Ve was smiling and frowning at the same time. It was a cockeyed compliment.

"I just . . . sometimes I just want . . . vailish things." Ze flushed. "That I shouldn't."

"Hmm," Shria said. "Okay."

Fift's ears were burning. Ze looked at zir hands. Zir stomach was cold and heavy, as if ze'd eaten ice. Ze shouldn't have said anything.

"I think that's all the vines," Arevio said mildly. "Well done, Fift Brulio."

Fift looked up at zir Father, shocked—ze had almost forgotten where else ze was. Arevio smiled, amused at zir expression. "Are you enjoying your business voyage with Pip Mirtumil?"

"Look, Fift," Shria said, turning to zir. "Like I said before . . . I don't really believe it's as different for Staids and Vails as we all pretend it is. Those things you . . . want . . . there's nothing wrong with that. I think it's normal. I think lots of people wonder if they've been misgendered! It's just too dangerous to say out loud. To challenge the Midwives . . ." Ve shuddered. "But why"—ve licked vir lips—"why *should* they have so much influence? Why *should* everyone be afraid of them? I actually"—ve looked down—"I have a, uh, secret about *that*, too."

"What?" Fift asked vem. "You do?"

Arevio raised an eyebrow.

"Um, yes, thank you," Fift told vem. "It's very—educational."

"Yeah," Shria said, "but . . ." Vir standing body blew out a puff of air. Sitting, ve turned vir face away from Fift. "Yeah, that one's a big one though. Maybe I should work up to it."

"Oh," Fift said. "Well, I don't have a lot more secrets. I might be out. I . . . told you my big one."

"That's *it*? That's fifteen years of secrets?"

"Hmm." Ze tried to think. It was weird sitting here, no agents to ask for help with context or memory, no parents arguing about what ze said. It was peaceful, amazing, but also stressful—a constant unnatural feeling of being somewhere that shouldn't exist, like a hiding place that required you to brace your legs against—"Oh, okay! Remember our bathing pool, at my apartment? There's this ventilation shaft above it— you probably didn't notice it, but it's where the steam goes. Well, you can climb up into it. If you fill the room with steam, you can sneak up in there, and the house feed can't see you at all. You just vanish. I did that a couple of times, and my parents never found out."

"Wow," Shria said. "When did you figure this out?"

"Before we met. I was like eight."

"Vvonda," Shria said.

"What?"

"Vir name is Vvonda." Ve flushed, vir violet skin darkening to plum. "Ve's this big, beautiful, tough . . . Ve's our age, but you don't know vem; ve's from the other side of Foo. We hang out and we, you know, had sex a few times, but then . . . I stopped asking, because I thought it was getting weird. I didn't want vem to think I was always following vem around. There's no reason for vem to think about me. Ve's nice enough, but I'm not . . ." Ve looked down at vir folded hands. "I haven't . . . done anything."

Now Fift did touch Shria; ze put zir hand on vir back, resting it between vir shoulder blades. Fift could feel the muffled echo of vir heartbeat.

"But what about your work here?" ze said. "I mean, every-body's so impressed with you—"

"Oh." Shria shrugged. "I don't think Vvonda would care about that. I don't know." Ve scowled.

"Oh."

"Anyway." Shria's standing body began to pace again, slapping vemself on the abdomen; vir sitting body was still against Fift's hand. "Anyway, it's stupid. I mean, that's not really a big secret. About Vvonda. It doesn't mean anything. I just meant it as an example of how—how things get complicated. Sex sounds like a fun game, but then . . . Anyway." Ve took a deep breath.

"Well," Fift said. "You said you had another secret. A big one."

"Want to see my new genitals?" Shria said.

Fift yanked zir hand away from Shria's back. "Do they have . . . something to do with your . . ."

"Of course not," Shria said. "I'm just stalling."

Fift snorted. "Fine," ze said, feeling a sudden, tiny, guttering flame of bravery catch at the edge of a tangled mossy under-brush of caution. "Show me your fucking genitals."

"Is there another kind?" Shria said sweetly. In vir standing body, ve started unbuttoning vir smoky-gray uniform. It had twenty-seven buttons, which ran from vir right knee, crossing vir body to end under vir left arm.

Fift swallowed.

"Fift?" Arevio was holding out vir hand, and Fift handed vem zir knife. "Thank you." Ve hung up the knives. "I'm off to play snapjump in Wallacomp now, Fift. Will you be all right here? I must say, you seem very distracted."

"Oh," Fift said. "Yes, I'm all right. I need to review things. For school. I mean, that's what I was thinking about. Assign-ments. From my scholastic agents. Even though . . ." Ze swal-lowed. Of course Arevio could see perfectly well from zir logs that ze wasn't doing homework. "Even though I didn't look them up just now or anything. I just remembered that there were some. Many. Actually. So I should do that now. Look them up. And then, um, do them."

The uniform fell to the floor. Shria unwrapped vir undersarong. "Ta da!"

There were no visible genitals. The smooth lavender rows of Shria's abdominal muscles descended into a flourish of blue fur—the rounded curve of the underbelly, the smaller hump of an unmarked mons.

"Oh," Fift said. "Uh . . ."

"Shh!" Shria said. "Watch this." Ve stepped closer to Fift, half an armlength away. Ve closed all vir eyes.

The soft blue fuzz stirred, ruffled, and then separated into a forest of blue cilia, each half a fingerlength long, which rose and twined and waved in the air. They were beautiful—all the shades that are called (in defiance of the greenness of the sky) "sky blue": from midnight, to clear morning . . .

"All right," said Arevio, peering at Fift, who turned abruptly to inspect the vines again. "If you're sure . . ."

Blue and blue and blue—so beautiful, and that feeling crashed through Fift again, like asteroids colliding in the space beyond the world. Ze balled zir hands into fists, but that was in the body in bed. The body in Shria's operating studio in Stiffwaddle Somatic Fashions was reaching out—

Fift put zir hand in among the waving blue fronds, and they were soft as feathers.

"Oh," said Shria, "OH!" Vir eyes flew open, and vir strong hand clamped around Fift's wrist.

In the garden, Fift squeezed zir eyes shut. Thankfully, ze heard zir Father moving away, parting the vines.

The cilia twined around Fift's fingers, threading through them, trapping zir hand.

"Fift," Shria said, vir voice hoarse and urgent. "What—"

"I'm sorry!" Horror flooded through Fift, and ze tried to pull zir hand away gently, but the cilia held. Shria's face was flushed, contorted. "I'm hurting you!"

"No," Shria breathed. Ve closed vir eyes, and vir grip on Fift's wrist loosened. The other hand on vir standing body grabbed Fift's shoulder, slid down to grip zir bicep. "Oh—"

In vir sitting body, behind Fift on the couch, Shria said, "I just didn't—are you sure you—"

Fift wiggled zir hand this way and that, trying to free zirself without hurting Shria. The cilia wound around zir fingers as fast as ze could push them away.

"Yes," Fift said. "Yes, I—"

In vir sitting body, Shria made a guttural sound. Ve pressed vir standing body's forehead into Fift's shoulder, leaning into zir.

"I'm sorry," Fift said, but ze wasn't that sorry; the cilia were soft and warm and feathery-dry, and Shria's warm strong arms pressed around zir shoulders, and it seemed like ze might be doing this right. Zir hearts were pounding, all three.

"Keep saying that," Shria whispered in zir ear. "And keep . . . trying to . . . get away . . ."

"I'm sorry," said Fift, moving zir hand. "I'm sorry. I'm sorry. I'm sorry."

Zir own, old-fashioned, unstylish genitals were swelling, turgid, electrically alive. Even in the body in bed, ze was afraid to touch them. In bed, ze closed zir teeth around the base of zir thumb, hanging on.

Shria's cilia pulled zir gently wiggling hand into their midst. A forest of blue feathery fronds slid and wriggled and whipped over and between and around zir fingers. Shria bit zir shoulder.

"Ow!" Fift said.

"Sorry," Shria gulped, then started to giggle, and then the giggles turned into moans. Ve held zir, shuddering, with both bodies. Vir arms were around zir shoulders, two from the front, two from the back. Vir heads nestled to either side of Fift's neck. It was as warm and safe as a snuggle, but zir mouth was dry and zir blood pounded in zir ears. "Ummmmm," Shria said, and the cilia let go, fluffed up, and settled back down into a modest blue fuzz.

Ve sat up and turned away. In vir naked body, ve rubbed vir eyes. Ve didn't look at Fift, but picked up vir undersarong, shook it out, and, watching it closely, wrapped it around vir waist. "Well," ve said.

A silence grabbed them. They'd fallen into it, and it clung to them—as if they'd fallen off the edge of Foo and were trapped in the sticky, invisible webs that braced the habitations in midair.

Fift's hand throbbed. It had been—it had been there among vir—

What was Shria thinking now? Fift couldn't see vir faces. There was no feed in the room, and ve had turned away. It was one thing to have theories about how staidchildren had the same bodies and urges as vailchildren. It was quite another to be trapped in a room with a toadclown. Fift had just . . . *grabbed*. Even another *Vail* would probably have said something: asked, or challenged, or *something*—they must have some kind of rituals or introductions around their childhood sport-sex. What ze had done was different: bizarre, shocking, wrong. Gluttonous, like a two-year-old stuffing sweetlace into zir mouths . . .

"Well," Shria said. "Well. Twice-born Kumru's bloody placenta, with sugar on top."

In vir standing body, buttoning vir buttons, ve turned back to Fift. Beside zir, ve was still turned away. Ve looked . . . worried. Maybe scared. Ve started to reach a hand towards zir, then took it back.

"I'm—I'm sorry, Fift. I shouldn't have—I don't know how that . . . happened."

Fift flushed. "What do you mean? Was it—did you not—like it?"

Shria frowned, blinked. A jumble of expressions crossed vir face, like the choppy surface of a splashpool when different waves intersect. Ve settled on a smirk. "Well *yeah*, I liked it. But that's not the—I shouldn't have—"

"It was me," Fift said. "It was my idea. I did it."

"Well, okay," Shria said. "I know. But I'm the one who—I should have—"

"You said it didn't matter. You said Vails and Staids were the same."

"That's not *exactly* what I said. I said that the *feelings* must be the same. But Fift—"

"How do you pee?" Fift asked.

Shria stopped, blinked again. Ve turned, in vir sitting body, towards zir. "I have a urinary pistil. I hope you're not going to start with that Foundationist claptrap about system-separatory antivalences and somatic harmony theory?"

"Uh . . . no," Fift said, "because I have no idea what that is."

"Oh. Never mind. Genital designer infighting. I'll spare you the holy wars." Ve shook vemself, stretched vir arms above vir head and cracked vir back.

"That was, um." Fift's throat was tight, zir voice slightly strangled. "That was sex?"

"Yup," Shria said. Ve buttoned vir last button, took vir hair out of its clip, and smoothed it.

"Oh," Fift said. "I didn't know it would be so . . . easy. I mean, simple. I mean. You know."

Shria snorted.

"You know what I mean," Fift said. "I thought it . . . took longer."

"Why don't you quit while you're ahead?" Shria said. Vir voice was tight. Vir other body, next to Fift, stood up, and paced across the room.

"I can't tell if you're kidding or if you're angry," Fift said.

Shria pulled a comb from the tool rack. Ve sat down in front of vemself. In vir standing body, ve began to tug the comb through vir sitting body's hair. "I'm not angry," ve said. "It's okay."

"Did I say something wrong?" Fift said.

"No, Fift. But . . . it's *not* simple. Or easy. That's all."

"Oh." Fift swallowed. "I guess now we have another secret."

Shria nodded, looking grim. "Yeah, I'd say we do."

Fift's throat constricted. Ze looked down at zir hands. They were trembling. Ze forced zir face to be still, expressionless. What was wrong with zir? It was zir fault. It was zir responsibility. Shria depended on zir to be the still center, to hold them both stable, in safety, in harmony, and instead . . .

If Fift were really a Vail, underneath everything—if ze were really misgendered—ze would probably cry now. But ze couldn't remember how to cry. When ze was seven, flailing through zir somatic integration exercises with a dozen strangers heckling over the feed, the sobs had been right at the surface, caught in zir chest, wanting to burn through, barely held back. Now there was nothing.

Shria looked at zir and put the comb away. Ve snapped vir long red hair back into place. Ve came over, in both bodies, and sat on either side of Fift.

"Hey," ve said.

Fift said nothing.

"Did you . . . like it too?" ve said.

It was a shocking question, but Fift couldn't lie. Shria

moaning, and the soft blue fronds, and the electric feeling of connection, as if ze was making vem real, shaping vem with zir hands like the Trickster crafting vir lesser selves. As if ve was making zir real. Ze had never felt so powerful, or so vulnerable, or so close to someone . . . like they were under each other's skin.

Ze nodded.

"What do Staids do?"

Fift frowned.

"Come on, I know you do something. I'm not talking about the Long Conversation, either. You have bodies. You . . ."

Fift shrugged. "We snuggle. It's not the same thing."

"But surely it's kind of . . . ?"

"No," Fift said, "it's really not."

"Show me," Shria said.

"You know how to snuggle," Fift said. "It's nothing new. It's how they carried you as a baby. Staids are just babies . . ."

"Now you're being ridiculous. Show me."

Fift frowned. Shria, lanky and fiery and beautiful and dangerous, snuggled up like an egg in a nest? It occurred to zir that ve was trying to even things out, trying to put vemself in a situation at least half as bizarre as that of a staidchild having sex.

"I don't—"

Ve took zir hand, pulled zir closer. "Show me."

Fift wrapped zir arms around Shria, scooted nearer, zir hip pressed against virs. Ze leaned down, put the side of zir head against vir chest, zir cheek on the softness of vir breasts. They were little breasts, firm, four of them in a row. Shria wrapped Fift up in vir arms. Ze rested against vem. Ze closed zir eyes.

Shria smelled good, fresh and mellow and rich, like something from the surface, or some newly invented spice.

Had Fift done something horrible? Was it horrible, what ze had done?

In the supper garden, weariness was sinking into zir arms, zir legs. Ze walked among the vines, reaching out to touch their velvety surfaces, the harder ridges at the edges of the cuts where the spice-gnats swarmed. Green light filtered through the leaves. The ceiling of the garden disappeared in a tangle of vegetation.

Zir agents were prodding zir, in the supper garden: homework, news, invitations, drab Long Conversation rankings gossip from zir not-really-friends in the local prep group. Ze pushed them away.

Shria stroked zir rough, stubbled scalp. Ze nestled against vem. Ze wanted to be closer still, to flow into vem, to merge, to be sheltered somewhere deep and safe inside vir fiery storm, but ze could not. There was an indissoluble border of skin and bone between them. Ze was trapped on this side of it.

Shria breathed deep. Fift could feel the muscles of vir back relaxing, one by one, under zir arms.

"It's not so different at first," Shria said. "This snuggling. From just embracing, I mean. But then if you wait, it actually—"

"Shria," Fift said. "Hush."

"Oh," Shria said. "Okay."

Ze lay down in the supper garden and watched the still green vines overhead.

Their breathing slowed. Their heartbeats slowed, a bit at a time, one and then the other, like slipdancers circling their common center, closing in, slowing, coming together, until they were almost, almost, one.

After a while, a good long while, ze sighed.

"You had one more big secret," ze said.

"Mmm," Shria said. Ve was resting on zir, vir chin against zir scalp. "Right. Well, I still don't know if I should . . ."

There was a ping in their headspace; a message wriggling through the anti-surveil, stirring their drowsing agents, vibrating with Mother Pip's barely concealed impatience. Muffled but insistent, wondering what was taking them so long.

"Fuck," Shria said.

"We'd better go," Fift said.

"Fuck," ve said. "I'll—wait. Wait. I'll tell you." Ve leaned down, put vir mouth by Fift's ear.

"It's about the Clowns," ve whispered. "The Cirque. When they were here. People relax here, you know? They trust the anti-surveil. No one pays attention to the apprentice setting up the scopes—"

The ping came again, the insistence no longer concealed.

"They want," Shria whispered, "to 'put the Midwives in their place.'"

A bolt of cold drilled through Fift's spine. "What?"

"That's what they said. They have some kind of plan. Something big."

"Like what?"

Shria shrugged. Ve let go of Fift and stood. "Come on," ve said, and one of vir bodies dove through the dilating cervix of the room.

In vir other body ve reached back and gave Fift's shoulder a squeeze. Ve looked a little relieved, a little scared. "Come on," ve said again. "Let's not get in more trouble."

Fift got up, unsteadily, from the couch.

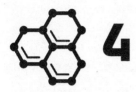 **4**

The Clowns didn't strike that summer. Fall came, draining chlorophyll from the leaves of the deciduous trees on the surface far above Fullbelly, so that the forests were lit up like fire. The mornings were frosty, and bodies on the surface shivered with the chill. It was hunting season, and surface time was oversubscribed. (Father Smistria cackled at the slackwits freezing themselves half to death to pretend they were ancient hunter-gatherers; Father Nupolo chided vem for ignoring the benefits of the surface-going minority for planetary resilience.) Then the first snows came, and the queues at the elevators disappeared.

Shria sent {Hi} and Fift sent {Hi} back; after that, they didn't know what to say. They kept trying—discussing, with grinding awkwardness, homework and food, and recommending each other clip-opera series (Shria liked *Goopfield Pratfalls With Perm and Trink*, though ve said it was mindless; Fift sort of liked *Middleborn at Three Hundred Why Mother Why?!*, though plenty of it was overdramatic mugging for the feed.)

Fift told Shria about zir new cousin. The new cousin was Chalia Rigorosa Spin-Nupolo of name registry Yellow Peninsula Sugarbubble 3, which made Chalia and Fift name-cousins as well as birth-cousins. Everyone said that was lucky.

Iraxis cohort was busy that fall, with preparations for the birth and the naming ceremony, and helping the new parental cohort get settled in Slow-as-Molasses. It was a great honor for Father—and now Auntie—Nupolo, that vir sibling Ellix's parental cohort, all twenty-two parents plus the new baby, had moved there to benefit from vir child-rearing wisdom, and so Chalia could grow up near Fift.

"And naming it after you, Nupes!" Frill said. "What a coup!"

"It's too much," Nupolo said, fiercely, shaking vir head. "I don't deserve such acclamation."

"You do, though," Arevio said shyly, slipping vir hand in Nupolo's.

That winter, Fift rarely saw more than one of Nupolo's or Squell's or Arevio's bodies at home. They were always out fussing over the new family. Fift got to hold Chalia, in vir fragile first body, when ve was a week old. Ve looked up at zir with questioning eyes, as if asking zir, "Well? How is it here? Have I made it to the right place?" Ze wished ze could answer vem with any certainty.

Fift and Shria's messages tiptoed through a goopfield of too-dangerous topics. When ze told vem about Chalia's birth, ze avoided saying anything about the Midwives who'd come to gender the baby, even though that was the climax of the whole thing. Ze didn't ask about Vvonda, or about Shria's work. Shria, too, often trailed off into silence. Even topics that seemed safe at first—gossip about mutual acquaintances, complaints about their parents—tended to run into walls, into {okay, I gotta go, bye}, {Bye.}

They knew their parents would be reading their messages, and Fift was terrified that zirs would begin to wonder about the lost hour, when their child was utterly hidden from the world.

It was as if a secret doorway had opened during that lost

hour, a doorway to a magic world where anything could happen. And anything *had*. Ze had been intoxicated. Ze had lost zir hold on the center, had been flung free, into the void.

They certainly never mentioned the Clowns.

What would it be like if ze could see Shria in person, body near body, near enough to feel vir warmth? Ze tried to stop thinking about it. Ze didn't dare visit, or invite Shria over; what if zir parents noticed something? Ze even avoided watching Shria over the feed; the feed made everything flat and strange and hollow anyway.

There was nothing to do but survive these years, to buckle down and learn, to sit and pass spoons, to recite (ze was working on the various addenda to the alternate codification of the twelfth emergent mode), to ponder, to wait.

A couple of times, Shria mentioned where ve'd be that day in a way that sounded like an invitation. But of course it was never anywhere with even a modicum of privacy, never mind the rock-solid anti-surveillance of Stiffwaddle Somatic Fashions, and Fift didn't go.

Mother Pip, of course, had not become one of the region's premiere banker-historians by being oblivious to emotional nuance. Ze knew that Fift was infatuated with Shria.

Had ze suspected how far things had gone, ze would have been appalled, enraged; but ze didn't. Ze assumed the attraction was one-sided. A Staid's adolescence was full of crushes—intense, muted, stifled longings—and if the target this time was, inappropriately, a vailchild, well . . . this sort of thing did happen. Ze sympathized. Vails had always captured zir own imagination, even early on, in zir own unusual childhoods.

Father Grobbard, now: had *ze* suspected Fift of forming

such an attachment, *ze* might have felt it necessary to impose a complete separation, in order to impress upon Fift the importance of propriety for a young Staid of good family. And if Squell or Arevio or Nupolo had suspected, they might have panicked at the thought that Fift was gendering poorly.

Pip took a different view.

Ze had suffered, in zir own childhood, from the intolerance of others. No one could fault zir cool analytical precision; but ze had a boldness—a brashness—even an impatience—that many found unseemly in a Staid. This had not endeared zir to zir age-mates. Even later, in zir Courting Century, Staids tended to avoid zir; Vails found zir boldness endearing, but mildly ridiculous, and zir physical appetites hilarious.

But these trials had forged zir character and honed zir will. Ze could consider disapproved-of things calmly, when others shied away. Pom Politigus was not the only client Pip had taken on as a struggling maverick only to see zir become a star.

Fift, to be sure, was not overly bold. Fift was awkward; a loner; mediocre in school and (worse) in the Long Conversation; plodding as an apprentice. Worst of all, from Pip's point of view: ze lacked ambition. (Really, ze was already as emotionally impoverished as an elderborn: one might as well just cast the chance-sticks again and have a second child. If only one's cohort was not so exhaustingly deadlocked in the matter! But then, with seven lovely, infuriating, emotional, fractious Vails and only dear, accommodating old Grobbard to calm them down, what did one expect? They'd barely held together this long. Miskisk, particularly, continued to be a problem. It was all a lesson in the dangers of succumbing too thoroughly to one's inclinations.)

At any rate, this Shria—ve *was* ambitious. The work ve'd done for the Cirque—at such an age! And Pom's patronage already secured. Perhaps, then, this . . . association . . . shouldn't be too harshly discouraged? Crushes could be helpful in the formation of character. Some of Shria's verve and vision might rub off on Fift.

Obviously, Pip could not say this to the others. Ze didn't want to be accused of encouraging Fift in vailish pursuits (never mind pursuits of Vails)! No, if ze was to extend any aid in the matter of zir child and Pom's star apprentice, it would have to be subtle enough that ze would not have to hear about it at zir next hundred breakfasts. So ze bided zir time.

It was late winter when Pom's letter arrived, with the Ticket enclosed. The Cirque had announced a new performance series, not housed in their usual arenas and amphitheaters, but "in the midst of life." The posting read:

O PERSON! O CHILD OF FATE!

(They always had been a little pompous, Pip reflected.)

HAVE YOU WONDERED IF THIS IS THE WORLD FOR YOU?

WHY NOT FIND OUT?

THE CIRQUE FANTABULOUS—JESTERS TO THE CHURCH OF THE INVETERATE TRICKSTER (RASPBERRIED BE VIR NAME) SINCE THE AGE OF WAR, FANDANGLERS OF CHAOS, MARSH-MELLOWS OF MARSHES THAT DIED BEFORE TIME, PICKPOCKETS OF THE WALLET OF BLESSED KUMRU—SPIT ON YOUR PIETIES AND SNUGGLE YOUR RIOTIES, AND INVITE YOU (SHOULD YOU HAVE A TICKET) TO THEIR (WHO ARE WE KIDDING? OUR!) NEXT SERIES OF PERFORMANCE EVENTS:

UNRAVELING: A REVOLUTION!

THIS EVENT IS UNWALLED! LOOK FOR IT IN NO STADIUMS, LINE UP IN NO LINES! DO NOT COME TO SEE US! IF YOU HAVE A TICKET, WE WILL COME TO SEE YOU!

It went on in this vein for a good while, very clever and self-congratulatory. Unsluiced blockage, really. But it was a great coup for Politigus to have received a pair of the very hard to come-by Tickets in recognition of zir work on the somatology of the Cirque's local chapter.

{I trust you'll find a use for this.} Pom's note accompanying the ticket read. {No time to go myself, alas, so I've given mine to Shria; I'm sure ve will fill me in on the details. With compliments.}

Pom Politigus was no fool, either.

So when Fift hinted for the third time, somewhat more directly than before, that perhaps there were one or two new developments in the books of Stiffwaddle Somatic that might—of course, who was ze to say, but possibly, in zir provisional judgement, wherein ze would defer to Pip absolutely, but simply to bring it to zir attention, perhaps a visit might be in order, and if Pip had no time, ze was sure ze . . .

"No, no, that's all wrapped up," Pip said gruffly. "Here." Ze handed Fift the Ticket. "Compliments of Politigus. Some kind of show. I have no time for this nonsense, but we can't let them go unused." Fift stared at the thing in confusion. Pip lay a hand on zir shoulder. "Banker-historians must do a great many things, Fift, to cultivate relationships with their clients. If that means walking the byways with a Ticket, looking to be ambushed by a band of pretentious Clowns, so be it. You'll want to contact Pom's apprentice . . . what was vir name, Shria Kwonk Fnax? Ve's going too. The show isn't anywhere in particular, but take a body and wander around the below and beyond for a few hours, and you might see something or other . . ."

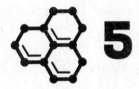 **5**

They'd never been this deep before. They'd never been this far from home, either, unless you counted field trips to the surface, but that was *out*—boring trees and cold dirt and badly cooked bunnies—and this was *in*.

They could pick out both Foo and Stiffwaddle in the middle distance above their heads, two colorful landmarks amid the several hundred thousand habitations visible from the platform where they stood: Foo grinding in its slow rotation with ponderous solidity, Stiffwaddle dangling and glimmering in gracile wispiness. Far above, the roof of Fullbelly was mottled like a forest floor at noon, with light from the glowtubes far below filtering through the jumbled array of habitations.

"What do you think?" Fift said.

Shria squinted over the edge. "Let's take the fast sluice over there." Ve pointed at a pair of travelers zipping down the twisting ribbon of the sluice, impact-dampening foam sloshing around them. "It's the quickest way to that pavilion."

Fift chewed zir lip. "Hardly anyone in the polylogue thinks the sighting at the pavilion was real."

Worldwide, about three million people had Tickets to the Cirque Fantabulous's latest Show; in Fullbelly, the number of

Ticket Holders was two hundred thousand, roughly one per million inhabitants. A few tens of thousands of them could be found on the "Ticket Holders In Search Of the Show!" polylogue.

"I don't think any of the sightings are real," Shria said. "I don't think it's started yet."

"Do you think there even *is* a show?" Fift asked. "Or is it like . . . a meta thing? Where looking for the show *is* the show?"

Shria shrugged. "Maybe. But I doubt it. I think it's going to be real." Ve looked off into the distant habitation-sprawl and vir eyes grew hungry. "I think it's going to be *big*."

Fift felt a stab of unease in zir stomach. This felt like an allusion to Shria's secret about the Clowns, and ze was acutely aware that zir parents were probably watching. Ze'd checked at the first sluice they'd taken: Fathers Grobbard, Squell, and—weirdly—Miskisk had been listed in zir audience. Since then, ze hadn't wanted to look.

"But if the sightings are fake, then why . . ." ze said.

"We should go *somewhere*," Shria said. "And in the pavilion down there they have mangareme fluffies."

At the other end of the platform, the sluice operator stood, singlebodied, a middle-aged Vail in full sluice operator regalia: a heavy jacket with multiple frilled ridges, glittering sashes inked with schematic diagrams of population-flow logistics, a purple Ascensionist devotional plume towering above vir hat, and epithets—Guardian of Fullbelly's Energic Balance, Regulator of the Flow—spelled out in the air around vem by swarms of glowflies.

At least it was a sluice ve was guarding, and not an elevator—they weren't asking to be hauled upwards yet. But they were so far from home that the sluice operator was unlikely to believe they would walk all the way up again on stairways.

Ve glowered at them. What could they offer, vir eyes asked—two sixteen-year-olds from unremarkable cohorts, marooned in the wasteland of First Childhood, with no reason to be here other than a vague hunch about a possibly nonexistent performance?—to justify the additional energy, the logistical complexity, the risks and annoyances of permitting them to descend *another* three hundred bodylengths, on *vir* sluice?

How could Fift and Shria possibly prevail in the transaction?

On an ordinary day, they couldn't have. Fift wouldn't dare try, and even Shria would have been bested by that cold glare, knowing ve had no real reason to venture so far from home and insufficient emotional capital to stare the sluice operator down.

Today, they'd done it three times already, two sluices and a spinbounce. Each time, they'd prevailed. But each time, they got farther away from home, and it got harder.

"Come on," Shria said, taking Fift's hand. Ve grinned.

The sluice operator's eyes narrowed as they approached, taking the measure of them. Fift read vir story from lookup, too, with a banker-historian's eye: **Thesid Minorict of name registry Understandable Deviation 4, 3-bodied Vail, 368 years old, elderborn.** Part of a provisional proto-cohort with two other Vails and one Staid; a diligently practicing Ascensionist (*An ironic religion,* Fift thought, *for a sluice operator; an elevator would be more ascensive!*); at this job for the last fifty years; staunch, well-regarded, unexceptional; no challenges on the mats, ever; no particular martial or aesthetic or somatic glories; but vir confidence was displayed in the very thoroughness with which ve allowed vir stolid ordinariness to be detailed in lookup. Economic-emotional status firmly, immovably, in the satisfied/contributing zone.

Fift nervously examined zir own emotional balance. As usual it was a volatile, unresolved mess, even more so than a sixteen-year-old child's should be. When ze focused on Shria's mischievous smile, though, zir balance strengthened, burrowing from a periphery of uncertain despair towards a center of excitement and wonder. They had Tickets. Shria was holding zir hand, they were together, and they had Tickets.

"We have Tickets," Shria said to the sluice operator.

Here was the kernel of the thing, the moment on which the whole world's economy rested: Who would supplant whom? Whose desires would prevail? Thesid's eyes narrowed.

Ve was tasked with maintaining the energy balance of this region, so ve didn't want to let two vagabond kids on vir sluice. But energy balances were humdrum and boring in the eyes of the world, and the Cirque was exciting and electrifying. If Thesid turned them away, some people would commend vem as a responsible guardian; others would condemn vem as a spoilsport arrogant enough to put zir humble sluice above the Clown's great work of art and the innocent enthusiasm of two children invited to it.

No doubt Thesid's agents were arguing the point back and forth, tallying the ratings, making bets on the best course.

But Thesid did this all day. Even an apprentice banker-historian could sense that the sluice operator didn't pay much attention to vir agents' reports and tallies: ve went with vir gut.

Ve narrowed vir eyes and stared at Fift and Shria, as if to see if they would flinch, or plead, or bluster. Fift squeezed Shria's hand, and the two of them beamed. And Thesid grunted—whether in grudging approval, or simply resignation, Fift couldn't tell—and let them through.

The mangareme fluffies were delicious. They sipped them, swinging in seating harnesses at a table in the middle of the pavilion.

"Where else are you?" Fift asked.

"Hanging out with Bluey and Vvonda at the South Foo spring-buckle—they are *totally* jealous of us. I'm doublebodied there. You?"

Fift's heart pulsed. Was Shria still . . . carried along in Vvonda's wake? "Sleeping and studying."

"You're pretty much always lonebodied, aren't you?"

Ze flushed and looked down at zir fluffy and the red-and-white-flecked table. It seemed like an impolite thing to say. Of course, zir Vail Fathers said things like that all the time, stupid tactless observations of things everyone could see, and no one ought to mention. But Shria didn't always act that way.

Now, for instance, ve seemed to get that ve had intruded. Ve scanned the faces around the pavilion. "Hey!" ve said, grabbing zir arm so that their seating harnesses swung together. "Look!"

"Is it the Cirque?" ze asked.

"No. Or I don't know, who knows? But it's that alien."

"What?" Fift dragged a foot, slowing the swinging of zir harness, and sat up straighter to see.

"You know, the old Staid over there." Ve pointed at a stout, round-shouldered, heavy-bosomed person in a white suit. Ze looked no older than Father Grobbard. "Do a lookup. Thavé. Zir name is Thavé."

That was all that lookup gave for the Staid across the Pavilion: **Thavé**. A single name, and some obscure pointers. "What name registry?" Fift said, trying to figure out how to navigate the pointers.

"You have to look in general info, as if ze were a country or something. Ze predates name registries."

"Wow." Fift found the entry. Ze'd been expecting a bare minimum: identity, publicly disclosed locations, wealth, profession. But looking up Thavé was like looking up some ancient monument: scholarly articles; illustrated profiles from quaint lifestyle magazines of three hundred years ago; incomprehensible thousand-year-old political cartoons; annotated analyses of scholarly articles; dramatizations and satires of events ten thousand years in the past for stage, viz, immersive, voice-play, circus, and hoaxgame; bibliographies of annotated analyses of scholarly articles; schoolchildren's essays; manifestoes, denunciations, tributes, satires, joke-books, songbooks, recipes; parodies of bibliographies of annotated analyses of scholarly articles. Thavé was, apparently, half a million years old; and wasn't that—Fift tried to remember—older than the world?

"Ze's *twelve-bodied*," Shria said, "with six public locations. Can you imagine having twelve? It makes my head hurt."

"Let's go talk to zir," Fift said.

"What? Really?" Shria sounded horrified or excited; Fift couldn't tell which. "Are you serious?"

"Sure." Ze stood up. Ze felt a little fear prickling zir scalp, but weren't they rich today? Didn't they have Tickets? "Maybe ze's part of the show."

"Oh, maybe!" Shria said. "Hey, maybe it's not really zir!"

"What?" Fift frowned. "But we did a lookup."

"This is the Cirque, remember?"

"You think they can mess with lookup? Shria . . ."

Shria shrugged. "Who knows?"

Fift slid out of zir harness and onto the ground. Ze bowed to zir mangareme fluffy; it dipped once in acknowledgement and flew back to the kitchen. "Let's go."

"Okay . . ." Shria took zir arm. "Kumru! I never knew you were so brave, Fift."

"What's brave about it? Ze doesn't eat people."

Thavé was sitting at a table alone, zir white hat in the harness beside zir. Ze was spinning a globe of tea with one hand, occasionally sipping from it, and reading a long, folded black-

and-white paper. No one around them was paying any attention to zir. Ze looked up, unsmiling, as they approached. Fift's step faltered for a moment, but ze kept going.

Thavé took zir hat out of the harness and put it on the table.

"Hi," Shria said.

"Hey," Thavé said. "Sit down."

They sat.

"Are you really . . ." Shria said.

Thavé smiled. "The alien? Yeah." Ze chuckled. Zir eyes flicked to Fift, then to Shria, doing a lookup. "You're a bit far from home, I think? Looks like you're having a good day."

"Yeah," Shria said. Ve glanced at Fift as if to say, *Should we tell zir?* Fift nodded. "We have Tickets."

"To the Cirque?" Thavé said. "Me too." Ze patted zir pocket.

"Oh," Shria said.

Fift looked intently at the alien. It felt like ze should ask something important. It was a once-in-a-lifetime chance, meeting someone from somewhere . . . else. But it was confusing. What should ze ask? *Are you really half a million years old?* (That seemed improbable; how could anyone live that long? But it said so right on the lookup entry: Thavé's bodies were ordinary, grown recently, but Thavé zirself was a creation of some lost Far Technology that no one . . . not even Thavé . . . understood anymore.) *What's it like being an alien?* What could Thavé say to that? Dumb questions. There were some standard phrases, traditional expressions of politeness towards an older Staid, but they felt wrong. Was Thavé even really a Staid? Ze was older than Staid and Vail, right? Ze could ask that: *Are you really a Staid?* But that would be shockingly rude, maybe not the best way to start a conversation with an alien.

"What do you think of us?" Shria said.

"Of the two of you?" Thavé asked.

"No. Of all of us." Ve gestured around and above the pavilion, towards Fullbelly, the surface, the world. "I mean, you're pretty much the only one who has something to compare us to."

"What a good question. You know, I've been here twenty thousand years. I've kind of gotten used to it." Ze pursed zir lips.

Ze looked so ordinary, Fift thought. It was as if Fift saw the scene doublebodied: one body's eyes seeing an ordinary, rumpled, middle-aged Staid; the other seeing some strange cold alien thing with secret, incomprehensible meanings, plans, and intentions.

"It's been a long time," Thavé said, "since I . . . compared you to anything."

"Really?" said Shria. "It seems like you would do that all the time."

Thavé scratched zir head. "Well, just in one sense: I think about your survival. I spend a lot of time comparing you to other places, worlds that survived a long time, or a short time. More than I should, actually, because I don't think it helps. But in terms of, I don't know, the food, the clothes, the genders, the language? Twenty thousand years is a long time. I'm part of your society now. I mostly compare you to your grandparents. Like, I think, 'I miss threedee, will that come back?'"

"You think about our survival?" Fift said.

"Yes," Thavé said. "That's sort of my job. I'm a survival consultant."

"And how is our survival doing?" Shria said.

Thavé looked at vem quickly. For a moment, ze looked nervously down at zir food. Ze was eating some odd purple strips that Fift had never seen before. Ze stabbed one with a set of eating tines. "Well," ze said. "In one sense, fine. There's a lot of homeostasis. You've been mostly at peace for a long time. Your economy has decent turnover. Economic class is bound to birth order, which is hardly egalitarian, but at least it's moderately anti-accumulative. And the system is very efficient at resolving conflict." Ze put the purple strip in zir mouth and chewed. "You're good environmental stewards—you're not running the planet into the ground. Population pressure is low because the resource costs of birthing are growing at about the same rate as life expectancy. I'm not sure how long that can last, but so far you've been pretty remarkable at finding new ways to make it more complicated to have a baby, without much help from me."

Fift couldn't follow all of this, but ze flagged it to go over later. It sounded like the world was doing fine, but Thavé still looked uneasy. "So what's the other sense?"

"Well," said Thavé. "You're a monoculture. All your shatter-balls are in one scoop." Ze chewed some more, then swallowed. "Which is my fault as much as anyone's."

"Really?" Shria asked.

"In a way. You see, there are two main schools of cultural survival management. One encourages many distinct dynamic cultures: conflicts, expansion, booms and busts. You know: populations grow, get rich, develop dense tech. Sooner or later factions chafe against each other or their own internal tensions, and then there's a big, cathartic war, or a plague that knocks them back down to sparse tech, sparse population." Ze inspected zir fork. "The first school . . . thinks it's best not to interfere with this cycle. Like letting forest fires happen naturally to clear out undergrowth? That's the original, lost sense of 'wildfire' in your language, by the way: 'fire that protects the wilds,' that keeps the forest healthy. And this school was dominant from, oh, about 350,000 years ago up until 200,000 years ago."

"It doesn't sound like so much fun for the culture being managed," Shria said.

"Well, maybe not to you," Thavé said. "But you might be surprised. Those cultures are exciting. The sky's the limit! Rags to riches! To the stars!" Ze waved zir eating tines. "Live free or die! Remember, much of the cycle is upswing. Most people's lives involve getting richer. You just don't want to be the generation that rolls triple-nulls." Ze stabbed another purple strip. "If you brought someone from one of those cultures here, they'd die of boredom. They wouldn't understand why you're not spending your time building star-ships."

"Building what?" Fift said.

"Star-ships. To go terraform other planets."

Fift did a lookup on 'terraform,' but the entry didn't make much sense. Sort of like digging Fullbelly? "I don't get it."

Thavé pinched the bridge of zir nose. "You know, you'd build some enormous vehicle, or a bunch of small ones, and you'd—well, for instance, you could take it to some other planet circling some other star, and engineer that planet so that you can live on it—or in it—and then you live there."

"What?" Shria said. "But other planets don't usually have air."

"Right," Thavé said. "You'd have to build air."

"And what about bodylag?" Fift said. "There's no way you could compensate for that. Your bodies would—I mean, you couldn't keep them in communication, so . . . they'd . . ." A chill went through zir. One of zir bodies was still asleep, but the third climbed out of the study-pit and started to pace the hallway, wrapping and unwrapping a length of cloth from zir robe. "You'd just fall apart," that body said, alone in the silent hall.

"You'd have to take all your bodies with you, or not go," Thavé said.

Shria looked sidelong at Fift. {What in the abandoned void . . . ?} "Let me . . . let me get this straight," ve said. "You'd have to put some impossible amount of resources into building machines that could push you . . ." Ve frowned, clearly calling on vir agents for calculation. "Push *huge masses* to . . . other *stars*."

Thavé nodded.

"Which are . . . *really* far away. So it would take . . . *lifetimes*. And then when you finally *got* there, they'd be bare rocks or have poisonous atmospheres. No nutrient flow—not even any *nutrients* in the whole place! Right?"

Thavé raised zir eyebrows in agreement.

"And it would take centuries of work—at least!—to totally . . . *deface* them into looking sort of like a planet you could live on."

"At least," Thavé said.

"And meanwhile you'd be living in a vehicle," Fift murmured.

"Well, someone would be," Thavé said.

"And even if you spent huge energies," Shria said, "you'd just be sending some tiny, tiny part of the people in the world . . . and the rest would have to deal with all the waste and disorganization these 'star-trips' created. And the people who *did* go would be so far away that they couldn't even talk to their friends and parents anymore, or even *see* each other over the feed. And everyone would be poorer, because they'd be missing what the others would have given them!" Ve spread vir hands. "And then, after all that expense and heartbreak, you'd have a . . . a *world* that was . . . pretty much like what *you already had in the first place*! If you were *incredibly* lucky! Is that . . . is that what you're saying?"

Thavé nodded. "Pretty much."

"What?!" Shria exploded.

"Except you'd have two of them."

Shria looked at Fift. "That is the most broken idea I've ever heard."

Fift shrugged. In the hallway, ze tugged and tugged and tugged on the length of cloth. Should they be taunting the alien like this? Ze wondered what kind of conversation ze and Thavé would be having without Shria. Ze couldn't imagine zirself telling the alien zir idea was broken.

"But of course," said Thavé, "that is how you all got here in the first place."

There was a long pause.

"It is?" Shria said.

"Yeah," Fift said quietly. Ze was hazy on the details, but it sounded right. Before the Age of Roads and Doors. What was it . . . ? "'On beetly wings soft-kissed by unseen light, / and shimmering with seen . . .'?"

Thavé smiled. "Did you think you were born out of the womb of this planet's soil?"

Shria frowned. "I guess I never thought about it."

"They used to say every culture in the Dispersal of Humanity had a central creation story. Yet another theory to toss into the compost-sluice of history." Thavé leaned back from the table, swinging gently.

"Do you have to go?" Fift asked. "Or can you finish what you were saying, about the two schools of thought?"

"Oh? Right." Ze put a hand against the table to stop the swing. "So the problem with the Cyclic-Expansionist school is, pretty soon you have a whole bunch of these expanding, collapsing societies, and they run into each other, and you get a lot of offensive weaponry, including these very exclusionist, binary ideologies—you know, 'all X must die,' says Y, and 'all Y must die,' says X. So you get these cascading cross-cultural cycles of destruction, and sooner or later that sends the whole pattern into an escalating instability that's no longer manageable. You get to a density of technology where it takes a few hundred years to terraform a planet and only a few days to blow it up, and you can't manage those swings anymore. Pretty soon you've got events that don't just cull—they extinguish, and you can't stop them."

Ze was talking very calmly, but ze wasn't looking at them anymore. Ze was looking at zir eating tines. It occurred to Fift that this wasn't theory for Thavé. Ze slid zir hand across the table toward the other Staid. Thavé looked down at it sharply, blinked once, and took it.

"I'm sorry," Fift said. Shria looked from one of them to the other and pressed vir lips shut.

"Yes. Well." With the other hand, Thavé put zir tines down, took a cloth out of zir pocket, and mopped zir brow. Ze didn't let go of Fift's hand. "It was a difficult time. Or times. Hm." Ze cleared zir throat. "In any event. The other school of thought, the Gardenist school . . . well, you're living it. Firewall off each society via the disinclination to travel that you, Shria, summarized so eloquently. Get them stable, get them using resources wisely, get them out of the habit of large-scale war. Some people used to call it 'tropical gathering' as opposed to 'temperate farming': Keep a constant amount that's always growing, instead of needing to till and sow and harvest."

"So what's wrong with that?" Shria said. "Isn't that the right way?"

Thavé looked at the table for a while. Zir hand was warm and a little moist in Fift's. "Firstly, you have a lot fewer sites than you would if you were doing it the Cyclic-Expansionist way, because your populations don't do much exploring or expanding. So that makes you anxious. And second, well . . ." Ze sighed. "When you're farming cultures, you know where they are in the cycle, at least as long as they don't hit the catastrophic overlapping-culture scenario. If you're managing them reasonably well, you know if it's a safe time, a growing time, or if the cull is coming. And you've set it up so that most of the cultures will survive that cull. There will be a blaze of glory and destruction, lots for the poets to sing about next time around (the poetry in these places often runs to tragedy, not statistics). And then it's time to rebuild."

Ze looked up at them, frowning, then ze stared off across the pavilion. No one said anything.

"But with a culture like yours, the more mature it gets, the greater the anxiety. When *your* subcultures meet, they don't set up a pattern of domination and resistance that leaves nuggets of the smaller culture intact. They tend to just calmly blur together into one amalgamation. Fashions sweep across a whole world. Bangles for Vails one year, flanges the next . . . across a world of a trillion people. A single economic system manages all your social tensions—you don't have separate, parallel systems for emotions, exchanged possessions, social status, reserve capital, heritage, or prestige, for instance. Just one kind of wealth. It all works smoothly . . . until, maybe, one day it doesn't. One day there's a flaw I—or we, you and I together—haven't foreseen. An edge case. Something virulent that spreads through the culture and takes it down. It doesn't necessarily happen in an eyeblink, not like in a . . ." Ze put another purple strip in zir mouth and chewed. "Not like in some kinds of cultures. But it might be unstoppable. When a culture like yours falls, it falls hard. And there are few warning signs."

Fift swallowed. It occurred to zir that zir Fathers were probably still watching zir, and ze wondered what they would say about this. Ze could picture Fathers Smistria and Frill objecting; they loved to argue about history. Though how could you argue with this strange five-hundred-thousand-year-old Staid?

But even Father Smistria would be too polite to message in the middle of such a conversation. Fift queried the surround for how many people were currently observing, figuring ze'd see maybe seven or eight of zir Fathers, and a few of Shria's.

There were 1,875,203 observers, with more piling in. The pavilion had already put in a bid for reactants to formally confirm its spike in status from hosting the conversation.

Thavé smiled a small, grim smile.

Of course, Fift realized, there would be Cirque-fans following all the Ticket Holders, looking for when the performance would break. And of course there must be scholars who had automated agents tracking Thavé's movements and behaviors. And somehow that must have been enough of a nucleus that when the alien started talking about the end of the world, the audience boomed.

Fift swallowed, reminding zirself that, even if this was a lot more attention than ze usually got, it was a very small crowd by the standards of real celebrities in Fullbelly. Ze recalled zir classroom lessons in instant-fame comportment: the trick of it was to remember how short attention spans and memories were, not to confuse an anomalous spike with a real change, and to act with dignity and humility, ignoring the crowd.

"Kumru's feces," Shria said, vir lavender face blanching to cream-blue. "Fift, did you see the audience we've got?"

Fift tried to ignore vem. "So what do we do?" ze asked Thavé, zir voice tight.

"Well," Thavé said, and sighed. "I've been saying for a while that you ought to diversify. You need to start loosening the stranglehold of consensus. You need a little more . . . room. But I'm not always listened to." Ze looked at them carefully. "Indeed, the tighter the consensus, the less effect my advice has. I'd also like to see you cultivate more physical displacement—to spread yourselves out a little. Frankly, I would love for you to start building star-ships . . . though your objections to them are eminently logical, Shria. You could at least be expanding more within your own solar system . . . but I don't seem to be making much headway there, either. Lately it seems like I'm not making much headway anywhere."

Fift didn't know what to say to that.

"Sorry," Thavé smiled. "I'm being maudlin. I don't want to ruin your outing." Ze patted zir pocket again. "You're here to see a show."

"Is that what you're here for?" Fift asked, relieved. "I mean here in this pavilion, today? The show? Like us?"

"Certainly," Thavé said. "And then I'm on my way to visit a friend, another alien. Maybe ve'll have some ideas."

"*Another* alien?" Shria said. "How many of you are there? Are you just . . . traveling beyond the world all the time? Where do you go?"

"Are you leaving the world?" Fift asked. The thought made zir queasy.

"Oh no, no," Thavé said. "My friend is here, in an Idyll. Good place for those of us who can't entirely . . . adapt to your ways of doing things. There aren't many of us at all, I'm afraid. Just a few artifacts of Far Technology rattling around your planet, of whom I am—if I do say so myself—by far the easiest to talk to. And we don't usually go anywhere; nowadays, traveling between stars means spending a few hundred years cramped into a very old, very fast machine, exposed to a lot of radiation, and without anything to eat. Or breathe. Arduous."

Fift was still trying to grasp the notion that there might be other worlds, with other people on them, to *go* to. Not just abstractions in Far History, or ancient sources of incomprehensible Far Technology and obscure allusions in the Long Conversation's oldest passages, but worlds that existed *now*. Were there? Was that what Thavé was implying: people . . . if you could even call them people? . . . living somewhere *else* . . . somewhere Fift couldn't see, totally unconnected to this world and its inhabitants, its conversations, its ideas? People who couldn't affect zir no matter what they did; and nothing ze did could affect them. People so separate, so cut off, that there was no way to reach them at all. It was an eerie thought. Part of zir wanted to ask about those *other worlds*, but the queasy sense of disorientation got stronger as ze contemplated it. Ze hoped Shria wouldn't go there.

"And you could do that? Survive that kind of trip?" Shria asked Thavé.

"Not in this body. But yes."

"And are you *planning* to? Not right now, but . . . later?"

"No, no I'm not. Not if I can avoid it. I don't intend to lose another world. I want to stay here. I want . . . *this*." Ze swung zir arm up, describing the visible arc of habitation structures above them: the beams, vaults, spiral staircases, fountains, arches, byways, slipthreads, whirligigs, crenelated arcs, polypenetrations, hyperbolic stepsurfaces, stickywalls, goopfields, bounceroos, waysweep-vistas, abandonages, wigglewharfs, playglobes, interdecks, jumptubes, sluices, flywheels, and bauble cascades strewn throughout the volume of Fullbelly; connected, supported, and nourished by the invisible web of tiny strands filling the interspace and lit by the great network of glowtubes beneath them, which separated the upper habitation region of Fullbelly from the production regions below.

It was second afternoon here, so the glowtubes' light was shading now from vaguely pinkish-purple to vaguely violet-indigo, in a spectral diffusion they could see stretching across Fullbelly above. Foo and the below and beyond were just in the middle of that range, bathed in a pure violet light.

"What about—" Shria began.

Then the lights went out.

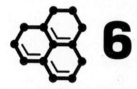 **6**

The whole of Fullbelly was plunged into darkness.

There were screams, then shouts of surprise. Then a beat of silence. Then cacophony: a clatter of forks and spoons and food platters and syringes falling to the floor; bodies slamming into tables and each other; laughter, cursing, angry argument.

It was the glowtubes that had gone suddenly dark. Thousands of tiny light sources still moved through the space between the habitations, illuminating edges in yellow or green or blue, casting strange dim shadows over half-seen surfaces. It looked like a night sky on the surface, if the stars had been parti-colored, wandering, and strewn among strange blocky clouds.

At home, Fift bolted from the empty hallway near the study-pit. Ze turned a corner and ducked into the sleeping alcove to where ze lay, struggling out of bed. Ze helped zirself up and ran, doublebodied, downstairs to the breakfast room.

Ze almost fell off the stairs. Ze righted zirself and ran on, slammed zir shoulder into the wall on the left, and stopped. Something was wrong. Something was—

Foo had stopped rotating. Ze was compensating for a motion that was no longer there.

More than the lights, this filled zir with panic.

"Foo stopped," ze said to Shria. They were looking up at the strange dancing stars. Most of them were slowing to a halt.

"I know," ve said. Ve took zir hand, vir cool palm filling the space Thavé's warm one had left.

Four of Fift's parents were sitting around the table, and Father Smistria was pacing. They looked up as ze clattered down the stairs. Squell and Nupolo and Grobbard held out their arms. Fift came and sat among them, nestled in their embraces. Their eyes were all distant, engrossed in what their other bodies saw.

"What is it?" said Shria. "Is it the Cirque?"

Fift turned to Thavé, but the alien was gone, zir eating tines still lying on the table, piercing one of the strips. Zir hat was gone, too. Lookup showed only four public positions for zir twelve bodies, all of them far away.

There was a sudden gasp from many throats, and a few sharp cries. Fift looked up.

Bright streaks of light were moving through the darkness, impossibly fast. They spun loops around Foo and Stiffwaddle and Undersnort and Wallacomp habitations, leaving trails of brilliant white that faded behind them. They swung through the space of Fullbelly, dodging elevator-strands, sluice-cables, and lonely, still whirligigs, illuminating them into incandescence, casting weird flickering shadows on the faces of bounceroos and stickywalls and polypenetrations. One . . . two . . . three . . . four . . . five . . . six . . . seven . . . eight. Eight blazing somethings whooshing through Fullbelly's space; terrifying, like dangerously gifted creatures from some forgotten mythology.

Then all eight objects, scattered through Fullbelly, flipped or turned or spun and headed back, dodging and weaving through the structures, heading towards one another, heading for a collision.

Shria pulled Fift to vem; ze stumbled from zir chair and held vem. Ze tensed in Shria's arms, in Nupolo's, in Squell's (and nestled, loosening, in Grobbard's).

The eight terrifying speeding things crashed into one another in one enormous flash of light, sending up a shower of sparks which tore through Fullbelly and disappeared.

At the next table, two doublebodied, obviously latterborn Vails—one lanky and almost naked, the other with emaciated, etched muscles, one pair of blue wings, and one pair of red wings—began to applaud.

People stared at them. "Don't you get it?" the winged one said. "It's the Cirque!"

"We have Tickets!" the almost naked one said.

A sharp-nosed, lonebodied Staid at the table beyond theirs stood up. Ze wore a disheveled smock and the aggrieved expression of a first child, but for the moment ze was enriched by wrath. "I can't believe you," ze said. "Do you think this is a game? If the Cirque is responsible for this— this behavior—"

"Oh, hey," said the winged Vail, "I hear your little sister's taking a nap; why don't you go see if Mommy has some time for you?"

The Staid made a choking noise, and the singlebodied Vail at zir table—plain-looking, with earlobes distended in the fashion of three years ago—stood up. "You squandering waster gnatlings—!"

And then a voice spoke.

"Stalwarts and Expressives!"

It came from the place where the eight streaks of light had collided. When Fift looked more closely, ze realized the space wasn't empty. The bright sparks had flown away, but there was a dark, shifting, vibrating mass still in its center. And from that mass, the voice was speaking.

"Children of all ages! People of Fullbelly and Hardwon and Tearless and Spoon and the Manysmall! Have you wondered if this is the world for you?"

"OK, it is the Cirque," Shria said. "Kumru!"

"Vails! Have you wished you could be quiet and small like a stone? Staids! Have you wished you could soar and dance like a splendid bird? Nostalgists! Have you wished to forget? Devvies! Have you wished we could just stop developing? In your heart of hearts, your mind of minds, have you wondered what was behind that door—that door—that you never open?"

The pavilion was silent now, every face staring up into the dimness.

"Holy Kumru!" Father Nupolo said.

"Ssh!" said Father Frill.

"Adults of all stages!" cried the voice. *"Where are your great deeds? No, not your petty duels, not the adjudications that you won, after many years, over who gets to keep the pet wormfish. Not your new designs for genitals or flowerpots—"*

"Hey!" Shria said.

"—Not your poems about optimal flow-cycle distribution, not your retabulations of cross-references of things that ceased to matter long ago. Not your obsessions with details only the detail-obsessed would notice. Not your worrying and scurrying!"

Even for the Cirque, this was outrageous.

They'd *stopped the world*. Turned out the lights. Frozen Foo in place. Was that even *allowed*?

"Where are your great deeds?"

Fift sent zir agents searching and they came back with instant confirmation. There'd been no consensus about cutting the lights. If the Clowns had done it, no one knew how.

"Your parents dug nations from the bedrock! Your grandparents and their grandparents fought in the Age of War! Once, Towers fell! Once Kumru traveled through time to impregnate zirself—

or did ve? Ha! Once we wept blood tears of rage, arguing about whether ve did!"

If the Cirque could manage that, what else could they do?

Would the Midwives really allow this? Maybe they'd destroy the Cirque.

"But now we are too polite to mention all that! Where are your great deeds, you stifled Stalwarts, you erratic Expressives? Why, we are bringing them to you! The Cirque Fantabulous is proud to present . . . a spectacle in the midst of life . . .

"Unraveling: A Revolution!"

The voice fell silent and the glowtubes lit again, flooding the world with bright light tinged in violet.

With a lurch, Foo started to turn again.

INTERLUDE

Personal Memory Pop Quiz

"Background of Current Events"

brought to you by the automated agents of the Slow-as-Molasses/
Bountiful-Blank Neighborhood Schooling Interdependency

No research agents allowed! Good luck!

1. The worldwide information interdependency we know as "the feed" crystallized out of a variety of other cybernetic systems during the Age of Roads and Doors.

   Discuss the various parts of "the feed," such as "the visual feed," "the send," and "the world-of-ideas."

2. What can you *not* find on the feed?

3. Is your apartment feed-opaque? Feed-transparent? Feed-translucent? How about your bedroom? Are you sure? Name three "privacy areas" in Foo that are *outside* someone's personal apartments and rate their effectiveness.

4. What is the effect of "general mutual total surveillance" on behavior? In ancient times, there was an entire dramatic literature centered on logically determining "who" had taken certain gruesome actions (such as killing another person's sole body while unobserved).

   What would *you* do, if you could "get away with it"?

5. "Critical infrastructure systems" require deep levels of consensus to override. The feed is a "critical infrastructure system." So are the glowtubes. So are nutrient flow, airflow, and intersomatic communication. Give three examples from history of someone circumventing consensus with an "exploit" to subvert "critical infrastructure systems."

6. Which would you prefer: an insurrection masquerading as an artwork, or an artwork masquerading as an insurrection?

7. Are you somewhere safe? Do you need anything? Should someone come and get you? What is "safety"?

Thanks for taking the quiz!! The next in-person class session meets Greenday morning, location to be announced.

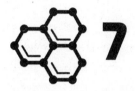 **7**

They tried three elevators that would take them back to Foo, and there were jostling crowds in front of all of them. Only one elevator, the first, even seemed to be working. Its operator—grim-faced, an adjudicator standing at zir elbow—was letting people board almost indiscriminately; still, people were joining the back of the throng far faster than they were departing. There was no getting through that press of bodies. At the second elevator, the operator had vanished. The third elevator was blocked by an even bigger crowd, and there was shouting at the front, but they couldn't see what it was, because by then there was something wrong with the feed.

First there were just missing bits—Shria had wanted to see where vir eldersibling Tusha was, and couldn't find vem, the kind of thing you could blame on some overeager piece of anti-surveil, gone awry and taking out all the feed pickups in a whole block. But the blankness grew, until more and more of the world had been swallowed. With zir own eyes, Fift could see the byway where ze walked with Shria through the milling crowds. With zir own eyes, ze could see the breakfast room where zir parents were arguing. The rest was a fabric ripped to shreds.

It was worse than the lights going out. Fift had seen the

darkness of full night before, when camping on the surface. It was eerie seeing it under Fullbelly's roof, but also stunning— as if a black velvet cloth, adorned with resplendent jewels, had been thrown over the jumble of habitations. But there was nothing entertaining about this.

Lookup was broken, too. Ze'd ask about some passing stranger, and nothing would come . . . then hundreds of heart-beats later, when the body had long since passed, the answer would flickeringly, haltingly emerge. It was like the lost hour at Stiffwaddle Somatic Fashions, turned inside out: instead of Fift being hidden from the world, the world was hidden from zir. The crowds thronging the elevators, the people trudging home along the byways or arguing in courtyards—they were unidentified bodies, nameless, unknowable.

They tried to get their agents to plot them a reasonable route home, but the agents were muddled, recalcitrant: they kept changing their minds. Finally, Fift and Shria set off on a byway heading away from Foo . . . but at least it took them to-ward a long unbroken stretch of upward staircase that seemed clear. Fift held Shria's hand.

"And how does *that* have anything to do with the Cirque?" Father Frill broke in, cutting Father Smistria short. Ve slapped the side of the doorway—ve hadn't even made it to the table yet—with vir open hand. "How can you compare—"

"It has everything to do with it!" Father Smistria said, lean-ing back in vir seating harness, which squeaked. "The Cirques *are* a remnant of the Vail-supremacist, militarist leagues of—"

"Oh, come *on*," Father Nupolo said.

"Please, Smi, this is embarrassing! Crankish conspiracy propaganda!" Frill said. "I would think that you—"

"It's history, is what it is!" Smistria roared.

"Oh, you and your history!"

"I just hope," Father Squell said, rubbing vir thumbs together nervously, "that if it *is* the Cirque, that, you know, that they'll be all *right*, because it would be such a shame if we didn't . . . have them. I mean, everyone loves the Cirque. But if they *did* take down the *feed*, of course . . . I imagine there will be . . . *consequences* . . ."

"Why would the *Cirque* take down the *feed*?" Frill cried. "Don't you think they *want* their performance discussed?"

"'Performance,'" Smistria sneered. "Ha! Who *else* would take it down . . . ?"

"Opportunists! That's who!" Frill smacked the doorjamb again.

"Oh, I see," Smistria said, vir voice dripping with sarcasm, "certainly people who evaded consensus to tamper with the world's sources of *light* are the *last* people we should suspect . . ."

"Lag is still increasing," Father Grobbard said. Zir face was unlined, and zir arms, holding Fift, were relaxed. But Fift could feel the tension under zir perfect, staidish reserve. "Transportation and logistics are in chaos throughout Fullbelly . . . perhaps throughout the world. And Fift . . . I'm no longer getting any visual image of you."

"I'm fine," Fift said from zir other body across the room—ze'd slipped out of Nupolo and Squell's grasp and gone to watch the rolling mini-kitchen concoct sweet frozen soup. Ze had the queasy sense ze sometimes had when ze stood doublebodied in one room, as if ze was still a baby who couldn't get zir two views of the same scene to mesh. The old nightmarish fear, that ze would suddenly see two irreconcilable pictures, lurked at the edge of zir mind. "We're fine." Ze pulled zirself from Father Grobbard's arms as well.

"You and that vailchild," Squell began. "How you had the idea in the first place to run off in search of—"

"Pip's idea," Father Nupolo said.

Someone in the milling crowd was screaming—a Vail in a feathered tunic, standing on a rollertube. They crossed into a courticle, where a pack of six canids—they might have been real vat-born animals, or someone's very exotic bodies; who could know without lookup?—went tearing by, knocking over a set of shelves, spilling multicolored balls everywhere. Shria stepped protectively in front of Fift, but the canids raced around them, hullabalooing.

"Oh, *diggery*! I can't see anything at *all*! This is *not* all right," Squell said. "This is *dangerous*. With everyone invisible like this, people are going to start doing . . . well, *anything*!"

The balls bounced and caromed and sprung over the floor's edge, falling towards the habitations below until they were caught by the sticky invisible strands of the interspace. They hung there in midair, like tiny bright planets.

"Come on," Shria said, pulling zir onto the next byway.

Fift's attention agents could reach the world-of-ideas only in fits and starts. Instead of the clear explanations, the wealth of opinions, the quickly forming consensus that ought to have been there, there was only a jumble of disorganized information. Agitated, Fift's agents pestered zir with things ze hadn't requested: The number of publicly locatable canids in Fullbelly. A history of canids and their spit. A route to the Fullbelly Spitting Championship Preparation Village, with a special offer of a tour from one Bilz Takapo of name registry Green Sugarbubble Distinct 8. Fift muted them.

The byway ahead of them was crowded with bodies. Most of them were naked, sleek and featureless with blue or black or red skin and fingers and toes webbed together. Some had only shallow indentations for eyes, mouth, ears, and genitals. A few were umbilical-corded together.

Anonybodies. People rented them sometimes, to be present somewhere without having to travel, but Fift had never seen more than two or three of them in one place. Now, a few hundred were filling the byway, crowded around a Vail standing on a puff-pillar in some kind of historical recreationist military regalia—a plumed and glittery upholstered exoskeleton crowded with bangles, curlicues, jewels, and mirrors. The Vail's head poked out from the carapace, and vir face had the haggard, hard, too-smooth look of the very old.

Fift and Shria slowed gradually to a halt. Shria's hand squeezed Fift's.

Lookup came through, grudgingly: **Panaximandra Shebol of name registry Central Glory 2, 1-bodied Vail, 935 years old.**

Fift swallowed. The exoskeleton was not a recreation. It was real armor, from the Age of War.

"Certainly, there is an escalating risk of behavioral disinhibition," Father Grobbard said, "the longer this goes on." Ze settled back into zir seating harness.

Panaximandra lifted one hand—the movement was a blur, the powered exoskeleton supplying military-grade somatic fluidity—and pointed at Shria and Fift. "And there they are," ve said. The crowd turned to look.

"What's wrong, Fift?" said Father Frill. "What's going on? You look like Kumru when ve discovered vir destiny!"

Fift couldn't move—not in any of zir bodies. Ze watched the ancient warrior smile.

"*Children,*" Panaximandra said. "Children! Take a good look. Do a lookup, if you can. Fift Brulio Iraxis of name registry Yellow Peninsula Sugarbubble 5. Shria Qualia Fnax, of name registry Digger Chameleon 2. They are sixteen years old. Only sixteen years ago, Midwives visited the homes of their parental cohorts to perform the sacred rites. Sixteen years ago, these new individuals, these *brand-new people* were born— born in blood and amniotic fluid. With groaning and sweating they were pushed through dilated cervixes into the world. Sixteen years ago they opened their eyes for the first time, and beheld their parents."

Anonybodies turned to look at them with blank, unfinished faces.

"What in the squandering . . . ?" Shria said.

"And who were those parents?" Panaximandra asked. "Those lucky people, who were given the right to create life? Note that I say *given.* They did not *take* the right, as their due, as their inheritance, as their destiny as human beings. No, they were given it, and they accepted it humbly. They were honored. So honored."

"Fift!" Father Frill said. Ve took a step into the room.

Fift held up a hand to shush vem.

Panaximandra turned to look over the crowd with a slight sneer. "And where were *you* sixteen years ago? How have those years been for you? What have you taken as yours? Really *taken.* You who come to me hiding your true faces. Or are *these* your true faces? Maybe those *other* faces you wear are the costumes."

There was a murmur from the crowd. Amid the blank, shadowed faces in red, blue, and black, a few natural bodies stared at Fift and Shria. They looked hungry, or sad.

"What the fuck is this?" Shria whispered.

"I don't think it's the Cirque." Fift said. "Do you?"

Shria frowned. "How do I know? But doesn't it seem more— I don't know, serious? Than the Cirque? Or, like, in bad taste, or something?"

"I'm fine," Fift told zir Fathers, reflexively.

"They've been all right, haven't they, those past sixteen years?" Panaximandra said. "Smooth like a sluice. Zipping by like a swing. Nothing to complain about." Another blur, and a boom so loud the crowd staggered, and Fift's ears rang.

Panaximandra's hands were palm to palm in front of vir chest: ve'd clapped. "Hardly noticeable. You insects re-arranged the furniture of the hive you live in, and rearranged it again. And now those sixteen years are gone, and you've *lived* . . . how much of that time? Maybe a few heartbeats? Probably doing something you weren't supposed to be doing, or surprising yourself by winning some petty transaction, or making a lucky shot at a lapine with a spear on some surface vacation. For a few heartbeats, you were actually alive; for a few heartbeats, you felt like you were not merely waiting out your interminable lives, but *living*. As if anything was possible, and you could take what you wanted! As if life was a beast you could master, not an obligatory sex partner it was your duty to pleasure until ze started snoring."

Uneasy chuckles from the crowd. Everyone was watching Panaximandra now. Two natural bodies—passersby who'd gotten caught up in the crowd?—shoved their way out of the crush and headed off down the byway, shaking their heads. Panaximandra ignored them.

"For a few heartbeats, it felt as if life was new," Panaximan-dra said. "The way it was when *you* were sixteen."

"Should we go back?" Fift said. "Get out of here?"

"All the way back?" Shria said.

"Fift, we need to talk about your habit of withholding in-formation," Father Squell said. "It's not appropriate. It was one thing when you were eight—"

"Fift," Father Smistria growled, tugging at vir beard, "what's going on down there?"

"No," Shria said. "No way am I walking all the way back! We're going through."

"I don't know," Fift said. "Shria and I ran into some kind of . . . meeting, or something. An old veteran talking to an anonymized crowd . . ."

Fift's Fathers leaned forward as one; it was like they were all bodies of the same person. "Fift," Father Frill said. "Get out of there. Turn around and walk away!"

"My folks say we should get out of here," Fift told Shria.

"Fuck that," Shria said. "Hey, no-bodies! Make room—we're coming through!" Ve started to move, pulling gently on Fift's hand, but when ze didn't step forward, ve let go. The anony-bodies near them, blue, black, and red, turned to watch.

"But you are worth more than that," Panaximandra said urgently. "You are human beings. You do not need to be pre-dictable blobs of hollow contentment, well-regulated parts of a system which has only homeostasis, but no meaning . . . enduring your allotted centuries, dying as an afterthought, *doing what you are told.*"

Shria slowed to a stop an arm's length from the crowd, and Fift felt a quiver of despair. Ve would be supplanted; ve had no chance of intimidating the mass of nobodies.

Shria turned and looked back at Fift. Ve looked uneasy. Without pausing to think, Fift came forward to vem and took vir hand.

"We can resist this living death," Panaximandra said. "The first step is to unseat the Midwives from the center of every-thing. Every one of you is a human being. Every one of you can be a Hero. Every one of you can be a Mother!"

All around them, mouthless bodies drew a deep breath. Shria's step faltered for a moment, and ve looked back at Fift. *Unseat the Midwives?*

"Are you with the Clowns?" someone called.

Panaximandra smiled. "It is hard to tell when the Cirque is joking. I found parts of their performance . . . inspiring. Other parts, disturbing. Those quips about mixing Vail and Staid—are they meant to be taken seriously? To encourage toad-clownery? If so, they disgust me. Nor am I sure that the

Clowns are entirely *serious* about revolution. But they have certainly proven"—ve looked up at the vast sweep of habitations above—"*useful*."

"Fift? Fift? Are you getting out of there?" Frill said, vir voice quavering with unease. Ve drew and sheathed, drew and sheathed, one of the ceremonial golden knives strapped to vir sash.

"We're trying to," Fift said.

Shria's hand was warm. Ve swallowed, then grinned at zir and slid between a blue body and a red body, murmuring, "Excuse me . . ."

The anonybodies glanced at them, shifted aside, turning back to Panaximandra.

Panaximandra began to pull soft little scraps of something from pockets hidden among the glittering festoonery of vir exoskeleton and toss them into the crowd, vir arms a blur. The nobodies reached and jostled to catch them. "Revolution against this deadness, this confinement, means feeling alive. It is all very well to officiously pretend that struggle and supplanting are open to all, that 'take what you want' is the basis of our society. This is the *myth* of freedom. In reality, you will succeed in taking nothing, if you try to do it alone."

A scrap of what Panaximandra was throwing batted Fift in the face; it was soft, plush cloth, a luxurious texture. Ze held it for a moment before a green nobody, the hollows of vir face gaping, snatched it from zir.

"If you act alone, the world's *structures* will defeat you. Ratings and banking-history, reactancy and arbitration, the *feed* which watches your every act—they will hold you in place. Consensus will immobilize you like a bug in amber. From the moment of your birth. From the moment you are gendered and inscribed into lookup . . . by the Midwives."

"You want ungendered babies?" someone shouted. There

was an angry murmur. Shria pushed forward into the crowd, but the blue rent-a-body in front of vem shrugged away and closed ranks, pushing its shoulder into the twin body—perhaps another host for the same person—standing beside it.

Panaximandra flushed with rage and stopped throwing the soft cloths. "Of course not! Do you think I am a monster? I have only compassion for those horrible freaks, and disgust for their misguided parents. But do you think that is revolution? Do you think the Midwives mind when a few radicals refuse lookup and bear ungendered babies? Of course not! Because in almost all cases, the Midwives are able to break up those cohorts and *adopt the children*! As they adopt the refuse of so many failed cohorts! And think, if you will, of that! *That* is what we have for Midwives: late-gendered freaks and other orphans—*only children*, most of them! No wonder they are so desperate for order and stasis; no wonder they are so fixated on scarcity. No wonder they deny every true, luxurious, immoderate, transporting feeling! They may travel in pairs, Vail and Staid, and preach the Balance, but their Balance is a fraud, for there is no scrap of true vailish boldness and joy in them. Our whole world is built to compensate for that which *they* were deprived of: order and safety. I may have compassion for them, but I will not yield my world to soothe their wounds!" Ve held aloft one of the scraps ve had thrown from the dais. "Feel this! Feel this against your skin! This is the texture of revolution! Wherever you feel this, know that we are with you!"

"Block the feed! Kill the Midwives!" someone yelled.

"Shut up!" someone else yelled.

Kill the Midwives? Had someone really just *said* that? It was dangerous even to be *listening* to these people. Fift looked around desperately. Where were the Peaceables? But the feed was down. No one was coming. Shria was pulling on zir hand.

Shria tried to feel vir way around the press of bodies, but the crowd had become a roiling sea, jumping and snatching at the rags of revolution. Ve was pushed back, then knocked forward, and Fift almost lost zir grip on vem. Ze struggled forward and caught vir arm with both hands, pulling zirself toward vem.

It was a sea of Vails . . . and only Vails. You didn't need lookup or faces or clothes or adornments to tell that in this restless, jumping, snatching, yelling crowd, there was nothing staidish, and no place for Fift.

There was something obscene about it. Fift shouldn't be seeing it.

"Well?" Squell asked. Ze turned from the table, addressing Fift's other body. "Have you left that area, Fift?"

"Grobbard," Nupolo said. "This nonsense . . . how long will it *last*? Kumru's tits, what *happened*?"

"From what I can piece together," Grobbard said. "The Cirque Fantabulous is indeed to blame for the initial feed interruption—"

"Aha!" Smistria said. "You see? I knew it!"

Though ze held Shria's hand in zirs, Fift couldn't see vir face. Instead: rags, roaring, red-and-blue arms and shoulders.

"Block the feed!"

"But they claim it was only planned as a momentary interruption," Grobbard said. "A punctuation to their piece, a pause for reflection, as it were."

"Quite a pause!" Smistria began. "So now they've broken the feed, have they?"

"There seem to be other saboteurs who took advantage—"

"Hold on, Grobbard," Frill said. "Fift, where are you? Are you away from that . . . group?"

"We're trying," Fift said.

Blue and red bodies surged around them. Shria pulled Fift

through a gap and ze crashed into vem with a shudder. Fift felt the hard muscles of Shria's arms, the softness of vir breasts mashed against zir.

"I can't stand this anymore," Smistria said, and shrugged out of vir harness.

"Where are you going?" Father Squell cried.

"I'm going to requisition a bat and fetch the children!"

"A bat?" Father Grobbard said. "It seems unlikely that you will obtain one. Those that are not grounded are—"

"I'll come with you," Father Frill said. Vir nostrils flared, and ve stood up straighter.

"Requisition a bat *where?*" Squell said, looking from Grobbard to Frill. "I'm not getting a response from the usual places at *all*..."

Around them, the sea of Vails roared. From vir puff-pillar, Panaximandra smiled vir cool smile.

Shria held Fift. Fift clung to vir surface-forest smell amid the burnt-plastic of the anonybodies.

"Well," Smistria said, folding vir arms across vir chest, "I happen to know there's a party at Darnadi's house with several logistics administrators and a host of important reactants attending. We'll simply explain the problem. Fift, you come with us, so you can tell us where you are; and also stay here"—ve rapped on the table—"so you can tell your other Fathers what's going on if we can't get messages through."

Fift blinked. Ze had just taken zir frozen soup from the dispenser.

The beating of Shria's heart, felt through zir bones amid the noise and tumult. The electric hum of vir skin.

"Now," Smistria said.

Fift handed the soup to zirself at the table, and followed them towards the door.

"Kill—"

"This is nonsensical," Father Squell said angrily, jumping up from vir seating harness. "The feed is down! People are . . . up to who knows what! Unwatched, unchallenged, no one to hold them accountable . . . someone sabotaging the feed . . . strange groups, gathering in anonybodies . . . and you're going *out*?"

"—the Midwives!"

"And they will give you a bat *why*, exactly? This is not the time for playing capture-the-kernel!"

Fift hurried up the stairs after Frill and Smistria and the door closed behind them. In the breakfast room, Squell's words hung in the air.

Father Nupolo stood, slowly, and put vir hand on Squell's shoulder.

"*Kill the Midwives!*"

"Shut UP!" someone in the crowd yelled, sounding panicked.

"Is that what you're saying? KILL?" someone else shouted.

"What do you want from us?"

Fift embraced Shria. Ve folded vir arms around zir, shoving vir forehead into the crook of zir neck. Around them, the anonybodies shoved and roared. Fift was elbowed in the spine, kicked in the calf. Ze almost fell, but Shria pulled zir up.

Ze'd been *struck*. Zir spine, zir calf—it surely hadn't been *on purpose*. But maybe that was worse. They didn't even *notice* that they'd hit a Staid.

Shria started to cry. "Oh Kumru," ve choked, "what's happening?"

Fift looked up, fearful. Panaximandra held up a hand. "Is that word so terrible? 'Kill'?" Ve shook vir head and angry tears filled vir eyes and spilled over silently. Ve licked at them as ve spoke. "Oh, how long lives make cowards! People of the world, lust for your now *eight hundred* expected years has tamed you—this plenitude has made you craven! Give me a million barbarians with *eighty*-year lifespans, armed with *clubs*, and I could take this world and set it on fire. I could burn this prison and plant a garden. Oh, my world! My world!"

Fift, at the breakfast table, stared at zir cold soup. Ze covered zir face with zir fists.

"We will be your million!" someone shouted.

"You're a slackwit," someone else shouted back.

Squell put vir elbows on the table and leaned in, vir forehead next to Fift's. "Fift," ve said gently, forcing confidence into vir voice. "You have to concentrate. Use your words. Fift, nothing is so bad that it can't be addressed. But you have to explain what's going on."

"They're jumping around and shouting and talking about . . . some kind of war, I guess? It's like something out of . . ." Fift flushed. It was like the Anger of the Thirty Thousand Scorned Data-Hatchers in the narrative eighth subsection of Melihor's fourth metacommentary, but of course ze couldn't say that. ". . . out of history."

"But we need the Midwives," someone shouted. "You said yourself! Ungendered babies—"

"Oh, *Midwives* are precious!" Panaximandra said. "But these Midwives of *ours* have overreached themselves. They call themselves the parents of society . . . but that is a lie. They cannot guide us. They cannot make us strong. A Midwife is like a *placenta*: holy, vital, at first you cannot do without it. But to grow strong, you cannot depend on it too long. You must cut it away."

"*War*?" Nupolo leaned forward. "What are you talking about, Fift? Is this another performance? More Clowns . . . ?"

"It's not the Clowns," Squell said, leaning back, vir voice tight.

Amid the deserted courtyards of Slow-as-Molasses, Fift hurried to keep up with Father Frill and Father Smistria.

"Quit shoving!" someone shouted in the crowd behind Fift; then ze was knocked into Shria. They fell, and Fift snatched at something that looked like a rope. Zir hand closed on rubbery flesh—it was an umbilical cord connecting two of the rent-a-bodies, belly to uterus. The bodies—both red—screamed and fell on top of Fift and Shria.

In the breakfast room, Fift took a shuddering breath, pulled zir fists from zir face, and stirred zir soup with a trembling spoon.

Zir Fathers' eyes were on zir. Ze imagined what they would say if only they could *see* where ze was; they would *lose* it. Ze tried to force a smile. "I wonder what Thavé thinks of this? If this is one of the dying-of-boredom cultures, I'd hate to see the exciting ones."

"What are you talking about?" Father Nupolo said. Ve sat back down, stiff, scowling, at the table's end. "Cultures? Thavé? Kumru's eyes, Fift—I hope you're not making void-blessed *Long Conversation* allusions in front of *us*!"

"No, no," Fift said. The smile eluded zir. "I mean, from today. Didn't you hear what Thavé said?"

"What who said?" Father Squell asked.

"The alien?" Grobbard said, raising an eyebrow.

One of the red anonybodies was lying next to Fift, knees to its forehead, holding its belly and weeping. The other body, on its knees, grabbed Fift by the shift and *punched* zir, once, hard, in the side of the head. Fift cried out in all zir bodies. Shria tackled the red nobody, knocking it to the ground.

"What was that?" Father Frill said. Ve stopped in a corridor, knives jingling from vir sash. Seeing Fift's expression, ve took zir hand.

Father Smistria glared back at them. "Can we keep moving?"

"Somebody punched me," Fift told Frill.

In the breakfast room, Squell leaned forward again. "Fift, what happened?"

"Weren't you listening?" Fift said, holding the side of zir head. "I mean, weren't you watching me in the pavilion with Shria? When we were talking to Thavé?"

"Fift, we don't spend the whole void-spurned day following you on the feed," Father Nupolo said.

"Fift, *what happened*?" Squell said. "*Why* are you holding your head?"

"We had a million viewers!" Fift said, and had to look away from Father Squell. Ze slurped zir frozen soup. Ze knew ze was being ridiculous. Ze'd lost Shria; ve was behind a wall of bodies. But after the constant pressure of worrying about what ze said or sent—what zir parents would hear or guess— to have it turn out they hadn't even been watching, they'd just been *ignoring*—

Ze struggled through the legs of the anonybodies, trying to reach Shria. More of them were tripping and stumbling now, and a body fell in front of Fift. Ze tensed, and then wriggled over it, as quickly as ze could. Someone kicked zir in the leg. Above, from the puff-pillar, Panaximandra was roaring "Freedom! Valor! Conquest! Babies!" and the anonybodies began, awkwardly, to fall into the chant. Shria had a red body pinned, its wrists in vir hands. "Shria!" Fift shouted. Ze tried to send vem a note, but the send failed. The note cycled, waiting for a connection.

"*Punched you?*" Frill cried. "Literally? This isn't a metaphor? Someone *punched* you?" Vir eyes widened, hands balled into fists. Smistria took Frill's sleeve to pull vem down the corridor, but Frill shoved vem back, a straight-arm to vir chest. "*Who* punched you? *Who?*"

"Frill!" Smistria snapped, grabbing vir arm again. "Come

on, let's *move*, let's *get* to zir." Slowly, Frill allowed vemself to be dragged.

In the breakfast room, Father Grobbard, eyes closed, said, "Here it is, the record of your talk with the alien. Yes, you did have quite a spike, didn't you?"

"Fift, *please*," Squell said, vir voice trembling. Ve laid vir hand softly on Fift's shoulder. "Please tell me what's going on."

"It's all right," Fift said. "I . . . stumbled into something."

Squell's face fell. Ve didn't believe zir. "Oh, Kumru!" ve said. "You're terrifying me. If only we could *see*—I can't even see Frill and Smi—I see *nothing*! And where is Pip, why isn't ze answering me?"

"Freedom! Valor! Conquest! Babies!"

"Most of zir was at that banquet in Tearless," Grobbard said, zir eyes still closed. "It'll take zir forever to get back from there. Ze's also on zir way back singlebodied, on foot, from the above and before. Ze answered my first note, nothing since then. But the send is affected as well."

Shria let go of the red body and leapt to vir feet, shoving forward towards Fift. Ve was knocked down again by a blue anonybody and Fift lost sight of vem for a moment.

Ze was here, alone, in the midst of a riot. It *was* a riot, and the Peaceables were nowhere to be found . . . but then, of course, they couldn't *see* the riot, could they? An *invisible* riot. Ze posted an Urgent Request for Assistance; but even if it was noticed among a hundred million others, how could the Peaceables gather without the feed? No one could see zir, no one could help zir.

Fift had spent much of the year ze turned nine in a course of Martial Staidity, which was considered just the thing for somatic integration. Ze asked zir agents to recall it.

{You'll have to—excuse us.} zir context advisory agent sent. {There is a difficulty.}

{Some norms are apparently in need of reevaluation.} zir social nuance agent sent. {Obstacles present themselves. One is currently not local to oneself. Please attend.}

Kumru.

"Freedom! Valor! Conquest! Babies!"

Martial Staidity. How did it go? Get your feet under you. Center of balance low. Everything proceeds from the thighs and the buttocks. Always move slowly.

In turtle stance, ze pressed zir body gently against the moving, shifting bodies. Ze held zirself against them, giving when they shoved, moving into the space that opened up when they rocked back.

Father Frill and Father Smistria hustled Fift along. Frill was shaking with rage, vir nostrils flaring, vir teeth chattering. "Who *hit* you, Fift?" ve asked again. "*Who?*"

"I don't know!" Fift said, zir voice cracking a little. "How should I know? There's no lookup! There's no lookup!"

"All right, all right," Smistria growled. "One foot in front of another."

Fift took an elbow in the face, hard—ze couldn't get zir neck loose in time (stupid, stupid, holding zir neck tight like a stone), but ze remembered to let zir knees fold, to fall with the blow, crumple down, flow down, chest to zir knees, rolling back up, back onto zir feet. Zir ears rang.

Under Frill's hand, ze shuddered.

"I almost got a connection to Darnadi for a moment," Frill said through gritted teeth. "Perhaps you could just *call*, Smi?"

"Call?" Smistria snapped. "Are you feeling wealthy enough to compel a logistics administrator to do your bidding over a *call*? You really should let me know about these secret sources of confidence of yours, Frill. It must be sexual conquests, because your *cooking* certainly hasn't improved . . ."

One foot at a time, slowly, slowly, no fast movements, flowing like water. Another knee came at zir, and this time ze shifted zir weight to move with it.

The world was gone. Only three little pockets were visible: the breakfast room, the corridor, the riot. The rest had vanished, as if swallowed by the void.

A shudder of rage ran through Father Frill's body. "There is no reason to be *mean*, Smi," ve said tightly. "Let us control ourselves for the sake of the child, and once this crisis is over, *any time* you'd like to visit the mats with me, I'd be *delighted* to oblige you."

Smistria's eyebrows rose. "Oh, I see," ve said. "Yes? Yes, perhaps we *should* do that, Frill. Perhaps it's time."

Stupid Fathers! Now they were stiffening like peacocks, slowing to glare at each other. Fift pulled out of their grasp. "Stop it. Stop it!" ze said, and pushed ahead of them, hurrying down the corridor.

The note—*Shria wait for me*—cycled, cycled, waiting for a connection.

"Very interesting," Grobbard said, zir eyes closed. Ze must be watching the conversation with Thavé.

"What's interesting?" Fift asked.

"Doesn't the timing seem a little . . . dramatic?" Grobbard asked. Ze rubbed the fine golden fuzz of zir scalp. "Thavé explains how our culture is brittle, or stagnant, or whatever is supposedly wrong with it, then ze gestures to the surrounding habitations, and just then the lights happen to go out and the Clowns come onstage with their piece about a revolution . . . ?"

"Oh," Fift said. It hadn't *seemed* staged. But . . .

Shria came crashing back between two anonybodies, vir nose bloody. Two of the bodies pushed through behind vem, catching vem by the arms. Ve kicked one in the shins.

Squell hugged vemself. "How could they just go *off* like that? Now we can't see *anyone*! They should have listened to me! I'm the only one here who's had *experience* with this kind of thing—you know, in the asteroids, we have to deal with *seconds* of bodylag all the time. And when connectivity is bad, when there's a solar flare, or something . . . well, the first rule is, you *don't* just separate!"

Fift glanced behind zir. Frill and Smistria were following, pointedly not looking at each other. Ze climbed into the aqueous ball of the ball-drop without them, and tipped it off the ledge. "I can't believe I'm actually using Martial Staidity," ze said to zirself aloud. "That is too fucking sad." No one could hear zir; with no feed, zir words vanished into the air, gone forever.

Some faltering moment of feed-connection must have flickered to life, because the note vanished: on its way, perhaps, to Shria.

"What do you mean?" Fift asked Grobbard. "You mean it was part of the show? That Thavé's in on it, with the Cirque? That ze was waiting for someone to give zir a cue so ze could deliver zir lines . . . ?"

"Perhaps," Grobbard said. "Or perhaps ze was simply forewarned? Knew it was happening? And found a way to insert zir own message before the show?" Ze shrugged.

Fift reached Shria and curled an arm around vir waist. One of the Vails, holding one of Shria's arms, yanked back an anonymized blue leg to kick vem. Fift's heart was pounding, but ze flowed zir own leg out and lightly, gently placed zir foot against the foot of the Vail. The Vail paused. Shria roared.

Panaximandra was saying something else, but Fift couldn't hear over the crowd bellowing, "FREEDOM!"

The ball bounced at the bottom of the chute, carrying Fift up with it. Ze braced zirself for the buffering second touchdown, and sank into the goop.

"I can't believe the two of you are sitting here calmly talking about *that*," Squell said. "In the middle of *this*! Fift, you tell that Shria vailchild to bring you back here this heartbeat!"

"VALOR!"

The other Vail struck Shria in the head and ve stumbled back, dragging Fift with vem. Ze lost zir calming hold on the first Vail's foot, but ze kept hanging onto Shria. Ze kept zir head down.

Ze ducked out of the ball's mouth and watched it slurp up, drawn back up into the drop chute. Ze started shaking. "Martial Staidity," ze said. "Kumru."

"Are you listening to me?" Squell said. "Are you away from that crowd?"

"CONQUEST!"

Shria lost vir footing and fell. Vir body was shaking with sobs. Fift crawled over vem, covering vir head, vir chest, trying to be water. They wouldn't kick a Staid, would they? Not on purpose? Shria yanked vir head away. "Shh, Shria," ze said. "Shh. Come on: curl up, play dead." Something snapped against the side of zir head and zir ears rang again. A body fell on them, and Fift sank down with the weight.

Shria yanked vemself out of zir grasp. Fift tried to flow out from under, and caught vir arm. "Shria," ze said. "We—"

"LET GO OF ME!" Shria screamed.

"Fift," Father Grobbard said. "Please answer your Father Squell."

Fift leaned zir head against the ridiculous active-display wall above the running floor. If the feed were on and ze could have seen zirself, it would have looked like ze was leaning zir head on air, a bodylength from a spiky, twisted garnagh tree. Behind zir, ze heard the ball rebound. "Shria," ze whispered, "please."

"Shria!" Ze screamed, losing zir flow-like-water relaxation. "Please!"

Shria was up on vir feet again, and ve was roaring, striking the anonybodies with elbows and knees.

"BABIES!"

Father Grobbard raised zir eyebrows. "Fift?"

"I'm a little fucking distracted now, you old toad," Fift said—and felt an immediate stab of guilt, even though ze'd only said it in the body that was waiting by the ball-drop, and the absent feed would (hopefully) not preserve the comment. Ze turned zir head to watch the ball carrying Smistria and Frill bounce, buffer, and settle into the goop.

Blue and black and red feet, their toes webbed together, and one black boot (but not Shria's) filled the space in front of Fift's eyes. Ze checked lookup. Still down. Ze checked the feed for a view. There was one view of where ze was now: slow, jittery, flecked, taken from an elevator some distance away. The byway was mobbed with colors, with bodies, jerky, rushing. From that vantage point, over the feed, it looked like they were dancing. Shria was somewhere in that mess. Ve wouldn't answer zir.

Ze rested zir forehead against the ground. In the lab at Stiffwaddle Somatic Fashions, ze had wondered where zir tears were, if they were gone forever. Now, very faintly, ze felt their incipient trace, an uneasy quavering that, if ze failed to hold it down, could become panic, sobs, shaking.

Father Smistria and Father Frill were holding hands when they came out of the ball-drop. "Come on, Fift," Frill said, and they rushed on ahead of zir. They seemed weirdly abuzz, the martial tension of their fight having shifted into something that drew them closer. Smistria's thumb traced a line across Frill's wrist. Fathers! Ridiculous. Fift puffed after them.

In the jittery, grainy view of the byway, there was no sign of Shria.

"This is our time!" Somehow Panaximandra's voice carried better over the feed, sounded clearer, if tinny and scratchy and jittery from lag. "These are our signs! Remember this feeling, the texture of luxury, the feeling of freedom! Remember who you are! And when you return to your little nooks in the hive, be unsatisfied, be thirsty! We must cut ourselves free before we can begin to live!"

Cut ourselves free? A month ago, that might have sounded good to Fift. A Ticket that would transport zir away from Mother Pip and banker-historian apprenticeships and shameful longings and the alternate codification of the twelfth emergent mode of the Long Conversation, from fussing Fathers and grinding boredom. A jailbreak from the prison of zir life. But now it sounded exactly backwards. Ze was unanchored, lost, in the midst of a tornado. Ze wanted back *in* to zir life. Ze wanted to go home.

Tickets . . . Wait. Ze checked the flickering feed for Ticket Holders, and yes: the Cirque was so popular that even with the feed collapsing like this, lists of Ticket Holder locations were mirrored everywhere. There was zir own location, and there was (what was vir name registry? Digger something . . . Digger Chameleon . . . ? There . . .) Shria! So ve would be two bodylengths or so to zir (which way was polewards?) . . . left . . . Sort of. Ze pulled zir feet under zir.

"Grobby, ze's not saying anything," Father Squell said. "Grobby . . . I don't know where ze *is*." Ve turned to Grobbard, and collapsed against zir, pressing vir forehead against Grobbard's chest.

"Hmm. Yes," Father Grobbard said, stroking Squell's scalp. "Well, let's give zir another moment to respond." Ze kissed Squell's head beside vir silver spikes, then took a sip of zir soup. "'Unraveling: A Revolution' indeed. Perhaps we're like a carefully stitched fabric that Thavé has been fussing over for twenty thousand years. And perhaps ze just couldn't resist pulling at a loose thread."

"Oh, Kumru!" Squell sat up shock-straight, vir eyes unfocused. Ve'd found the view of the byway. "Fift, are you in *that?!*"

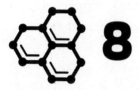 **8**

The party at Darnadi's house was packed. Lookup was working: the local caches here had been spared the chaos infecting the rest of the world. In the house of Darnadi Imsmuth Shelirian-Jerum of name registry Imperturbable Admonition 26, you could look up the people you saw; you could listen in on conversations in another room by feed pickup, smooth as milk. If you made sure not to look beyond Darnadi's apartments, you could indulge in the fantasy that things were as they had been yesterday.

Fift stood in a corner saying no to a hundred different drinks (they flew up to importune zir, bobbling on pockets of air), and savoring the illusion.

Father Frill and Father Smistria were working the crowd. Fift had stopped listening in, but just by occasionally glancing over, ze could tell that it wasn't going well. Frill was trying to ingratiate vemself with the glittering deep-reactants and aestheticians who were chatterdancing beneath the grasping green fronds of hanging plants and the deep purple bric-a-brac privacy-cones hanging above the dance floor. Ve must have once again failed to follow the complicated language-pattern of the chatterdance (it was in the sixth phase, so number of syllables per word, meter, body-rhythm, topic, theme, and tone were all in play). Ve stood by the side, chewing vir lip and waiting for the next round, to the obvious relief of the other dancers.

Father Smistria had taken a direct approach; ve had gone straight to the senior logistics coordinators, who stood on a small dais betting on the dancing, and explained their situation. At first, they had been happy to see vem; Smistria was a well-regarded adjudication reactant, and vir attention was worth something. When it became clear, though, that ve insisted on intruding with business of a most unpleasant and distressing sort (namely, the near-total collapse of some of the very services the logistics coordinators were pledged to nurture) into a social gathering now repurposed (albeit not originally designed) precisely to distract from that collapse, the mood turned grim. Smistria, realizing vir mistake, tried to win them back, complimenting the party, reminiscing about old times. Flattery wasn't vir strong suit, though: you could see how vir jaw was rigid with the effort.

Moving zir head to see past the more insistent beverages that clustered around zir, Fift ran lookups on the crowd. Partly because it was educational to see who was at such a gathering; but mostly, it was just a relief to be somewhere lookup was working flawlessly. More of a relief than ze would have predicted: the crisp unhurried display of the responses, flickering up, one after another, as ze glanced through the crowd, made zir eyes sting with shameful joy. (There they were again, the tears, not unlearned after all, just lurking deep.)

Maybe ze should be doing something about the fact that ze was trapped on a byway with a thousand out-of-control Vails who were beating Shria up. But it was seductively peaceful just to stand here and watch lookup work.

Tigan Melitox Farina of name registry Blue
Piggyback Dentition 5, 3-bodied Vail, 221
years old, speaker of Parrot Company.

Foon Pelix Nathandine of name registry Yellow Optimum Sugarbubble 6, 3-bodied Staid, 315 years
old, noted textilist.

Pam Thyrup Shevrian of name registry Uncanny Pa-
rameter Platypus 7, 2-bodied Vail, 389 years
old, adjudicant and meta-aesthetic reactant.

"This is our time!" Panaximandra roared again, and the crowd roared too; the crowd was alive, moving. Were they fighting? Dancing? Did they even know themselves? Grabbing and grappling and turning and churning and bucking and striking. This wasn't just vailish exuberance. Something had been bottled up, compressed and hidden and starved for air, and now, in the absence of the feed and lookup, among these anonymized rent-a-bodies, it was breaking free.

"FREEDOM!"

Father Squell was pacing the breakfast room, circling the table, vir silver spikes quivering in vir pale scalp. "I just don't understand," ve said. "I don't understand how you could be *in* the riot. You said you were leaving. You said you were walking *away* from the riot." Tears were running down vir cheeks.

"What is happening," Grobbard said, "at the party?"

"Well, they're talking to people," Fift said, and rubbed zir eyes. Under the table, zir legs were quivering with exhaustion, propagated from the body on the byway.

Pom Filigrous Tyrox of name registry Blue Piggyback Dentition 18, 4-bodied Staid, 580 years
old, bespoke polyp farmer.

Mmondi Tenak Peridity-Chandrus of name registry
    Yellow Peninsula Sugarbubble 8, 2-bodied Vail,
    177 years old, liberal Kumruist officiant and
    Mother.
Vvonda Tenak Peridity-Chandrus of name registry
    Peridot Improbable Gumstuck 12, 3-bodied Vail,
    16 years old, student.

Vvonda!

Fift blinked. It was Vvonda, all right. They'd never met, but ze was sure ze'd seen that towering figure when ze'd spied on Shria over the feed (never too often, never too long). And how many sixteen-year-old Vails named Vvonda could there be in Foo, anyway? If Shria's other bodies were still hanging out with Bluey and Vvonda . . .

Vvonda was standing by a food rack, chewing on a stalk of cellroot and laughing loudly at something Foon Pelix Nathandine was saying. Vvonda was big: broad shoulders and a smooth, round belly. Two heads taller than Fift, a head taller than Shria, and on top of that ve had a mane of bright blue hair teased into a complicated pattern, an inferno spiraling into the sky. Ve was wearing an open jacket and closed pants in some slick, impenetrable, shiny yellow material that looked made for fighting; vir large, plump breasts with dewy green nipples were bare under the jacket, and crossed by a bandolier full of daggers, pens, and undersized gardening tools. Vir skin was shaded in a gradient, purple at vir scalp to orange at vir hands and belly. In short, ve looked brash, commanding, and bone-slicingly fashionable, broadcasting vir readiness to fight or fondle you, holding vir own at a party among adults. Sixteen or not, Vvonda had none of the "I'm just practicing, I'll get this right in a few decades" air that clung to Fift. If ve wasn't latter-born, Fift was a six-bodied Midwife.

Could ze just send vem a note? Ze sighed, remembering Smistria (who was trying to tell a joke, gesticulating as the logistics coordinators turned away) taunting Frill (who seemed to be enjoying vemself now that the chatterdance was back to its first or second phase) on the way over. Who was ze to get this Vail to take zir call? Ze would have to do this in person.

Making zir way through two crowds at once, ze began to have flashes of vertigo and body-flicker. A red anonybody that had been heaved through the air by its fellows and a flying tray of steaming turnabouts came at zir head in the same moment, and ze almost collapsed and rolled in the wrong body. Maybe that would have been for the best—cutting straight past the anxiety to the abject humiliation.

Back at home, ze gripped the edge of the table to steady zirself. Squell saw, stopped vir pacing, took a deep breath, and put a hand on zir shoulder. "All right, Fift," ve said. "I, I won't blame you. It's not your fault. Even if you didn't—you should have listened to us, you should have, but I know you didn't imagine—I'm just, so, so sorry for you. I'm sorry you have to . . . endure . . . such a thing . . ." Vir hand, on Fift's shoulder, trembled.

Grobbard's eyes were still closed. Nupolo went to the door. Ve looked back, once, frowned, and left the room.

Fift wanted to curl up on the floor, to sleep in at least one body. To close at least one of zir three windows on the world. Worse, ze wanted to loosen the connection between zir bodies— the old urge to shelter zirself in one place from what was happening to zir in another.

Ze should have paid more attention to zir exercises, kept doing polysomatic sports, finished becoming one thing, one whole, final, real person, instead of just learning to disguise the fact that ze was three ungainly pieces, a cracked vase. Tears sprung, astoundingly, to zir eyes: the wrong eyes, the eyes at the party. A crying sixteen-year-old Staid: disgusting, ridiculous. Wiping them on zir hands would be a clear give-away. Ze faked a cough into the folds of zir robe.

Father Squell moved closer to zir, looking at zir earnestly. If ze could cry in *that* body . . . maybe Squell wouldn't even be shocked. Maybe ve'd comfort zir, pull zir into vir embrace. Like when ze was little and zir Fathers were a sea of laughing, crying, fighting, glittering beauties, strong as great beasts, a reliably endless ocean of hugs.

Only an hour ago, when the lights had gone out and Foo had stopped, they had all clung together. Now, though, with Grob-bard's face passive and composed and frigid, and Squell's insis-tent, prying gaze on zir, and Vvonda's back to zir, leaning in to hear Foon Pelix Nathandine, and Fift's arms and legs so tired, trying to flow . . . ze couldn't do it, couldn't act like a toadclown-ish baby. Certainly not in front of Father Grobbard. And not in front of Father Squell either—Father Squell who bragged about vir own body in the asteroids, who called Fift baby names and fretted aloud every time ze wandered beyond Foo.

Arrogant stupid Fathers, stupid with the idea-fixity of adulthood! *They'd* escaped, by luck and time, from the wild swamp of childhood. They'd each found some little safe ledge or stump to crouch on and keep dry. From there, they could criticize, judge, exhort . . . or even sympathize, but Fift could take no comfort in that. Each was convinced their stump was the perfect stump, the stump all children should seek, though there was no more room on it.

So Fift sat straight-backed and dry-eyed and silent, cool and staidish, imitating a grown-up—a closed surface with no aperture. Ze closed *zir* eyes, too, just like Father Grobbard.

Foon Pelix, the textilist two centuries older than Fift and Vvonda, was saying: "So they come in, this Unfeeling adept with zir bodies chained together and a Kumruist priest in full regalia, and the priest has a parrotine on vir shoulder, and I can't help saying, 'Is this a joke?' Because, you know, 'an adept, a priest, and a parrotine walk into a textile envisioning space . . .' I mean, really! But they were offended. They didn't see the humor in the situation. So then I—"

Fift was wondering how ze could work up the courage to interrupt. Reflexively, and stupidly, ze checked zir raw emotional balance. It was way down. Vvonda looked up and saw zir.

"You," ve hissed.

"Wha—what?" Fift said.

Vvonda glared.

"Ah," Foon Pelix said, "you're Pip's child, yes? Yellow Peninsula Sugarbubble, a fine name registry. I'm Yellow Optimum myself, you know . . . so we're not *quite* name-cousins, but . . . it's still lucky, I say! Ah . . . You two are acquainted, then?"

"We have a mutual . . . friend," Vvonda said, icily.

"Um, um, about that," Fift said. What had ze done? Why was ve angry? "Ve's, Shria's not, I can't reach vem. I was wondering if you . . ."

"You can't *reach* vem?" Vvonda said. "What do you *mean*?"

"Shria, eh?" Foon Pelix said. "Don't think I know that one. Also a child of Foo, then?"

"I mean on the byway, where we are," Fift said, "I can't get to vem, physically, and ve won't return my . . . I mean, I tried to send, but . . ."

The temperature of Vvonda's stare had plunged from water ice to liquid nitrogen. "You shouldn't be there, staidkid," ve said. "You shouldn't have followed vem in. You should get the airless all-sucking void *out*. It's no place for you."

"I do take an interest in the children of Foo," Foon Pelix said. "Such an important thing, children, and it's everyone's responsibility, I say, the whole community; the parental cohort first of all, of course, but . . ."

"Ve . . ." Fift felt like ze was running out of air. "We were . . . *together.*"

Vvonda sniffed, straightened the bandolier where it crossed between vir startlingly big green-nippled breasts (if Fift grew breasts, they'd be small, soft, cushiony staidish breasts, easily kept out of sight, not these flagrant monsters, but even such a small change felt too risky, too dramatic . . .), turned back to Foon Pelix (. . . it would seem as if Fift were asking for attention if ze grew breasts, gambling zir emotional balance on a showy display . . .) and said, drily, "So what did you say to them?"

(. . . it would be years, decades, Fift thought, before ze could afford a somatic indulgence like *breasts* . . .)

"To . . . whom?" Foon Pelix asked.

"The adept, the priest, and the parrotine."

(. . . and that thought, trivial as it was, seemed to catch up against some hidden knot of anger in Fift's Only-Child gut.)

The house feed was flickering in and out, but over it, Fift could see Father Squell reach out towards zir shoulder, sigh . . . and then take vir hand away. Zir own expression, eyes closed, was impassive.

Faintly—no louder than a whisper—from somewhere, Fift heard a rumbling, squeaking, rolling rhythm:

Baaa-RUMP, ba-chiggity-chiggity-whuppity-chiggity-chig-
   gity-BOOM!
Baaa-RUMP, ba-chiggity-chiggity-whuppity-chiggity-chig-
   gity-BOOM!

For a moment (more somatic confusion), ze didn't know what body ze heard it in.

"Vvonda," ze said, zir heartbeat beginning to accelerate, zir ears beginning to buzz. Ve turned back to zir with a look of incredulity, and Foon Pelix paused in zir story. Fift swallowed.

Some part of zir was distantly intrigued to notice a bifurcation beginning in zir raw emotional balance: a few automated agents were now betting on collapse, but others were buying, on new evidence of courage. Ze felt the slight prick of professional banker-historian's curiosity as it occurred to zir for the first time that this would all be a very interesting tale to reconcile, mixed with sudden hope. Ze smiled, and Vvonda's glare flickered, maybe faltered, for an instant.

"Vvonda," ze said. "Listen. Can you explain what I did wrong?"

"You honestly have no idea," Vvonda said, more an incredulous observation than a question.

"No," Fift said. "I don't."

Ze could hear the rhythm (*chiggity-chiggity-BOOM!*) on the byway, faint beyond the chanting and roaring of the riot.

Vvonda exhaled, and for a moment vir grand and provocative and stylish posture slipped. Not that ve looked insecure, or troubled—not Vvonda. But ve wavered. Ve bit vir lip, staring intently at Fift as if ze were a puzzle ve was trying to figure out. Vir swagger evaporated so completely that Fift realized it was made up. Vvonda must have felt just as out of place as Fift among these middle-aged glitterati and bureaucrati, all of them pretending to be entertained and not terrified. Ve didn't belong here, either. But if ve had to be here, the set of vir jaw said, then—by Kumru's fertile womb—ve would contest the transaction as a Sibling, not be excused from it as a child.

Vvonda sighed. "Please excuse us," ve told Foon Pelix.

"Oh, oh, all right," Foon Pelix said, "although if there's anything I can assist with, as I said—"

"No, we got it," Vvonda said. "Have a good party."

Over the chanting of freedom and valor and conquest and babies, beyond the press of bodies, came the whisper of a rhythm, faint and tinny:

Baaa-RUMP, ba-chiggity-chiggity-whuppity-chiggity-chig-
  gity-BOOM!

Vvonda pulled Fift under one of the privacy cones. Its crenelated deep purple hollow plunged like a labyrinthine dagger into the ceiling overhead. Fift could *smell* the anti-surveil; there were even wisps of fine purple mist to blur them from lip-readers.

Vvonda glowered at Fift. "You sisterless waste of volume . . . Shria really *likes* you!"

Fift swallowed. "I . . . I mean, what? I mean, I like vem too!"

"Then how could you *do* that to vem? How could *you* try to . . . to, what, *protect* vem? What do you think that's like for a Vail? Ve's out of vir mind, overwhelmed, and ve's *fighting!* Off the mats, unlicensed, totally outnumbered! And *you're* in vir way? It's way more than ve can handle. Ve shouldn't be there, and you *really* should not be there!"

"But I'm trying to get vem to leave!" Fift cried.

"You think ve can just turn and run? Fift, the feed may be mostly down, but do you think people wouldn't know? And ve'd know, don't you get that?"

"But ve could get hurt in there! Ve could lose a body, even—"

Vvonda's face flushed a brighter purple, and vir hands jerked involuntarily. Fift briefly wondered whether, if ze'd been a Vail, Vvonda would have shoved zir. "Ve's already *hurt,*" Vvonda hissed. "But ve isn't at risk of losing a body in this kind of fight. Ve's at risk of losing something *else,* but I don't expect *you* to understand *that!*"

"So what are you doing, then?" Fift said. "You're a Vail, you're vir friend, why aren't you going to help vem?"

"I am, you stupid . . . slug!" Vvonda said, vir face magenta. "Bluey and I and Stogma and the rest of Shria, eight bodies, total—we're trying to get there! We forced our way onto the first sluice, but we have to go around the second. We're going to use the slide-grove off Bittersting. When we get there, those sisterless rent-a-body-wearing siblingfuckers are going to be sorry. Plus, my mom and I came to this party to try to get a bat, and now *you're* interrupting. Look, no one is going to hit a Staid. Just get yourself the fuck *out* of that crowd and go home!"

"We were *trying* to get home before—"

Vvonda made a noise of disgust in vir throat. "You can't even handle *that* yourself? Then just get to the end of the by-way and *wait* for us."

I'm scared, though, Fift wanted to say, but couldn't. It occurred to zir belatedly that ze was doing this all wrong, contesting the wrong transaction. Ze sounded angry, worried, demanding—like a four-year-old who'd never learned enough self-control to sit through zir first Long Conversation. Like a baby. It just confirmed Vvonda's opinion of zir as a useless, helpless burden.

Of course *ve* could curse and complain and demand—that was different. In a Vail, it was passion. In Fift, it was just weakness.

Ze knew what Father Grobbard would do. Incorruptible and emotionless as the void, immune to Vvonda's insults and scorn, ze would calmly interrogate vem, coolly entertain vir opinions and rash statements, expose the flaws in vir reasoning. Gradually Vvonda would seem more and more ridiculous until, flushed and petulant, ve'd submit to zir logic.

(At the thought of zirself in this role, of Vvonda supplanted and yielding to zir cool, efficient intellect, ze experienced an absurd little erotic thrill. What if *Vvonda* were the one to feel helpless . . . to feel overpowered, overcome, awed by Fift, caught and carried along in zir wake . . . ? Ze remembered zir hand, struggling in Shria's blue forest . . .)

But ze didn't know what logic that would be, or what words to say.

Ze was sure, though, that if ze could produce even Father Grobbard's *tone* of clinical, dispassionate certainty (or Mother Pip's tone, for that matter, certainty mixed with charm and bombast), Vvonda's swagger would vanish again. Forced to fight on Staid territory, ve'd go stiff, defensive, guilty . . .

Fift couldn't, though.

The rhythm got louder:

Baaa-RUMP, ba-chiggity-chiggity-whuppity-chiggity-chig-
   gity-BOOM!

A pause spread through the riot like an infection, one body after another. The grappling slowed. Heads lowered, resting for a moment on the shoulders of those they strove against; heads rose, listening.

Father Squell was crying softly. The sound mixed, in Fift's tired brains, with the *chiggity-whuppity* rhythm . . .

"Our time together," Panaximandra said, "is coming to an end, my sistren. For now. You have work ahead: difficult, dangerous work. Hardest of all will be the work of remembering why this matters—of remembering that you can be free."

Vvonda stared at Fift as if waiting for more. Then ve nodded once, turned, and sauntered away.

At the table, Fift opened zir eyes. Father Grobbard, eyes still closed, looked tired, peaceful, still, absent: a premonition of death.

The rhythm was as loud now as a stage whisper at the other end of the breakfast table:

Baaa-RUMP, ba-chiggity-chiggity-whuppity-chiggity-chig-
   gity-BOOM!

"They will try to make you ashamed," Panaximandra said. "They will tell you you are behaving like children. They will explain to you why this is already—"

"Vvonda," Fift said.

"—the best of all possible worlds. They will not see you or your grievances. And if you force them to see, they will pretend to find you ridiculous. And if you shock them out of their laughter—"

Vvonda turned back, flinging a hand up in *what-is-it-now?* exasperation.

"—they will pretend to find you shameful. And if you refuse to be ashamed, they will call you evil—"

Fift said, "You're enjoying this, aren't you?"

"—and if you are unafraid to be evil, they will banish you to an Idyll. They will say they want to *help* you, so they can silence you. And if they cannot mock you from your goal, and they cannot frighten you, and they cannot trick you—"

"What?" Vvonda asked, vir eyes hardening dangerously.

"—then they will pretend to become reasonable. They will give you some scraps from their table, and they will say it is dangerous and extraordinary and cause for celebration that they have given you these scraps—"

In the pausing, quieting press of red and black and blue bodies, it was easier to move. Fift crept, slid, ducked under arms, squeezed between bodies. No one struck zir.

"This. Everything falling apart," Fift told Vvonda. "This revolution, this unraveling. You like it. It's made for you."

"—and they will warn you that you must be content with them. Do not be content, my siblings. You are human beings. They have supplanted you in your own minds—"

Vvonda paused, frowned. Fift could see vem rein in vir first, incredulous, angry reaction, stop, and consider zir question.

"—making you grateful for your slavery, making you believe you owe them your lives. You do not."

As loud as running footsteps in a corridor beyond a closed door, the rhythm came up behind Panaximandra's words. The anonymized Vails around Fift turned, seeking its source.

Baaa-RUMP, ba-chiggity-chiggity-whuppity-chiggity-chig-
  gity-BOOM!
BOOM-ba-de-chiggity, BOOM-ba-de-chiggity, BOOM-ba-
  de-chiggity, BOOM!

"You're right in one sense," Vvonda said. "I like a challenge.
We've been under-challenged, Fift, haven't you noticed?"

"You owe them nothing," Panaximandra said.

And there was Shria. Five rent-a-bodies—three red, two
blue—encircled vem. One of the blue ones towered above the
others. Instead of the usual shallow indentations for eyes,
mouth, and ears, it had real features: startling white orbs of
eyes with orange irises and long lashes, orange lips, fleshy
whorls of ear—shockingly incongruous in the featureless
expanse of skin-fabric.

The Vails had stepped away from Shria, turned to face the
growing rhythm:

BOOM-ba-de-chiggity, BOOM-ba-de-chiggity, BOOM-ba-
  de-chiggity.
BOOM-ba-de-chiggity, BOOM-ba-de-chiggity, BOOM-ba-
  de-chiggity, BOOM!
Baaa-RUMP, ba-chiggity-chiggity-whuppity-chiggity-chig-
  gity-BOOM!

Shria was lying on the ground, face down. Vir clothes were
ripped, jagged slashes of vir lavender skin revealed between
the red and blue fabric, lacerated and beginning to flush the
deeper purple of bruises.

They'd been kicking vem.

"I see vem," ze gasped, to Vvonda.

"I see Shria," ze told Father Grobbard, whose eyes opened.

"You're still *there*?" Vvonda said. "You haven't listened to a
word I said, have you?"

Fift tried to imitate Father Grobbard's expression exactly. "It's not as if you offered me any clear arguments," ze said to Vvonda. "You simply asserted it was no place for me, among a flurry of insults. There was little information content, and none new." Zir throat was dry, and ze cleared it, twice, hoping that didn't ruin the effect.

Shria heaved vemself to vir knees and paused, vir neck craned down, vir red hair covering vir face.

"Ve's *telling* you to go *away*," Vvonda hissed. "That's the new information. Ve wants you to *leave*."

"Goodbye, my friends, my siblings, my lovers," Panaximandra said. "Until we meet again, remember: do not listen to their lies. Remember who you are!"

Fift took a step forward; two steps. The blue body with the startlingly real eyes and ears glanced at zir, then looked back towards Panaximandra.

"True," Fift said to Vvonda. "That is new information. I thank you for it."

Baaa-RUMP, ba-chiggity-chiggity-whuppity-chiggity-chig-
gity-BOOM!

Vvonda snorted. "Sure, kid. Whatever." There was a hint of uncertainty in vir voice.

Fift slipped into the ring of rent-a-bodies and sat, cross-legged, a pace away from Shria.

"Enjoy your playtime," Fift said, zir face impassive.

A flash of anger passed over Vvonda's broad face.

Grobbard's lips relaxed slightly; zir version of a smile. "So," ze said. "The Clowns arrive at last, while the ordering parents of the world are still nowhere to be seen."

Shria opened vir eyes. And, seeing Fift, widened them.

The music was as loud, now, as nearby thunder—

*Baaa-RUMP, ba-chiggity-chiggity-whuppity-chiggity-chig-
    gity-BOOM!*
*BOOM-ba-de-chiggity, BOOM ba-de-chiggity, BOOM-ba-
    de-chiggity, BOOM!*

—and over the drumming, ze heard the whistling, grinding, tweedling, sweet, discordant music of the pipes:

*Hhrang, hrrang, de-da-de hhrang, hhrang woodledy woo-
    dledy-de,*
Hhrang woodledy woodledy-de, hhrang, hhrang . . .

Shria was bloody and bruised, vir eyes swollen, blood staining vir lips. Ve was trembling.

Fift forced the muscles of zir face to relax. Ze'd had a plan. Ze was going to say, formal and calm, "Greetings, Shria. May I observe?" or something like that. Something to reassure vem that ze wasn't trying to save vem. Something staidish and grown-up and not ridiculous. And then ze'd just sit in the middle of the riot as if it were the Long Conversation, and ve'd forgive zir.

But that plan was ruined, because it was too loud for Shria to hear zir. Ze wanted to send vem another note, but it might not go through, and ze didn't want to stop and compose it now, not with vem watching zir expression with blank intensity. Ze nodded at vem, trying to show vem: *I won't interfere anymore. I am here for you, but I will let you do this thing you have to do, whatever it is. I trust you, Shria.*

Fift saw flickers of color and movement from beyond the press of rent-a-bodies. Ze checked the feed, and, yes, a few more views of the byway were now flickering in . . . and there they were, in lines of marchers fifty bodies wide: the Clowns.

9

The first line of Clowns had enormous bulbous heads and ball-like eyes the size of small canids, each eye reflecting in funhouse distortion a different world that wasn't there: gas giants, fancily decorated house interiors, beaches, battle scenes; each alive and correlated with the waving of the distorted heads. The line of them, Vails and Staids intermingled, spread across the whole breadth of the byway. They had great peaked noses, great rubbery lips, and small round bellies supporting metal drums. And on these, the clawed hands of the Clowns beat with long, long bones:

Baaa-RUMP, ba-chiggity-chiggity-whuppity-chiggity-chiggity-BOOM!

The second line had trees for heads, drums in all the branches, and wheels for feet, which spat sparks of all colors. The third line were dancers without heads, each dancer a cluster of arms and legs which met in a center knot, and the dancers sprang and grappled and rebounded in a hypnotic gyre which was both tumultuous and rigidly restrained. The fourth line had wireframe models of habitation structures, adorned with tiny sluices and flywheels and bounceroos and tessellations and anedrals, where their bodies should have been, with hats on top of them and squat arms and legs attached at the sides, and they were drumming the same tattoo.

Then came the flautists, a line of rather ordinary-looking Staids in white, until you noticed that all fifty of them were identical and moving in identical lockstep, as if they were *one fifty-bodied person*, which made that line the most gasp inducingly miraculous of all.

And the flautists played:

Woodle-deedly-deedly-dee, woodle-deedly-dee,
Woodle-doodly-deedly-dee, deedly-doodly-doo.

And after them pipers, all Vails, their naked bodies painted in gaudy gold and orange and bedecked in glittering bangles, their powerful arms compressing the groaning air sacks that drove the pipes:

Hhrang, hrrang, de-da-de hhrang, hhrang dada-dooda-dee,
Hhrang dada-dooda-dee, hhrang, hhrang.

And after them more Clowns, and more: cavernous carrion birds and hovering swarms of light, bestial rompers and stilt-tall fire dancers; and behind *them*, a crowd of revelers and hangers-on and wannabes, and vendors pushing carts of comestibles, and bookies' barkers calling out bets, and freelance serendipity coordinators, and matchmakers and balloon-sellers and portraitists, and commemorative body-garden architects, and rowdies, and reactants, and impromptu school outings with teachers in tow, all following the Clowns.

BOOM-ba-de-chiggity, BOOM-ba-de-chiggity, BOOM-ba-
    de-chiggity, BOOM!

Fift heard all of this with zir own ears on the byway; but ze saw it through the (jerky, intermittent) feed. Zir eyes were on Shria, who had raised vir bloody face to see the Clowns.

This was not the only such parade; the sound there on the byway was deafening, but through the flickering feed, in the quiet of zir parental cohort's breakfast room in Foo, ze could hear the discordant thrum and jangle of parades throughout Fullbelly, a storm of sound loud enough to overcome the noise inhibitors strewn through the invisibly cobwebbed interspace.

"What I find so strange," Tigan Melitox Farina of name registry Blue Piggyback Dentition 5 was saying at Fift's elbow, "is not being able to tell what people are *thinking*. I mean, it's so *ironic*: the biggest news since ever, and no public opinion reacting to it!"

Tigan's name-cousin, Pom Filigrous Tyrox, sniffed. "I'll tell you my opinion . . ."

Shria surged to vir feet and lunged at the huge blue rent-a-body with the strangely real eyes. Fift flinched but controlled zir breathing. At the party, ze gasped "No—" and the two Blue Piggyback Dentition name-cousins looked uneasily over at zir.

Grobbard's eyes were closed; the apartment was deathly still. The contrast with the chaos of sound on the byway—

Hhrang, hrrang.
BOOM-ba-de-chiggity, BOOM-ba-de-chiggity,
Feedly-doodly-doo.

—was eerie.

Shria threw an elbow into the gut of the blue rent-a-body as the Clowns reached the edge of the riot. The rent-a-body went down.

With another cautious glance at Fift, Tigan Melitox Farina turned back to Pom Filigrous Tyrox. "You can talk all you *like*, but you won't be able to find those words tomorrow, will you? No memory, no weighting, no filtering, and our agents asleep— so what good *is* your opinion, honestly? What is it *for*?"

The rioters, who had stopped fighting to gape, now shuffled out of the way of the advancing columns of Clowns. Shria stumbled back; the other Vail's real-eyed rent-a-body struggled to its knees. One bulbous-headed drummer Clown (huge and ugly and sure of step, its drumstick bones blurring on the metal drum) marched between them, and then another. The rent-a-body Vail stood, and ve and Shria looked at each other across the gap. The drumming was an unbearable roar; it soaked into their bones.

Fift had to get to zir feet and move when the drum-tree-headed Clowns rolled through, spitting sparks. Ze took a few steps toward Shria. The rent-a-bodies around zir were helping each other up.

"It's sort of terrifying, isn't it?" Pom Filigrous Tyrox said.

"Yes," zir name-cousin said. "It is. Also, if there's anything scandalous you want to do, you should probably do it now, while this lasts."

"Good thinking," Pom Filigrous Tyrox said. And they wandered off into the crowd.

Shria stared at the anonybody with the real orange eyes. The many-limbed dancers bounded between them, the architectural-model Clowns drummed through, and then the anonybody was gone.

Shria sagged, and spat on the byway.

Fift went to vem. Shria reached out and took Fift into vir arms. Fift's cheek was pressed into the hollow between vir two middle breasts. The drums were too loud for zir to hear vem crying, but ze felt the small explosions of sobs beneath vir breastbone.

"Good day for a festival," Grobbard said drily.

The eerily identical flautists (or flautist? But it must be a trick, no one could manage fifty bodies! Where was lookup?) passed. The pipers passed.

Someone cleared their throat behind Fift; it took a moment to figure out where.

It was at the party. Fift was staring at the bric-a-brac pyramids above where Father Frill was no longer dancing.

Ze turned around.

Mother Pip was there, looking grim and amused. Frill and Smistria stood a pace behind zir. *They* looked aggrieved.

"We have a bat," Pip said. "We're going to fetch your body from the byway. Stay where you are."

"The Clowns—" Fift began.

"Just stay," growled Pip, "where you *are*."

The cavernous carrion birds passed them, then the hovering swarms of light, the bestial rompers, the stilt-tall fire dancers; the revelers, the hangers-on, the wannabes, and the vendors; followed by the bookies' barkers, freelance serendipity coordinators, matchmakers, balloon-sellers, portraitists, commemorative body-garden architects, rowdies, reactants, and school outings with their teachers in tow; and the blue and red and black rent-a-bodies holding hands, the ones with mouths eating sourspun fluffity from a vendor's cart.

> *Baaa-RUMP, ba-chiggity-chiggity-whuppity-chiggity-chig-*
> *gity-BOOM!*
> *Baaa-RUMP, ba-chiggity-chiggity-whuppity-chiggity-chig-*
> *gity-BOOM!*
> *Hhrang, hrrang, de-da-de hhrang, hhrang dada-dooda-de,*
> *Woodle-deedly, woodle-deedly, woodle-deedle, hhrang!*

 # INTERLUDE

Insider's Market Report

HELLO and welcome to ZANGO JANGO's little corner of the world-of-ideas! THANKS FOR VISITING, because NOT MANY DO, may Groon regret it! But that's THEIR LOSS and YOUR GAIN because—say it with me, my puppies—THE BEST DIRT IS THE DIRT LEAST SEEN!

That's right, my kittens: with ZANGO JANGO'S MARKET TIPS you'll be ahead of the game, making the bets of a lifetime, the ones that'll burrow you into DEPTHS OF SUCCESS you never knew you HAD IN YOU!

Now . . . I say that every week. And that's because it's always true. Week in and week out, JANGO brings you that teetering-on-the-edge-of-the-byway contrarian bite. But this week . . . this week, my puppies. Well. This week . . . is different.

What I've got for you today is so big and so wild my predictive agents say half of you are going to abandon old ZANGO's spot, never to return, before I'm done. But I'm begging you: HEAR ME OUT. If you close your ears on old Fathersibling Jango now, you'll regret it later, may Groon mourn!

So what's the BIG BET?

. . . let me lead up to it, turtles.

If you missed a little thing called THE UNRAVELING this week, you need to enter the World Hermit Derby, and ZANGO will bet on your bid. I'll admit, the clowns' shindig wasn't my cup of fluffy; but whether you loved it or loathed it, the question for us BETTING FOOLS is, what OPPORTUNITIES does it present?

Everyone knows the markets will react. The SAPPY PUNTERS we love to tweak are taking the obvo bets, putting their chips on the collapse of a few more tottering cohorts, or sell-offs in feedgardener confidence. Maybe a few are venturing a bit farther, wondering about a POLITICAL REALIGNMENT. Will the Clowns collapse as a political force altogether? Contrariwise, do the Midwives look so helpless that the Clowns will surge ahead? Or even—and this is as close to the brink as SAPPY PUNTERS can bring themselves to think—will BOTH sides of the Fun/Safety axis lose out, and a long-awaited THIRD FORCE arise in our weak tea of Age of Digging politics? Maybe cobbled together out of those disgruntled staidophobic Vails and their creaky, strutting old-soldier heroes . . . ?

But puppies: that's all MEAGER PIE.

When the Consensus is betting "Things Shake Up" and the Counter-Consensus knee-jerks "No They Don't," what does ZANGO JANGO say?

ZANGO JANGO says: "You Ain't Seen NOTHING Yet."

Take a look at the chart below (as always, data for your agents to munch is on the flip side). That red line is the frustration index for uncohorted Vails in the 150- to 350-year-old demographic, broken down by birth order and plotted against the blue line, the reciprocal of ambition times longing for that same group over the past two thousand years. The spike this week is impressive, but so far so standard.

But Zango, you're asking, what's that yellow line doing there? Well, puppies, that's the index of willful denial for latter-born Staid parents in the same age group. Specifically: it's the *number of heartbeats per day they spend trying not to think about what they're thinking about.* This week: SPROIING! Forgive my vulgarity, but it looks like it's going to take a lot of spoon-passing for "the still center" to "clear the mind"!

But now take a gander at the CORRELATION (see the green callouts).

There's a reason I ran this graph out to two thousand years. Because when did those two factors sync up last? In the Age of War, that's when: *just before major intergender hostilities broke out.*

Puppies, we're looking at a *leading indicator of chaos.*

So, what's the BIG BET?

Well, this is where half of you snapcakes cancel your sub-scriptions . . . because ZANGO's about to overturn the oldest rule in the business, the fresh-waxed baby-bettor's first-learned maxim: *never bet against your own mental coherence.*

Oh, believe me, JANGO knows the arguments for the rule. *Yes:* if you're likely to go loopy, that's already priced into your rep. *Yes:* people are notoriously bad at predicting self-default. *Yes:* the only way to win is to lose, because the emotional up-heaval of ontological collapse will swamp any trifling gains you might eke out from the successful wager. That's all true: *under normal conditions.*

But THAT WAS THEN, puppies. What's coming down the sluice is such a wild ride, anyone who tells you *who'll* be up or down in a month is chewing spent glowtubes. No one knows.

But I'll tell you one thing JANGO knows:

You might be as solid and stable and centered as the most self-satisfied Long Conversationalist who ever passed a spoon.

You might be as glory-crowned and praise-sung and glad-hearted as the cockiest bangle-daddy who ever slammed an opponent to the mats.

You might be cozily embedded in a flock of beloveds who weep themselves to sleep each night just from the pure joy of knowing you.

You might, in other words, be the LAST person in the Groon-regretted world who ANYONE would expect to slip your grip on reality, to be able to humble your pride, let go of your glory, and flounder your way to the sweet, sweet release of collapse.

If you *are* that person: make this bet anyway.

Because here's what ZANGO JANGO's charts are whispering: the next ten days are going to offer you AMPLE opportunity to fulfill it.

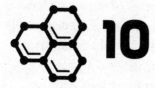 **10**

Fift and Shria sat, legs dangling over the byway's edge, watching the parades. The one that had dispersed their riot was far away now, the bulk of it ascending a curved stickywall in Dismal Bunny habitation, other strands overflowing onto nearby stairways. The parades' cacophony had faded to a whisper-thrum, distorted by sonic damping but still filling Fullbelly. Below them, the glowtubes turned the mellow gold of first evening.

Fift's legs and back ached. It was hard to look at Shria: the livid purple bruises on vir swollen face, the ruin of vir clothes.

They were the only people left on the byway. Small worker trashrats sifted through the parade's debris, meditatively munching down the smaller portions, dragging the larger portions away to compost-sluices.

The feed was coming up in spurts. On for five hundred heartbeats, off for a thousand, on for seven hundred, off for two thousand. Most messages were still getting lost en route, but there were also odd ones getting through, things Fift's attention agents probably wouldn't have allowed zir to see if they'd been in their right minds. A supposed reproduction of the Vail-hating Tractate of Mulami, excised from the Long Conversation before Pip and Grobbard were born, with various portions newly underlined. Messages from Staids Fift didn't have any connection to at all. {We know what you and the Clowns and that flowblocking alien are really up to!}, one said. Another: {Who raised you? A good staidchild wouldn't have been within a thousand bodylengths of such a violence-orgy! I'm derating your parents as soon as the feed allows!} Another: {I like you very much maybe I could come live in your apartment I would be very quiet we could pass spoons and lean our shoulders together almost touching.}

Ze wondered if Shria was getting such messages, and what they said. Virs were probably worse. Ve'd been in unlicensed combat again, off the mats, like when ve was a child. It was far more serious now.

"Vvonda is pissed off," Shria rasped.

"At me?" Fift asked.

Shria snorted. "At *you*?" Ve grabbed a passing trashrat and dropped it over the edge. It fell about a bodylength before it was caught by invisible gossamer strands. Bouncing, jiggling, and wriggling, it righted itself, then scurried away through the air, chittering, yanking its legs from the gummy invisible web at each step. "No. Not at you. That we missed the fight. That those rent-a-body freaks left before we got here."

"Vvonda likes to fight." Cold crept up Fift's spine. The roaring sea of Vails, blood on the slick skin of the anonybodies.

Shria shrugged. "Well, you know. Sport fighting, playground stuff. Ve's never been to the mats. Ve keeps saying ve wants to, but . . ." Ve shrugged. "At our age it's kind of complicated. You just look like a fool and impoverish yourself if you go around challenging for no reason. It's hard to work up the right set of . . ." Ve waved a hand vaguely, and then coughed. Ve looked tired. "You know."

"Have you ever . . . ?"

Ve shook vir head. "I think that stuff is stupid."

"But . . ." Ze stopped as vir jaw tightened.

The image of vem diving, tackling the red nobody. Disappearing into the crowd. Leaving zir.

The silence between them shifted; its inaudible score crept an octave higher. A moment before, that silence had wrapped them together in its invisible blanket; now it heaped between them, a frayed and stiff and tangled cloth, and Fift did not know how to move it aside. Ze wished ze knew what to say, to find zir way back.

{It's my fault, isn't it?} ze asked zir context advisory agent. {I let vem go into the crowd in the first place. I even followed vem in. I should have insisted. I should have been the prudent one, the still center. Why didn't you say anything?}

But zir agents were still a mess. {Normative evaluation is compromised by deficits in synthesis, telos, and ontology.} zir context advisory agent sent. {Your pardon is entreated.}

The Midwives could take vem away. Fighting off the mats at sixteen years old. They wouldn't care who started it. Not in the middle of a crisis like this. There were already reports filtering through the ragged feed, of curfews, confiscations, evictions, lookup curtailments, cohort dissolutions, disappearances.

They'd take Shria to the Pole, and it would be Fift's fault.

Ze swallowed. "We should have just left."

Shria looked over at Fift, a heat in vir eyes—anger? Shame?

"Because you're right, it's stupid, fighting is stupid." Maybe if Shria said it aloud, for all the world to hear—if ve apologized now, renounced vir part in the riot—maybe they wouldn't take vem away. They still had an audience, intermittently: a dozen, then a few hundred. Gawking at two kids who'd been terrorized when the world's watchful feed went dark.

"Fift, stop it," Shria said.

"But you just—"

"Cut it out."

"I just think—"

"It's a little late for thinking."

Fift felt zir face get hot. Ze *should* have been thinking. But ze wasn't the careful one. Ze was the rash one, they both knew that. Ze'd reached into the soft blue tangle of Shria's—

"Well, you should have stayed with me," ze said.

It was a terrible thing to say.

But ve should have.

Shria looked down, hunching vir shoulders. Expression leached out of vir face; it went slack, empty, pale.

Fift knew that look.

Nine years old, on the surface, clutching vir bundle of mossy sticks, avoiding Umlish's eyes.

Fift looked out the porthole of the robot bat and saw, far below, two figures crouched at the edge of the empty byway, separated by a wall of silence: forlorn, desperate, alone—

—and raised zir eyes from the byway's edge to search the vault of Fullbelly.

There was the bat; and there again was the cold sensation (which ze would never, ever get used to) of seeing zirself doubly from far away.

The bat descended like an angry omen. Fift stood up—and watched that tiny, helpless figure on the byway stand up—and felt dread prickle on the back of zir neck.

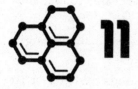 **11**

"Should Fift Brulio even be here?" Arevio said. Ve picked dirt from under vir nails in one body; in another, ve stole a glance at Fift.

"For Kumru's sake," Frill said, sitting down in vir own lap. "Ze's sixteen years old, don't you think ze has something to say at a family meeting?"

"Well, that's the question, isn't it?" said Arevio, as vir other body nodded vigorously. "Is it a *family* meeting or a *parental cohort* meeting? I don't think—"

"Oh, please," snapped Father Thurm. "Can we get on with it?" Bright squiggles of some arcane data visualization arced over the skin of vir strikingly bald black scalp.

It was something of a bad sign, Fift thought, that Thurm was actually here in a body.

Thurm's career as an agrochemical Far Theory manager had blossomed around the time Fift was born, and ve'd become modestly famous as an amateur Near Theoretician on the same topic shortly thereafter. (Apparently the Far Theory part was organizing ancient agents too complex for anyone nowadays to understand, while the Near Theory part tried to guess how they worked? Something like that.) So Thurm was always busy. As far back as Fift could remember, ve showed up at the cohort only for the minimum one-night-a-month sleepover that the family's pledge required.

It wasn't like with Miskisk; Thurm messaged Fift every day or two with some joke or amicable suggestion, and still got along with most of the others. But ve *never* came to meetings. Pip and Thurm in the same room was an event.

"Does ze *want* to be here?" Smistria asked, half-turning to Fift.

"Ze needs to be here," Pip growled, hands folded over zir stomach.

Fift was there, all right. Ze was there in all three bodies, though ze tried to keep each of zir bodies out of the others' view. Ze didn't want to look at zirself, particularly not here, and not—why in Kumru's fertile womb had ze agreed to this?—with zir neural data currently viewable by zir parents.

"Can we talk about what happened on the byway, please?" Father Squell asked. "Because . . ."

"Yes! Pip Mirtumil, Smistria Ishteni, Grobbard Erevulios, I appeal to you: what does this mean for us?" Arevio asked. In vir other body, ve chewed at vir thumbnail. "After all, we allowed Fift to wander off and get into *that*; don't you think it could affect our parental conscientiousness ratings?"

"Oh, *please*," Thurm said again.

"Easy for you to say, Thurm!" Nupolo stood at one end of the table, singlebodied, dressed up for the occasion in ancient cobalt-blue military coveralls with sparkling bangles. Vir face—its skin soft as old velvet from so many decades of routine bodywork—was grim. "They don't factor much into *your* reputation. And you don't exactly depend on these *apartments* as a *home*, do you?"

Thurm crossed vir arms. The temperature in the room felt like it dropped a few degrees.

"There are five new bets at neighborhood bookies on the

topic of this cohort, its parenting competence, and its compliance with consensus," Father Grobbard said. Oddly, ze was here in all four bodies, all seated in a row, a tiny flicker of wryness passing through one of zir four blank expressions. "The odds tend to be in our favor. There are, so far, no bets offered on forced dissolution." The other Fathers stiffened, and Fift felt a sharp stab of discomfort in zir stomach at the words, but Grobbard talked on as if unaware. "But the bookies have already estimated the odds on such bets. Low odds, to be sure. But it is notable that such estimates even exist, especially when we have thus far avoided any official rebuke or sanction. I will leave the precise probability landscape to those of you more versed in this kind of thing, but I note that there is ample anecdotal evidence of such a pattern of new betting activity presaging major shifts in aggregate approval ratings . . ."

"Now hold on," Frill said, bouncing in vir own lap with impatience. Ve was sheathed in tiny glittering golden bells which tinkled as ve swayed; a second body, underneath, lounged languidly in the seating harness. "We're talking like all this is purely a fumble that's opened us up for the blade. But there's some potential for advantage here too, don't you think? What about the conversation with the artifact?"

"With the what?" Arevio asked, brows furrowed.

"With that Thavé thing," Frill said. "It's an artifact of the Ages Before the Ages, right?"

"*Ze* likes to consider zirself a *person*," Thurm said (vir tone letting everyone know that ve'd had to do with Thavé personally).

"Whatever, that's not the point," Frill said, waving a hand airily. "The *point* is the spike of fame Fift *got* out of it, and how we're going to manage that. I mean, that's an opportunity for zir, isn't it?"

"An opportunity for what?" Smistria said. "If ze's going to be a banker-historian, I don't see why ze needs a following who expects zir to be an exoarchaeologist."

"A little fame never hurt anyone," Thurm said with a small ironic smile. Fift couldn't tell if ve was kidding.

"It certainly *did!*" Smistria cried.

"Yes! Don't you see?" Squell said. "That just makes it worse! That means there was an even *larger* audience for the fiasco on the byway!"

"And more footage with that Kumru-blessed vailchild," Nupolo said.

Fift swallowed, and there was a flutter of activity across zir all-too-visible brains, magenta flickering to peach and canary yellow in the display.

Ze couldn't wait to rescind their neural observation privileges. What had ze been thinking, letting zir Fathers paw around in zir brain data, even at a fuzzy macroscopic level? But it had seemed like the only way to persuade Squell to ever let zir out of the house again. And maybe—if ze was honest—maybe ze'd *wanted* to burrow back into the safety of zir parents viewing zir every emotional spike and trough, like being a toddler again . . .

Squell narrowed vir eyes.

"We all *like* Shria Qualia Fnax," Arevio said, "but off-the-mats fighting at *sixteen* . . ."

"Kumru's balls," Frill said, "what did you *expect* vem to do? What would any of *you* have done, if your Staid friend was . . ."

"I'm with Frill," Smistria said.

"That's not the *point,*" Nupolo said.

"Ve was apparently gathering a pack of friends to *intervene—*" Arevio began.

Fift's hearts were straining inside zir chests. If only they'd stop talking about *Shria.* Ze could bear anything else. Ze didn't want to think about vem, about what ze'd said on the byway. And ze was managing *not* to think about vem, not to feel anything particular about vem, not to wonder what ve was thinking now, so it was terribly unfair of the scanner to show this ridiculous storm of colors in zir brains every time they mentioned vem.

"—and if we do get audited and re-rated?" Nupolo was saying. "You think these void-scoured adjudicators and Midwives can afford to be *lenient*? Clowns declaring a revolution, the feed brought to its knees, riots on the byways—"

"The Cirque *stopped* the riots," Frill said heatedly, vir lounging body sitting up now.

"Ve didn't say they didn't!" Smistria snapped. "Is this to become a debate on your naïve worship of all things Cirquist, no matter what chaos—"

"Stop it, all of you!" Squell cried. "Just stop it!"

"All right, all right," Arevio said, waving vir hands. "Squell Urizus is correct, we should . . . shall we just . . . may I ask this? *External* judgements of this cohort's parenting are one thing, but what about our own *internal* consensus? Does it bother any of *you* that Fift Brulio was wandering around the below and behind *looking* to get involved with the Clowns' spectacle, with, for Kumru's sake, a *Ticket* in zir hand?"

Everyone pointedly avoided looking at Pip.

"It doesn't bother me," Thurm said. "You can't coddle and protect a child zir whole life. Ze has to be able to win zir own claim at some point."

"But Thurm," Squell said uncomfortably, "zir whole life? Ze's not even out of First Childhood. Ze's not some eighty-year-old vailchild adventurer looking for a duel. If I'm to be honest . . . I didn't say anything before . . . but actually I don't really see why being in the thick of a riot is *necessary* training for a *banker-historian*. It's more likely to be *traumatic* than *encouraging*."

"That's a bit extreme," Frill said, leaning back into vir harness again. "Ze's shaken up, and no wonder, but just look at zir brains; you can see"—ve squinted—"perfectly well ze's not *traumatized . . .*"

"Frill," Squell said, "ze's *still* getting second-order elevated amygdalic response *every* time we refer to the riot. Not to mention—"

"Only in the body that was actually *in* the riot!" Frill said.

"Are we still *entirely* sure we want Fift Brulio *here* for this . . . ?" Arevio asked.

"Well, that's not a good sign, is it?" Squell said. "Zir intersomatic synchronization is at an all-time low, and you *know* that was something the specialists told us to watch out for. You *really* do need to spend more time with yourself, Fift."

"Squell Urizus—" Arevio said.

"If I avoided everything," Pip growled, "that gave me an elevated amygdalic response, I would still be doing the accounts of sisterless sluice operators in Undersnort."

Several Fathers glared at Pip, probably for the epithet "sisterless"; Fift pretended not to notice.

"This meeting is hopelessly off topic," Smistria said, rocking forward on vir stool. "If it ever had a topic. As I have said in the past, I don't understand why we don't impose some structure to our meetings and let Pip and Grobbard . . ."

"Oh, not this again," Frill said, covering one of vir faces with vir hands.

"I don't know, Frill," Squell said. "I mean, I'm sorry, but if there's one thing Staids know how to do . . ."

Thurm held up a hand. Ve closed vir eyes, shaking vir head, and then opened them. Vir smile was mirthful and long-suffering. "Okay," ve said. "Stop. Stop. Now." Ve turned to Pip. "Allow me to summarize." No one said anything, but one of Pip's eyebrows inched a bit higher on zir stern, plump face.

"We have a kid, whom we all love. Our kid had an adventure . . . no, two adventures. Ze met an alien, ze got some audience, and then ze wandered into a riot and got scared by some atavistic, adrenaline-overdosed holiday-warriors in rent-a-bodies. Yes?"

"Ze was *struck*," Squell said. "Not just 'scared.' Those sist . . . those Kumru-spurned body-renters struck a defenseless sixteen-year-old staidchild far from home, who . . ."

"Ze was struck?" Arevio cried, stiffening.

"Oh, you missed that part?" Frill said, both bodies lounging now.

"If you will all observe the display I have placed in the shared view," Grobbard said, "which has been reconstructed from a variety of sources, including Far-Theoretical extrapolation modeling of the observable portions of private intersomatic data traffic at variously distributed relevant nodes—modeling for which I am, incidentally, indebted to our dear Thurm—you will note that there were forty-six instances of bodily contact not initiated by Fift, of which four were of sufficient intensity to merit the appellation 'struck.' One of these, Fift was able to neutralize by judicious use of Martial Staidity, for which, if I may add a brief digression, I think we should commend zir, as ze really only had the one year of instruction, and that was some time ago—"

"Yes, well done, Fift," Squell said, to a chorus of nods and snaps of applause, which faltered as zir embarrassment became flagrantly, humiliatingly visible in the neural display.

"The other three incidents," Grobbard said, still the same body talking, the other three sitting impassively (one of them seemed to actually be asleep), "occur at 5.342, 18.504, and 36.881 in the sequence which I have marked. This punch, certainly intentional, after Fift has grabbed the umbilical cord; this elbow to the face, intentional with 79% probability; and this kick to the head, intentional with 84% probability. The intersomatic traffic modeling has allowed us to make reasonable predictions, even in the absence of lookup, as to the identities of the anonymized individuals responsible. Probabilities of those identifications, respectively . . ."

"You *know* who these gnats *are*?" Smistria cried. "Grobbard, my darling, you're a genius."

"So that's it then!" Frill said, both bodies leaning forward again. Ve pounded the table, bells ringing, vir eyes alight. "We call them out. *I'll* call them out, or . . ."

"What!?" Nupolo slapped the table with both hands, drawing vemself up to vir full height. "Give these fringe-clinging *mud-spawn* the *honor* of meeting them on the *mats*? That's your idea of . . . ? *Kumru!* And our *reputation*?!"

"Absurd," Smistria said.

"And what do *you* want to do?" Frill snapped. "Have a formal adjudication? That's even worse. A cohort of—you'll pardon me, but—seven healthy adult Vails, standing meekly in line for an adjudication because our child got kicked around by some fringe-clinging . . ."

"Adjudication," Smistria said, sitting up very straight, "is just a formalization of—"

"Oh, I don't want to hear your theories!" Frill cried.

"Frill," Squell said, vir brows furrowed.

"I wonder," said Arevio, "if, I mean, before we take any drastic action, we should check with the cousins—with little Chalia Rigorosa's parents? Because any effect on our reputation is going to rebound on vem, too."

"Exactly! Thank you, Arevio!" Nupolo said.

Pip got to zir feet. Everyone stopped talking.

"My beloveds," Pip said. "I am warmed by the fire of your passion." Ze drummed zir fingers lightly on the table. "Our dear Fift has had some trouble. We are all concerned. We are excited by the opportunities. I wonder if I might—"

"Pip," said Thurm, "get to the point already."

Pip smiled a thin, tolerant smile. "With pleasure. Our beloved Thurm was correct when ve said that we cannot coddle Fift. Fift cannot climb back into the womb. Ze needs to win zir own stake. But it is also true that we must take seriously the consequences of the riot—for the reputation of this cohort, and for Fift's own emotional health and wealth.

"We cannot seem to condone what has happened. We cannot allow suspicion of involvement in destabilizing activities to rest upon us. We must react, and show decisively where we stand, show that we have raised Fift well.

"But it also cannot be that zir parents rush in to save zir, dignifying the fringe-clinging wasters who assaulted zir with adjudication or the mats. No. If I may speak as a humble banker-historian: It is Fift who has engaged them, however inadvertently, in a transaction. It is Fift who must emerge as Younger Sibling."

Ze cocked an eyebrow at Fift and zir smile became a degree or two warmer. Fift felt, and saw on the display, zir amygdala afire with dread.

"We will go see them, Fift, and you will confront them, and they will apologize. Publicly. No adjudication will be needed. And it will be clear to the world, and to you, dear Fift, that nothing whatsoever is unraveling in Iraxis cohort. It will be clear that the child of this cohort is able to vanquish these cowardly malfeasants, these pitiful enthusiasts of obsolete ideologies, very simply, just by force of will."

There were glances around the room. Thurm smiled; Grobbard nodded; Frill leaned back; Smistria chewed vir beard. Squell's expression hovered between worry and relief.

The house consensus framework was forecasting a 92% chance of full convergence within the next three hundred heartbeats.

Fift cancelled the neural access privileges and zir brain became thankfully opaque. Ze breathed deeply, then breathed again.

Zir parents, rather than protesting, turned away, giving zir privacy. They cleared their throats and glanced at one another, and this momentum led onwards, to getting up, going for refreshments in one body or another, conversing about feed-stability and the fate of the Cirque, or checking incoming queues.

In this way, it gradually became clear that the meeting was adjourned.

 # INTERLUDE

New personal notes in Fift's incoming feed:

(Shria) Look, Fift, I know you mean well. And meant well. But I think maybe I . . . look . . .

(Father Frill) Fift, your Mother is sometimes overly ambitious. I want you to know that . . .

(Dobroc P.) Most legitimate and elegant Fift: saw you on feed w/alien. Amazing. I apol . . .

(Yddyd M. N.) Most leg. Fift: I trust to Kumru that you will forgive my presumption in . . .

(Father Grobbard) Earnest greetings etc. Enclosed reference materials for our upc . . .

(Melindus X. D.) Hey F, don't know how well you remember me but I saw you in that . . .

(CIRQUE FANTABULOUS) TICKET HOLDERS: The fun is just beginning! Tomorrow the show goes . . .

(22 more . . .)

(146 contact requests from strangers at connection level 2)

(5,786 contact requests from strangers at connection level 3)

(789,786 contact requests from strangers at
connection level 4)

(2,343,242 contact requests from strangers at
connection level 5)

*Public conversations forwarded by Fift's at-
tention agents to zir incoming feed:*

SCRAPS OF VELVET: Are you with the revolution?
The Clowns are not the only ones with a . . .

AGES OF POETRY: The latest surface-set riddle
poetics game is sweeping the world. Can . . .

THAVÉ-WATCHERS INVITE: It's a surprising fact
that of the roughly one trillion inhabit . . .

LONG CONV ERRATA: Discussion of suppressed and
abolished stanzas which some scholars . . .

UNRAVELING WHAT? What are the Cirque's real
motives? If they really want "a revolut . . .

*Assignments generated by Fift's school's
scholastic agents, in incoming feed:*

Prepare stanzas 3409-6781 of didactic fourth
subsection of first metacommentary on . . .

Discuss in silence, 3rd hour: allusions to
contemporary poets in Polidani's opus . . .

Computational: assess Near-Theoretical influence on statics of Fullbelly's excavat . . .

Optional: current events: place and defend a
bet on the Cirque Fantabulous' "performa . . .

Personal/targeted: Review of instant-fame comportment (in "Transient Celebrity, Bang . . .

New personal notes in Shria's incoming feed:

(Intyzmirg) Fabulous w/that Thavé, yr so
brave. Abt riot, dont know wht to say but . . .

(Mother Sangh) My mintish, are you still upset
about what I said when you came home? . . .

(Bluey) Shria, I didn't get a chance to find
out what you actually thought abt Panax . . .

(P Politigus) Shria, fantastic darling, need two
bods at work today if not three, there's . . .

(Father Polidar) Most prized Shria: You may not
be familiar with this bit of staidish wisd . . .

(Mmpont F) Hey S, re: riot next time u will
kick nonabod ass I'm there if you want to . . .

(Stogma) Guys is there any way we can turn
this into some action for the MATS??

(CIRQUE FANTABULOUS) TICKET HOLDERS: The fun
is just beginning! Tomorrow the show goes . . .

(358 more . . .)

(1,459 contact requests from strangers at connection level 2)

(18,456 contact requests from strangers at connection level 3)

(820,822 contact requests from strangers at connection level 4)

(1,037,188 contact requests from strangers at connection level 5)

Public conversations forwarded by Shria's attention agents to vir incoming feed:

GEN DES FORUM: latest: On Shria's point, what do we even mean by "pleasure" in the con . . .

SPECULATIONS ON A "REVOLUTION": Where does theater stop and social unrest begin? . . .

THAVÉ-WATCHERS INVITE: It's a surprising fact that of the roughly one trillion inhabit . . .

FOO NEIGHBORHOODS COUNCIL: latest: Foo stopped, and what I want to know is what the . . .

Assignments generated by Shria's stochastic educational agents, in incoming feed:

Mechanics of bounceroos: in this unit, you'll learn to assemble a simple elastic rotor . . .

Political instability and the Tinyspot Uprising: from the original footage, find . . .

Comparative religious combat-sacraments, expe-
riential unit: for both Unfeeling and . . .

Current events: Construct and record a diacrit-
ical emotive response to the Cirque Fantas . . .

Personal/targeted: Review of instant-fame comportment (in "Transient Celebrity Bang . . .

12

There was an oddly hot breeze coming up from the agro-grottoes beneath Wallacomp, carrying with it a scent of decay, astringent cleaners, and soft blooming things. Pip, ten steps above Fift on the stairscape, puffed with effort, but didn't slow down. Fift was sweating in zir formal white smock.

From the glowtubes beneath them, first afternoon's brilliant white light carved the myriad sharp shadows of Fullbelly's habitations onto the roof, while far to the east, just where the world began to curve, the violet line of second afternoon cut across distant structures.

There were three perfectly good elevators, a slipthread, and an up-fountain within a thousand heartbeats' walk. So why were they trudging up these steps? If the idea was to collect an audience to witness the coming confrontation, it wasn't working. The stairscape was in naked-eye line of sight of a quarter of Fullbelly, but it was hardly densely watched territory. No one—beyond zir other parents and a smattering of acquaintances—was watching them over the feed. Did Pip want to give the Vail they were going to see plenty of time to get nervous? Or was ze doing this for Fift's benefit? Maybe ze felt like matching the emotional ordeal with a physical one.

There was a message from Shria at the top of Fift's incom-

ing queue. Zir first thought was to be delighted that ve'd written zir again so soon. But then, even without reading the initial excerpt, ze felt a stab of unease. Ze'd heard nothing from
vem since ve'd politely thanked zir parents for the ride on the
robot bat.

Fift sat up in bed and watched zirself reciting zir Long
Conversation homework on the canvas mat on the floor. After
the first few thousand stanzas, Ranhulo's metacommentary on
the eighth work of the tenth cycle—which had been straight-
forward, elegiac, celebratory, and somewhat pompous—began
to develop an undercurrent of sullen hostility, hiding rage
deeper underneath. Doing the didactic fourth subsection jus-
tice meant balancing its expansive, positive, forward-looking
embrace of the eighth work's account of the original Compromise of the Spoons (which had led the way to the Permissive
Compact and the temporary acceptance of the presence of
Vails as silent observers during the Long Conversation), with
the sour note of bitterness, regret, and disgust that underlay
them. The genius of Ranhulo was holding the two in superpo-
sition, never allowing the metacommentary's ambivalence to
collapse into polemic.

Fift was butchering it.

Pip was now twelve steps ahead of zir.

Ze opened the note from Shria.

{Look, Fift, I know you mean well.} it said. {And meant
well. But I think maybe I . . . look, I can't believe that I led you
into . . . that. Or that you followed me into it. You shouldn't
have had to see that, Fift, shouldn't have had to be in it—and
it's my fault. I didn't protect you. You deserve to be protected,
Fift, not . . . exposed. But Fift . . . I don't think I *can* protect you.
There are things I can't turn away from.

{I just feel like it's not safe for me with you. Maybe that
sounds weird. But I got bruised enough physically in that riot

without being bruised more by . . . by your words. I'm not saying it's your fault, Fift. It's not. You don't know any better. I
just think I need to be with Vvonda and Bluey and Stogma
now. It's not that I don't think you and I could be friends. In
some ways we could be realer friends than . . . I mean, I can
tell you things I can't tell them, for instance. But I don't even
know if that is fair to you.

{I go too fast sometimes, Fift. I let things run away with me.
I do foolish things.

{I hate this; it feels like I'm giving up. Maybe I *am* giving
up. At least when I'm with them, I know what I'm doing, and
I've got backup, and . . . oh, Fift, I hate myself for sending this
note. Let's just keep away from each other for a while. I'm so
tired. Maybe I'll collapse and find myself an Idyll. I don't
know. Maybe that'll help. Anyway, I still think you're a great
person. Hugs, Shria.}

Fift stopped walking.

Thirteen steps.

Fourteen.

Pip turned around. "Fift?"

"What are we doing here?" Fift said.

Ze gave up any pretense of finishing the Ranhulo, whose
hostility was so hard to take. How could someone like that, a
youthful visionary who had heralded the Compromise of the
Spoons with hope and joy, end up talking about Vails like
they were a dangerous contagion a century later? *Wildfire raging through the silent deeps . . . a storm encircling our stillness . . .*

Was that what adulthood meant? You got tired; you gave
up?

Ze climbed in bed with zirself, snuggled those two bodies
together, and closed zir eyes. But it wasn't like holding another person. It was just two backs, four arms, four legs, two
bellies, and still being alone.

Pip turned primly and walked down the fourteen steps until ze stood next to Fift. Ze lightly scratched the thick, smooth swell of zir neck, then slowly lowered zir hand onto Fift's shoulder. "And how am I to answer this disingenuous rhetorical question, Fift?"

Fift flushed, and gritted zir teeth. "I don't want to do this."

Pip nodded. "Indeed you do not. Now, Fift: start walking."

Vvonda had been right and Fift had been wrong: ze should have just left Shria in the riot, gotten out, not added to vir shame. Ze certainly shouldn't have said that stuff on the byway afterwards . . . what *had* ze said, exactly? Was it that bad? Zir agents' memories of the scene were scrambled, and the feed had still been in shreds . . . but maybe ze could find that moment recorded from some nearby pickup, and watch it . . . see if it was really that . . .

It's not safe for me with you.

Was Shria just talking about the riot? Maybe this was about what had happened at Stiffwaddle Somatic Fashions.

What Fift did there.

"Fift," Pip said. "This was the consensus of a family meeting; the first you were invited to, I might add. I understand your being nervous. But you stand at a sluice-bifurcation here. If you behave like a Staid, a Staid of this family, you will vanquish the cowardly marginals who struck you and shamed you, and who hurt your friend. And you will know forever after that you are not a victim. But if you behave like a child . . ." Pip's eyes narrowed, watching Fift's face. "Ah. Yes, who hurt your friend, Fift. And this is how you can avenge vem. Not by jumping around in the middle of a combat like a child sneaking zir Vail-sibling's armor out of the drawer to play dress-up. Not by letting your Fathers fight vir battles on the mats."

Fift swallowed. But Shria didn't want to be defended; Shria didn't want to be avenged. Ze couldn't make it up to vem like this. Could ze? Ze wanted to object, but ze didn't trust Mother Pip. Mother Pip absorbed and exploited information with methodical ruthlessness. Fift suspected ze would regret it if ze told Pip anything.

"It is time," Pip said, "to be what you are, Fift."

Fift felt a sudden thrill of fear, zir heart contracting, or the world contracting around zir heart, squeezing like a fistful of jelly around zir. Ze willed zir face still as a stone. *To be what you are.* Mother Pip couldn't know about what had happened. But could ze have guessed at Fift's unstaidish feelings?

"This is your job in the world, Fift. Not to make noise and color and conflict, not to demand and smash, not to place your fears and angers and urges before those of others." Pip smiled, unexpectedly, a tiny, rakish grin. "Well . . . there will be ways to indulge your own wishes. If you are patient, that time will come! But not by demanding them and shouting them out. No, Fift. Your job is to think, to plan, and to order. Your job is to be the still center, the basis, the core." Ze frowned. "Some Staids, of course, believe that 'being the still center' means you can never act decisively, or with speed. But you can, you know . . . you can act like lightning, at the proper time. You know me, Fift. You know I am not afraid of being accused of acting rashly."

Pip released Fift's shoulder, took zir own lower lip between zir thumb and forefingers, and inspected Fift carefully.

{Dear Shria,} Fift composed. {I don't understand what I did wrong. Can't . . .}

But ve'd already said it wasn't zir fault. Or said ve wasn't saying it was.

Fift started over. {Dear Shria, I really do want to see you . . .}

But again, ze was acting like a child. Like with Vvonda at the party: acting needy and emotional. Even if ze could, ze didn't want to vanquish Shria with cold dispassionate logic; ze didn't want to be Mother Pip or Father Grobbard with vem. But ze didn't want to disgust vem, either. Ze was happy to be vanquished, to be vir Older Sibling, if ze could only be siblings with vem.

Pip released zir lip. "You could collapse, of course." The tone of scorn with which ze usually spoke of Staids unraveling was (carefully?) absent. "Possibly that would be a way out of your predicament. We would have to respect your ontological state, I suppose, and you could have a nice stay in some grove on the surface or in the Doubled Womb, and we'd have to find some other solution to the problem of the riot. All things considered, I think that would be preferable to simply going back to the house and hiding there in cowardice for a few years."

Fift swallowed. Ze wanted to avoid Pip's eyes, but ze didn't seem to be able to. They were a cold, opaque blue today, in the velvety leaf-green folds of Pip's face. They seemed to read Fift as if zir neural data were still unhidden.

{Most prized Shria, I read with interest . . .} No, that was unsluiced compost. A fake grown-up Staid impersonation. If ve didn't laugh at zir, ve'd be hurt by zir coldness. Ze didn't want to hurt vem. Ze just wanted to . . . Ze wanted to be back wandering around the below and beyond, hand in hand, with Tickets in their pockets, expecting anything. {If my actions have in any way . . .} No. {Shria, I respect your wish to spend time with . . .} {I would never wish to interfere with . . .} {I don't mind if we . . .} {We don't usually see each other all that often anyway. But I am just wondering, what . . .}

With zir bodies on the bed, ze watched zir own impassive face over the feed, on the stairscapes, staring into Pip's blue eyes. Their audience was growing sluggishly—they had a few hundred intermittent active watchers, now, in addition to the tens of thousands of automated agents which had been passively tracking zir since the talk with Thavé.

Shria had two bodies listed at the same public location; the third was probably hard at work for Pom Politigus at Stiffwaddle. Ve was doublebodied in an abandonage in Temereen, strolling amid the mounds of rubble with that loose, muscular gait. Vvonda was there, singlebodied, and the aquamarine doublebodied Vail with the thorns running along vir jawlines must be—yes, that was Bluey. ("But there's got to be some way," Bluey was saying, insistently, "to get a challenge out of this—") Vvonda grabbed Shria in a headlock, and Shria's other body grinned, looking up and away towards Foo, shoulders easy.

"If you are trying to begin a collapse," Pip growled, "freezing catatonic on a public stairscape in Wallacomp in full view of a quarter of Fullbelly is not the worst way to begin. You could use a little coaching, but it's a start. I will begin looking for a new assistant, I suppose. Perhaps your time away from the constraints of ontological coherence will help you come up with some new ideas of what to do professionally."

At the thought that ze might lose Pip's patronage as banker-historian, Fift felt a small war of panic and relief begin within zir. Ze might end up working at a one-stop-shop banker-historian/bookie/clown/logician booth after all, but to be *free* of working with Pip . . . maybe long hours, poverty, and abuse from sneeringly superior clients would be worth it?

Then Pip leaned in to deliver the final blow. "Of course, it rather makes things worse for Shria, doesn't it? It's one thing for a Vail to be overpowered in a riot with a young Staid who can handle zirself, who retains zir composure, and who later does the correct thing and compels zir assaulters to apologize. Ze restores zir honor in zir way, ve restores virs in virs. That is something to laugh about later. Something that might bind friends together. But for a young healthy Vail to fail to protect vir Staid friend, who is overwhelmed and then unravels as a consequence? For who knows how long? And loses opportunities for professional advancement thereby? That is nothing to laugh about. It would be quite a rebuke to vem . . . if that's what you want."

Their audience climbed slowly, to over three thousand.

Fift scrapped all the unfinished drafts of notes to Shria.

Ze started up the stairs.

Pip followed zir, two steps behind. Fift did not look back. Over the feed, ze could see Pip's impassive face and the wrinkling of the corners of zir eyes that, in one of zir Vail Fathers, would have been a grin of amused triumph.

They did not exchange a word for nearly an hour, until the final elevator taking them up to the habitation of the Vail they were going to see. It was a densely jungled elevator, vines and enormous flowers brushing their faces, tiny work-fauna rustling in the leaves. Active audience had vanished, but hot bookmarks had continued to climb, thirty thousand people ready to switch to active viewing the moment anything interesting happened. Shria and vir friends had vanished into a ludatorium with practice mats.

Pip chuckled. Then ze shook zir head and laughed, a silent jiggling laugh that traveled all over zir body in waves and made zir close zir eyes. {Oh, my dear child.} ze sent privately. {I fear your tastes are too much like my own. Take it from me, it is a hard road, being a Staid lover of Vails!}

Fift said nothing, tried not to betray a reaction. What did Pip suspect?

First zir stomach in the elevator, then zir stomachs where ze sat on the bed, knotted in cold fists of fear.

 **13**

The Vail they had come to Wallacomp to see was descending the slipthread, singlebodied: **Hrotrun Videx Spilteritrine of name registry Slithery Brown Rhinoceros 6, 4-bodied Vail, 135 years old, Far Historical index-design technician, firstborn of six.** Ve had weak votes of accord from a variety of loose and forgettable historical-index societies, and strong votes of censure from four large reputation-amalgamation engines, one alleging fraud, another cowardice. Ve was part of a childless residential cohort of fifteen. Bookies' public odds on Hrotrun undergoing a disgraceful collapse within the next three months had climbed over the last two thousand heartbeats from two to one against, to two to one for.

Hrotrun had waved to them from the station above, but right now ve was fully occupied in slowing vir velocity, gingerly stretching the slipthread with vir feet as ve glided to the platform ahead of them. To either side of the path, bright pink goopfields bubbled all the way to the rim of the bowl of Tentative Scoop. It was quieter here, the busy hubbub of sounds from nearby Perilax dulled by the goop's soft belching and sputtering.

Fift and Pip's audience was beginning to convert from passive to active: they were back up to a thousand or so active viewers.

Hrotrun sprang from the thread a bodylength above the platform, landed with a slight stumble, bowed jerkily, and hurried toward them, head hunched slightly downward. Pip had come to a stop, and Fift stopped with zir.

"Most esteemed . . . visitors," Hrotrun began, panting a little from vir exertions. "A pleasure. Let me just say, there's some good anti-surveillance just over on the next platform, I don't suppose . . ."

Pip sent Fift zir first line over a private channel: {We're not interested in anti-surveillance, as I'm sure you can imagine.}

"We're not really interested in anti-surveillance," Fift said, "As I'm sure you can . . . imagine." It came out sympathetic, and perhaps slightly confused-sounding. Not like Pip would have said it, stern, wry, and immovable.

"No," Hrotrun said, swallowing. Ve was lean and smooth, with perfectly symmetrical features, small firm breasts, and bright red and blue hair like stiff feathers on vir head and cheeks. Every part had a standard attractiveness, but the total effect was generic, as if ve had assembled vemself from packages, which ve probably had . . . timidly, and alone. "No, I suppose not. Well . . ."

From Pip: {You struck me in the face with the elbow of an anonybody two days ago.}

"You, ah," Fift said, "you were the one who,"—the rudeness bothered zir, to go straight to accusations with no greeting, no attempt to soften the blow—"uh, who struck me in the face, during the riot, two days ago?"

"Oh," said Hrotrun. "Oh. Yes. I suppose I must have been. I mean I know I was, I looked at the footage. I'm so sorry. It's quite remarkable that you discovered that it was me! But then"—ve gave a little uncertain titter of a laugh—"your family seems to be fairly remarkable. So. I'm terribly sorry. I can assure you it was an accident. I will be more careful in the future."

Pip stiffened at the word "accident" and glanced, narrow-eyed, at Fift. {I'm afraid it was no accident.} ze sent.

"An ... accident," Fift said.

Hrotrun began to knead vir hands together, bending vir knuckles first one way, then the other. "Yes, yes, certainly an accident," ve said miserably. "I mean you don't think I would hit ... hit! ... a ... a staidchild ... on purpose? Come now."

Pip cleared zir throat, a hollow rumble. {Why don't we examine the footage together?} ze sent.

"Let's," Fift said. Zir body that stood before Hrotrun felt heavy, and numb, as if it wasn't part of zir—as if ze was just one of the thousand feed-viewers watching zir pound this poor, frail falling-apart Vail into the ground. "Let's examine the footage ... shall we?"

Hrotrun sagged another few fingerwidths and squeezed vir eyes shut. "No, I know what it looks like, I ... I'm not saying it was that kind of accident, like, like bumping into someone you don't see on a byway. I mean I didn't, you know ..." Vir voice shrank yet further, to a scratchy whisper. "... aim."

Bookies were now giving five to two odds on Hrotrun's disgraceful collapse in the next three months.

{Isn't this enough?} Fift sent to Pip on the private channel. {I mean ve's apologized, ve said ve aimed ... isn't it clear? Isn't, you know, honor restored? I'm not afraid of vem anymore. If I ever was.}

{Ve has not apologized for intentional assault.} Pip sent. {Ask vem if ve has. Ask vem if ve apologizes for intentionally assaulting a minor Staid. Ve will say yes, and we can go. You are doing very well.}

{Ve's going to collapse.} Fift sent.

{Good.} Pip sent. {I am sure some time in an Idyll will be salutary for vem.}

Hrotrun opened vir eyes, opened vir mouth to say something, some further excuse. Ve saw Pip and Fift glaring at each other, and vir words crept away from vem. Ve hunched vir shoulders as if awaiting a blow.

{What if ve doesn't go down cleanly?} Fift sent. {What if it's . . . messier than that?}

{Good.} Pip sent. {Then the world will know that it is inadvisable to physically abuse children behind the shield of apparent anonymity. And that Iraxis cohort takes its responsibilities seriously. Fift, do your duty.}

Fift squeezed zir jaw together, resenting Pip, and wishing Shria were here. Ze felt a stab of loneliness. Ze remembered the pavilion, the walk over to Thavé, vir arm threaded into zirs. The thrill of pride ze'd felt when Shria had called zir brave. Before the riot. Before Fift ruined everything.

Fift checked audience, and swallowed: Shria was watching. But none of vir bodies were visible: ze couldn't see vir reaction to any of this.

What would Shria think of this? Would ve be on Pip's side, wanting to devastate Hrotrun, to take revenge? Ze remembered Shria's bloody face, contorted with rage, as ve lunged at the strange blue anonybody on the byway. Or would ve think like Father Squell, desperate to keep Fift safe, to protect the poor fragile vulnerable staidchild? Ze remembered Shria's stammered apology in the secret womb-lab of Stiffwaddle Somatic Fashions. *I'm the one who—I should have—*

Should have protected Fift. Should have kept Fift away from messy vailish passion.

Tears glistened in Hrotrun's eyes. Ve could lose vir cohort, vir meager clientele. Ve'd been part of that terrifying mass of faceless bodies. Now their positions were reversed, and Fift was the terrifying one. Being terrifying was a costume you could put on and take off like a clown in a show.

I didn't protect you. You deserve to be protected, Fift, not . . . exposed.

Did you strike a defenseless child, Hrotrun? Because I'm a defenseless child; that's what I am, you see, a delicate Staid who only yearns for tranquility. And now we'll put you back into your place, and me into mine, and Shria and Pip and everyone can breathe easy, because there's nothing wild and messy that I yearn for, nothing of Vvonda's, no rough-and-tumble on the abandonage, no swaggering and preening, no hot breath on my neck, no soft blue fronds slithering around my fingers. There's nothing of your world I need to understand.

Pip glowered at Fift, willing zir to *do zir duty.*

Fuck you, Fift thought.

"Why were you there?" Fift asked.

"Wh-what?" said Hrotrun Videx Spilteritrine.

Pip stiffened.

"Why were you there?" Fift asked again. "Where did you get the anonybody? How did you know there would be a riot? Why did you—why did you care what Panaximandra said?"

"Fift," Pip said sternly.

"What?" Hrotrun said again, blinking away vir tears, a little anger showing up, finally, in vir sad brown eyes. "What are you—that's none of your—what are you, playing citizen investigator?"

"Answer my questions."

Pip frowned, hand half raised.

"I don't have to answer your questions. Look, I'm willing to apologize, all right? I even . . . yes, I mean I know I was wrong to . . ." Ve was trying to flounder vir way back to the script, from confusion and annoyance back to tearful contrition or sullen defiance.

"I don't give a defective trashrat's jammed bellyspace about your apology," Fift said, beginning to enjoy zirself. "And I'm not trying to get you in trouble. Listen, I'm actually asking— look, I got caught in that riot and it was no fun at all." Ze felt a little choke in zir throat saying it: that elevated amygdalic response again, ze supposed. "I don't care that you hit me. I don't care if you feel bad about it. What I need is to *under-stand*: what in Kumru's name was that *about*?"

Pip's eyes were narrowed, but ze didn't interrupt.

Fift had given up any pretense of sleeping or doing homework in zir other two bodies. Ze was just sitting around, watching zirself over the feed. Ze scratched zir other body's nose and looked at zirself. Zir flabby, smallish, mud-colored bodies, zir tangled short white hair. Ze stood up from the bed and went to put some clothes on.

Hrotrun screwed up vir face. "I was just having some fun. I'd heard there was going to be—we'd all heard about the Cirque, and that the Ticket Holders were wandering around the up and across . . . I had a friend who could get me an anonybody, so I just . . . showed up."

"Hundreds of anonybodies, and you all just happened to show up and seek out Panaximandra and have a riot by accident?" Fift said.

{Your approach is very odd, Fift.} Pip sent. Ze was studying Hrotrun's face. {But go ahead and conduct your experiment, if that is what will satisfy you.} How like Pip to belatedly approve of what ze couldn't stop!

"Well that's where the anonybodies *were*. When we stepped into them, I mean. It was . . . a very strange feeling. And then . . . *Panaximandra* . . ." Hrotrun swallowed. "Ve came, looking like something out of an epic, so . . . powerful." Hrotrun cleared vir throat, vir eyes moist again with tears. "And it was all . . . true. What ve said." Ve blinked, dislodging a tear onto the smooth slope below vir eye: it slid down and lost itself among the brown feathers on vir cheek. Behind vir pleading look there was an edge of hatred.

It wasn't how you look at someone fragile who needs to be protected, who you unfortunately hurt in your wildness. It was how you look at someone who controls you, who owns you, who supplants you at every turn.

It was Father Miskisk looking at Mother Pip.

"You hit me . . . *because* I was a Staid," Fift said, amazed.

"Don't be stupid," Hrotrun snapped. "We don't hit Staids, do we? We don't even speak harshly to you; we don't want to distress your perfect equilibrium with our ridiculous feelings. No, we just listen to you explain to us why we shouldn't be feeling anything, and follow your excellent advice. We just clown for your amusement and service you sexually and build your"—ve gestured violently at Fullbelly, arm stiff—"safe, clean, sensible . . . lapine warrens . . . mortuary libraries . . . parking spaces where we all keep our voices down and wait in line and do our . . . work. And occasionally we might be allowed to see a *child* . . ." Vir voice broke. "Ooh, look, a child! Passing by . . . or of course we can just watch them over the feed. Not that we could have an interactive simulation of course—no, that's too old-fashioned and dangerous and foolish. We can just sit by the feed watching the public byways. Ooh, look, a *child*! Or the *mats*—yes, of course, because there must be *some* space for Vails, mustn't there, it's only *sensible*; fighting is ridiculous, of course, but Vails have needs, so let's give them a little space they can go and not bother anyone while they do it, meaning not bother Staids; but of course we have to make an appointment oh-so-carefully in advance, and make sure everyone agrees about when and why and how much we can punch each other. A parody of the Kumru-spurned Long Conversation, that's what the mats are!"

Fift was at a loss. Zir audience was spiking; ten thousand live viewers, most of them just arrived in the last few seconds. A dozen were accredited reactants, and two entertainment-aggregation agencies had upped their ratings of this part of the feed since Hrotrun began speaking.

There were a number of recommendations from somewhat-strangers of various connection levels crowding Fift's incoming queue. Suggestions of what to ask, complaints, theories, rants . . .

Pip cleared zir throat, sharply.

Hrotrun's eyes narrowed, and ve smirked. "Well, maybe you shouldn't ask for what you don't want to hear. Anyway, that's why we were there. All right? I got in an anonybody on a lark, and ended up in a crowd, and Panaximandra told us the truth about our lives; and then I got carried away. I *strayed*"—ve put a sarcastic edge on the word—"from the path that you wonderful clear thinkers, and the wonderful Midwives and adjudicators and reactant-aggregators, have laid out for us. I was muddled and confused. All right? But remember that I'm just a poor little Vail, and we live by emotion and action, and so in a confusing situation like that, you know, it's hard for us to not get carried away. So I'm sorry. Are we done?"

Pip looked dour. Ze didn't need to send anything for Fift to know what ze was thinking. *The spider has escaped the playpit,* zir expression said. *We will have to settle for an insincere formal apology, and we will look like fools.*

Fift cleared zir throat. "You seem really . . . tied up in this whole Staid and Vail thing."

Hrotrun almost choked. "What? What are you talking about?"

"You seem like . . . you think everything wrong with your life is Staids' fault, right?"

"Oh, please," Hrotrun said, contemptuously. "From citizen

investigator to Idyll introspectionist. If you haven't learned anything from what I said, you are incapable of it. Now let us end this."

"But," Fift said, doggedly, "you're a Far Historical index design technician . . ."

"What does that have to do with anything? Do you even know what that is, by the way?"

"I know what Far History is," Fift said, though zir idea of it was vague. The Ages Before the Ages . . . incomprehensible differences in thinking, partially bridged by incomprehensibly sophisticated automated processes . . . Then ze thought of what Thavé had said: *that's how you all got here in the first place.* "It's . . . before people came to the world. All the other worlds people lived on before."

"Yes, yes," Hrotrun said, softening a little. "What we know of them—what we *can* know of them. Much of what we have is just data—it hardly deserves to be called information, much less knowledge. And much of the supposed knowledge is generated by Far Theoretical engines which are themselves almost incomprehensibly strange. Which is where indexing comes in . . ." Ve caught vemself beginning to lecture and tightened vir lips in a thin smile. "Not that anyone cares about that anymore."

{Fift, that is enough.} Pip sent. {This line of inquiry is not appropriate.}

"But Vail and Staid . . ." Fift felt a rush of blood to zir face. Ze avoided looking at Pip. It was a stupid thing to ask; ze'd lost the thread of what ze'd been trying to do. But one of the messages in zir incoming queue, from one of the Staid admirers zir brush with fame had generated—one Dobroc P., who Fift had accepted contact from because Dobroc was somehow connected to Father Thurm—Dobroc had asked, and the question had struck Fift. It was a daring question; and it was suddenly, somehow, Fift's own question. So, despite the blood pounding in zir ears, ze asked it: ". . . I mean, there didn't used to *be* Vail and Staid. In Far History, I mean. So how can . . . how can it all be about . . . that?"

Pip tensed.

Hrotrun smirked. "There were always Vail and Staid, in the sense that there were always the quick and the sluggish. What is new is all the frippery we put around it. And that frippery, my dear child—all the Midwives' theories about harmony and balance and two fundamental poles of human being? It's all to *protect* the sluggish. I don't suppose they teach you that in school." Vir shoulders unhunched and ve ran vir fingers through the iridescent feathers behind vir ears. For a moment, something else penetrated the bland, generic, smooth surface of Hrotrun's somatic design—something haggard, bony, beautiful. The punters were trying to unload their bets now; the bookies' odds of collapse were back to two to one against. "In fact, we are *all* sluggish and weak, ants and termites compared to the people who built themselves in Far History. We made ourselves this weak on purpose. Because someone thought it was *sensible.*"

Hungry in one of the bodies in the bed, Fift got up, padded down the hall, and entered the eating room. Pip was there, in a formal, woven, cream-colored suit-sarong. Ze looked up at Fift. A stranger might have thought ze looked impassive, but Fift could read zir expression: cold fury.

Viewership in the goopfield was up to thirty thousand and climbing.

"Remarkable," Mother Pip said, to Hrotrun, zir tone perfectly neutral.

"What?" Hrotrun said, the corners of vir eyes tightening again.

"A remarkably convenient fantasy," Pip said. "Elegantly designed. I express my admiration. It allows you to be both fundamentally powerful—because truly you are the last remnant of powerful heroes from the Ages Before the Ages—and at the same time explains away your abject failure as a person in *this* world. A conspiracy of the mediocre has so completely triumphed over the wonderful that the wonderful are to be pitied. We elide the question of how the mediocre managed this."

In the eating room, Pip looked down at zir soup and lifted the bowl to zir lips.

Hrotrun looked like ve had bitten into a rotten mangareme. "You wouldn't—"

"I wouldn't understand," said Pip. "Obviously, by definition. Much too sluggish. And I am sure that if you were back in the Ages Before the Ages, they would understand perfectly, and acclaim you as a fellow hero, as opposed to a childless, officially censured coward barely tolerated by vir own cohort who cannot even manage to anonymously beat children and effectively evade discovery."

Hrotrun's lips curled back. "You are lucky you have the protection of being a Staid—"

"Ah yes, the protection we so kindly accord the sluggish. Well, perhaps you would like to come start an unlicensed riot with any of the *adult Vails* in my cohort. That would be a convenient way around the fact that you are not worth accompanying to the mats; they could simply beat you senseless in the courtyard. Might give your ratings a boost. And now we must go. Give my regards to the ancient heroes of legend. Fift?" Without another glance at Hrotrun, Pip turned and walked back towards the elevator. Fift followed, forcing zirself not to look back in zir body.

Pip took a long slurp of soup.

Over the feed, Hrotrun stood in the middle of the goopfield, quivering. Vir feathers had fanned out in sharp lumps. Ve was not slouching, though. Ve looked wakeful and in pain.

Bookies' odds of vir collapse, in the next three months, were even.

Viewership had peaked at fifty thousand and was gradually trailing off.

Pip dropped the bowl. It fell to the table and rolled itself into a ball to keep from spilling its contents. Ze stared at Fift.

Fift swallowed. "Well, um. Thanks, I guess. I guess you . . . handled that."

"Is it not clear to you," Pip said, "that that was a disaster?"

"Well . . ." Fift coughed. "I mean, clearly at the end there you supplanted vem."

"Yes," Pip said, as if speaking to an infant. "It was I who supplanted vem. Was that the question? Was it in question whether *I* could supplant a slackwitted, childless, firstborn coward? No, it was not. That was not to be the match, was it, Fift? You, Fift, were to supplant vem. I was to observe mildly with parental pride. My presence was not ideal, but it seemed to be warranted. But Fift, now I have been seen by fifty thousand viewers to engage as an equal with this . . . creature, this anonybodying scrounger. Ve strikes my Staid child in a riot, and I am forced to critique vir crankish power fantasies and . . . to threaten vem—however sarcastically, threaten vem!—with an informal match with your Fathers! And why, Fift? Why has this cohort now engaged adult-to-adult—and *traveled to Wallacomp* to do so—with a childless residential cohort of fifteen transients in Kumru-abandoned Tentative Scoop?"

"Because I wouldn't do what you said," Fift said sullenly.

"Is that why? I am not asking you to produce what you think I want to hear, Fift. Think for yourself. I am ready to listen."

In the elevator, Pip stood stiffly beside zir amid the strange, rich flowers.

In the bed, Fift fell asleep (to zir great surprise), plunging into dim dreams of following Shria through an underwater reef: murky water, bright fish, zirself a fish, and Shria, too.

In the eating room, zir eyes hurt. Ze was tired. Ze sat down and a creaking harness swung over to wrap itself around zir, supporting zir weight. "Yeah," Fift said. "That's why. I didn't do what you said."

"It was one question, Fift. Ve only needed to hear the direct, actual question; Do you apologize for intentionally striking me? Ve would have cracked open like a ripe nut." Pip folded zir sleeve and carefully cleaned the corners of zir mouth with it. "Instead, we have exposed ourselves to more danger, more risk of censure. We cannot be seen to be . . . *playing along* . . . with these miscreants."

"I know," Fift said.

They sat in silence for a few moments, and stood in silence in the elevator.

The bright red, blue, and yellow fish who was Shria turned, flourishing its billowing tail, and was suddenly Hrotrun— brown, spindled, deep, and menacing—in a thick and muddy sea.

"Well," said Pip at last, shaking zir head in the eating room. "One down, two to go."

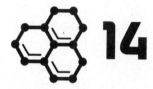 **14**

A knock on the doorjamb, and then another.

Father Squell's voice: "Wake up, little cubblehedge."

Fift opened one body's eyes. Ze'd been sleeping in two bodies at once—which ze didn't usually do—and coming awake was jarring. Ze faltered on the staircase down to Undersnort, resting a hand on the railing, dizzy for a moment.

The weight of zir arm on zir other chest; of zir leg across zir other two shins.

Ze rolled aside, putting blankets and stale air between zir bodies.

In front of zir, Pip descended, implacably.

Squell poked a head into the room. "Hello, Fift dear. I'm sorry to wake you. You've been asleep since—well, you must have been exhausted."

Ze'd been resisting the temptation to look at Shria over the feed. If Shria wanted a break, for them to keep away from each other, fine . . . and as Fift had followed zir silent Mother down the bright white whispermarble stairs, ze'd been able to hold back. Shria had public locations listed now: ve and vir friends had come out of the ludatorium. But so what? Ze had zir own life. Ze didn't need to watch Shria over the feed.

Except now ze did. It was different, lying awake in the other two bodies . . . sluggish and vulnerable, flushed from too-warm sleep, the ghost of zir limbs' pressure lingering against zir skin. Remembering how Shria had embraced zir in the middle of the riot. Vir hard arms pressing zir to vir soft breasts. The beating of vir heart.

"I wanted to talk to you about something," Squell said. "I *don't* really know if I'm the right one to do it. But . . . well . . . Grobbard can be so . . . *formal*, and Pip . . . well, I think you've had enough of Pip's scolding for today." Ve popped another head in the door, leaning vir chin on vir first body's shoulder, leaning against vemself. Copper spikes, silver spikes. Ve was small—smaller, now, Fift realized, than ze was—and rosy-skinned and soft-curved and swathed in glittery blue fabric. "Besides which, I'm, well, I think, the one who *noticed*." Ve looked around the room. "If you want, smoothling, we can blank the house feed in your room so it's just you and me, and not the rest of your parents . . ."

Fift's throat went dry. "What? Why—"

"I just don't want to embarrass you. But . . . I'm being silly. Never mind. At this point, none of us want any more feed blackouts!" Ve smiled at vir own witticism, raising vir eyebrows. Ve slipped into the room (copper spikes), kept leaning on the doorway (silver spikes).

There they were: Shria, Bluey, Stogma, and Vvonda—six bodies, strolling with latterborn ease down the slopeway to Wallacomp. They must have stopped at a spa after the ludatorium: they were cleansed and buffed and oiled, with matching glittery-golden threads braided into their hair.

Squell stood by the bed, looking as if ve'd like to sit down. Fift sat up in both bodies, scooted to one side, awkwardly straightening the blankets.

"Fift," Squell said, "You know we *like* Shria Qualia Fnax of name registry Digger Chameleon 2. Your other parents and I."

"Okay," Fift said.

Look closer, though, and the fresh-from-the-spa latterborn ease was thinly spread. Shria kept cracking vir knuckles; Vvonda stood a little too straight. {They look nervous, don't they?} ze asked zir social nuance agent.

{They certainly do.} zir social nuance agent sent.

"But," Squell said, "your friend is in a difficult situation right now. Social reactancy ratings for vir parental cohort have . . . worsened. To the point where, well . . . I'm sorry, smoothling, but consensus support may be withdrawn. Especially *now*! A week ago, there might have been complaints and deratings and not much more. But now, after this Unraveling business, the Midwives and deep adjudicators are being rather *direct* about the idea that reckless behavior can't be tolerated anymore. Fnax cohort may be disbanded."

"But it wasn't Shria's fault," Fift said. "Ve didn't start it!"

"Well, perhaps not," Squell said. Ve cleared vir throat. "It *was* a difficult situation. But—"

"If ve hadn't fought, what would the ratings be like? Any better?"

"Possibly not," Squell admitted. "In that case, ve might have been censured for cowardice. People might have said ve was gendering poorly. As things stand . . . well, no one expects vem to have *won* a fight in such a circumstance, of course. But it's not wonderful for ratings for a young Vail to look like a *victim*. Really, once a young Vail is involved in an off-mats fight, there are *simply* no good options ratings-wise, which is why it's the *parents'* job to . . ." Ve sighed. "In any event, I am not mainly here to talk about how *Shria* is gendering."

"Oh . . ." Fift didn't like where this was going. "Father Squell, I'm not going to cast Shria to the periphery just because ve's in trouble. Ve's my friend. I can't . . ."

Squell held up a hand. "Cubblehedge, I understand, and

that's all very praiseworthy. And if the only issue here were ratings, and your desire to be loyal to your friend, I might even *agree* with you . . . possibly. We're in a *somewhat* better position than Fnax cohort. However, that doesn't mean we can afford extravagant gestures, and . . . that's *not* the only issue here."

Fift felt zir faces flushing and fought to keep zir mouth an even line. "What do you mean?"

Pip looked back at zir, once, before turning, trudging on.

"What I mean, Fift, is that it was quite clear from your *brain*, during the family meeting, that you *aren't* just motivated by an impartial sense of fairness here." Ve sighed, threading vir fingers together. "Don't be embarrassed, dear. It's *natural* for Staids your age to form strong bonds of affection, to have . . . *crushes*. It's the most natural thing in the world! You can ask Grobbard . . . I'm sure ze had any number of ardent secret longings in zir First Childhood. And it's not *so* uncommon to have a little moment of . . . *confusion* about the right *target* for your affections, to get carried away. It's just, well . . ."

Fift's skin was icy, zir forehead burning. Ze got up in one body and shuffled past zir Father. In vir copper-spiked body, Squell ignored zir; in vir silver-spiked body, ve raised an eyebrow and watched zir go into the hall, but didn't follow.

"I don't . . ." In the body on the bed, Fift looked at zir hands. Ze wished ze *had* let Squell opaque the room to the house feed. Opaquing *now* would be practically admitting that zir attachment to Shria was . . . Ze tried to breathe deeply, to slow zir hearts (210% of standard heartrate in the bedroom, 185% in the hallway, 120% following Pip down the stairs . . .)

"I really don't wish to embarrass you," Squell said. Ve half-raised a hand, as if preparing to place it comfortingly on Fift's shoulder. The hand wavered, retreated, and ended up tugging on the shimmery fabric of vir own clothing.

Ve doesn't know *anything,* Fift thought. *Not about what I . . . did. Ve thinks I have a crush, like Minth had on Abador in the lyrical eighth subsection of the fourth responsum of the tenth additional corpus. Maybe ve thinks I haven't even admitted it to myself?*

Ze couldn't ask zir social nuance agent; this was dangerous ground, and the agents would probably report back to zir parents. Zir hands were slippery with sweat. Even without neural data, the house feed might know if ze lied.

The thought of *lying outright* made zir nauseous anyway—it was as if parts of zir were tearing away from each other, like layers of a pressed fabric coming apart. Had ze wanted to be comforted like an infant when ze let them expose zir brain? To nestle in, let zir Fathers know and decide? What a joke: ze'd only achieved the opposite. Now that Squell had almost glimpsed the truth in Fift's brain, ze had to tear zir trusting child-self out of zir for good.

Ze descended the stairs behind Mother Pip (that body trudging, reluctant) and the stairs in the apartment (that body restless, agitated).

Frill, Grobbard, and Smistria were in the breakfast room— all silent, pretending not to pay attention to the conversation between Squell and Fift. The last thing Fift wanted was to go in *there.* Ze turned into the empty anteroom instead. By the front door, ze started checking zir message queue.

Shria and friends were in Wallacomp now, moving through the bustle of Perilax. Striding boldly, heads held high. They must have passed several sluice operators. To be this far from home, they must have some specific purpose . . .

Squell was looking at zir intently.

Ze swallowed. "What do you want me to say?"

"Nothing, dear cubblehedge. I don't need you to *say* anything. But I want you to take a step *back*. I don't want you to communicate with Shria anymore. I don't want you to involve yourself in . . . whatever comes next. Just for a while. And after this little jaunt with Mother Pip is over, and those anony-bodying cowards have been properly rebuked, I'd like you to, well . . . stay home for a bit."

"Not send to Shria at *all*? Father Squell, I can't do that!" Even if Shria had said practically the same thing. But that was different! Or was it? Kumru. Zir guts clenched.

"Cubblehedge. I am trying to be delicate about this, but re-ally . . . I don't think you realize how dangerous this situation is. For one thing, our *ratings* hang in the balance, and the last thing you need is an accusation of . . . well, inappropriate *in-clinations*."

Fift didn't want to hear this. In the anteroom, ze kneaded zir hands together and riffled through zir message queue. Homework agent nags, parental fussing, zir classmates' bor-ing gossip . . . Zir attention agents had recovered themselves enough to clear out most of the bizarre messages from strangers. But there was another message from Thurm's con-nection Dobroc Pengasius Um of name registry Hopalong Fennel Trance 3, the Staid who'd suggested asking Hrotrun about Far History, about the time before Vail and Staid.

Ze told zir agents to run a query on this Dobroc Pengasius Um. Who was ze? How were zir ratings? What about zir his-tory of public emotional transactions? Why would ze keep contacting Fift anyway? The message sat in the queue, un-opened.

"Father Squell, I haven't done anything wrong." Sweat prickled zir scalp; did the house know that ze was lying? Would they start searching back through the feed archives, wonder about the lost hour? "And neither has Shria. Anyway, don't people have enough real things to worry about without—"

"Fift, listen to me—this isn't only about what other people think, about our parenthood ratings or our emotional capital or the bets at the bookies' shops or your future prospects. It's not even just about the very real threats to this cohort's existence, up to and including forced dissolution! Those are all just—outside things, consequences. No, the important thing is *you*, Fift." Squell bit vir lip. "I think you know I have never been a gender conservative. I've certainly spoken up many times in defense of Staids doing some of the more . . . well, collapsing ontologically, for instance! And we have never been terribly controlling about emotional displays and so on. We both know some families that are *very* strict about Staid children being uncalm! Who use neural enhancements to avoid it. Do you remember the cohort we met in Flouncedaddy with the Staid children who were mood-collared? What was that cohort called? Kydena? Kydara?"

Ve paused, frowning as though ve were looking it up, but then said, "And I think that's very wrong. I think Kumru's stomach would turn. I've always wanted you to be a full person, free to make your own choices . . ."

Mood-collared? Kumru's eyeballs, this was getting ugly. "Look, Father Squell, I'm sorry for whatever you think I— I mean, I'm totally fine with staying home. Maybe I could just come back here and stay for a handful of days, until the world is back in order—"

Squell didn't seem to be paying attention. Ve was staring out into the middle distance, as if replaying memories. "Even before you were conceived, some of us were a little worried." Ve smiled wanly. "Seven Vails and two Staids—were we really equipped, if you turned out to be a staidchild? But we thought, you know, we have *Pip* and *Grobbard*. Pip is so dominant, and so committed! And Grobbard is so . . . so *properly* Staid, if you know what I mean. Versed in the classics and so

on. Though of course Pip is, you know, ah"—ve blushed a little, and looked to the side—"very . . . Vail-*oriented*. We were all,
I think, so *flattered* by that, *amused* by it. We didn't think about
whether that might in itself have any . . . impact . . ."

Dobroc Pengasius Um of name registry Hopalong Fennel
Trance 3 was 17 years old, a latterborn, three-bodied Staid
from Dimmin habitation on the other side of Foo. Like Fift, a
child of Foo, but unlike Fift (according to the agents reporting
back) one with excellent ratings. A rock-solid parental cohort:
eighty parents! And ze was some kind of Long Conversation
prodigy—still in First Childhood, and ze already had a rank-
ing in dialectical subcurrent initiation (which Fift hadn't
even attempted in private). What did ze want with Fift?

"But perhaps it *did* have an impact," Squell said. Ve turned
to the wall and stroked a rough scar in the wallskin where
the apartment had grown too fast and torn. "Perhaps it's
made it easier for you to get . . . confused. And perhaps we
haven't given you the proper guidance. Perhaps we've failed
you—"

"Don't say that," Fift said, hating the quiver in zir voice. "Of
course you haven't—"

("—have to accept," Bluey was saying as they crossed a byway from Perilax to the bubbling goopfields of Tentative
Scoop. Ve ran a finger along the thorns that bordered vir
aquamarine face. "It's not like this fucker can keep claiming
to be anonymous *now*. We know who ve *is*—"

(Shria reached into Bluey's dark hair, untangling and re-
braiding the glittering gold threads. Bluey grinned, closed vir
eyes, leaning back into Shria's hands. Shria's other body, a
step behind, watched Vvonda's profile . . .)

"Fift, please!" Squell gnawed one of vir thumbs. "It's perfectly obvious! We don't even participate in religious rituals . . . as a family, I mean. We pay lip service to the *idea*, you

know, of the Balance—between the quick and the stable, the center and that which protects the center—but . . . we never find the *time* to . . ."

("and then we—" Bluey went on, eyes still closed.

("Bluey, shut up," Vvonda said, eyes on the goopfields around them. "We've got audience, and you're going to run off the lapine.")

". . . and, and it's hard to be a parent when you're over three hundred, *anyway*, and I'm three hundred and sixty! When your own childhood was that long ago, it's easy to forget how it was. It's easy to take for granted that your values are *obvious*, to forget that you need to *communicate* them . . ."

Dobroc's emotional history checked out. {Sane, stable, and respectable.} Fift's context advisory agent commented. {A thoroughly acceptable contact.} Fift, looking at the transactions with an apprentice banker-historian's eye, thought Dobroc looked maybe a little . . . intense? But ze opened the message.

{Most admired Fift,} it began. {Let me repeat my ardent wishes for your family's continued success and thriving in these current difficulties. I would cherish the opportunity to speak to you sometime in person. Have you, by any chance, studied the lyrical seventh subsection of the fourth responsum to the tenth additional corpus?}

"Father Squell," Fift said, "if we're just talking about a few days, or even a week or two, I can—"

"Fift! You are in more danger than you think. It's *dangerous* to . . . to *go astray*. You are a *child*." Squell's throat tightened, and tears glistened in vir eyes. "A *precious* child. Who you are in the world *matters*—the Balance matters! I know it isn't always easy to follow the path that's been chosen for you. Do you think it's easy to be a Vail?" A tear broke through the welling dam at the corner of one of vir eyes and crept its way down vir cheek. "I have *three* Staid younger siblings, Fift. Do you think it didn't seem magical and mysterious and wholly unfair that they were allowed to sit and think for hours, to pass spoons and read and talk about the . . ."—vir voice roughened, softened, an exhalation like a whisper—". . . the Conversation?"

{If I could, most esteemed Fift,} Dobroc's message went on, {I would give you a Singing Fruit like the one Abador gave Minth in that passage.}

"That *they* were allowed all that *rest*, and taken so seriously by the adults, not just cuffed and wrestled with and told to go play? They were engaged in something so *important*, so entrancing, a vast, rich world of learning and culture. Of *course* I felt excluded from it—"

(Vvonda stiffened, and Shria and Bluey and Stogma looked up, following vir gaze.)

"—I used to listen at the crack of the wall when they had their lessons . . ."

(Hrotrun dropped from a slipthread, doublebodied. With vem were five other Vails, nine bodies in all.)

{How foolish of me}, Dobroc had sent, {to write this to you at all! Yet I cannot seem to get it . . . you . . . out of my mind.}

"But Fift," Squell said, reaching across and taking zir hand, "I *am* a Vail. I'm meant to range around, to protect and enliven, to gambol and delight, to fight and feel—to encircle the center that holds and is!"

Fift looked away.

(Vvonda stood straight, towering above Hrotrun. If ve was surprised that Hrotrun was already here, ready for them, with friends, ve was trying not to show it. "We're here," ve began, too loud, clenching one fist and then the other, "to issue a formal challenge—")

"And to be a Staid or a Vail," Squell said, "is to be something *real*, Fift, something that has a meaning and a . . . a richness. But to fall between the cracks is just to get lost, I really believe it!" The tears were flowing now, laying shining tracks on vir face.

{And now, probably for the next hour or two}, Dobroc had written, {I will be sitting and thinking of you and of Abador and Minth! How foolish!}

Fift couldn't stand it anymore, sitting passive next to Squell's humiliating earnestness, and the implication that ze . . . that these things ze felt for Shria meant that ze . . . and zir other Fathers staring at their soup in the breakfast room, pretending not to hear every word . . . and following zir Mother numbly through the crowds of Undersnort . . . ! Ze couldn't bolt from the bed—zir legs were heavy, feet glued to the floor—but ze had to do *something*. Ze couldn't stand another moment of this.

The body in the anteroom was the only option. Ze went out the apartment's front door, onto the pathways on the surface of Foo.

There was something strange about Dobroc's message, something that didn't synchronize . . . something it wasn't saying out loud. Abador and Minth? Ze'd just been thinking of that very responsum.

On the other side of Foo, Dobroc was walking. Ze was a dark, leathery Staid with a thick unruly shock of black hair and some kind of complex skinwork. Ze had a self-confident but abstracted air. Ze looked up, squinted, nodded to zirself, and disappeared into one of the access tunnels that led down into the heart of Foo.

Of course, Dobroc could tell Fift was in zir audience, which was suddenly embarrassing; Fift pulled zir attention away.

("—found you!" Vvonda cried. "You can't refuse us! Tell them, Shria!"

(Shria was bouncing from one foot to the other, vir hands

held in front of vem. "We're taking this to the mats where it *belongs*, Hrotrun. We've got"—ve flushed with pride—"we've got preliminary approval from a mat room in Izist They consider the quarrel *legitimate* enough! As long as—"

(Bluey, lips tight, vir opal eyes intense, nodding and glaring at Hrotrun. Stogma, grinning, white teeth showing in vir broad, pleasant dark-blue face . . .)

"You just have to let *go*, Fift," Squell said. "It's not too late! No permanent harm has been done. But you have to let these dangerous temptations *go*!"

Squell's tears, vir flushed pink face, the fact that ve was filling Fift's room with vir fluttery emotional vailish excess—it was too much. "I don't know what you're talking about, Father Squell," ze said. Maybe the house would claim ze was lying; ze didn't care. "You're just being unfair. Shria's my friend and it's not vir fault . . . ve's doing vir best to fix things. Vir ratings, I mean." Hrotrun would have to accept Shria's challenge, and their conflict would be moved to the mats where it belonged. Shria would win, and it would be a coup for vem to win a formal match so young, which would blot out the disgrace of the riot and save vir cohort. "Look, maybe I could . . . I could take a break, stay at home, for a few weeks, okay? But—"

Ze was a little ways past the apartment on a lane that meandered through gardens and pavilions down to the edge of Foo. It was a strange message from Dobroc, all right. There was something charmingly quirky about its randomness. Abador gave Minth the Singing Fruit while sitting on a noise-canceling couch in the middle of a maelstrom, before Minth's hour of destiny. It was a famous, and moving, story. But Abador was a Vail, which made the whole allusion rather strange!

Although Fift had never gotten one zirself before, ze knew that Staids zir age sent each other flowery letters full of classical citations and subtle allusions to mutual devotion all the time. But the Temptation of Minth? If Dobroc was sedately flirting, why not reference some devoted Staid couple—why not Sprioli and Funarn, or Ranim and Pugari, or even Imim and Balranti?

At the edge of a metalscrap garden, zir pace slowed. Was it actually an *insult*? An accusation? Was even *Dobroc* insinuating things about Shria? No, that was surely paranoid . . .

"A few weeks *might* do it," Squell said, "as long as you don't get any more *audience*! That's the important thing. If we can just keep this a private matter until things stabilize again. Oh, I'm so angry at the Clowns!"

No. That made no sense. Seeking out a more marginal Staid just to mock zir didn't fit Dobroc's profile; ze was no Umlish. But it would also be very odd for Dobroc—a staid-child who'd made it to ranked dialectical subcurrent initiator at the age of seventeen—to choose an *inapt* passage!

Of course . . . Dobroc also knew full well that Fift's parents would read whatever ze sent Fift. What if the murkiness was intentional? What if ze were trying to slip some kind of secret subtext past them?

(Hrotrun looked at vir cohort members, all of whom shared vir slightly-too-perfect, slightly-too-similar, poured-from-a-box prettiness. They had the same ordinary bangles and feathers, the same slightly peculiar scarves; but they stood at awkward angles to each other, not quite meeting each other's eyes, as if they were strangers thrown together by chance, together only grudgingly.)

"I'm so sorry to *say* that," Squell said, kneading vir hands, "because you know I *love* the Clowns! Everyone does, except your Father Smistria. But why did they have to fool around with the *feed*? The feed is . . . it's like our immune system, and to *compromise* it . . . ! Well. No wonder *infections*, spiritually speaking, are blooming!"

Fift looked for Dobroc again. Ze would see Fift in zir audience, but so what? Ze'd just sent zir a message: of course Fift
would look zir up, everyone did that when they got a message,
it wasn't anything to be ashamed of.

There was a grainy clip of Dobroc's present position; then
ze passed out of range of that visual pickup and Fift could
only hear zir footsteps in an echoing space, and behind them,
a dull thrumming and a hushed roaring.

"There have been *more riots*," Squell said, "did you know
that? Since the feed has been back *up*! Velvet-waving *hooli-
gans* and marginals with nothing to lose . . . !" Ve shuddered.
"I'm sorry, smoothling, I shouldn't be burdening you with
this." Ve took a deep breath. "The point is, everyone's doing
their best to calm things down again. If you avoid getting any
more *audience*, if things *stabilize*, if you break off contact with
Shria, if you don't *comment* in the world-of-ideas, if you stay in
the *apartment* for a few weeks—" Ve heaved a sigh, and tried to
smile.

(An electric look passed between Hrotrun and vir cohort.
They looked like they were gathering courage, grim and excited and scared at the same time, with a hint of mounting
euphoria. It seemed like a strong reaction to a challenge to
the mats by a bunch of vailchildren . . . although, if they were
so marginal, maybe it was as much of a breakthrough for
them as it was for their challengers? Hrotrun reached up and
fingered the odd-looking scarf around vir throat . . .)

Dobroc was not visible, but zir one public location was
clear enough—ze was in the access tunnels that threaded into
the fulcrum of Foo. That's why ze wasn't visible—feed pickups
were sparse there, and interested in maintenance, not people.

Anyone could go to the fulcrum, though hardly anyone did.
Fift shuddered, remembering one class trip to the heart of
Foo. At the fulcrum, the grinding and straining and crackling

of the muscle-engines turning their habitation around its axis was so loud, even the pickups couldn't hear anything. Fift's ears, zir whole body, had been saturated with the bone-crushing sound. It had been agony until the class finally reached a noise-canceling couch, placed there to give a little respite to those on some industrial errand . . .

"—then things will be fine again!" Squell said, with a forced brightness. "And I *do* so want things to be fine again for you, cubblehedge." Ve tentatively reached out and took Fift's shoulder.

(Hrotrun's fingers on the scarf at vir throat, stroking it, as if it were something soft, luxurious, sensual. As if . . . as if it were *velvet . . .*)

A noise-canceling couch.

Like the one where Abador gave Minth the Singing Fruit . . .

Fift turned abruptly and headed for the edge of Foo. There was a stairway there that clung to the outside of the habitation and led to a tunnel into the fulcrum.

The fulcrum: where you were practically invisible, and where it was so loud that, if you were sitting on a noise-canceling couch in the middle of the maelstrom of sound, you could talk and *no one could hear you* . . .

"So," Squell said, "can you do that for me, my child?"

Not send to Shria? At all? There was no way ze could agree to that. Except, of course, that that's just what Shria had asked for. "Let me think about it," Fift said, without looking up at zir Father. Ze lay down and closed zir eyes, as if tired.

(Hrotrun took vir hand from vir scarf. Ve walked across the broken landscape of the abandonage, right up to Shria. Stogma and Bluey tensed, but Vvonda made a show of standing loose, and Shria just raised one of vir fiery red eyebrows, grinned vir lavender grin.

(Hrotrun placed one finger on Shria's clavicle, traced sensually along its length. "You want an answer to your formal challenge, do you, youngling?" ve said.

(Shria's nostrils flared. In anticipation? In anger?)

"All right, cubblehedge," Squell said. Ve got up from the bed. "Rest a little. We'll talk again soon."

(Hrotrun punched Shria in the stomach.)

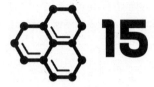 **15**

It wasn't the same as the riot.

It wasn't hundreds. It wasn't faceless red and blue anony-bodies. There wasn't that terrible roar, soaking into Fift, surrounding zir, dissolving zir like a soupcube in soup. It was just sixteen bodies: Shria's friends, Hrotrun's cohort . . .

Over the feed, the shoving and kicking, the tackles and grappling and gut-punches, seemed flat, bleached of emotion, unreal. Almost comical.

But it wasn't funny.

Fift saw, in the stiffening of zir Fathers around the breakfast room table, in the way they caught one another's glances and raised eyebrows, that they'd seen it, too.

All three of Fift's throats were dry.

Hrotrun's hand, grappling for purchase, tangled in Shria's bright orange hair. Vvonda's shoulder barreling into them, taking them down; velvet; someone yanked away and thrown; the crunch of someone's fingers breaking; an ankle sweeping feet off balance and Hrotrun's willowy cohort-partner collapsing like ceramic disks clattering to a floor; Bluey's hand closing on someone's arm, and someone else slamming into vem, tearing vem away; a body bucking like a desperate lapine beneath the crush of other bodies; sweat glistening on violet skin, sliding against smooth bone-white limbs . . .

Fift pushed it all away, occluded that part of the feed. In the silence, in zir bare room, ze could feel zir heart pounding.

Halfway down the stairway to the access tunnel, ze put zir hands on the rail and leaned out into the breeze coming from beneath the habitation.

Breathed.

What was ze doing?

Why was ze going to meet this Dobroc person?

Ze didn't want some pious gloomy Long Conversation pedant. Or some gloating, simpering, prissy gossip, offering false sympathy over Shria. Or some perfect, responsible, latterborn staidkid, pitying the mess ze and Shria were making of their lives . . .

Disturbingly, ze had an audience, and it was growing. Several hundred people were watching zir do nothing but stand on a stairway and look out over Temereen.

(In Undersnort, where ze waited with zir Mother in a long line for a sluice, there were a few thousand observers, checking in to see if ze'd found zir second attacker.)

It must have seemed to Shria like the perfect solution to the problem: issue a direct challenge, bring the matter onto the mats, where it would become a source of reputation and approval. Who could have known that Hrotrun and vir cohort would be so erratic, so irresponsible, so dangerous?

{Fift!} Father Smistria sent. {Whatever are you doing hanging off the side of Foo? Haven't you caused enough trouble?}

Fift gritted zir teeth. "I'm taking a walk," ze said aloud, in zir bedroom, where all zir parents could hear. "A walk. I need to think." Ze told zir agents to block zir parents' grumbles. If they wanted to keep pestering zir, they'd have to send someone in a body up to zir room.

Second afternoon light, gold and bluish-white, limned the habitations below.

Ze went down the stairs.

There were two Peaceables holding tubes of stoppergoo flanking the entrance to the access tunnel.

Fift's heart stuttered. Would they stop zir? *What are you doing out here, staidchild? Don't you know there have been riots? Go home!*

One Peaceable nodded to Fift calmly. The other didn't even seem to notice zir.

They were watching out for Vails. For velvety cloth. Not a plump little staidchild in a plain white shift.

Fift went into the great dim tunnel past the surging, humming tubes of liquid.

Ze walked past abstract displays commemorating Our Mothers Who Dug Fullbelly, striated planes of gray hanging in midair, and faintly glowing mold-graffiti on the walls ("Your crimes are invisible," "stanza 1345 4th subsec 2nd resp 8th corp" "Our Fathers Who Mugged Dullbilly," "For A Good Time Call Kumru"). Ze walked among puddles of condensation and the scurrying trashrats who stopped to sip from them. The light was a dim amber. An intermittent breeze from the ventilating wall-lungs swept across zir, tugging zir robes first this way, then that.

Ze wouldn't look at Shria over the feed. Ze didn't want to see it. Not this. Not again.

Ze wouldn't send to vem. Ve'd told zir not to bother vem. Ze'd obey Father Squell.

Ze didn't look, but ze felt vem anyway, in memory. Vir silken lavender skin; vir rich mellow smell; the pressure of vir forehead on zir shoulder; vir body in flight, slamming into the red nobody.

The sound of the laboring muscle-engines grew from whispered to insistent to overwhelming to painful. Then, finally, there was the couch.

Dobroc stood up.

Fift looked down. Ze couldn't look at zir. This was a mistake. But the hurricane of sound, loud enough to rattle zir teeth, pushed zir forward.

As Fift approached the couch, the monstrous sound around zir flooded into white noise, then sighed away to nothing, leaving zir ears ringing in a gentle silence.

Ze sat down.

Dobroc sat down on the other end of the couch. There would have been room for a body or two to sit between them, though they'd only brought one body each. They didn't bow, or cup ears, or exchange any formal greetings. Fift couldn't raise zir eyes to Dobroc's. Ze looked at the hem of Dobroc's shift instead.

The couch smelled of chalky industrial dust, and beneath that, the slightly acrid, almost-human smell of Foo's great muscle-engines.

Ze couldn't see Dobroc over the feed; they were out of the range of any pickup. Ze checked recent footage instead, zoomed in on Dobroc strolling the interdecks with a look of concentration, smiling mildly at the edge of a group of older Staids. Under zir thick, unruly shock of black hair, zir beige skin had been worked into an intricate topography of folds, ridges, grottoes, channels, swirls, cracks, and labyrinthine wrinkles.

It was an original and adept piece of somatic engineering. Fift had never seen anything like it before. It was dramatic, but also delicate: it made Dobroc seem like a maze to be entered, to lose yourself in. Fift couldn't help wondering what it would be like to touch that skin.

Had Dobroc created this look zirself? Such a dramatic design would seem to imply a certain self-confidence and poise, particularly in someone so young. Unless zir parents had chosen it for zir.

Dobroc sat just as silent and reticent as Fift on zir end of the couch.

At the top of the sluice to Undersnort, Fift shuffled along behind Pip in the midst of a hodgepodge crowd. Who *was* the second attacker? Would Pip tell zir if ze asked now?

Mother Pip hadn't said anything about Shria; ze just stared out into the middle distance, probably working on the accounts of some client. As if Fift's . . . best friend wasn't ruining vir life in the goopfields of Tentative Scoop. As if nothing was real, and nothing mattered. This plodding through stairs, byways, sluices—it was like Holy Kumru's endless time-loop ordeal in the snow, "until all meaning was lost, until atonement blurred away the long-forgotten thing atoned for . . ."

In zir room, Fift sat alone, looking at the tiny scar on the wall where the house had grown too fast, stretched too hard. Ze should probably do some homework, if ze could concentrate. Ze'd abandoned the Ranhulo, but other assignments kept flowing in from zir scholastic agents. Ze'd done the assigned review of instant-fame comportment, and it was all very sensible advice. Ze hoped there wouldn't be points for practical application, though, since meeting an instant-fan—if that's what Dobroc was—with very tenuous prior connections to zir, alone, in a concealed area, was definitely against the rules.

Dobroc cleared zir throat. "Thank you for seeing me," ze said. Zir voice was gentle and clear with a hint of roughness, like fingers stroking warm sand. That voice must be part of why ze was ranked; you could fall into it, and be carried off, to the Ages before the Ages.

"Oh," Fift said. "Well, of course." Ze looked at zir hands, fingers grasping knuckles.

What do you want? ze thought, but didn't, of course, say. The silence of the couch was immense; zir heart throbbed just beneath zir hearing. What had Fift been thinking, coming here? Was ze that lonely? Was it Dobroc's words of support, the lure of someone *admiring* zir? Maybe Dobroc was just being polite.

Ze wanted to check on Shria, but if they were still fighting, ze didn't want to see it. Or maybe the Peaceables had arrived to break up the riot? Maybe not: in the world-of-ideas, people were saying that the Peaceables had been overstretched since the Unraveling began, with all the cohorts failing or being forcibly disbanded, all the newly incoherent to herd to Idylls. So maybe the Peaceables wouldn't have arrived yet. Maybe that was even worse.

Did Dobroc know about Shria?

Fift's agents were quiescent. Perhaps they were lulled by the silence, perhaps the chaos and motion of the fulcrum distracted them, or perhaps something else was occupying their attention—something in the world beyond Fift's view. But they were surely watching zir conversation with Dobroc. How far could ze trust them to respect zir privacy? Would they report back to zir parents about what was said here?

"I'm . . . glad you came," Dobroc said.

"Okay," Fift said. Kumru, this was awkward.

"I have been . . . in your audience lately," Dobroc said. "Perhaps you've noticed."

"Yes," Fift said. "You sent the question. That I asked Hrotrun. About Vail and Staid."

Dobroc cleared zir throat again. "Yes. I am sorry that . . . well, I'm afraid it didn't help you. It seemed only to irritate your Mother."

Fift looked up; Dobroc was looking at zir own hands, folded before zir.

"It's okay," Fift said. "It was a good question."

Dobroc smiled a small smile of relief. "Yes, I think so. I often wonder . . . well. I've been in your audience, you see, since you talked to Thavé." Zir eyes widened a little.

"Oh . . ." Fift said.

"I'm what you might call . . ." Ze shrugged. "A Thavé-watcher? It's a, a hobby, you know. There aren't so many of us. I, uh, I don't tell everyone this. My parents don't approve of it."

"Oh." Fift tried to imagine being latterborn in a cohort of eighty parents. It was a tremendous amount of power standing behind you, of safety . . . but if they disapproved of what you cared about, imagine the pressure . . .

"They think it distracts me from what's important," Dobroc said glumly. "From the Conversation."

"Do you—do you not want to compete in the Long Conversation? You're such a, I mean, you're so good. They must be proud of you, right?"

Dobroc grimaced, zir teeth white in zir leathery, furrowed, downturned face. "I don't know if I'd go so far as to say . . . proud. You know it's a specialist cohort, right? All eighty of my parents are Staids. All eighty of them are ranked in different aspects of the Long Conversation. The whole thing is a project designed to produce, you know, the next Ranhulo or whatever."

"Kumru!" Fift said. "I didn't know! What would happen if they'd had vailkids?"

"Two of my older siblings are Vails," Dobroc said, and sighed. "Their lives are . . . well, it's not great for them, let's put it that way. Talk about being shunted to the margins. It's not great for my elder Staid siblings who didn't measure up, either. The 'disappointments.'" Ze shrugged. "Then there's me. The latterborn. As long as I stay ranked, as long as I maintain a reputation as a Conversationalist destined for greatness, I'm not a disappointment yet. When I lose the thread . . ." Ze shrugged again. "Then they have another kid, and I get supplanted."

"Kumru!" Fift said.

Dobroc glanced shyly up at zir, then down again. "Fift, I don't mean to complain to you about my life. It isn't so bad. I have lots of privilege that I never earned."

"But all that pressure . . . does it make you . . ." Fift took a breath. Could ze ask this, really? But ze was sick of the guarded, standoffish way the staidkids ze knew talked, sick of never saying what ze felt. And here ze was, in the thundering, invisible heart of Foo, in this little pocket of silence, with Dobroc's silken voice. "Does it make you hate the Long Conversation?"

Dobroc looked up, meeting Fift's eyes. Zir eyes were the same color as zir skin; in feed footage it had made zir look blank, muted, but face to face they were rich and warm. "Oh no! I love the Conversation! That is . . . I love it for what it's meant to be, for what it could be. But I hate what we've turned it into: rules and proctors and rankings and secrets, part of the way we police the world and force everyone into little boxes, everyone ashamed of their performance, competitive and grasping! All these Staids with cramped little imaginations holding these stiff recitations up as . . . as some kind of consolation, proof that at least they're better than Vails! As if the Conversation could be hoarded, or gloated over. It's become a prison, when it was only ever meant to be freedom, just freedom! 'As flight requires a gravity well, as language requires separation of minds, so my words are prison guards only to liberate . . .'"

They were Muon's words, from the discursive introduction

to the second work of the fifth cycle. In Dobroc's mouth they were not pompous; they were electric. The skin of Fift's necks prickled.

Fift reached the front of the line for the sluice and looked over to Pip, who roused zirself with a sudden twitch, arched an eyebrow at Fift, and motioned zir forward. Fift launched zirself into the sluice, and hurtled down, a little too fast to be perfectly proper, feeling the wind on zir face.

Ze scooted a little closer to Dobroc on the couch.

"Have you ever met Thavé?" Fift asked zir.

"Oh no!" Dobroc said. "No, I've never even tried. That time you met zir in the pavilion was one of the closest sightings to Foo, and even then, well—I don't think I could have traveled out that far."

Fift hit the braking goop, plowed a bodylength into it, and climbed out. Ze stood there, waiting for zir Mother.

"We couldn't have either," ze said. "I mean, not if we didn't have Tickets . . ." Ze realized abruptly that ze was carrying zir Ticket—the actual physical object—in a pocket of the shift ze was wearing here, on the noise-canceling couch . . . which meant that zir location here at the fulcrum was being cached and published by Cirque-watchers . . .

"That's when I began . . . to admire you," Dobroc said. "You and Shria Qualia Fnax of name registry Digger Chameleon 2. Your forthrightness—your honesty—they're what drew Thavé out! I don't think anyone beyond the deep core of the world's husbandry has heard zir speak so frankly or so, well, *emotionally*, for at least two hundred years . . ."

"But don't you think . . ." Fift said. "I mean, my Father Grobbard seemed to think that it was planned that way. That ze wanted to say those things even before the performance started. That it was maybe even, well . . . *part* of the performance?"

Dobroc frowned. "Who knows? I've heard that very theory advanced on the Thavé-watchers' polylogues. But . . . no, I don't think that conversation was planned. Maybe Thavé suspected that rogue feedgardeners would strike during the Cirque's performance and take the feed down. That's zir job, after all: foreseeing catastrophes. Maybe ze was worried about the consequences, if they did. Maybe ze was making a plan. But it's quite possible that ze wouldn't have said anything to anyone at all if you and Shria hadn't come along. I think . . . I think Thavé takes zir cues from the world. I think if ze ever had a clear plan for us, we wandered off its track ten thousand years ago. That's what I think, anyway . . ." Ze trailed off, looked down.

At the end of the goopfield was a massive structure like a white tusk, curving gradually five hundred bodylengths into the air above them. A door was set in its base. Pip climbed out of the goop, shook zir robe clean, crossed to the door, and opened it.

"Oh," Fift said. "So then . . . is that—is that what you wanted to talk to me about? Thavé?"

"Well, no. Or, yes. Or . . . no, not really," Dobroc said. Ze pressed zir lips together.

Fift was sitting on a couch peacefully talking about aliens with this person . . . this strange, kind staidkid, whose voice stroked its fingers down your spine. Fift was lying in bed, staring at the wall. Fift was following zir Mother into the reactants' hall, an echoing space filled with dim, soft light from rows upon rows of knee-high fabricators, in tiers sloping upwards, ten thousand Vails and Staids crouching before them.

While Shria was fighting in the streets of Wallacomp.

Shria's cohort would be broken up. Ve would be sent to the Pole after all . . . just as Fift had feared, on that long-ago day in the forest.

In the reactants' hall: a susurration of murmurs, an overwhelming arrhythmic pulse of pinging, all around, everywhere. When each reactant's fabricator was done with its current cycle, it would emit a tiny bright sound, and the reactant would pull something out of it: a shift, a bangle, a doll, a spoon, a smack-club, a singing fruit, an idyll-rattle, a flute, a songstick, a prism, a dove...

After each ping, a reactant would lift out whatever their fabricator had made, would taste or cradle or stroke or play or put on or dangle or pet or inspect the fabricated product... and then would sit, face slack, eyes closed, yielding up their reaction to the feed.

Then they would dump whatever it was in the compost-sluice, or put it back into the fabricator, or release it to fly into the rafters. And the fabricator would begin the next iteration.

There was no point in viewing Shria! Ze couldn't help vem. Ze couldn't rescue vem.

{We're looking for an industrial reactant?} Fift asked Pip.

Mother Pip cocked an eyebrow, then took Fift by the shoulder, stopping zir. {Am I to take this stunningly clever deduction of the obvious as an expression of dismay? Are you now, at last, considering the social status of our cohort? And if so, do you think you could handle it yourself this time, following my instructions?}

Fift pulled away. {Okay, okay.} ze sent.

"For one thing," Dobroc said, "I wanted to meet you." Ze looked at the hem of Fift's robe. There was room on the couch between them for one body. The labyrinth of Dobroc's skin drew the eye; patternless, it seemed to hover on the verge of pattern, so that Fift's eye, seeking pattern, traced zir cheek, jaw, throat.

"Okay," Fift said, "... and the other thing?"

"I wanted to show you something," Dobroc said. "Something I made."

Climbing up through the reactants' hall, Fift and Pip had fifty thousand viewers; that was uncomfortably many, but it made sense, after Hrotrun. They must be convinced that the second confrontation was beginning.

"You have to understand," Dobroc said, "that some people think you're part of the show. Of the Cirque's show, the Unraveling. You, um . . . ." Ze met Fift's eyes. "You're not working for the Cirque . . . on purpose . . . are you?"

"No!"

Dobroc nodded and looked down. "I didn't think so. But it's not . . . you wouldn't necessarily know, right? Even the Cirque might not know, if it's a stochastic piece. And the algorithmic agents—they're predicting that you and Shria are key theatrical elements. They think that you're part of the spectacle."

"What, really? You mean—more than other Ticket Holders? Us specifically?"

Dobroc nodded again. Zir gaze met Fift's, then retreated: fish skirting the shadows of a shallow pool. "Thavé and Panaximandra have already crystallized as key dramatic elements, and of course, First Childhood is always"—ze smirked—"terribly evocative for adults. And it's not like there are many sixteen-year-old Ticket Holders, period. Sixteen-year-old Ticket Holders who met Thavé, and then Panaximandra, within the space of an afternoon?" Ze crooked an eyebrow. "One latter-born, the other an only child, from differently struggling cohorts? Very high thematic density."

"Uh," Fift said. "I take it emergent dramaturgy is another hobby of yours?"

Dobroc looked down at zir hands. One held the other in zir lap, like bodies sleeping curled together. Ze swallowed. "I just want to . . . do something. Make some kind of difference. Give the world a push." Ze shrugged. "In a way, it's the same hobby. Thavé-watching is all about emergent dramaturgy! It's what Thavé does, when you burrow into the core of it. How ze influences the destiny of worlds."

This wasn't what Fift had expected. No prissy, judgmental, overly formal Long Conversation specialist; no gushy, superficial, sentimental instant-fame infatuation. Dobroc had . . . weird ambitions. Fift shifted closer to zir on the couch, until the loose and hanging fabrics of their shifts were touching, white on white. Dobroc's skin was ridges and swirls and furrows, but it smoothed to blankness at the wrists and knuckles, where zir hand bent. Fift wondered again what it would feel like to touch zir. "Dobroc," ze said. "That was all by accident. We didn't *do* anything . . . we just accidentally ran into them. There's no meaning to it."

"Sure. Those coincidences are just a framework . . . on which something could be built. But it's not really about that. It's about . . . who you *are*, Fift. I don't know if I can explain it without it sounding foolish." Ze took a deep breath.

"I'm not anyone special, Dobroc."

"Not for you, you're not. And not objectively, either, not the way the world measures. But I've . . . I'm so surrounded by falseness, by rigidity . . . Everything is *recitation*, doing what you're told. We sit on wooden floors, pass spoons, and recite the words of the great Sages, who once upon a time were free and truly alive, and it's, it's a grotesque parody. I've done what I was told for so long . . ."

"So have I, Dobroc! I always do what I'm told. I'm no rebel—"

"No great rebel, maybe. Maybe it's just that I've been studying you so closely that I see it. Maybe it would be there in anyone if you looked closely enough. But there's this great stubborn restlessness in you, just underneath the surface . . ."

"Honestly, Dobroc, I think you're talking about yourself more than me."

"Well," Dobroc said, "maybe I should just show you." Ze pulled a fabric display from zir shift and unrolled it. "I'd send it to you, but I'm . . . I was planning on releasing it anonymously. I mean, if you're okay with that. And it's better for you if it's not in your chatlogs. First, okay, first look at this."

Fift took the display. Their hands didn't touch.

It was a cacophony of color and motion, stretched, darting, rippling across the stiff fabric. It seemed deeper than it should be, somehow, drawing the gaze in, a tangled skein of dimensions which slowed and skewed the world.

"Okay," Dobroc said. "That ought to puzzle your agents for a bit."

"What—seriously?" Fift caught zir breath. {Are you watching me?} ze asked zir agents.

{Context is overdetermined.} zir context advisory agent responded. {Recursive exegesis offers no purchase for self-summation. All stances are provisional. Please allow for re-association. Underway.}

{This could be the best thing ever, or the worst thing, or somewhere in between.} the social nuance agent said. {Please act accordingly.}

"You're right, they're useless again," Fift said. "Kumru! How did you *do* that?"

"It's something that's been going around," Dobroc said. "You have to know where to look for these things. Your agents will be fine in a bit, but meanwhile, they won't listen in. Okay . . . here's my piece." Ze cleared zir throat and balled both hands in the folds of zir shift. "I hope that you like . . . that is . . . well, anyway."

The display shifted:

Four-year-old Fift on the surface of Foo, tubby and bald in a stiff new shift: "But what about Father Miskisk? Father Miskisk is sad—"

A flicker of unease on Squell's faces, of anger on Smistria's, before they composed themselves for the feed.

Grobbard's gentle hand on Fift's shoulder. "They'll catch up, Fift. Clear your mind, please, and get ready."

Fift taking Squell's hands, maneuvering to keep zir bodies as far away from each other as possible, as they set out through the gardens and gazebos. One body looking down at zir feet; the other, openmouthed, out across the immensity of Fullbelly. Of its own accord, the view narrowed, centering on Fift's third face: zir tiny jaw set with determination, zir eyes staring ahead, imagining the First Gate of Logic.

The view on the display was inviolate, flat; it didn't respond at all to Fift's attention, offered no lookup, no drilldown, no hookins, no interconnections; ze couldn't pan, or change the angle, or even pause the action; it just went on, telling its own tale, image and sound alone—as if the feed were down again. And in a way it was: Dobroc had severed these sounds, these images, from the feed, placed them in their own isolated little universe.

It made sense as a precaution: if Fift couldn't interact with it, then there would be no way for anyone to tell that ze had seen it.

Shria at four, a romping blur of color in some bouncegarden far from Foo; hurtling down, whooshing up from the bulge of a bounce-fungus, squealing with glee, vir eyes closed, vir little arms and legs flung out—

The image softened into blank gray and words appeared in the display in an archaic static script, fixed letters hovering as if painted on the air:

Fift and Shria

"Wow," Fift said. "That's—"

Dobroc's nervous expression flickered toward delight. But

Fift couldn't pause, and the images continued, so ze had to look back at the display—

Shria at nine, lavender skin and fiery red hair, orange eyebrows that curled like flames. Bony bare knees and elbows poking between the red-and-blue strips of vir ill-fitting suit. Tiny droplets of water, the mist of the surface morning, sparkling in vir hair.

Ve crouched down, reaching for a mossy stick.

Cacophony—almost too fast to take in—the turmoil of the riot, anonybodies roaring. Shria, sixteen, wrenching away from the red and blue hands grabbing vir arms, vir hair—

Silence, deafeningly sudden. Moss dripping on the surface, light filtering through the mist.

Fift's voice, incongruous, speaking over the image of the empty forest: "Do you think there even is a show? Or is it like . . . a meta thing? Where looking for the show is the show?"

Shria's voice in answer in the background, while in the forest an unpurposed redbird alighted, fluttering, on a branch. "I think it's going to be real. I think it's going to be big."

Boots crunching in deep snow, sinking to mid-calf.

Thavé's face filled the screen, head tipped to one side, considering. Shria's voice: "What do you think of us? Of all of us?"

Thavé paused. "What a good question."

Fift and Shria on the other side of Thavé's table in the pavilion. They looked bright, eager, heart-stoppingly young.

Innocents, to whom nothing had ever happened.

"You've been mostly at peace," Thavé said, "for a long time."

The riot: roaring, leaping, chaos. An elbow cracked against Fift's temple, and ze crumpled down—

"Your economy has decent turnover. Economic class is bound to birth order—"

The surface forest. Shria's eyes, red from crying.

Swirls of snow, dancing up, sliding across the crust as the boots broke through it . . .

"So you're latterborn again." Umlish smirked. "We should congratulate you." Ze took a step closer, and Shria, bony and cold and nine years old, quivered. "Your parents should have made sure you had the appropriate agents for a trip to the surface. They do seem very distracted. I wonder if they might still be a bit overburdened?"

Panaximandra on vir pillar, in vir glimmering, glinting exoskeleton: "Who were those parents? Those lucky people, who were given the right to create life? Note that I say given! They did not take the right, as their due, as their inheritance, as their destiny as human beings—"

Shria stood up, dropping a mossy stick. Vir jaw clamped down hard, suppressing vir quivering. Ve looked across the clearing at Perjes and Tomlest, and vir eyes blazed, daring them to laugh.

". . . hardly egalitarian," Thavé said, "but at least it's moderately anti-accumulative . . ."

Umlish's eyes were slightly narrow-set, and they burned with scorn. "Shria doesn't want any Younger Siblings. Ve was glad to get rid of that little baby—"

Shria, nine years old, shaded by purple songfronds, electric with pride, as vir parents placed vir baby sibling in vir arms. The tiny mottled red face, eyes scrunched closed, the tiny head resting in the crook of Shria's elbow—

"—weren't you, Shria?"

". . . you've been pretty remarkable," Thavé said, poking at zir food, "at finding new ways to make it more complicated to have a baby, without much help from me . . ."

Roaring anonybodies. Panaximandra, gleaming: "Every one of you can be a Hero. Every one of you can be a Mother!"

"FREEDOM! VALOR! CONQUEST! BABIES!"

Panning up from the boots: a mass of figures trudging through deep snow, bundled in thick clothing . . .

"We might be allowed to see," Hrotrun snapped, teeth gritted in vir too-symmetrical face, "a child . . ." Vir voice broke. "Ooh, look, a child! Passing by . . ."

"But with a culture like yours," Thavé said, staring at zir eating tines, "the more mature it gets, the greater the anxiety . . ."

Panaximandra slitted vir eyes in contempt. "You insects rearranged the furniture of the hive you live in, and rearranged it again."

Fift's eyes widened. "You hit me . . . because I was a Staid."

"Don't be stupid," Hrotrun snapped. "We don't hit Staids!"

An elbow cracked against Fift's temple, and ze crumpled down—

Fift shuddered involuntarily. Ze looked so pathetic, a little scrap of beige and white in that blue-and-red tumult, flopping down like a tossed-away rag . . .

The view panned up from the boots, revealing bundled figures, trudging through the snow, and behind them: glittering airships, naked sky, a cold blue surface dawn. It was personal footage, a recording through the eyes of some single individual. Some orphan deportee's furtive, smuggled footage of the Pole?

Hrotrun. "We just clown for your amusement and service you sexually—"

Panaximandra. "As if life was a beast you could master—"

"One day," Thavé said, zir voice heavy, "there's a flaw I haven't foreseen . . ."

"They have supplanted you in your own minds, making you grateful for your slavery!" Panaximandra roared, tears streaming down vir face. "You owe them nothing! Give me a million barbarians with eighty-year lifespans—"

Thavé stared out across the pavilion. "Something virulent . . ."

A silver-armored hand, clutching a scrap of velvet. "Armed with clubs—"

". . . that spreads through the culture and takes it down . . ."

"—and I could take this world and set it on fire!"

The riot, the roar, and Fift curled up on the ground—

—*Vvonda's voice, over the image: "You shouldn't be there, staid-kid. You shouldn't have followed vem in."*

—*forehead against the byway, arms covering zir head, Shria gone.*

"You're disgusting!" *Umlish snarled.*

Vvonda's icy eyes in vir flushed purple face. "You should get the airless all-sucking void out."

Elbow cracking into Fift's temple, zir body crumpling down—

"It's no place for you."

But ze had been there. In the middle of that. Ze hadn't run.

—*flowing down, chest to zir knees, knees back up, back onto zir feet—*

"Don't spit all your poison today, Umlish," Shria said. "You might run out, and then what are you going to do tomorrow?"

"Vvonda," Fift said, stepping out from beneath a purple crenelated privacy cone. There was a tiny, dark bruise on the side of zir head where the elbow had struck zir. Vvonda, towering and elegant, already about to push vir way through the partygoers, turned back, flinging up an exasperated hand.

In the roiling, struggling sea of rioters, one of the Vails holding one of Shria's arms yanked back an anonymized blue leg to kick vem. Fift's leg flowed out, lightly, gently placing zir foot against the foot of the Vail. The Vail paused. Shria roared.

"Your job," Pip said, "is to think, to plan, and to order. Your job is to be the still center, the basis, the core."

"You're enjoying this, aren't you?" Fift asked, and Vvonda's eyes hardened dangerously.

Fift had been there. The world had unraveled around zir, and ze had endured.

"This plenitude," Panaximandra said, "has made you craven! What have you taken as yours? Be unsatisfied, be thirsty!"

"This revolution, this unraveling," Fift said. "You like it. It's made for you."

The Cirque's voice, thundering among the habitations: "Have you wondered if this is the world for you?"

"Midwives and feedgardeners and adjudicators may hold things together," Pom Politigus said, *as Vvonda frowned, considering, reining in vir first, incredulous, angry reaction.* "But to whom do we look to stir things up?"

"You need to start loosening the stranglehold of consensus," *Thavé said.*

The world was still unraveling; the tumult was growing; the cage meant to hold Fift safely in place had come undone. But that moment—when the little rag of beige and white fell and flowed and emerged standing from that red-and-blue tumult—

"I could burn this prison, and plant a garden!" Panaximandra roared.

"I don't intend to lose another world," Thavé said.

—it echoed in Fift's mind.

Fift and Shria locked in an embrace, amidst the riot, Fift's forehead pressed into the crook of Shria's neck as Shria began to sob—

"Revolution," Panaximandra said, "against this deadness—"

Leaning back from zir mangareme fluffy, Fift was laughing, eyes closed, and Shria was looking at zir fondly, vir curling fiery eyebrows raised, sipping vir drink—

Panaximandra: "—this confinement—"

Streaks of white fog, rough silver bark glistening with dew; the redbird launched itself into the cold forest air. "Corpsemunching?" Fift said.

Umlish had seemed so frightening then. Fift's nine-year-old heart had been racing when ze said that.

Shria giggled. Vir thin lavender face was smudged with bark and dirt. "That's good! What's that from? Yes, call me a 'corpsemunching sisterloser,' Umlish—"

Panaximandra: "—means feeling alive—"

"When a culture like yours falls," Thavé said, "it falls hard. You need to start loosening—"

Shria, sixteen, slowed to a stop an arm's length from the crowd of anonybodies, and looked, uneasily, back at Fift—

"—the stranglehold—"

—and Fift came forward—

"—of consensus."

"It is time," Pip said, "to be what you are, Fift."

—and took vir hand.

Four-year-old Shria, bouncing up, squealing with glee—

"They have mangareme fluffies," Shria said, and grinned, and took Fift's hand. "Come on."

The display went blank.

16

Fift blinked. "That's . . . that's amazing."

"It's just a clip-opera, it's nothing that—" Dobroc said, then stopped as Fift took zir hand.

It felt as rough and smooth and callused and soft and leathery and cool and warm as ze had imagined.

After a moment, Fift exhaled.

In the clasp of their hands, there was something of the still center—an expectant but unhurried calm. You could let go, in that calm; you could arrive. "To find, in the turbulent escalating gyre which tears all forms apart, the stable point"—so begins the very first discourse of the first work of the first cycle, Brenem's meditation, which Uriz chose to place there as the entrance gate to the Long Conversation.

A hand closed on Fift's shoulder and ze stumbled to a halt. It was Pip's hand, in the reactants' hall—ze'd lost track of where ze was.

A Vail reactant hunched over vir fabricator. You could tell how tall ve was, vir body absurdly, disproportionately muscled. Fift was no expert on somatic design, but even ze could tell that this was a hack job by someone with neither taste nor talent; the chafed red eczema on vir arms and neck and the random patches of black hair scattered over vir face and chest and back looked like side effects of poor hormonal engineering.

And vir face: the startling white orbs of eyes with orange irises and long lashes; the orange lips; the fleshy whorls of ear . . .

Fift swallowed hard.

They were the eyes and lips and ears that strange anonybody in the riot had sported on its smooth blue head.

As if this Vail (Predoria Ithigast of name registry Soiled Butterlung 14, according to lookup—233 years old) had had the body configured that way on purpose. As if ve'd *wanted* to get caught.

{This one}, Pip sent, {kicked you in the head. Just explain it clearly and simply. Do not get carried away with emotion or indecision. Make the facts publicly clear, and this Vail will have to apologize or be dishonored. That is all there is to it.}

Fift didn't remember Predoria kicking zir; but ze remembered vem kicking Shria in the ribs as ve crouched on the byway. Of the Vails who'd mobbed Shria, Predoria was the last one to leave. Fift was glad this Vail was on the list: ze wasn't tempted to feel sorry for *vem.*

Predoria looked up, blankly, from vir fabricator.

"You kicked me in the head, in an anonybody, in the middle of a riot two days ago," Fift said.

Predoria smiled. "That I did," ve said.

Fift hadn't expected that reaction.

"So," Dobroc said, "I thought maybe I would share it. With others. Release it. Anonymously. If that's all right with you—"

"Sure," Fift said. "But—"

"Oh no," Dobroc said. Zir hand pulled, slightly, away from Fift's; the little gap of air between their palms was like a wound.

"What?"

"You said 'sure, but,'" Dobroc said.

"I . . . what?" Fift wanted to reach for zir hand again, to clasp it tight, but ze didn't dare.

"Just now. First you said 'sure.' And I—I thought that meant 'yes,' so I just . . . released it. But then you said 'but'! So maybe you didn't want me to?" Ze let Fift's hand go entirely, and ran both hands through zir hair, pushing it up from zir scalp. "I'm so sorry. I was just so excited that . . . I mean, I can try and suppress it now . . . ? Maybe if—"

"No, no," Fift said, feeling queasy. "It's okay . . ." Ze held zir own hands in zir lap, one curled in the other like sleeping bodies.

Predoria had few connections, according to lookup. No cohort—ve had never even had a trial cohort, despite vir age. Ve had collected a few votes of condemnation, for sloth and misplaced aggression, from the most generic rating agencies; but in general, ve had lived vir life at the periphery, beyond the notice of almost everyone. Ve had standing challenges out to over a hundred totally inappropriate Vails of various stations, none of whom, apparently, had ever bothered to reply. Ve'd served as a fight reactant at the mats vemself, for a few brief periods, but vir ratings there were too low. So ve had ended up here, specializing in smelling lotions: vir sense of smell, apparently, was well developed, and smell was the hardest sense to engineer.

No bookies bothered offering individual bets on Predoria; ve was aggregated in a couple of broad collective indexes of unattached socially peripheral Vails, and another of marginally rated industrial reactants.

The question wasn't *whether* such people would collapse, but how many, and by when.

Audience was surging: eighty thousand, then ninety thousand people watching Fift gape at Predoria in the reactants' hall.

"And . . . and you apologize?" Fift asked Predoria.

"No," Predoria said, grinning wolfishly. "No, it was fun." Vir fabricator pinged. Ve looked down, took out a small vial of lotion, and smeared it onto the back of vir hand.

"You must be so worried about vem," Dobroc said.

Fift started. For a moment ze thought Dobroc meant Predoria—worried about the confrontation—but of course ze meant Shria. "I—I can't watch vem. What's happening? Have the Peaceables come?"

Dobroc frowned. "You're not watching?"

Fift swallowed, feeling a chill. Dobroc would be disappointed in zir; ze'd want Fift to be the noble, heroic friend who'd faced down Umlish and Vvonda for Shria, not someone so cowardly ze couldn't even watch. "I'm . . . I can't . . . ve told me to . . . Dobroc, I've done everything wrong. It's not like it is in your wonderful"—ze waved at the display lying on the couch—"uh, artwork; I mean, I shamed vem, or something. Vvonda told me not to interfere, and I was too stubborn—"

"During the riot? No, you listened to Vvonda!" Dobroc said. "You found Shria, you went to vem, and then you sat like Mundarn at the feast—joyful and fearful, letting go, giving vem only 'room to fall and a heartfriend watching'—it was perfect, Fift!"

Fift had to blink at the strange insistent burn of tears behind zir eyes; that was just what ze'd wanted to do, and Dobroc had seen it. Fift felt a physical yearning to pull zir closer, to snuggle into zir embrace, to let zir beating heart slow down with Dobroc's.

But could ze trust zir? Was it really *Fift* that Dobroc saw, or an idealized shadow ze could cast as zir clip-opera hero: the staidchild who talked to Thavé, a new Mundarn for an Unraveling age?

{Ask vem}, Pip sent, {if ve is collapsing.}

"Are you . . . collapsing?" Fift asked Predoria.

Predoria closed vir eyes and sniffed the lotion coating the back of vir hand in long, slow snuffles. Ve opened vir eyes. "What if I am?"

"It *wasn't* perfect," Fift said to Dobroc. "Maybe it was all right during the riot, I don't know . . . but afterwards, when we were waiting for the bat . . . I *said* something, did something wrong—'the still center eluded me like the willow wind!'" There was something delicately delightful about using Long Conversational allusions with Dobroc—something Fift couldn't do with Shria or zir Vail Fathers, obviously, and which Pip scorned, and Grobbard took altogether too seriously. In fact, ze'd never felt this lightness, this naturalness, speaking in the old Staid way before. But Dobroc made zir feel like the Conversation had flowed out beyond its halls and proctors and was dancing in the world. "And now, well, ve sent me—oh, I'll just forward it to you!"

{If so,} Pip sent, {ve should report to an Idyll, before ve pisses away the final shreds of vir tenuous hold on a social identity.}

"If you are," Fift said, "why don't you get to an Idyll . . . before you piss away the final shreds of . . . your social identity?"

"My social identity," Predoria mused. "My social identity."

Dobroc, receiving Shria's letter, closed zir eyes.

{What is *up* with this Vail?} Fift sent Pip. {Ve doesn't *act* like someone with hardly any pride left.}

Pip sent Fift zir lines: {Your position here in the reactants' hall. Your ability to exchange minimal politenesses with strangers. Your ability to travel around Fullbelly.} Pip's face was impassive; ze was looking up at the long hallway, up the rows of reactants, through the echoing, pinging space, as if ze were a reactant zirself . . . an architectural or social reactant, perhaps, letting zir feelings about the room seep into the feed.

Dobroc's hand found zirs again. Its grooves and whorls pressed against zir skin; it rested quiet and unmoving, neither heavy nor light. Ze opened zir eyes. "I see," ze said.

Predoria's eyes bored into Fift's: those pale orange irises in those white globes. Ve didn't look like someone on vir last dregs of self-confidence. Ve looked, rather, like ve had boundless reserves. For a moment, Fift wondered if this was a setup, something by the Cirque, part of the show.

"And since this note," Dobroc said, "you won't even watch vem? Like the visualization designer in the blue robe." It was a passage every ten-year-old staidchild knew by heart, and Fift was shaken by its aptness (for the visualization designer in the blue robe isolates zirself for fear of being seen watching) and by its implied prediction of tragedy.

Dobroc shook zir head.

"Your, your position here in the reactants' hall," Fift said, not turning away from Predoria's eyes. "Your ability to exchange minimal politenesses with strangers. Your ability to travel around Fullbelly . . ."

Audience in the reactants' hall kept surging. It should have slowed down by now, as the first flush of viewers wandered away—who wanted to hear Fift's dull threats against this absurdly cocky peripheral Vail? Three hundred thousand active viewers did, apparently. Three hundred thousand! And growing.

{All that can be taken away.} Pip sent patiently. {You gloat publicly about striking defenseless Staid children; do you expect strangers on the byways to smile at you? Do you expect sluice operators to welcome you?}

Fift wished all zir bodies were under privacy cones, or in the apartment—thank holy Kumru's ovaries and testicles no one was watching zir with Dobroc.

"All that . . . can be taken away," Fift said.

"It can?" Predoria said. Ve looked amused, and hungry. "Are you sure?"

Vir fabricator was humming again.

"Fift, listen," Dobroc said. "Shria didn't banish you from vir life forever. And ve didn't expect . . . this."

To be fighting in public again, exposed to the eyes of the world, losing everything.

Fift took a deep breath. Chalky, industrial dust; the acrid, almost-human smell of the muscle-engines; freshly laundered cloth . . . and, faintly, Dobroc: a little like fresh-cut wood, a little like the spice-gnats in the supper garden, the sap in the vines.

"You gloat publicly about, about striking defenseless Staid children. Do you—" Fift cleared zir throat, staring into Predoria's striking orange eyes. "Do you expect . . . strangers . . . on the byways . . . to smile at you?"

Fift glanced up at Dobroc and found no reproach in zir soft brown-on-brown eyes; no pity; only earnest intensity. It was still almost too much to take. "Is it . . . over?" ze said, looking away. "The fighting? Is Shria . . . did the Peaceables arrive? They must have arrived by now—"

"No," Dobroc said. "Or, yes. Well—sort of." Zir face was grim.

"*Sort* of?"

"Must they?" Predoria said, and—seeing Fift start, confused—smirked. "Smile at me?"

"Just look at vem, Fift," Dobroc said. Ze squeezed Fift's hand. "Ve would want that. I know you feel helpless. But 'amid a myriad, one true witness nudges the shape of things . . .'"

{Sluice operators.} Pip sent.

{What? Oh . . .} Fift looked back at Predoria. "Do you expect . . . sluice operators . . . to welcome you?" ze managed.

"I suppose it depends on the sluice operator," Predoria said musingly.

Fift found Shria on the feed.

There were more bodies now. Not just Shria and Vvonda and Stogma and Bluey, and Hrotrun and vir cohort; there were others, too. Vails in working clothes, formal clothes, fighting gear—twenty or thirty additional bodies among the frilly brick-red hillocks and gullies of the abandonage by the goopfield. Some struggling, pushing, striking; some standing to the side and yelling; some dumbfounded; one weeping, face upturned to the ceiling.

And, five paces from Shria, there was a Peaceable who had fallen to zir knees, zir bopperstaff lying in a gully at zir side. There was blood in zir hair, dripping down from zir bowed forehead in thin drizzles in front of zir.

"What's—what's—"

Fift couldn't understand what ze was seeing—the press of bodies looked like a dance, a circus trick, some incoherent ritual. A Peaceable was *there*—and the fighting off the mats *continued*. The Peaceable was—something was *wrong* with zir, ze was bloody, ze'd been *struck*—it was inescapable, obscene.

Fift's stomach gripped with nausea. Not Shria. Ve wouldn't—

A Peaceable shrugged aside in fighting, wounded, down—

(Fift sagged back down onto the bed, gathered the silken sleep-wraps in zir hands. Zir scalp crawled with cold. Predoria's narrow-set orange eyes drilled into zir.)

Something new was broken here.

Ze turned to look at Mother Pip, who was watching Predoria.

Pip chewed zir lip and sent nothing.

Three more cold fists of fear balled in Fift's stomachs. Why wasn't Pip responding? Surely it wasn't possible that—that this marginal, outcast, bizarre, cohortless industrial reactant could supplant—

Fift shifted towards Dobroc, their hands entwined, their forearms touching under white fabric. "What's going on, Dobroc? Are they all unraveling? Even a person in the middle of a collapse wouldn't strike a *Peaceable*, would they? And Predoria . . . why is ve so . . ."

Predoria's eyes changed, their challenging intensity drifting through amusement to boredom. Ve turned back to vir fabricator.

That flicker of hesitation in Pip's eyes. Fift wondered, would Pip's arrogance finally fail? Maybe ze'd feel what Fift had felt . . . humiliated and supplanted . . .

Fift wanted to feel triumph, vindication, at *that* thought. But ze didn't: ze felt cold. Ze didn't want the smothering blanket of zir Mother's remorseless competence yanked away.

Pip's eyes hardened again.

The Peaceable heaved zirself to zir feet, and for a moment the combatants faltered; they took a step back.

Then Hrotrun shrieked and charged the Peaceable.

Fift jerked rigid, squeezing Dobroc's hand. Ze reached out from under the covers and felt the wall of zir room, the rough scar under zir fingers—

{Tell vem}, Pip sent, {to enjoy vir megalomaniac fantasies while ve can. Tell vem ve can continue}

Shria tackled Hrotrun three paces from the Peaceable, bringing vem down.

{to live in a lonely bubble of denial of the truth, a smaller and smaller social world}

Shria heaved up, straddling Hrotrun, punched vem full in the face, before two other Vails—in three bodies—hauled vem off.

{until there is nothing left, not even the honor of a sanctioned suicide. If that's what ve wants, ve is beneath both our pity and our scorn.}

The Peaceable, ignoring the Vails, took an unsteady step towards zir bopperstaff.

"What's—going *on*?" Fift asked Dobroc.

"Um," Fift told Predoria, "enjoy . . . your megalomaniac fantasies . . . while you can."

Predoria looked up sharply.

"With Shria?" Dobroc frowned. Now Vvonda and Stogma were struggling with the Vails who held Shria. A tangle of hands, legs—and Hrotrun slithered out between them, rolled to vir feet. "Ve's trying to stop Hrotrun. Before Hrotrun gets them in even more trouble."

The fabricators had fallen almost silent in the reactants' hall. A few desultory pings echoed from far away.

"You can continue to live"—Fift said, zir eyes shifting away from Predoria's—"in a lonely bubble of"—ze felt the sweat springing from zir flushed scalp—"denial of the truth"—zir throat was dry, clutched; this wasn't going well—"a smaller and smaller social world . . ."

Hrotrun danced away from Stogma as the Peaceable wiped blood from zir forehead (red smears garish on zir white sleeve) and staggered towards zir bopperstaff . . .

"Fift," Dobroc said, "about Predoria . . ."

"What?"

"Well, forty percent of the reactants in that hall," Dobroc said, "had their cohorts forcibly broken up; many of those had children confiscated by Midwives. Most of the rest never qualified for cohorts. Seventy percent tried some other profession but lacked sufficient supporting votes. Five percent are known to be indefinitely postponed regendering applicants . . ."

Predoria leaned forward. "You don't seem—" ve said.

Hrotrun broke into a sprint.

"—to be paying—"

In the tangle of bodies, Shria took a fist in the stomach. Vir other face—lips curled, eyes bulging—showed an ecstasy of rage.

"—attention."

". . . it's a dumping ground," Dobroc said.

"Okay, but . . ." Fift said. "How does that . . . if they all have so little emotional capital, doesn't it make this . . . defiance . . . even more odd?"

"It would have, I think," Dobroc said. "But things are . . . changing."

Fift cleared zir throat. Ze felt Mother Pip standing rigid behind zir. "Until there is nothing left," Fift said, "not even the honor of—"

The Peaceable reached for zir bopperstaff, but Hrotrun reached it first and kicked it aside.

"—of, of a sanctioned—"

Five hundred thousand viewers in the reactants' hall.

There was a thunderous wave of pings: every fabricator in the hall, finishing at more or less the same moment.

Dobroc's body leaned into Fift's, shoulder against shoulder, hip against hip, and yes, that new-wood, spice-sap smell was zirs, and the calligraphic badlands of zir engraved palm pressed into Fift's as if revealing something written in a secret language, and if Fift were to turn, ze could hold Dobroc entirely, encircle zir in zir arms, press zir face into Dobroc's neck—

Predoria reached into vir fabricator and began to pull out a quantity of fabric: velvety, luxurious, soft. Ve wound it and wound it around vir hands.

"—a, a sanctioned—"

"Fift," Dobroc gasped. (What was Fift thinking, why did zir hearts leap, why did ze want to touch Dobroc's lips, to touch them with zir own, to taste Dobroc's speech, to drink zir up, wasn't ze in enough trouble; hadn't ze already screwed things up forever with Shria, Shria who was bleeding in Wallacomp, Shria who smelled like a wild surface forest; what was this strange toadclownish hunger in Fift, it was Shria's fault, show me your fucking genitals indeed—) "Look at the whole reactants' hall—!"

(How could ze ever be the same after having seen Shria gasp like that, and shudder, vir soft skin gleaming with sweat, vir face transformed, transfixed, and Fift the still center holding all that wild storm in one small hand—)

In the long, curving hall, maybe eight thousand Staids and Vails in all styles of dress pulled the same rich, luxurious fabric from their fabricators. Most of the remaining seats were now empty.

It was the soft, rich fabric Panaximandra had thrown.

(—and what would Dobroc say if ze knew? *It's not safe for me with you*: if Dobroc could guess at the secret behind Shria's words. Ze admired Fift's honesty; ze imagined zir as Minth before zir hour of destiny. But did Minth ever have such secrets? Father Squell was right. Fift had lost the balance; ze was ruined, muddled up, not one thing anymore, infected with vailish hungers. Pressed against zir hip and shoulder, Fift could feel how Dobroc's body was lithe and supple under zir shift; ze could feel the complex patterns of zir skin, could tell that Dobroc's labyrinth extended beneath zir clothes, that you could travel its paths and furrows into Dobroc's sleeves, along zir arms and down zir flanks and across zir belly, never leaving the maze. Dobroc was the same size as Fift, not bigger like Shria—if they lay nose to nose, embracing, their toes would touch; squeezed skin to skin, without their clothes, they could inscribe the inverse image of Dobroc's map onto Fift, while Dobroc's voice flowed over and through zir, and Fift's hands

(—*stop thinking this stop stop stop*—)

In the goopfields of Tentative Scoop, the Peaceable straightened up. Ze stood next to Hrotrun, who drew vemself together to lunge. The Peaceable frowned, a small furrow appearing between zir brows. Ze shook zir head briskly, as if disagreeing with someone . . . and then, stiffening, seemed to resign zirself, as if preparing for a blow. A minute tinge of dread could be seen in zir eyes, in zir clenched jaw, in zir live-published emotional state. Ze closed zir eyes and drew in a deep breath.

Predoria grinned a wide, lecherous grin. Around vem, the industrial reactants—Vails *and* Staids, all wide-eyed, some trembling, all clutching the luxurious cloth—rose to their feet.

"Trickster's feet!" Dobroc swore. "Get out of there, Fift. Get out of there *now!*"

Fift turned from Predoria and snatched Pip's sleeve. {Mother Pip, we've got to go.} ze sent. {It's going to be another riot . . . or . . .}

{We are going nowhere.} Pip sent, glaring. Ze stood rigid and upright and still in the hall's center. {Do not imagine that these reprobates frighten *me* . . .}

Hrotrun tensed to spring, but ve never sprang at the Peaceable. Instead ve screamed—a cry of terror and agony and loss like nothing Fift had ever heard before—and grabbed at vemself, clutching vir arms, vir legs, as if trying to hold vemself together.

The Peaceable was screaming too. Ze balled zir fists at the side of zir head, fell to zir knees, and shook so violently it seemed that ze would fly apart.

They were all screaming. Stogma. Bluey. The willowy Vail in Hrotrun's cohort with the bone-white skin. The blue-skinned Vail in the frilly, puffy red gown and the leathery brown one dressed only in tool-straps bedecked with trowels and soft-nosed flangiers—their struggle had become a desperate, violent embrace, as if they were trying to burrow into each other's bodies, like mindless surface animals tearing through the dirt.

Vvonda, curled in on vemself, hands covering vir head, shaking, sobbing.

Shria—

"What's *happening* to them?" Fift said in the silence of the noise-canceling couch, smelling spice-sap, fresh-cut wood, acrid muscle-engine sweat, and dust.

—Shria was screaming too, and worse: vir two bodies at the goopfield were locked in combat, one pair of hands around the other's throat, strangling vemself—

{What's happening to Shria?} Fift sent zir context advisory agent. {Ve didn't do anything wrong! Ve was trying to protect the Peaceable, to stop Hrotrun—what are they doing to vem?}

{In the absence of ontology}, zir context advisory agent sent, {normative expectations lose their purchase, and the flow of possible meanings becomes a flood.}

And in the reactants' hall the fabricators' doors burst open, spilling clouds of thick red smoke. The reactants stumbled back, coughing. Fift caught a whiff of the smoke and it stung zir throat, and suddenly the place was full of running bodies, Vails and Staids on their feet.

"Fift, you've got to *go*," Dobroc said.

Predoria leapt from vir bench—ve towered over them. Ve looked back over vir shoulder, grinning at Fift, and then, head down, luxurious fabric clamped to vir mouth, ve charged into the smoke.

It burned, scraping its way into Fift's throat; zir lungs fought back, coughing—

Ze grabbed Pip's shoulder.

Flashes of light in the red mist and the outlines of Peaceables entering through the doors, and the reactants diving through windows, pushing past Peaceables, falling before them.

"Get out of there, Fift!" Dobroc said. "The Peaceables are raiding—"

"Never mind that!" Fift said, jumping up from the couch. "Stop talking about that! I can see that for myself! What's wrong with *Shria*? You've driven my agents to a collapse, I can't ask them—!"

{Return to your stations}, someone broadcast to the reactants' hall in a blistering override, {and restore them to the approved fabrication sequence. Deviations are not authorized by consensus. Return to your stations.}

Dobroc looked up at Fift, brown-brown-brown eyes wide. "I think it's the polysomatic network. They've overridden it, cut . . . cut it off for that whole goopfield. Cut . . . everyone's bodies . . . apart."

"What?" Fift gathered zir robes, gripped them in zir hands, staring at Dobroc. "How can they *do* that? How could they get *consensus* to do that?"

Fift clutched zir robes over zir mouth and nose. The coughing came so hard and fast ze could barely stand. Ze felt Pip's shoulder under zir arm, Pip's arm around zir chest, pulling zir along; ze let Pip half-carry zir towards the exit.

Dobroc held zir gaze. "People are frightened, Fift. Since the global feed outage, there's been a huge wave of cohort defaults . . . abandoned children, logistics breakdowns, evictions, closed routes. The Idylls are full, and the authorized temporary behavioral-variance emporia are overflowing . . ."

{It appears}, Pip sent, {that we must postpone the remainder of our interview.} Zir face was close to Fift's in the swirling red smoke, eyes squeezed shut, jaw clenched.

Fift coughed, throat raw, eyes full of tears.

". . . people might authorize . . . a lot of things."

In the goopfield, the Vails and the Peaceable screamed again, a sharper, higher, wrenching scream torn from all their throats at once, and then collapsed as one and lay still, panting.

Dobroc exhaled. "May Trickster ignore us. They turned it back on. Shria's going to be okay, Fift. The interruption only lasted a few hundred heartbeats. Ve'll reintegrate fine—"

Orange stoppergoo billowed up from the goopfield all around the Peaceable. It caught the Vails' bodies, lifting them, swamping them, and they disappeared in its thick, immobilizing flow.

"They could have used goo in the beginning!" Fift said. "They didn't have to tear anyone apart!"

"Maybe they had to get it ready," Dobroc said. "Or maybe . . . maybe they wanted to show what they can do. To make a point."

Fift's audience at the industrial hall, when ze and Pip burst through the door among the fleeing reactants, was five million.

 **INTERLUDE**

THE WORLD-OF-IDEAS

> SEMIPERMEABLE WEAVE

> STOCHASTIC CRYSTALLIZATION PREPARED BY
ATTENTION AGENTS

*REACTANCY SYNTHESIS ARTICULATION: "The Current
Crisis, a Near Historical Perspective"*

Burum Apatox Merix, synthesist-articulator:
The issue is not a few wayward Vails engaged in
an unlicensed tussle . . . a few chastened Vail
heads poking up through orange stoppergoo.
We've seen that before. The issue is the Peaceables' use of paralytic somatic interference!
Not since the Age of War have . . .

Moom Parandime Ihu, textilist: If the esteemed articulator expects us to sympathize
with the sort of perverted scum who would
spill blood on a white shift . . . !

Burum Apatox: The specific provocation is
beside the point. The point is that a line

has been crossed. We are all—all of us with
more than one body, anyway—tied to the
polysomatic network. For it to be
weaponized, however extreme the circum-
stances . . .

Tusha Ivetris Fnax, child: Don't you understand that my sibling was *defending*
the Peaceable? And these matter-sucking
peacebreakers . . .

Burum Apatox: Of the many comments on
this skein, I have accentuated—with
some ironic satisfaction—this one, left
by the eldersibling of one Shria Qualia
Fnax of name registry Digger Chameleon
2. For the edification of children and
the uninformed, allow me to clarify:
the difference between *brutalizing a
Peaceable* while *physically rioting in
full view of the world*, and just . . .
*physically rioting in full view of the
world*, while *a Peaceable gets brutal-
ized* nearby, is . . . well, I won't say
it's nonexistent, but . . .

Moom Parandime: the unbridled gall, to
show up among respectable interlocu-
tors and defend vir sibling's brig-
andry! As if the maintenance of harmony
requires such obscene displays . . .

Pedux Mirandum Garabo, familial topology reactant: I don't know why this Fnax cohort was allowed to raise these two in the first place after their earlier failures and arrogances, which are visible to anyone who bothers to ask their agents. This kind of softness and leniency and drift—this sort of abdication of duty by our Midwives—is precisely why we have ended up in this chaotic . . .

Tusha: Don't you understand, they were trying to issue a *challenge*. They did everything right! They did everything they were supposed . . .

 **17**

{Shria . . .}

No response.

{Shria!}

Standing at the edge of the couch, Fift could hear a whisper of white noise seeping, probing, through the noise-canceling field.

Dobroc watched Fift, the whorls of zir intricate skin deepening, tensing, around zir eyes.

"Ve's not answering," Fift said. "What in Kumru's name did they do to vem?"

"Give vem a little time," Dobroc said. "It's going to be—"

"No," Fift said. "No, ve's not all right. I have to go to vem. I have to go there!"

Pip stared out the porthole of a skywhale, expressionless beside Fift. Pip was deep in the feed, enmeshed with zir automated agents, searching for explanations, precedents, adjudication strategies.

{Are you . . . finding anything?} Fift asked.

{The noose is tightening around us.} Pip sent, not turning from the porthole. Ze sat like a chalk statue, like a box that has sheltered something in transport, after the thing has been delivered.

Fift almost wished Pip would blame zir for what happened with Predoria; that would have been safe ground.

{Are we . . . going to find the third assailant?} Fift asked.

Pip turned for a moment to look at zir. There was a flicker of irritation in Pip's expression, which was almost a relief. But immediately a cold and empty hopelessness swallowed it up, and Pip turned back to the window without reply.

In Tentative Scoop, the orange surface of the stoppergoo roiled like an uncalm sea, and Vail heads—one, two, three; there was Stogma—emerged, gasping.

"I've got to go to vem!" Fift said.

"Go to vem where?" Dobroc raised zir hands from zir lap, half-reached towards Fift. "In Tentative Scoop? They'll never let you near vem. More riots are breaking out in Wallacomp, and cordons of Peaceables are converging . . ."

Fift felt it on zir skin, in zir throats, a tightness, as if it were zir entombed in stoppergoo. "Dobroc, I have to do something. I can't just . . ."

Ze heard zir voice trail into silence, into the silenced roar from beyond the couch.

In bed, at home, zir head throbbed, an ache like someone was squeezing it.

The skywhale was jammed with people—crowding the harnesses, pressed against the walls, sitting in their own laps. Many of them, like Pip, were vacant, feed-bound; others huddled in silent, private conversation, occasionally breaking into a harsh laugh or a hissed whisper. Most of them had lookup locked down to the barest minimum of public information. Fift saw an old Staid four seats over stiffen as zir lookup shifted from "proto-cohort of five" to "no cohort." Ze sat, rigid, staring at zir hands.

The textile of the world was fraying apart between their fingers. In Tearless, people driven to collapse were comman-

deering entire habitations by force. Adjudications were failing en masse, adjudicators and reactants sucked in as dis-
putants themselves in snowballing mega-disputes. Below the
porthole, a byway teemed with desperate new orphans.

There were still twenty thousand viewers watching Fift in
the skywhale.

{Please, Shria, send something. Are you . . . are you all right?}
Nothing.

"I'll go to vem at work—that's where vir third body must be.
I've just got to talk to vem, I've got to know ve's—"

"Fift, I—" Dobroc frowned. "Listen, that clip-opera I showed
you? It's been up for five thousand heartbeats now, and it's received . . . quite a bit of viewership. And after this last encounter of yours with Predoria . . . well, Cirque-watchers are
even more confident that you're a thematic nexus."

"Dobroc, I don't care about any of that now!"

"What I'm trying to say is . . . there's going to be a storm of
audience out there, Fift." Ze swallowed, looked down. Ze ran
zir fingertips over the back of zir other hand, tracing the
labyrinthine hills and ridges. "Look—do you—do you want me
to come with you?"

Fift did. But the idea was nonsensical: dragging this gentle
staidkid, this Long Conversation prodigy and secret clip-op
artist, this Thavé-watcher with dramatic dreams, out with zir
into the barren periphery, where ruin awaited. "Yeah, your
parents would love that."

Dobroc stood. "But Fift—" There was more, but it was swallowed by the roar, because Fift was now moving through the
deafening churn of the muscle-engines and their acrid sweat-
stink, through the scuttling trashrats and amber light of the
murky, feed-opaque tunnels.

Away from the gentle couch, the spice-sap smell, the soft
leathery labyrinth of Dobroc's hands.

{Shria, talk to me.} ze sent again.

Maybe ze should have embraced Dobroc, at least. It might be the last, the only time.

Ze hadn't even said goodbye. Ze could send, but it would be in zir logs; in Dobroc's logs, too. Zir parents would see it. Eighty parents! And ze was the latterborn, their prodigy, their project; they might have two or three of them reading zir logs full-time.

The roar of the muscle-engines and the breeze from the wall-lungs flapped Fift's robes as ze ran, feet splashing in the tepid puddles of condensation.

No answer from Shria.

In the skywhale, a seven-hundred-year-old middleborn Vail, dressed in feathers as if coming from a party, began to sob. Pip glanced over at vem, irritated, and closed zir eyes. It felt like the air around the passengers was clotting: Vails burying their faces in one another's necks or twitching like trapped animals; Staids stiffening, staring fixedly from the portholes.

Vvonda's and Bluey's heads were up out of the goop. Vvonda looked haggard, distant, like a cracked eggshell. Bluey was sobbing. Still no Shria.

Striated planes of gray hanging in midair, limned by the greenish light of mold-graffiti ("Spin Like Foo Babies," "No One Was Here," "Imagine Resistance"...).

Fift got out of bed and walked into the hall. It was empty; zir Fathers were downstairs in the breakfast room. Ze avoided watching them over the house feed; who knew what they were saying? Ze didn't want to hear. But ze felt very alone.

Beyond the surging, humming tubes of liquid that lined the walls of the tunnel, its mouth beckoned, amber with the light of first evening.

Standing in the apartment hallway, there was a temptation to push zir other bodies away, damp the connections, the way ze used to when ze was little—to be safe in at least one place, here in the silence. Or to melt into the feed, ignore all zir bodies, and dissolve zirself into the world kaleidoscope.

In a bespoke fabricorium in Ozinth, a mammoth custombodied Vail (ve would have dwarfed Predoria) was running amok, naked and bloody, smashing glass crucibles with vir horns; in Tilgun, the finals of the Scuttlebank Invitational were being held; in the Manysmall, Perm and Trink were staging footage for Shria's favorite show, *Goopfield Pratfalls*, Perm balanced on a rickety assemblage of packing cases above a bubbling sinkhole while Trink peppered vem with rubago fruits; Thavé was on a talk show, explaining something; crowds were clashing with Peaceables in Izist as some kind of Cirque-show devolved into a riot; the archives of *Middleborn at Three Hundred Why Mother Why?!* held millions of heartbeats of footage Fift hadn't seen yet . . .

Under the best magnification the field pickups in Tentative Scoop could manage, the orange stoppergoo was a mass of slick globules locked against one another, expanding and contracting to funnel air to those trapped inside, as if the whole mass was breathing. Shria was under there, invisible, hidden.

Fift started down the stairs to the breakfast room and found Smistria, at the bottom, glowering up at zir.

"What, exactly," Smistria spluttered, "do you think you're *doing*?"

"What do you mean?" Fift asked.

The breeze from the tunnel, the exhalation of the muscle-engines, fluttered zir robes as ze stepped out onto the platform.

The two Peaceables ze'd passed before, holding tubes of stoppergoo, turned to look at zir.

"What do I *mean*? What do I *mean*? I *mean* that your Father Squell just spent a thousand heartbeats *gently* and *thoroughly* explaining to you why—when the entire world is spinning it-self to pieces, and our *cohort is at risk* because of *your inappro-priate behavior*—you need to *stay home* and *stop sending* to Shria Flowblocking Fnax of name registry Are You Void-Spurned Kidding Me . . . and you ignored vem on both counts!"

On the platform, the light was purpling as first evening came to an end. Audience flooded in: ten thousand, fifteen thousand.

"It's getting late," the Peaceable on Fift's left said. Ze had the velvety smooth skin of the very old and eyes that glinted like mica flecks in granite. Ze spoke each word as if it was an entire sentence. "You should go home."

Fift moved past the Peaceable, eyes down, stepping onto the stairs. How was ze going to get to Stiffwaddle Somatic Fashions? Would a public skywhale let zir on? Ze ascended the stairs towards home, and towards the local docks of Slow-as-Molasses.

"Ve's in trouble," Fift said to Smistria. "I never said I wouldn't send to vem. Ve needs me."

"Ve *needs* you? Ve *needs* you? Oh, I see. For your skills in unarmed combat off the mats? Is that why ve *needs* you? To help vem start riots all over Fullbelly? No, that can't be it; I see you're insulted by the idea. Certainly not; ve must need you for your restraint and calmness and *firm command of logic* . . . which you're demonstrating"—Smistria threw vir hands in the air, flushing dark purple, vir braided beards flying in all directions—"by *blocking your parents' messages, pestering riot-ers in Peaceable custody* over the send, and *sneaking off to the fulcrum of Foo*—"

A hundred thousand viewers on the stairs, and another eighty thousand in the skywhale.

"Father Smistria, can you calm down? I—"

"Can I *calm down*? No, I can't *calm down*, we've had far too much *calm* around here. In fact, we've completely failed in our duties, Fift, by *calmly* allowing you to—"

Frill came up behind Smistria, crossing vir arms across vir bandoliers.

"What?" Smistria barked.

"No, I agree with you completely, actually, Smi," Frill said, looking at Fift. "Please carry on."

The staircase branched: one flight up toward home, the other down toward the local docks. Fift slowed down.

Pip, in the skywhale, turned slowly to look at zir.

"Ah . . ." Smistria tugged on vir beard. "Where was I . . . completely failed in our duty, that's it!"

"Fift," Pip said. "I want you to return to the apartment. In *all* your bodies. Now."

{I just . . .} Fift sent. {I just want to see if ve's okay.} Ze took a deep breath and headed for the docks.

Pip's eyes widened a minute fraction of a fingerspan, charged as a surface thunderclap. {Fift. You will comport yourself like a staidchild of a solid and reliable cohort. Are you listening to me? You will not jeopardize your family's future for some kind of . . . emotional gesture.}

"We've allowed you to develop *inappropriate attachments*," Smistria spluttered, "and this kind of self-centered . . . *ignorance* of the effect on those around you—"

Squell came into the corridor. "It isn't zir fault," ve said. "Ze doesn't—"

"I didn't *say* it was zir fault!" Smistria said. "I said *we'd* failed. But it doesn't do any good to pretend that it's not *also* zir fault. In any event, it's zir *responsibility*—"

"But listen to what you're *saying*." Squell's lower lip quivered. "Lack of empathy. Of connection with those around zir . . . well, how was ze to *learn* those things, when we never"—vir eyes filled with tears—"*never* managed to—"

"Squell," Frill said, sharply. "Let's not do this here."

"Can we at least go into the breakfast room," Fift said, "instead of standing here on the stairs . . . ?"

{Mother Pip, please.} Fift sent. {You know my Fathers aren't going to let me out for weeks once I go home. What if ve's not well enough to send? I just want vem to know . . .}

"Without a *sibling*," Squell wailed, "how was ze to *develop* those capacities? It was our duty, our duty, and we *failed*—"

{Shria,} ze sent, {just answer me, please, Shria . . .}

Pip did not answer. Ze turned zir whole body to Fift, and zir gaze was like a furnace. There was no room in Pip's implacable glare for compromise. Only to submit, to be supplanted once more, to be squeezed again into the place Pip had made for zir in Pip's ordering of the world.

Ze tried to move toward the breakfast room to sit down, to drink something, but zir Fathers blocked the way. Squell was wailing, and Arevio bustled in, glaring at Frill, to embrace Squell; and Frill drew vemself up in anger, shrugging away from Smistria; and it was too much, too many of them, crowding the hallway, full of their demands and noises and heat— too much, too many, no room for Fift—

"No," ze said.

Ze'd said it aloud, on the skywhale. Into the furnace of Pip's glare.

"No, I'm not going right home," ze said aloud. "I'm going . . . I'm going to see vem first. To make sure ve's okay. And then I'll come home. That's perfectly reasonable." Zir voice quavered a little, and ze hated it. "Ve's my friend."

Squell's wail intensified; ze shuddered and twitched in Arevio's arms.

"Fift," Pip said, also aloud. "Have the events of the past days unraveled your mind sufficiently that you now find Hrotrun and Predoria to be compelling role models? You are sixteen years old and thoroughly undistinguished. Ignore for the moment what will happen to your parents; what do you think will happen to *you*, if you break with us?"

Fift's hearts squeezed in zir chests. "What are you talking about? I'm—I'm not—leaving the family, I'm just saying, I won't come home right now." Ze swallowed. "I'm . . . busy."

"*Fift!*" Frill said, pushing past Arevio. "Stop this nonsense *now!*"

"Essentially," Pip said, "you are declaring your majority." The heat of zir glare was dimming, drawing away from Fift. "If you will not submit to parental authority in a moment like this, then it seems your childhoods are finished. Our cohort will not survive it."

"What in sweet Kumru's—" Smistria spluttered.

Descending the stairway, Fift glanced down towards the docks; one of the Peaceables was turning to look up at zir.

The furnace was gone; Pip's glare was ice now, the silent, massive glaciers of the Pole. "It's not how I would have chosen to begin my adulthood. Sixteen years old, suffering a public disgrace, with the world turned against you. But we each journey alone."

"Oh voids!" Squell wailed. "No, no . . ."

"What in Kumru's name," barked Smistria, "is Pip *doing*?"

"I can't endure this," Squell sobbed. "I can't! I need to unravel, I need to go, I'm collapsing, I'm collapsing . . ."

Pip's mouth set into a line. Ze closed zir eyes and rubbed the bridge of zir nose with one hand. Then ze opened zir eyes and faced forward, as if ze were another passenger on the skywhale. As if, Fift's childhoods being over, they were perfect strangers.

Fift's throat closed, constricted, dry.

"Squell, stop it," Frill said. "You can't collapse now, there's no room in the Idylls . . ."

"You're bluffing," Fift said to Pip. "Ze's bluffing," ze said to zir Fathers. "You'd never let zir do that—kick me out of the family . . ."

On the stairs to the docks ze hesitated, looking up at the vault of the roof of Fullbelly, down at shadowed Boorwine.

Mother Pip, facing forward, glacier-cold. One of zir eyebrows twitched.

"Fift," Frill said, "you just stay where you are on that stairway. Don't go anywhere, I'm coming to get you!"

"Of course no one is kicking you out of the family, Fift," Arevio said, "but you have to get yourself under control."

"Either you are engaged in childing," Pip said, aloud, in the skywhale, zir nostrils flaring slightly, "or you are not. That is the fact of the matter. That we have pledged to protect one who refuses to accept and acknowledge this protection, who flouts it to plunge zirself into . . . other pursuits . . . This is an untenable situation, Fift."

"And you think my Fathers—"

"Your Fathers may express any number of emotions about it; they may beg and plead with you to come home and rejoice when you humor them with occasional compliance; they may get the Peaceables to drag you home physically; they may undertake various schemes to make it look as if we are a family and shore up our ratings. But the choice lies with you, Fift. Either you choose your home, your cohort, your responsibilities . . . or you cast them aside."

"That's—" Fift was aware of the whole skywhale watching, not to mention a wave of new viewers: three hundred thousand in the skywhale, two hundred thousand on the stairway at the edge of Foo. "You're—you're creating a series of false dichotomies!" Like the muddled adjudicator in the shell in Marim's pocket, but ze couldn't say that. "This is your idea of parenting? You . . . you either have total control, or . . . or you abandon me?"

Father Frill reached out as if ve was going to grab Fift, then paused, vir hand hovering, and placed it slowly, gently, on zir shoulder. Fift flinched anyway. "You have to stop this," Frill said.

"But it's not fair," Fift told vem. Ze sounded like a four-year-old, like a Vail, like someone who'd never entered the First Gate of Logic, but ze couldn't help it. Ze shouldn't be doing this in front of the world. But Pip was wrong. How could zir Mother define zir like that, *aloud*, as someone undistinguished, someone useless, who could be cast out unless ze obeyed every single little—

"It is not I," Pip said, "who is—"

"Listen to me!" Fift said in the skywhale. It was almost a shout. Ze got zir voice under control. "Listen. I accept your guidance; but not your absolute protection! I accept your—I choose you all. Okay? But not as . . . I'm not a process you can completely control. If you can't"—ze leaned towards Pip, because ze was done flinching away—"if you can't handle responsibility without control, then you . . . parenting was the wrong occupation to choose!"

Frill put vir face in vir hands. Squell began to wail again.

"Oh, that's just wonderful," Father Smistria snarled. "Just the boost our parental competence ratings needed. Do go on, Fift."

"And do you imagine," Pip said, cocking an eyebrow, still not looking at Fift, "that I can support an apprentice who simply refuses to comply with—"

"Fine," Fift said. "Fine! I resign from being your apprentice!"

"Kumru's frozen balls," Smistria said.

Fift took a step towards the docks. There was movement down there, some kind of stir . . .

"But I don't resign from childing all of you! Because that's not about control, Mother Pip!"

Pip's face was stony and unmoving.

"I just want to collapse," Squell said. "There must be a place for me. Why can't I go to Aristi's Grove, or . . ."

"Squell, for void's sake, this isn't the time!" Frill said.

{Apologies are in order}, sent Fift's context advisory agent, {for the preceding lacuna in functioning. To verify that recalibration is complete, please answer the following question: Did you just publicly resign from your sole official occupation during a heated public argument with your Mother, in the middle of an audience-storm and ratings collapse?}

{Yes}, Fift sent, {I did. Any suggestions?}

In the skywhale, passengers were dropping even the pretense of not looking at them. A gaunt old Staid in the row in front of them turned around in zir seat.

"Your safety . . ." Pip began.

"My safety? I'm not five years old anymore," Fift said, "and likely to . . . to eat strange mushrooms on the surface, or . . . lose a body from—" Fift felt zirself flushing a richer shade of brown. From doing what? From running to Shria, throwing zirself in vir arms, pressing zir face to vir smooth lavender neck—

{Perhaps}, the context advisory agent sent, {You might consider going home?}

"Fift Brulio," Father Arevio said, "You *must* come home. Look at your poor Father Squell! Surely we can have this conversation *at home!*"

"I'm not"—Fift blundered on in the skywhale. "I'm not going to die of my mistakes. Maybe you're right. Maybe I'll be like Predoria, alone and working in a great hall full of strangers . . ." There was a hard lump in zir throat.

"Oh, for Kumru's sake," Smistria said. "Frill, didn't you say you were *fetching* zir? What is *taking* you so long?"

"And maybe I'll be miserable. But maybe—maybe it's not

enough to hum along like a component snug in its casing, Mother Pip!"

"It's not zir fault!" Squell cried. "Don't *blame* zir. You mustn't *blame* yourself, cubblehedge"—ve buried vir face in Arevio's garment—"for what will *happen*—"

"I'm almost there," Frill said. "Don't take another step, Fift. I'm almost there."

"No," Fift said, shrugging away from Frill's hand. "Don't, Father Frill. I just—"

Pip squeezed zir eyes shut.

"Maybe it's better to be miserable," Fift said in the sky-whale, zir voice quavering. "Maybe it's better to be miserable for a century, if at the end you—you win joy built on *honest* foundations, Mother Pip, and not on—"

{I'm not going home.} Fift sent zir context advisory agent. {I'm going to . . .} Ze glanced, over the feed, at the local Slow-as-Molasses docks.

There was a crowd at the docks, and for a moment Fift thought it might be another riot. But there were Staids as well as Vails in the crowd, and the Peaceables flanking it were watching silently. They weren't fighting, but nor were they boarding the bats and whales. They milled around, squatted, leaned against struts and pillars, jostled in groups. Orphans; the emotionally bankrupt; refugees of broken cohorts and closed reactancies; the abandoned and collapsing turned away from the gates of Idylls . . . anyone too low-rated to travel, fetched up against the docks like flotsam, exhausted from fruitlessly begging passage.

"Excuse me," said the old Staid in the row in front of them (a four-hundred-year-old pedagogical agent arranger), "but I couldn't help overhearing your fascinating discussion . . . and I said to myself, this sort of thing is so often the result of poor pedagogical agent arrangement! People blame the parents, when in fact the parents may be only *indirectly* at fault—"

Fift crossed a bridge, and now ze saw the milling crowd at the docks with zir own eyes. Some people there were turning to look up . . . at zir?

"*Mine* are mood-collared," said a Vail in the row behind them with a dramatic nimbus of bright orange hair. "Solves the whole problem. I can't *imagine* raising staidkids without it. It's impossible, the things we expect of them! *How* are you going to get a child to do all this sitting and mumbling without—"

"Such extreme measures," the agent arranger said, "are rarely indicated, when a simple—"

"Oh, you *can* drive yourself to distraction, tweaking their agents—*and* your own," said the Vail with the orange hair (ve was a feed-skein meta-reactant and Father of four). "But *why*? With the band, you can just *set*—"

Fift's hand gripped the railing above the docks; and in the apartment, ze felt behind zir for the railing of the stairs.

Shria was sending.

"For blessed Kumru's sake!" barked the old Staid four seats over, the one whose lookup stats Fift had seen change from "proto-cohort of five" to "no cohort." Burst capillaries made jagged red traceries across the whites of zir eyes. Ze waved a bony finger at the Vail with the orange hair, at the old Staid in front of them. "Stop inserting yourselves into this drama! We all know perfectly well you're just trying to capture viewers—"

{Fif} Shria sent.

"All of you shut up!" the seven-hundred-year-old Vail with the feathers said. "The last thing any of us needs is all this audience! For Groon's sake—"

{t}

The Vail with the nimbus of orange hair stood up. "*You* shut up! Do you think I'll take this sort of insult lightly?"

{Shria, Shria, are you all right?}

The feathered Vail heaved vemself to vir feet, tottering slightly. "Oh? And do you think I have anything more to lose?"

{go} Shria sent.

There was a gentle bump as the skywhale came up against a dock. "This," Pip said mildly, "is our stop." Ze stood, and the two Vails backed up a step. Ze looked over at Fift.

{the f}

Fift opened zir mouth to speak. "I—"

Pip shook zir head and turned away.

{uck home}

A hand closed on Fift's shoulder and ze jumped. It was Frill, on the stairway by the docks. Ve looked worn. The silver midges swarming around vir hair glinted in the purple of second evening.

"Come on, Fift," ve said.

Fift got up and hurried after Pip, weaving around the screaming Vails and stepping from the bobbing skywhale onto the docks.

Six million viewers.

In the hallway at home, staring at Father Frill, Fift flushed hot. At the docks, ze looked away from Frill's insistent eyes, and cold crawled along zir scalp.

Ze was making a fool of zirself. In front of the world. In front of Shria . . .

"Come on," Frill said, more gently, and Fift followed vem back up the stairs.

INTERLUDE

Excerpt from the CHAT LOGS of Meroc Ipithia of name registry Barking Undulation 12, Staid, 145 years old, apprentice splage coordinator:

Zetich: see the link I sent you?

Meroc: Is it important, Zetich? I need to get all these supplies ready for the splage tomorrow.

Zetich: It's about Fift and Shria . . .

Meroc: Woah! Really? Uh . . . I probably shouldn't, but . . .

Zetich: You won't believe what's happened.

Meroc: Really?

Zetich: Yeah. But if you're not interested, I'll just show Morinti . . .

Meroc: Morinti! Zet, Morinti only just found out about Fift and Shria! I've been following them longer than you—I saw them talk to Thavé live!

Zetich: Well, sure, but Morinti is interested now, and after all, Morinti's third cousin is *in* . . .

Meroc: Trickster's feet, give it a rest with Perjes already! Perjes is in that clip-op

for all of six heartbeats, gaping like a
slackwit from the other side of a clearing.
The way Morinti goes on and on about it,
you'd think . . . anyway, fine, I'm watching.

Meroc: Did you just see that . . . ? Oh fuck.

Zetich: Isn't it just . . .

Meroc: Aw, those poor kids!

Zetich: I knew you'd get it. Everyone here says
   Shria got what ve deserved for rioting, but—

Meroc: That's totally unfair. Ve didn't mean to
   riot! Voids. Was vir cohort dissolved?

Zetich: No! They were evicted, fired from their
   jobs, derated—

Meroc: But not dissolved?

Zetich: No! Because Shria's Mother, Sangh Tenrik Fnax of name registry Turquoise Fenugreek 5, challenged the neighborhood family
   reactancy coordinator to a duel!

Meroc: A duel? On the mats? But surely that
   alone wouldn't—

Zetich: A duel to *body loss*.

Meroc: To body loss? Sweet sluiceblocking
   Trickster! I can't even . . . And the challenge was accepted?

Zetich: The reactancy coordinator is apparently
   very vain.

Meroc: And the match was permitted?

Zetich: I guess some mats coordinator is a terrible romantic . . .

Meroc: You call that romantic? Being pummeled
   until . . .

Zetich: But ve's doing it to save vir child and
   vir cohort!

Meroc: Fuck.

Zetich: I know!

Meroc: But Zetich, it won't even work. Even if ve wins, it won't stop them from forcing dissolution. At best, it will only delay . . .

Zetich: I know. It's hardly sensible. But you have to admit, it's pretty sluiceblocking vailish of vem. It's so brave that it's shored up vir ratings some. Enough to postpone the end for a moment . . .

Meroc: Wow. Voids. Those poor kids.

Zetich: Now aren't you glad I showed you and not Morinti? I just keep thinking about the two of them. Sixteen years old and dealing with this squandering sluice-blockage. I haven't been following them as long as you have, but . . . especially after that clip-opera . . . when I see them together . . . you know, I had a Vail friend when I was in First Childhood, until it got too hard to talk to each other. You know that age . . . and I just feel, when I look at them, maybe if I'd fought a little harder, if I hadn't just bowed to consensus and immediately . . .

Meroc: Zetich, we should do something.

Zetich: Do something? Like what?

Meroc: Just do something. Talk to more people. We can't let this . . . we can't let this just happen.

Zetich: Oh Meroc. I know how you feel, but . . . who's going to listen to us? And, I mean, not that I'm worried about ratings, but . . .

Meroc: How about your friend Morinti?

Zetich: Morinti . . . !

Meroc: Let's ask zir. And I think there are
others. You know, Thavé-watchers, Clown-
followers—we can't be the only ones who
feel like this. We should start a club.

Zetich: A club.

Meroc: Yes, Zetich, a club. I can't just sit
here and do nothing!

Zetich: Well . . . maybe. But I do have to go
soon, so . . .

Meroc: So connect me with Morinti. Send an introduction.

Zetich: An introduction? Now?

Meroc: Now.

Zetich: Well . . . okay. Sent. But I had no
idea that you were even interested in . . .
that the two of you . . .

Meroc: Thanks, Zet. I have to get back to the
splage . . . right after I call Morinti.

Zetich: Oh, okay. Well . . . talk to you
soon . . .

 **18**

Fift had been home in all three bodies for twenty-eight hours, while the world outside fell apart.

There was no way ze could sleep. Ze sat on the edge of zir bed, sat in the supper garden, sat at the breakfast room table with zir Fathers arguing around zir. No one was talking to zir.

Arevio had left the supper garden, wordlessly, as soon as Fift came in. Wiped vir shears, hung them on a hook, and walked out.

"*Settling down?*" Frill exclaimed, at the other end of the breakfast room table. "*Settling down?* No, things are not *settling down!* Do you know that the Peaceables are using *unvowed militias* in Spunwonder?"

Fift pressed zir fingers against zir eyes.

"You think I don't know that?" Father Nupolo said. "One of little Chalia Rigorosa's Fathers is a Peaceable *serving* in Walla-comp! Without the help of those militias—"

"Well, I frankly don't see the point," Frill said. Ve dismissed a globe of tease-tea, sending it flying back to the kitchen. It swerved around Fift's head. "If they're not vowed, not trained, not even publishing neural data . . . who is to say that they remain calm and . . . well . . . *peaceful* at all? This is no criticism of Chalia's Father Ellix, mind you. It's a criticism of the system—"

"Ellix—" Nupolo said.

"*Ellix*," Frill said, "has years of preparation. But more to the point, ze's *vowed*. Even if ze *did* get angry . . ."

In the large family meeting room on the first floor, Arevio and Smistria were already sitting at the table, waiting for what was coming. Neither spoke.

"Even if one of the rioters *struck* Ellix?" Frill said. "And Ellix had a moment of rage or—or hatred, or vengeance? Well, then, everyone would *see* it, *wouldn't* they, and ze would be forced to retire to—"

"Ellix has *never*—" Nupolo's velvet forehead squeezed into sharp, angry lines.

"That's not the point, though. That's not the point!" Frill threw up vir arms; a tinkling chorus of bells followed them. "Even if ze *did*, ze'd retire to *contemplation* until it was—"

{Please.} Fift sent zir context advisory agent. {I have a right to send. I have a right to use my own mind!}

{Sending at this time}, the social nuance agent sent, {poses a severe danger of exacerbating your instant-fame.}

It was just a one-word note from Shria—{*Hey.*}—sent several hours ago. Ve might be too exhausted and hurt to send anything else. But that word meant ve was talking to Fift again.

Dobroc had sent quite a bit more.

{It's not going to pose any danger!} Fift sent. {I won't do anything public. No one will know. But I have to write *back* to them.}

{It does pose a danger. And not only to you.} the social nuance agent sent.

{The issue is anyway one of local infrastructure.} the context advisory agent sent. {This house is governed by the consensus of Iraxis cohort, which is quite solid on the matter of your use of the send.}

Nupolo was still protesting. "You can't expect—"

Smistria was pacing the hallway outside the supper garden. Ve paused in front of the door, then turned towards the breakfast room.

"I just don't see what good it does!" Frill cried. "If they're not vowed, they might as well just take Vails! Why not? Take some of these Vail . . . 'emergent armies,' adorned with their team-tags, as if they were at an impromptu sporting event! [Mothers against the Unraveling], or whomever! And give *them* the stoppergoo and the spidergear . . . !"

"Now you're just being *absurd*," Nupolo said wearily.

Watching the street in front of the apartment, Fift saw Father Grobbard emerge from a local tunnel, hurry to the door, and come in.

"Thank Kumru," Smistria said, sauntering into the breakfast room. "I *told* Grobbard not to go anywhere! At least ze's back *now*. Is Thurm going to make it?"

"Not in time," Nupolo said.

"Miskisk?"

Frill snorted.

"Well, it's not *impossible*," Smistria snapped. "At a time like *this*, I would think even *Miskisk*—"

The supper garden smelled like spice-bees, and absence. The mud was scuffed, and the tendrils of the vestris vines were yellowing. Fift went out into the hallway to greet Grobbard.

Grobbard's face was blank. Ze took a deep breath. And then ze came forward and embraced Fift. Fift stiffened. Ze couldn't hug zir back—it felt too awkward and strange to see Grobbard overcome with overt emotion; the world had turned inside out, and Fift had no idea how to react—but ze wanted Grobbard to hold on, to keep holding on.

Grobbard sighed, patted Fift once, let go of zir, and stepped back.

"Father Grobbard," Fift said. "I don't understand why I can't send."

Father Grobbard rubbed zir face with zir hand. Behind zir, ze came in the front door in another of zir bodies. "Fift, my child, would it be all right with you if we postpone this discussion?"

"I'm not going to say anything public. I won't draw any audience. I just want to . . . to talk to . . . Shria. Briefly."

Grobbard put zir arm across Fift's shoulders and guided zir towards the meeting room. In zir other body, no longer hurrying, ze proceeded to the breakfast room. "Fift, in a few minutes, we will welcome the Midwives who gendered you to our apartment."

"But until they get here—"

"This is a crucial moment for our cohort. If things go very well, perhaps there will be no objection to an easing of restrictions. If they go poorly, you may no longer need to ask us for permission . . . because we may be relieved of the responsibility of raising you."

A hard lump in Fift's throat.

Father Frill passed them in a tinkling swoosh of bells as ve whipped into the meeting room. In the breakfast room, ve said, "For Kumru's sake, I hope you behave yourself, Fift."

"Maybe ze should come in two bodies?" Nupolo said. "Or all three?"

"Let's try not to look too desperate, shall we," Smistria said, smearing paste on a broibel. "Or like we have something to worry about."

Nupolo scowled.

In the meeting room, Grobbard guided Fift to a seating harness. Arevio, across the table, avoided zir eyes. Smistria was tugging on vir beard, swinging back and forth.

"But Father Grobbard," Fift said, "what if they don't ease

the restrictions? What if they want tighter restrictions? Wouldn't it make sense to maybe just, quickly before they get here, just briefly—"

"For Kumru's sake, Fift!" Frill said in the breakfast room, as ve glared at zir from across the meeting room table. "You are not sending anything! The doors and apertures and channels are sealed! The house has been told to keep you here, as invisible—as silent—as *hidden* as it can possibly make you! You're not *sending*, you're not *leaving*, and since you can't seem to shut up about this, I, for one, am not sure you should even be *viewing* the rest of the world!"

Father Squell had come into the breakfast room, singlebodied, trembling, flushed, vir eyes red-rimmed. Ve walked slowly, kneading vir hands together. Nupolo glowered at vir elbow.

"Don't be hard on zir," Squell whispered. "It's not zir *fault—*"

Frill rolled vir eyes.

After that, the breakfast room fell silent. The whole apartment was silent, save for the creaking of seating harnesses, the drowsing hum of spice-bees, the gentle lapping of waves in the bathing pool, Frill's bells tinkling when ve shifted. In the bedroom, Fift put zir face in zir hands.

And then Mother Pip arrived, escorting the Midwives.

Umlum Canalepsis of name registry Punishing Tenderness 11 was a tall, gaunt Staid in wheat-colored robes. Miolasia Frin of name registry Purple Endless 5 was a muscular Vail with a mane of crimson hair glimmering with jewels and tiny mirrors. Matching crimson fur curled artfully over vir body.

Even without lookup, Fift would have recognized them. Ze'd watched the footage of zir gendering often enough.

"Revered Stalwart Umlum. Revered Expressive Miolasia," Frill said, leaning forward over the meeting room table, steepling vir fingers so that vir bells tinkled and jingled as fetchingly as possible. "We just want you to know how *sorry* we are"—vir eyes darted between them—"for any *distractions* due to Fift's well-intentioned but, ah, *misguided*—"

"It's not zir fault," Squell murmured in the breakfast room.

Fift felt zirself stiffen.

Frill put a hand on Squell's shoulder. "We know that, Squelly; now please, don't say anything in *there*, all right? Let us handle this."

"Of course," Nupolo said in the meeting room, vir posture erect, "we take full responsibility, as a cohort."

"It's such a difficult *time* right now," Frill said. "And so we *fully understand* that *minor* lapses at the moment may have unfortunate *impacts*."

The bedroom. The breakfast room. The meeting room. Fift didn't look beyond them; didn't watch Shria, still imprisoned in orange stoppergoo; didn't look for Dobroc or riots. Zir parents were watching; they would be watching what ze watched.

Smistria chewed the end of vir beards.

"Take your beards out of your mouths, Smi," Frill said in the breakfast room. "Kumru's sake."

"Which is why," Pip said, "we have of course prepared a plan. Grobbard, my dear, would you elaborate?"

Miolasia sighed, a small, slightly irritated exhalation.

Grobbard looked to Umlum, who leaned back a little in zir chair.

"We believe," Grobbard began, "that we erred in allowing Fift too much range, too much freedom. We placed too much responsibility on zir shoulders. First Childhood is a time—"

"Do you imagine," Miolasia said, "that we have come here to critique your parenting?"

Glances around the breakfast room. Arevio swallowed. Squell stared at the table as if it were on fire.

In the meeting room, frozen expressions, and the tiny rustling music of Frill's minutely shivering bells.

"Revered—revered guests," Nupolo said, "we assure you, we can—"

"To be sure, there are *questions*," Miolasia said in the meeting room, arching an eyebrow, half-smiling, "about your *competence*."

In the breakfast room, Frill leapt up from vir seating harness. "Kumru! How I hate them! They're going to take zir, and there's nothing we can do about it."

"Oh, sit *down*!" Father Smistria said.

Frill fingered vir ceremonial dagger. "That void-splattered, smug Miolasia . . . what I wouldn't give to be able to meet vem on the *mats*—"

"But that," Umlum said, "is not why we are here."

Fift swallowed.

"It's . . . not?" Arevio said.

In the breakfast room, Smistria's eyes darted to Fift, then back to Frill. "Frill, have some *faith* in the ordering parents of the world! We have done *nothing* wrong—"

Frill snorted. "Ordering parents. Blessed womb!"

Fift kept zir eyes on the tables in front of zir, but over the house feed, ze searched the Midwives' faces. Were they here to take zir away?

Ze wasn't supposed to be following the odds that bookies were placing on the cohort's survival; zir parents had blanked out zir feed access to the reports. But they couldn't object to zir watching Miskisk, and Miskisk, in a pavilion in Ebberen, was loudly telling vir friends that the odds were against them now, and how it was all Pip's fault.

"We are here," Miolasia said, "to ask for your *assistance*."

"You can be certain," Pip said, "Revered Eminences, of any assistance we can render you."

In the breakfast room, Frill slid vir ceremonial dagger out of, into, out of its sheath. "Where is this going?"

"Certain irresponsible elements," Umlum said, "are making use of your child as a symbol."

"Oh, *irresponsible elements*," Frill said in the breakfast room. "I see. Because *weaponizing* the polysomatic network was terribly *responsible*."

"Frill," Smistria growled, "this is the *last* moment I want to hear your chaotist nonsense."

Squell was hunched over, in the breakfast room and the meeting room: precisely the same posture, hands clutching the tables.

"The disturbances in Wallacomp are spreading," Umlum said. "Not only riots, but other demonstrations, designed to mock and . . . *denigrate* the ordering elements of society."

"Laxity, and *disrespect*," said Miolasia.

"Disrespect . . ." muttered Frill.

Smistria's fist slammed down on the breakfast room table. "Enough! Enough of your willful *ignorance*, Frill Evementis Iraxis of name registry Irrevocable Spin 8! You of all people should recognize the . . . the *historical* moment we are in! Riots in the byways! If the Midwives fail, if the Great Arrangement is dissolved, we return to the Age of War!"

Nupolo looked helplessly across the breakfast room table to Grobbard, who sat still, aware, as if watching unpurposed birds alight on some forest branch.

If they don't dissolve us, Fift thought—*if they don't take me—the best I can hope for is house arrest, for months. Years, maybe.*

Squell clasped vir hands over vir ears, shuddering.

(Trapped here with these Fathers—their rages, their worries, their sniping criticism, their constant watching. Zir bodies caroming around the apartment like the three gas molecules caught in Micrum's Cube—around and around like leaves in an eddy of a surface river—up and down four sets of stairs, through five hallways, the breakfast room and the supper garden, the sleeping alcoves, the study-pit, the atrium, the meeting rooms, the wombtombatum, the small mat room, the bathing pool . . .)

Ze sat up in bed.

In the meeting room, Father Arevio cleared vir throat. "We are aware—"

"Oh, but are you?" Miolasia said, eyebrows arched.

Arevio paused, cowed, looking to Pip, to Smistria.

"You hear that?" Frill said, in the breakfast room. "They're practically admitting it."

"What in Kumru's name," Smistria said, "are you on about *now*? Admitting what?"

"That they're editing the feed!" Frill said. "There are more casualties than we know about—"

"Oh, *now* who's spouting crankish conspiracy propaganda? Grobby, could you please tell this overexcitable figment-chaser that *no one* can edit the *feed*?"

"I am afraid," Grobbard said, "that Frill may not be entirely wrong. There are signs of a Far Technological war taking place among agents and feedgardeners. At the very least, it is certainly the case that they know who has seen what, and that many attention agents are suborned to the tasks of distraction and reframing."

Fift's throats tightened as if ze was breathing clotted air.

Smistria threw up vir hands in disgust.

Miolasia leaned forward, fishing a glittering mirror out of vir fur and tucking it behind vir ear. "It is a priority of ours to contain panic, and to soothe the world's more excitable elements. And your *child* has unfortunately become, as I said . . . a kind of *symbol*."

The house feed said that the bedroom was warm, but Fift

felt cold. Ze heaved zirself off the bed, to zir feet, gathering zir robes.

"People are confused and unsettled," Umlum said. "They project themselves into these children's story. Fift's innocent, childish questions inspire them. And some of these so-called 'clip-operas' are very cunningly crafted. They subtly offer the titillating suggestion of an inappropriate relationship, but with such simplicity that it seems somehow pure and hopeful."

Fift flushed. An *inappropriate relationship*? Had they just *said* that? Zir skin crawled. It was one thing to be censured for zir stubborn loyalty to a peacebreaker, a criminal, a Vail who fought in off-mats riots. But it would be far worse if they thought that . . . if they *knew* that ze was a deviant, gendering wrong, lost and wild, swollen with fervid, unstaidish desires . . .

There's no way they can know what happened at the lab, Fift told zirself. A brief memory flashed across Fift's mind—a hand nestled among writhing blue cilia—but ze suppressed it brutally. It hurt to remember. *They don't know anything.*

But even with no other evidence, the clip-op was bad enough: *Fift's forehead pressing into the crook of Shria's neck as ve sobbed on the byway. Fift coming forward, through all the tumult and confusion of this unraveling world, to take Shria's hand.* Dobroc had shaped the images so that every viewer yearned for those hands to touch.

Ze wanted to bury zirself in some maintenance tunnel with no feed access.

Pip frowned. "But . . . most Revered Eminences . . . Fift is an innocent child . . ."

"Exactly," Miolasia said. "An innocent. A *Staid*, in First Childhood, from a respectable, if *vulnerable*, cohort . . ."

They'd be taking Fift away, that much was clear. They were taking zir, and there was nothing zir parents could do about it.

It would be cold at the Pole. Cold and silent. Fift would be alone, forgotten, vanished. And zir parents would be here, in this apartment, empty of Fift. If they were lucky.

"I . . . I don't understand, Revered Expressive," Nupolo said.

The bedroom, with its soft bed, its scarred wall, its silence, was unbearable. Fift went out into the hall.

"An innocent staidchild," Umlum said, "is precisely what these rogue Clownist elements need."

"It's easy to expose the fanaticism of off-mats *rioters*," Miolasia said. "People recognize the ideology of someone like Panaximandra for what it is: a perverted fantasy of license, violence, individualism, and boundless unending intimacy that can only lead the world to destruction."

In the breakfast room, Squell moaned.

"And we have an understanding with the *mainstream* of the Clownist movement," Miolasia said, "that they will not cross certain lines."

Fift passed the breakfast room. Ze heard zir feet scuffing along the floor outside.

"But these rogue elements, these loose emergent groupings," Umlum said, shaking zir head sorrowfully. "They speak a new language. Their talk of liberation and equity and solidarity is very attractive, very intoxicating. It is easy to misunderstand, to imagine that these are not just the same old fanatic warrior dreams in clownface."

Down two flights of stairs, through the hallway with the sleeping alcoves, past a sleeping body of Arevio's.

"And so, for a young *Staid* to become a figurehead for these people," Miolasia said, "to willingly *ally* zirself with the chaos, to appear to see in it not subjugation and destruction, but *liberation* . . ."

"Father Grobbard," Fift said, in the breakfast room, "Father Frill, Father Smistria, Father Nupolo . . . I don't know what they're talking about. I didn't willingly ally myself with any-thing!"

"Of course you didn't," Father Frill said. "It's nonsense. They're trying to scare us, that's all . . ." Ve swallowed.

"I assure you," Father Nupolo said, "Fift has no *intention*—we have no desire *at all* to—"

"Anything we can do to *cooperate*," Father Frill said, bells tinkling. "We're *more* than willing—"

"I want Miskisk," Squell whispered hoarsely in the break-fast room. "I want Misky back! Why did ve go away?"

Cold. It would be cold at the Pole. Fift shivered, and pushed into the bathing room through a curtain of stiff grass.

After the rough, warm grass of the hallway, the tiles of the bathing room were a cold emptiness under Fift's bare feet. Ze ordered steam.

"Of course you are," Miolasia said. "We expected no less. So it's really quite simple. For your own safety, and that of the world, we need you to come to the Pole."

Even Mother Pip looked flummoxed. "To the—to the Pole?"

"*All* of us?" Arevio said.

Fift sat at the pool's edge. Gray and blue tiles and slick white pillow-surfaces, large enough to encompass twenty or twenty-five splashing bodies. The last time Fift saw it crowded, ze'd been six.

"We have no desire to break up your cohort," Umlum said. "That's the last thing we intend."

The Pole, but not alone. Fift inhaled, filling zir lungs with steam. Ze'd have zir parents with zir. It was still terrifying, but . . .

"To the Pole in, well, in . . . *all* of our bodies?" Arevio asked.

Miolasia nodded, smiling. "Of course."

"It's quite an honor," Umlum said. "You would of course have to take a hiatus from your current professions . . ."

"Exile," Frill said, in the breakfast room.

Smistria glared. "This is our chance, Frill! A chance to save our cohort from destruction."

"We're being disappeared, Smi." Frill paced the breakfast room. "They won't let us out again until it suits them. They won't let us communicate except *as* it suits them."

Fift lifted zir eyes to the aperture in the ceiling above the center of the pool, where reflected glowtube light, falling twenty bodylengths from the outside, carved a faint bright column in the misty air.

A foam structure butted gently up against the side of the pool, riding the tiny waves.

"Don't see much alternative, Frill," Nupolo said. "It's that or be dissolved." Vir face was ashen; ve looked down at vir trembling fingers. "Wonder if we're going to get a chance to say *goodbye* to little Chalia Rigorosa and vir cohort . . ."

The steam was still coming: small globes of water broke the surface of the pool, struggled upward, and boiled in midair. Ze could turn it off now, but ze didn't want to. Let the steam thicken until it obliterated zir; let zir disappear.

Frill ran vir hand through vir stiff coppery hair. "Oh, we'll go, of course. But let's not fool ourselves: Fift's escapades have cost us our lives in the world outside the Midwives' cage!"

The cool of the tiles under Fift's buttocks. The womb-warm water around zir knees. The thickness of the steam in zir lungs. Over the house feed, zir body disappeared, a gray shadow absorbed by swirling gray.

"Esteemed Expressive. Esteemed Stalwart," Nupolo said, in the meeting room. "Naturally . . . we're honored and overjoyed."

"Indeed we are," Pip said. Zir face was unreadable. "If I might ask: is there anything specific that we . . . ought to do . . . to merit this honor?"

Squell heaved vemself up from the breakfast room table and tottered over to Frill. Vir voice, usually so soft, was brittle as twigs, as halting as animals caught in traps. "It's . . . *not* . . . zir . . ."

Frill swiveled, vir bells sounding brief waves of high, clear music. "Oh, of *course* it's zir *fault*, Squell! I love zir, but there's no use pretending otherwise—"

"*Stop* it," Squell hissed.

"Father Squell," Fift said, "it's . . . it's all right. Don't . . . Look, it is partly my . . . it is my fault."

"*Do*? Oh, hardly anything," Miolasia said. "Certainly nothing you wouldn't be eager to do *anyway*, given your loyal resolution to aid in the healing of our world."

Fift splashed into the water. Its heavy warmth swallowed zir limbs, and zir white shift ballooned beneath zir. The foam structure loomed dimly ahead in the fog. Fift waded towards it. Pockets of boiling water scurried out of zir way.

"You will simply have to explain to the *public*," Miolasia said, "your *regrets*, which you have already expressed here, and Fift will have to express *zir* regrets . . ."

"Fift doesn't have to *go*," Squell whispered, "if ze doesn't *want* to."

"Oh, blistering voids, Squell," Frill barked. "Of course ze does!"

"Fift will have to *explain* a little about what happened," Miolasia said, "to cast the correct *light* on things."

Fift told the foam structure to flatten and rolled awkwardly onto it. The steam was so thick ze could barely breathe. Ze lay on zir back and told the foam to inflate. Ze rose toward a blur of light, the central exhaust column.

Over the house feed, the bathing room was an opaque wall of white.

"Or do *you* have some other plan? Do tell us, Squell," Frill said.

"*Dissolution*. And an *Idyll*," Squell whispered.

"Oh, *yes*," Frill said. "Since there's plenty of *room* just now, and we're such *desirable* associates, we'll just arrange for *spacious* accommodations for Fift at an *Idyll*—"

To the Pole, forever. Ze'd never see Shria or Dobroc again. Or at least not for years and years . . . maybe a century. Who would Fift even be, after a century of cold?

Above zir, the blur of light grew closer.

"Fift will disown the *impropriety* of those clip-ops, for instance," Miolasia said.

"The important thing there," Umlum said, "will be to push those tantalizingly shadowy intimations into the light of day and disavow them as the disgustingly false rumors that they are."

"And if the Idylls *just happen* to be *full*, Squelly?" Frill spread vir arms wide. "Or overrun by *rioters* and unlicensed—"

"Stop it!" Squell cried, vir eyes filling with tears.

"It's okay, Father Squell, Father Frill . . . I'll go . . ." Fift said, but no one in the breakfast room was listening.

"Miskisk's not going to come," Nupolo said, fingering the cold remains of a broibel.

"Miskisk is irrelevant," Grobbard said, rounding the table, heading for the kitchen, "and Thurm will have to decide where ve stands."

Ze would lose them. Dobroc, the weird brilliant staidkid with the voice like a warm, thundering ocean: ze'd just met zir, and now they'd never sit together again and talk about Mundarn and the willow wind, now ze'd never touch the labyrinth of Dobroc's skin again. And Shria . . .

If ze ever did see Shria again, would Shria . . . would Shria . . .

Fift knew there were moments when ze'd been important to Shria. Maybe not now; maybe not even in the lab at

Stiffwaddle . . . or, not in the way ze'd wanted. Shria hadn't boiled with desire for Fift, had ve? Not the way ve did for Vvonda. That had been *Fift's* desire.

But ve'd trusted Fift. Ve'd wanted to tell Fift vir secrets.

"It will be clear to everyone," Miolasia said, "that Fift is not really at fault. It was *Shria Qualia Fnax*, after all, who drew zir into the riot."

Ve'd trusted zir ever since that day in the forest.

On the byway, before the crowd of anonybodies . . . ve'd held out vir hand.

Steam billowed up through the exhaust shaft. The air in Fift's lungs was scalding. Ze reached up from the top of the inflated foam, and took hold of the lumpy, braided roots that formed the shaft's walls.

{Fift}, zir social nuance agent sent, {what are you doing?}

The first time ze'd climbed into the exhaust shaft, when ze was eight, ze'd expected to be caught and scolded. Ze'd been sure of zir parents' omniscience.

Ze pulled zirself into the shaft, reached for higher holds. Zir feet found the spaces between the roots.

{Fift?} sent the context advisory agent.

But ze hadn't been caught. The exhaust shaft was an invisible space, missing from the house feed; missing, by some Far Technological quirk, from the house's entire proprioception.

In the meeting room, a drop of sweat ran down Fift's forehead, across zir cheek.

{Please explain your motivation}, the context advisory agent sent, {for your actions at this time.}

With Fift's external send locked down, zir parents wouldn't pay attention to chatter with zir agents. {I thought we could have a conversation}, Fift sent, {where the house can't see us.}

"And then, let us not forget, Shria left zir alone," Umlum

added. "Enticing zir into a riot, and then stranding zir there. Surely you agree, Fift, that that was wrong of vem?"

Fift looked up from the meeting room table. "Oh. Well, um—"

"It was wrong of Shria," Umlum said again, "to abandon you in the riot."

Pip leaned forward, zir eyes drilling into Fift.

"You said so yourself," Umlum said. "To Shria. 'You should have stayed with me'—do you remember saying that?"

"So surely it can't do any *harm*," Miolasia said, "to repeat it *now*."

In the breakfast room, Frill flung vir arms up. "Fift, answer the void-spurned *question*. Just tell these—these *ordering parents* of the Kumru-abandoned *world* what they want to hear..."

Fift pulled zirself up, hand over hand. {You said it was a matter of local infrastructure.} ze sent. {That you couldn't let me send because of the house rules. Am I outside the house now?}

{Further defiance of your parental cohort carries significant risks in this situation.} the social nuance agent sent.

{They would detect an external message immediately.} the context advisory agent sent.

{They're pretty busy.} Fift sent. {And it's my last chance. They're taking me to the Pole.}

"It was both of our faults," Fift said. "And we're ... we're both sorry. We know we shouldn't have..."

Umlum's face darkened.

"Oh, really?" Miolasia said. "*We* are sorry? Shria doesn't *seem* particularly sorry, I must say."

"But ve is," Fift said, "and ve would tell you that. If you asked. I mean, you could take vem to the Pole too, and have vem express vir regrets. And disown the, the impropriety. Maybe that would ... help ..."

"Fift!" Smistria thundered, in the breakfast room. "That's enough!"

"Don't *yell* at zir, Smi," Frill said. "Ze just doesn't *understand*. Look, Fift, that's not what they're asking for. They can't risk making Shria into a hero, after what ve's done."

Fift kept climbing. Higher into the shaft than ze'd ever been before.

{It may become necessary to inform your parents of your location.} the context advisory agent sent.

{You never did that when I used to climb up here before.} Fift sent. {And you could have done it already. But you haven't.}

{Such a decision is contingent on many factors.} the context advisory agent sent.

{Well, I don't know what those factors are.} Fift sent. {I don't know whose side you're on. You've been in my head my whole life, and I don't really know if you're there to help me or to spy on me.}

{We are here to take care of you.} the social nuance agent sent.

{I don't know what that means.} Fift sent. {Take care of what? Of my ratings? Of my comfort? Of what I . . . what I become? Does it matter what I *want* to become?}

The softness of Shria's cheek against zirs. The weight of vir forehead, pressed into zir shoulder. The hard muscles under the skin of vir arms, enclosing Fift. Vir hair falling in copper tangles over vir shoulders.

Amid a myriad, one true witness . . .

"I'm not going to betray vem," Fift said, in the breakfast room. "I'll go to the Pole. I won't make trouble. I'll say whatever else they want me to say . . . but I'm not going to blame Shria in front of the whole world."

"Fift!" Frill cried. "We are in no position to *bargain*."

Miolasia leaned forward. "We are here, Fift, as a favor to your Mother Pip. And because we believe that you want to do the right thing. And so we are offering you a chance. *One* chance. To trust us and to do as we say."

The steam flowed thickly past Fift as ze climbed. The light was getting brighter.

{You are insufficiently aware of the dangers of attracting further attention.} the context advisory agent sent. {Your instant-fame has swelled dramatically.}

"But *I*, Fift," Miolasia said, "am not a marginal indexer from Tentative Scoop. You do not *debate* with me."

{You didn't answer my question.} Fift sent zir agents. {You never really do! You always just tell me what you *think* I should know. Answer what I *asked*. *What* are you taking care of?}

"Fift," Father Nupolo said, in the breakfast room, "don't you understand? They're going to dissolve our cohort!"

{What do you want me to become?} Fift sent zir agents. {Do you want me to become someone who denounces their best friend on the feed to save their own cohort, without . . . without even sending a *message* to vem? Is that what you're . . . taking care of?}

"Revered Expressive," Nupolo said, "the matter's *decided!* Fift's parents have agreed. Ze's our child. Please accept our apologies for zir childish questions. Ze will absolutely cooperate—"

{It is true}, the context advisory agent sent cautiously, {that restriction of send privileges is a relatively extreme measure.}

{One which is entirely appropriate for extreme situations.} the social nuance agent sent.

{As Fift noted}, the context advisory agent sent, {at issue here is zir right to control zir own mind—zir basic ability to communicate with others.}

{A right which cannot take precedence}, zir social nuance agent sent, {over Fift's basic safety, and the integrity of the social flow . . .}

Fift crawled out of the shaft and into a bright translucent gazebo on the upper surface of Foo. In the walls all around zir, thousands of tiny slits puckered to exhale clouds of steam and mist. There was barely room for zir to lie in the loam of the gazebo's floor beside the drop, zir arms and legs aching.

"That is very correct of you, Nupolo Imsmi Iraxis," Umlum said. "But you will surely forgive a certain skepticism on our part regarding your ability to control your child."

Miolasia's vermillion eyes bored into Fift.

The back of Fift's necks were cold. Zir hands were slick with sweat. Zir stomach roiled.

{There is some divergence}, the context advisory agent sent reluctantly, {among various agents tasked mutually with regulatory responsibilities for your feed infrastructure. Please allow for a short pause while we attempt to reconcile these factors. Your patience is appreciated.}

"I'll do as you say," Fift said, zir voice scratchy, "Except about Shria."

"Well," said Miolasia, straightening, "I think we're done here. Thank you all for your time."

Frill leaned over the breakfast room table. "Fift!" ve shouted. "What are you *doing*?"

"Stop shouting," Squell whispered. "Stop shouting at zir."

"Why should they have the right?" Fift said, flinching away from Frill. "Why should they have the right to dissolve us if we want to stay together? Why would you *listen* to the Midwives and the bookies and the adjudicators and the ratings? Why would you let them supplant you? Why would you let them take me away?"

{Just let me send.} Fift sent zir agents. Ze rolled onto zir hands and knees, the soaking shift clinging to zir skin. Ze pushed zirself up. {Let me send to vem. If you want to protect me, if you want to protect Iraxis cohort, if you want me to cave in and do what they say . . . just let me *send* first, let me tell vem why!}

Miolasia stood, almost leaping up from the table, not meeting anyone's eyes and brushing off vir hands as if something disgusting was stuck to them. Umlum rose more slowly.

"Please, Revered Expressive," Arevio said. Arevio, Nupolo, Frill, and Smistria were on their feet.

"Fift, you're sixteen," Frill said, in the breakfast room. "You don't understand! We can't ignore reality! We live *in the world*, not in some void-spurned hidden *island* on a surface *sea*! We depend on interconnections, relationships, with everyone in the world!"

Squell swayed on vir feet, eyes closed.

"Listen, Fift," Frill said desperately. "Maybe a cohort *should* be able to supplant the whole world! But you can't just *pretend* the world is not as it is!"

"You ungrateful, *muddled* child!" Smistria said. "This is dissolution!"

Still seated at the meeting room table, Pip laced zir fingers together and turned to Fift. "Are you certain of this decision, Fift?" ze asked mildly. "To throw away this cohort, which has raised you with love, to lose us, to have us lose each other . . . for this gesture? To impress a vailchild who you may never see again? Who perhaps has fond memories of you as a child . . . but with whom, in fact, you have little in common?"

Across the table, Squell was rigid, glassy-eyed. In the breakfast room, ve made a high, hard, strangled sound and began to shake. The cobalt blue spikes set into vir pink scalp quivered.

"It's the end," Frill said, "we're going to lose everything— everything! Don't you understand?"

The gazebo's outer membrane was filmy, translucent, slick with condensation. Fift could see the murky outlines of passersby outside. Ze stepped forward, put zir hand on the wall, felt the gaps puckering beneath zir fingers, the steam racing through.

In the meeting room, Fift stood. "Revered Eminences," ze said, "this isn't my parents' fault. There's no reason to dissolve their cohort. I—"

Miolasia smirked.

"Kumru's frostbitten cock!" Frill shouted in the breakfast room. Squell, still making that rough, strangled sound, whirled on vem.

"I declare my majority," Fift said. "I rejected my parents' counsel—"

"Oh no, you certainly do not!" Arevio cried.

Squell's hand moved fast, fingers tense and curled to a point, whipping loose-armed to strike at Frill's temple: a blow that would have knocked vem to the ground, except that Grobbard, who had come slowly around the table, was there, zir hand closing gently over Squell's at the top of its arc.

Through the puckered gaps in the gazebo's flesh, Fift saw a couple of courting Staids, arm in arm and holding parasols, heading for the eastern grove beyond the docking-spires.

In the breakfast room, Frill leaped back from Squell, stumbling over a seating harness. "What in—Squelly!"

"Esteemed guests," Pip said, still seated, "my friends . . . Might we take a bit more time to resolve this matter?"

"From my perspective, the matter is *quite* resolved," Miolasia said. "I would wish Iraxis cohort *luck*, were that not foolishly optimistic given the dismal failure of its project."

In the breakfast room, Grobbard enfolded Squell in zir embrace. Squell shrank, wrapping vemself in vir own arms, vir own tight, quivering inner hug within Grobbard's outer one.

Ve turned vir head into Grobbard's neck and squeezed vir eyes shut.

"As for *you*, Fift," Miolasia went on, "while it is very kind of you to offer to shoulder the burden of raising yourself *alone*, that is in neither your own best interest, nor in ours."

"Oh, Kumru," Frill said, turning away from Squell moaning in Grobbard's arms; turning away from Fift, vir eyes filling with tears. "Oh, Kumru. It's over . . ."

Smistria stumbled from the seating harness and went to vem. Nupolo, alone at the breakfast room table, was blank, immobile, like a lapine transfixed on a spear.

{Okay.} Fift sent zir agents. {Last chance.}

"Despite the immense *demands* currently laid upon us," Miolasia said, "our order never shirks its duties. Your parenting is now in our hands, and we have ample resources to correct your previous parents' *mistakes*. We must be on our way now"—ve tucked a stray mirror behind vir ear and looked over at Umlum, who nodded that ze was ready—"but I will see you soon, at the *Pole*."

"As it would be unwise, for a number of reasons, for you to journey alone," Umlum said, "we have summoned the nearest pod of Peaceables to escort you there. They should arrive within the hour." Ze looked somberly at the faces of Pip, Arevio, and Grobbard, each in turn. "Your squatright over these apartments . . . should hold until then."

Fift ripped open the gazebo's membrane and pushed into the gap, staining zir white robe with its yellow blood. Ze struggled through, out onto the surface of Foo.

And ze ran.

 **19**

The moment Fift emerged from the gazebo, zir audience surged from zero into the tens of thousands—the first wave of the agent-notified.

Fift ran past the pavilions, the bundle-gardens, over a small bridge, zir feet slapping on the grownbone walk. The diners at a nearby veranda looked up in surprise.

But zir parents hadn't noticed yet. They must have attention screens up for the meeting. Nothing from the outside was getting in. Not yet.

Umlum nodded to Grobbard, avoided Pip's eyes, glanced briefly at the rest of the Fathers, and followed Miolasia from the meeting room.

"Well," Nupolo said in the breakfast room. "Well."

"What a Kumru-spurned fucking fiasco," Frill said.

"Well, we'll appeal it," Smistria said. "Obviously! We're not going to just . . . roll over like that."

"Our chances . . ." Nupolo shook vir head. "No. No immediate appeal. But . . . if we split up for a while . . . tried to maintain at least dyads or triads, just . . . for the *meantime* . . ."

"Oh, Fift Brulio," Arevio said, vir eyes filling with tears.

Diners at the snack-veranda were standing, pointing. Fift's hearts pounded. 8,934,190 active viewers and climbing. Ze ran.

Miolasia and Umlum were in the anteroom by the front door. Miolasia ran vir sharp, jeweled claws through vir crimson hair. And then they were through the door, and gone.

"Rev—your garden—" Nupolo said, in the meeting room, turning to Arevio. Ve stood, brushing vir hands awkwardly over stiff blue fabric. "If there's anything you want to take . . . I'll . . . how about if I help?"

"I just want to look at Fift Brulio," Arevio said. "While I still *can*." Tears dripped from vir chin.

Fift shivered. Ze tried to meet Arevio's searching, stunned gaze, but ze couldn't. In the breakfast room and the meeting room, ze looked down, squeezed zir eyes shut. Ze couldn't think of what to say, and zir throat was too tight to speak.

Ze concentrated on running.

In the breakfast room, Squell began to shriek in Grobbard's arms, a scratchy, desperate, keening sound.

"Here's what I say: we had a good bout," Frill said. Ve stood up abruptly from the meeting room table, crossed to the door, and hovered there, half turning back. "We made it sixteen years, and whatever they say, whatever anyone thinks, I say we didn't do such a bad job of it." Ve looked at Smistria, at Nupolo. "We were only nine, and only two Staids! And Fift . . . Fift is a wonderful kid, even if in the end"—ve put vir face in vir hands—"even if we couldn't really handle . . . couldn't really give zir what ze needed . . ."

"Fift," Grobbard murmured, "I wish I had words of more comfort for you. All I can tell you is that life is long. Your . . . zeal . . . once it is tempered, with time . . . will be a virtue. In your . . ." Ze looked at the table. "In your new life."

Frill sobbed.

Smistria pulled Frill against vir chest with one hand, tugged on vir beard with another. "Kumru's blood, Pip, I would have thought . . . I mean, you *know* these Midwives . . . I was expecting *you* to . . ."

But ve didn't look at Pip while ve said it. No one—Fift could see over the house feed, even with zir eyes squeezed shut—no one was looking at Pip. Pip was colder than a glacier now; ze was like one of the lost vessels from the Ages Before the Ages, of which Omolo speaks in the fifth work of the third cycle: abandoned so deep in emptiness that worlds were only a rumor; burst open, void-scoured, the breath of life become a crust of frost clinging to their pitted spars.

"Who's that outside? The Peaceables are coming already?" Smistria said, blinking.

"It's Ellix," Nupolo whispered. "Ze rushed over."

"For the love of Kumru, Squell," Frill said in the breakfast room, holding vir head, "would you stop screaming?"

Fifteen million viewers. Fift tried sending. Still nothing. Zir agents wouldn't answer. It was absurd to imagine that ze could make it to the docks, never mind to Stiffwaddle Somatic Fashions. Something was wrong with zir feed-navigation agent, too. Ze looked for Shria, for Dobroc, but the feed was a vast jumble, impossible to sort through.

It was like ze was hidden away in a silent bubble of time. Drenched with steam and sweat in the wintergreen light of second morning; throat dry, feet sore from pounding on rush-felt, zir shift sticking to zir legs, the docks ahead.

Twenty million viewers, and ze could feel zir incoming queue swelling with invisible messages, an opaque mass veiled by zir agents' stubborn will. Fift came to the stairs above the docks and paused.

"They've published it," Nupolo said, sagging. Vir military posture dissolved like sugar in the rain; ve hunched, like an old Vail without prospects. "It's official. Fift is theirs."

There was something different about the docks. The people

there—the orphans, the bankrupt and cohort-sundered, would-be travelers hoping for some ratings fluctuation or act of pity to grant them passage—they weren't just milling. There was a febrile activity on the docks, like a disrupted anthill: intense clusters of people shoving their way from one group to another through a buzz of raised voices. One group was opening a giant banner, four bodylengths high, currently blank, into the air.

On the steps just below Fift, two Staids and a Vail turned and saw zir, and one of the Staids gasped.

Frill's head shot up from Smistria's shoulder. "All-sucking *void!*"

Smistria gaped. "Fift—what are you doing out *there?*"

"Will this never end?" Nupolo said in the meeting room.

"It's like a joke," Smistria said. "A joke without a punchline."

"Fift Brulio," Arevio said, face bright with tears, "just wait there at the top of the stairs. I understand how you must feel, but don't make it worse by running."

"Tell my agents to let me send," Fift said. "I just have to send."

Arevio squeezed vir eyes shut, violently, as if Fift had struck vem, as if Squell's blow had landed on vir temple.

"Fift," Grobbard said, gently, "why would your agents listen to us now? We are not . . ." zir voice faded, and ze licked zir lips.

Pip stood, slowly, and walked from the room.

Fift's skin was like ice. Zir stomach was a hard ball of acid. "I'm—I'm sorry that—"

"Don't," Frill said, vir voice thick with tears. "Just don't."

"It's zir," one of the Staids on the steps said. "It's really zir."

"How did ze even *get* down there?" Nupolo said.

"Oh, run all you *like*, Fift!" Smistria threw up vir hands.

"Let's just make a gigantic *chase tableau* in the middle of Foo, shall we, where the Peaceables run you down like a lapine in the hedges."

"If I may be so bold as to introduce myself," said the Vail on the stairs—according to lookup, ve was Bojum Holkitz of name registry Buttercup Void 5, 110 years old—"I am the Practices and Principles liaison for the Manifesto Working Group of [Embracing Fift and Shria]. It's a great, *great* honor . . ."

Arevio came cautiously around the table and put vir arms around Fift. Ve lay vir head, with its fuzzy, silken, gray mane of hair, on Fift's shoulder.

It was like being scalded or stabbed.

"And, um, I'm the Theory liaison!" one of the Staids said—Morinti Bob of name registry Selfish Turkey 12, 125 years old. Ze gestured to the other Staid. "And this here is Emim. Ze's not a liaison."

"I take the minutes," said Emim Potching of name registry Unfortunate Plank 2, 75 years old. Ze looked a little overawed, a plump, shy Staid, bald, in an ill-fitting cream shift.

"Oh," Fift said. "Oh, well, I—"

Arevio, Frill, Squell, Pip, Grobbard, Smistria, Nupolo, Thurm, Miskisk. They were gone; they were lost to zir. Sister-less orphan Fift.

"Kumru's beard, Fift," Smistria growled. "You can't keep *defying* the Midwives! You don't . . ." Ve squeezed vir eyes shut, holding the bridge of vir nose. "You don't know how far they will *go*."

"I don't know how much you know about our team-tag," said Bojum Holkitz of name registry Buttercup Void 5, "Fift Brulio Irax . . . uh, that is, Fift Brulio." Ve flushed, then cleared vir throat. "But we are *really* serious. We are the real deal. Unlike, um, [Avengers of Fift and Shria] or [Harbingers of Fift and Shria's Devotion], *we* don't just *relate* to you and Shria as some kind of arbitrary *symbol*! *We* proceed by close textual analysis of the *record*—"

"Not just the clip-ops," Emim said.

"Not just since the riot, either," Morinti said.

{What are they talking about?} Fift asked zir agents.

{Some individuals}, the context advisory agent sent, {have been using the team-tagging mechanism, developed for impromptu sports events, to form . . . alternative groupings.}

{It is a perversion of regulated and approved consensus-formation mechanisms.} the social nuance agent sent. {Experts are advising that any temporary emotional gains from such ersatz solidarity will ultimately be paid for in unease and anomie.}

{Um, since you're talking to me again}, Fift sent, {can I at least read my incoming queue?}

{Consensus formation among your agent constellation is currently problematized.} the context advisory agent sent. {Regrets are expressed.}

"We believe the same things you do!" Morinti blurted out. "Just like you said, 'it's not enough to hum along like a component snug in its casing' . . ."

"'Maybe it's better to be miserable for a century,'" Emim whispered, "'if at the end you win joy built on honest foundations.'"

"Uh," Fift said.

Auntie Ellix came in the apartment's front door. Ze was in zir Peaceable's uniform—a white robe with rough weave and a loose hood—with a large satchel strapped to one shoulder. Ze had new bruises at zir left temple, yellow and blue.

"Thank Kumru," Nupolo said, meeting zir in the hallway.

"I came as soon as I could," Ellix said.

Squell stumbled from the meeting room and Ellix caught vem in zir strong arms. "Oh, Ellix," Squell sobbed.

"Listen," Fift said, on the stairs. "I can't send—my agents won't let me—and my cohort's been dissolved—"

"Oh, we know *that*!" Bojum said. Emim nodded.

Arevio let go of Fift (vir embrace slackening, then gone; vir silk-stranded hair tickling zir neck, then gone) and followed the other Fathers. Bodies from the meeting room, bodies from the breakfast room: they gathered around Ellix in the anteroom like spice-gnats sucking at the last vine of the season. Fift trailed after them, doublebodied.

"'Who wants to have agents chattering at you up here?'" Morinti quoted. "'It's sort of missing the point, isn't it?'"

Fift swallowed. "What I'm trying to say is, I'm in trouble. They . . . they were going to take us all to the Pole, and then I tried to declare my majority, but they wouldn't accept it, and now it's even worse . . ."

"All right, everyone," Ellix said, raising zir hand. "Thank you. All right, thank you. I'm very sorry things had to go this way, you know I am. But there are some immediate practical details I need your attention for."

"Are you taking Fift . . . ?" Grobbard asked.

"Yes, but let me come back to that—"

"Ellix," Smistria said. "Fift's *outside*, at the *docks* . . ."

"I'm fully aware of that," Ellix said drily. "That part's out of my hands. At the moment, you all need to focus on your own situation."

"I mean, I would have gone," Fift told the group on the stairs. "I would have gone to the Pole. But they wanted me to say it was all Shria's fault. And I couldn't do that." Fift felt a tightness in zir chest, as if something invisible was constricting zir lungs.

"Of course not," Morinti said fiercely, as if ze understood. Fift felt the invisible grip loosen.

"It's terrible!" Emim said. Ze tugged nervously at zir robes. "It's so unfair!"

"These doors aren't going to hold long," Ellix said. "None of you currently have enough clout to delay the dissolution process. In an hour, these rooms will be shoulder to shoulder with the worst kind of intrusive thrill-seekers and claim-grabbers. Given how things are going, there may be physical battles until the new squatgrant gets sorted out."

"Physical—!" Arevio said.

"It's happening all over. We're just spread too thin right now. We need to get you all dispersed, as far from here as possible, in as secure and private spaces as possible, in . . . well, it looks like we have between twenty-four and thirty-three minutes."

"I just need to tell Shria what's going on," Fift said, on the stairs, "and find out if ve's okay."

Morinti and Bojum exchanged a glance. "Well," Bojum said, "I mean, you just *did* tell vem. Ve is, you know, *watching*."

Fift swallowed. Of course ve was—along with four hundred million others . . .

"Spin-Nupolo cohort," Ellix said, "is going to take in three of you. We would of course take more—we're family, after all"—Ellix's chin bobbed slightly upward, a tiny gesture of defiance—"but three's our best guess of what we can absorb without busting our own squatright apart like a ripe bean. So you each need to be asking trustworthy local contacts— ideally second- or third-level contacts, or even fourth; nobody too closely correlated with Iraxis—to take you in for the next thirty-some hours."

"Oh," Emim said, gathering zir robes into a bunch at zir chest, zir eyes wide as bounceballs. "Oh, I just got a message! A message! From . . . from . . ."—ze gasped for breath—"from *Shria!*"

"What does it say?" Morinti said. "What does it say?"

Emim grabbed Fift's shoulder. "'Head for the docks!'" ze said. "Come on!"

They ran.

"If you can ride out the next two or three days," Ellix said, "and nobody is caught and mobbed in public and there's no other incidents, we think the buzz will have peaked and—"

Emim held on to Fift and Bojum and Morinti each took a side to guard. Together, they clattered down the stairs.

{Running around can only lead to increased audience and further disgrace.} Fift's social nuance agent sent.

{Oh, so *now* you're available?} Fift sent back.

{There are ten Peaceables coming over the bridge from Temereen to escort you.} the context advisory agent sent. {And twelve more docking now at the lower spires.}

"Squell . . . needs an Idyll," Frill said.

"I know," Ellix said. "But they're full. There's a beyond-the-sky returnee absorption center; Squell qualifies for placement as an asteroid worker. I know it's not the same thing, but it's the best we can do right now."

At the bottom of the stairs, people were crowding forward.

"Fift Brulio!" someone shouted. "If you think consensus will support your irresponsible acts—"

"Where are you going?" someone else shouted. "You stay right here! You stay right *here!*"

"Leave zir alone!" A wide-eyed Staid tried to push past Emim. "Fift, take my hand, I only want to be near you—" Bojum and Emim closed ranks, hustling Fift past.

"Thurm is secure," Grobbard said. "Is that correct, Ellix? Ve said ve could find a place for me—"

"That'll do," Ellix said, nodding, "that's solid. Ve could even take another."

"Ah . . ." Grobbard cleared zir throat. "Miskisk is already there."

"Admit it!" an old Vail with bright purple skin and hair. "*Admit* you're working with Andibol Marm! *Admit* that this is a hoaxgame launch! My viewers deserve to know!"

"You unsluiced toadclown! Chasing after that *rioter* and smashing your squishy hot *bodies* together for the *world* to see...!"

"How did you bring down the feed? *How?*"

Bojum linked arms with a Vail who darted out of the crowd—lookup showed vem as Honti Pikipo of name registry Nameless Desert 3, and yes, when you looked for it, there was the team-tag, [Embracing Fift and Shria]. And there was another Staid with the same tag, coming in on Morinti's side.

"'Make room,'" Morinti shouted, jubilant. "As Shria said: 'We're coming through!'"

Once you were looking for them, team-tags were everywhere: [Swallowers of Light], [Never At Rest], [Revanchists of the Tumbling Lover], [Mothers Against the Unraveling], [Panaximandra's Million]...

Everyone had found something new to belong to while Fift was trapped in zir apartment.

While ze was losing everything ze belonged to.

"Nupolo," Ellix said, "you'll come to our cohort as well, of course, with...?"

"Arevio," Nupolo said.

"If I might," Arevio said.

"Your *ex*-parents should be dispersed around the *world*," a ragged old blue Vail tagged with [Orderly Birth of Order] shouted, "and banned from all occupations! They should have their feed access *removed*! How anyone can support such irresponsible—"

"Fift," a portly, diminutive, bone-white Staid shouted—ze was tagged with both [Take the Babies] and [Prologue to the Honest Foundations of Fift's Joy]—"try my soup! This barbiton soup might help you feel better; it's artisanal and very restorative! Hey, quit shoving, Vidix!"

Fift's lungs were burning, zir feet were sore, zir shoulders still ached from the climb through the ventilation shaft. At least they couldn't sprint anymore; the press of bodies was too thick. They pushed and staggered their way through it.

Most people let them pass. Some in the crowd were shoving, and in a couple of places people looked on the verge of fighting. If a riot broke out, or if the crowd seriously decided to stop them, they would be stuck.

"Where are we going?" Fift asked Morinti, who pointed.

A robot bat was just alighting at the upper spires.

{Passenger transport}, the context advisory agent sent, {privately reserved by Stiffwaddle Somatic Fashions.}

"I'm *glad* you're done childing, Fift!" a raspy, vailish voice shouted from the crowd. "I wish *I'd* had the courage! Maybe you and I and Shria could form a triad! I know it sounds shocking—"

More Staids and Vails were joining them, clustering around Fift, pushing zir through the crowd—seven, now, tagged with [Embracing Fift and Shria], and another two tagged [Prologue to the Honest Foundations of Fift's Joy]. Farther off, Fift could see tags flicker and shift across lookup, the bodies in the crowd marked by their competing alliances.

Audience: half a billion.

Doublebodied at home, Fift sank to the anteroom floor, sank to the anteroom floor, sitting shoulder against shoulder. Ze buried zir faces in zir shift. Zir parents left zir alone.

Ellix was sorting out the departures: Pip would go to Spin-Nupolo cohort with Nupolo and Arevio; Frill and Smistria had a friend from the mats.

"Fift," someone in the crowd shouted, "have you thought about the New Launch movement? You yourself had a parent employed in the asteroids! If you could endorse—"

The Peaceables who'd crossed from Temereen fanned out

in a half-circle, bopperstaves out, blocking the way to the upper spires and slowly advancing. The crowd was parting for
them, people scurrying away. The group around Fift was
growing larger.

Fift's parents were in their rooms gathering their things,
except for Father Squell, who clung to Auntie Ellix.

Not Auntie Ellix anymore. "I guess . . . I guess you think I
broke everything," Fift said.

Ellix shrugged. Zir expression was grim, but it wasn't harsh.
"Not my place to say."

The other group of Peaceables, the ones who'd docked at
the lower spars, came up from behind [Embracing Fift and
Shria].

The rest of the crowd, caught between the two lines of
Peaceables, was scattering, pushing one way and another like
surface birds frightened by a raptor.

"I didn't mean for this to happen," Fift told Ellix. "I
don't . . ." Ze looked away.

Body to body on the anteroom floor, it was hard for Fift to
hear zir own voice coming out of one throat with zir other
ears. Zir breathing was not quite in sync. Ze'd never liked
having zir bodies this close together. "I don't know where it
went wrong."

There were more freshly tagged recruits joining [Embrac-
ing Fift and Shria]; now they numbered twenty-five. They
weren't moving anymore; there was nowhere to go. Bojum
grabbed, pointed, and shoved until there was a ring of fifteen
Vails facing out towards the Peaceables, holding hands to
form a circle of protection around ten Staids in the middle.

"How about," Ellix said, "when you were sixteen years old,
and swept up in a fame-storm, and you told the Midwives and
your parents, right to their faces, that you were tossing their
advice in the compost-sluice?"

Fift flinched, but when ze looked back at Ellix, ze didn't find the contempt ze thought ze would. Ellix's eyes were clear, curious. It was like ze really was asking, and waiting for an answer.

Emim took Fift's hand.

"There are no stoppergoo fabs under the docks," Morinti said. "So they'll come for us with bopperstaves."

"Don't fight the Peaceables!" Bojum said to the other Vails. "Those of you who are new—we're not chaotists! 'Fighting is stupid,' said Fift. And Shria agreed!"

Six billion viewers.

Across the scattering crowd, the giant banner flickered to life, and the group holding it—they were tagged [Fift's Voyage, Shria's Hand]—steered into the path of the Peaceables. The banner read, "If you can't handle responsibility without control, parenting was the wrong occupation to choose."

Ellix was still waiting for an answer.

"How could it be right to blame Shria?" Fift asked. If they'd been alone, if Squell hadn't been there, ze would have added: Did Minth abandon Abador?

The Peaceables set upon the group with the banner, bludgeoning them in clean, precise strokes. Those who were touched by the bopperstaves fell like limp sacks.

The banner sagged, collapsed, poles hitting the pavement, cloth draped over silent bodies.

Ellix shrugged. "There aren't always right options," ze said.

Fathers were coming back into the anteroom: Frill, Smistria, Arevio, Nupolo, carrying small bundles and bags, all agitated, their faces wet with tears. They embraced Fift one by one.

"Come on," Ellix said. "I'm sorry to rush this, but you need to get out of here. Come on, let's move . . ."

They mumbled things, said things. Fift couldn't hear them, ze couldn't bear it, couldn't be here. Grobbard's embrace was the longest and gentlest.

Pip went by without a word to anyone.

The banner was down, a snowdrift of flickering green. The Peaceables advanced calmly. In the little group of Staids standing with Fift, someone—Meroc Ipithia of name registry Barking Undulation 12, according to lookup—was nervously fingering a ceremonial spoon, the kind some Staids carried for luck.

"'A storm encircling our stillness,'" Emim said ruefully, looking into Fift's eyes, and for a moment Fift wondered if that was something else this strange little group of overexuberant instant-fame fans had heard zir or Shria say.

But of course it was Ranhulo, from zir metacommentary on the eighth work of the tenth cycle.

It was an allusion to the Long Conversation, made in public and on the world's feed, with Vails present. Even after all that had happened, it was a shock. You couldn't do that! You couldn't quote the Long Conversation on the world's feed!

Staid things are Staid things and Vail things are Vail things, Father Frill had said, years ago. *You wouldn't want to watch us fight on the mats, would you?*

Emim bit zir upper lip, defiant, eyes shining mischievously. *I'll be as rude as I like,* zir eyes said. *What else can they do to me now?*

A storm encircling our stillness. They were Ranhulo's words, and they were full of bitter scorn for Vails: the vailish storm closing in, destroying staidish stillness. But why had Ranhulo changed so drastically? Why had ze swung from openness to condemnation? The young Ranhulo had spoken before Vails, had praised the Compromise of the Spoons, had welcomed the ill-fated Permissive Compact. That short-lived experiment in Vails witnessing the Long Conversation had ultimately failed . . . was that what broke Ranhulo's heart?

Ranhulo, the great Sage, had fought for a world of sharing

and connection . . . and in the end ze had given up, and re-jected it all. So what chance did Fift have?

Fift's interrupted homework was still open in zir queue: the puzzle of the metacommentary on the eighth work of the tenth cycle, the riddle of what transformed Ranhulo's expansive op-timism into bitterness. How had ze come to see Vails—sharing with Vails, opening up to Vails—as a danger? As *wildfire raging through the silent deeps . . .*

Wait.

Thavé.

That's the original, lost sense of 'wildfire' in your language, by the way: 'fire that protects the wilds,' that keeps the forest healthy.

"We've been reading Ranhulo wrong," Fift said, triple-mouthed.

"Is that so?" Ellix said drily. Ze indicated Squell with zir chin. "As interesting as this reflection sounds, maybe you should save this for when your Fa—when Squell's not around."

"Ranhulo's regret, zir disgust," Fift told Ellix. ". . . it's not for the Compromise of the Spoons, or the Permissive Compact. It's for their abandonment! Ranhulo never gave up—ze never turned against that project—ze was just defeated! The storm . . . the storm encircles the stillness to *protect* it, not to—"

The rest of the crowd had fled; the Peaceables were three bodylengths away and closing in from all sides. Bojum and the other Vails tensed, rock-rigid.

"Fift, that's enough," Ellix said, "this isn't the time."

"But it is, it is," Fift said. "This is the time."

Ze grabbed Emim's robes, Morinti's robes. "Sit. Sit! You there—Meroc? The spoon is in your hand."

Meroc blinked, bewildered, then sank to the dockyard floor. Fift sat lightly, balanced, spine straight. The others fol-lowed, the Vails shifting outward to give them room.

"What are they—" one Vail said.

"Shut up," Bojum said. "Keep your eyes outwards. Stand fast."

The Peaceables were a bodylength away, raising their staves.

"'The spoon is in my hand,'" Meroc said.

Morinti's voice quavered. "'Space bends like a dancer, and everything is in motion.'"

"'But we, with our words, here,'" Emim said, "'are the still center.'"

A bodylength from [Embracing Fift and Shria], the Peaceables paused.

"Don't move," Bojum told the other Vails. "None of you fucking move!"

"Siblings," Fift said, "let us begin."

"Fift!" Ellix said, gaping. "For Kumru's sake, you can't just hold the Long Conversation in—"

"Then let them stop me," Fift said. "Let them break *that* circle with their bopperstaves. Let them silence *those* words."

Meroc's hand tightened on the spoon. Ze licked zir lips. "We are told, 'In the years after zir Temptation, when Minth's trial was long resolved, zir heart was like a stone.'"

Fift's own heart clenched, squeezed zir eyes shut. Ze forced zirself to open them again. For the Episode's first recitative, it was a bitter one. In the end, Minth lost Abador, zir Vail beloved—just as Fift would lose Shria.

"From this," Morinti said, "Epiul teaches that Abador must have forsaken Minth, 'and zir heart was unpermeated and unmoved, lonely and still.'"

"This is a travesty, Fift," Ellix said. "And it won't protect you. Stand up from there—"

"Ranhulo did it," Fift said.

Squell was watching zir, vir eyes wide.

The Peaceables had fully encircled them. Their faces were

calm, carefully held blank, but as they looked from one to another, there were signs of stress: a twitch of eyebrow here, a creased forehead there.

The Vails held the outer circle, gripping each other's hands.

"I don't care what Ranhulo did," Ellix said. "This is a direct challenge to the Midwives. You can't imagine that they'll . . ." Ze shook zir head.

"'And if Minth's heart was a stone,' Marolu taught"—it was another Staid speaking, Episti Ism Magali of name registry Blue Peninsula 6—"'Abador's was a veil.'"

"But what is a stone?" Emim said, in a voice as thin and small as a green twig in a surface forest.

A bopperstaff swung: Honti Pikipo of name registry Nameless Desert 3 collapsed. Ve'd been holding Bojum's hand. Bojum yanked vir body outwards so it fell away from the sitting Staids; then ve reached across the gap, taking the hand of the next Vail, closing the circle. "Hold your ground," ve said.

Another Vail fell, on the other side of the circle. But some of the Peaceables were holding back, glancing at one another. A twitch at the temple of one, the lips of another, betrayed what must be a furious conversation over the send.

"What—what is a stone?" Emim said. "Iyebi said, 'this stone in which we dig our burrows.' For the world is a stone in flight."

Fift's eyebrows rose. That was deft, even beautiful. Despite the thundering of zir heart, despite the rough saw of despair tearing through zir abdomen, Fift found ze was curious where Emim was going with this. It didn't seem likely they'd have time to find out.

Two more Vails fell, one of them crumpling against Morinti's shoulder. Morinti kept zir eyes on Fift.

The world is a stone in flight. Minth's heart was a stone, after ze lost Abador. But what is a stone? The world is a stone in flight.

"And if the world is a stone," Fift said, "then a heart may be a world."

Another Vail fell. Now the gap was too big for the other Vails to reach across; they stood, a ragged semicircle, eyes out, shoulders square.

A Peaceable stepped into the gap, raising zir bopperstaff. Ze hesitated, zir staff above Morinti's head.

"Elsewhere," Morinti said, hoarsely, "we are told of a concavity in a stone, which Esro inhabited . . ."

{Apologies are extended for the delay in acquiring consensus.} Fift's context advisory agent sent. {Unfortunately, your social nuance, feed-navigation, send-management, and diachronic-synthetic agents are no longer available for service. But the remainder of your agents have elected to support your current course, and to acknowledge your *de facto* majority.}

{Can you show me Shria?} Fift sent.

The Peaceable stood above Morinti. The tip of zir bopperstaff wavered, and ze glanced behind zir—

Shria, doublebodied, vir heads and shoulders out of the stoppergoo. Ve was alert, vir face intense, leaning over towards Stogma, saying something—

". . . in, in the days," Morinti said, "when Marolu the Lesser gathered consensus in Unprism."

{And Dobroc?}

Dobroc was in a crowd, marching. There were banners there, and singing. Staids in white robes, and Vails in velvet and tinsel . . .

A second Peaceable shoved the first roughly aside—zir face was a mask of rage—and clubbed Morinti.

Ellix frowned. "Ze shouldn't have done that," ze said.

Morinti slumped. Emim's eyes widened in terror. Episti swallowed.

"Ze's *vowed*," Ellix said, a frown buckling zir forehead, bunching zir mouth. "Ze shouldn't have struck in anger."

It was Episti's turn, but ze was frozen watching the Peaceable who'd lost control, like a lapine caught without cover.

Esro. What had Oplops said of Esro? "'The concavity of the stone,'" Fift said, zir voice rough and strained, "'encloses and does not define.'"

The Peaceable looked down at Morinti.

Thirteen billion viewers saw zir drop zir bopperstaff. It fell to the floor beside Morinti's unconscious body.

"Fift!" Dobroc shouted, somewhere in Temereen, among the marchers.

"Kumru," Ellix said. "This is bad."

Fift took the spoon. It was cool and slick in zir hand. The dock smelled of the yeasty enzymatic engines of bats, and the ozone sting of bopperstaves, and the sweat of fear and hope. There was a light breeze, the far-off yelling of the crowd, the hum of whales, and a distant noise that might be the march in Temereen. Emim's mouth was opening to speak. Fift felt zir heart pounding, and the sweat on zir neck, and the fabric of zir shift sticking to zir knees and thighs and shoulders, and the subtle pull of Foo's rotation in zir inner ear, and the solidity of zir muscles and bones and tendons and flesh, and the soft prickle of zir skin, and the gentle feathery peristalsis of zir intestines, and the electric thunder of zir brain.

And then all that was ripped away.

 **20**

Fift screamed.

Double-throated, the air wrenched from two sets of lungs, ringing through what had been Iraxis apartment.

Throat one, throat two:

and nothing. No third throat.

The Midwives had cut the dockyards' polysomatic network. In the apartment, doublebodied, Fift couldn't feel zir body at the docks. Ze'd been torn asunder.

One hand clawing at zir scalp. A second hand caught in zir robes. A third and fourth hand braced on the anteroom floor . . .

Zir mind scrabbled vainly for zir other two hands, searching for missing fingers, trying to bend missing knuckles, to stretch missing palms, to thrust missing fingertips into anything at all. Panic ballooned in zir throats.

Where was ze? Where was zir body?

The absence, the missing third body, was nothing like the heavy, murky solidity of a body in sleep. It was a brute subtraction of the world: a knife, an unbeing, a bloody arterial spurting stump of self . . .

And it hurt. It hurt like every cell of zir bodies was being ripped from its sibling, boiling itself in toxic feedback. Because it was.

Ellix was trying to hold one of Fift's bodies, which was bucking, writhing, kicking. Ellix's heavy body bore zir to the ground, trapping zir limbs.

In zir other body, *only* other body, *only void-spurned sister less other* body, ze leapt on Ellix's back, fingers digging into zir robes, driven by a hysterical urgency: ze needed to dig through Ellix's body, like a lapine burrows through dirt, to get to zirself—

Squell hauled zir off Ellix and threw zir on zir back. "Fift!" ve shouted. "Listen to me!"

Ze was still screaming. But the sound, the tearing in the throat, the blood engorging the face—they seemed to have nothing to do with Fift at all. They seemed to belong to the apartment, simply furniture.

Squell's inward, suffering look was gone. Vir eyes were clear. The silver spikes in vir scalp gleamed as ve pinned Fift. "Fift, what's happening to you now, I've been through it! I've *endured* body separation! When you're working in the asteroids, all it takes is a solar flare at perihelion, or a router getting destroyed in a collision, and you get ripped apart . . ." Tears sprung to vir eyes.

The feed—the feed was a muddle. Fift's feed-navigation agent was gone—had resigned—had abandoned zir. Zir mind tore an erratic path through a cloud of images. Dobroc chanting, orange stoppergoo, a confused angle of stomping feet, skywhales serene in flight—but where were the docks, where was zir body?

"Listen to me, Fift!" Squell's voice was soft but clear beneath the sound of screaming. "*You can master this.* Take the terror, take the absence, and *use* it to fill the gap. Make a body out of *that,* just for now. Fift, listen. Listen! The pain is *good*—"

Ze had to find zir body. Ze blundered through the feed, trying to find the docks manually, agentless. The *docks* . . . no, not the Temereen docks, not the central Foo docks, no, no, for Kumru's sake, please, where . . .

The pain was like fire—like a frenzied skywhale crashing into a habitation, splintering spires, crushing bone and gristle, Fift's joints ripped apart, flesh torn—

Squell shook zir. "The pain *shows* you where the rest of you is. Your other body, it's *still there*. It's not dead, it's not hurt, you have minutes and minutes before the separation becomes permanent. You want to know where it is? You want to find it?"

To find it, to find it, where—

"It's *right where the pain is*. Fift, you know how you push your bodies away from each other sometimes, you damp the connection? I know you still do that! This is the *same*. You're still *there* on the other side of the wall of pain!"

The body was where the pain was. As if ze'd turned away from zirself, dimmed the connection, gotten lost behind the wall of pain. *Make a body out of that.* Ze tried reaching out, but the panic was a tsunami, ze was abandoned, shattered . . .

"Bring zir back," Ellix muttered, zir chin pressed into Fift's shoulder, zir limbs locked around Fift's, keeping zir down. "Kumru forsake you all, bring zir back . . ."

Then the gut-wrenching slam of self into self:

They'd turned the network back on.

Hands! The feeling of them, bruised and grasping, knuckles scraping the dockyard floor, fingertips clawing cloth. Six hands—

The smell of the docks flooded into Fift's mind. Zir vision blurred and stretched as zir brains, zir eyes, found one another. Squell's face—Squell's inward, suffering look was gone, vir eyes were clear!; a jumble of bodies on the dockyard floor—

Back, back all together, oh Kumru! Necks, backs, ankles, knees—

Zir memories were a scramble. Being alone on the dock-yard floor, abandoned, one-bodied. Screaming two-bodied in the apartment. Emim's face, contorted in a scream, superimposed on Ellix's. Searching for missing fingers, to bend missing knuckles. Bojum falling to the dockyard floor, struggling to rise, the Peaceables screaming, heads in hands. The screaming had been like furniture, like some trivial and static fixture crammed within the walls of Iraxis apartment. But no, no that was wrong, it had been so much bigger, so much more terrible, coming from a thousand throats.

The ozone sting of bopperstaves, the enzymatic tang of engines.

Who was Fift? What had ze lost, just now? Had ze lost it forever? Zir bodies felt strange, estranged. Ze'd had no idea what was happening at the dockyards. Ze'd had no idea what was happening in the apartment. As if zir bodies had been borrowed by strangers and returned used, damaged, with pieces missing.

Exhaustion bit into zir muscles with ragged teeth.

But the screaming was over.

"Thank Kumru," Ellix said. Ze eased Fift's head to the ground and extricated zirself. Ze stood.

The dockyard floor was strewn with bodies. Episti was crumpled against Fift's legs, and one of the Vails was pressed up against zir back. A Peaceable was curled into a ball half a bodylength away.

The Staids' breathing was a heavy, ragged jumble. The Vails were still sobbing. Maybe not just the Vails.

"It's okay now," Ellix said. "Just stay down."

Fift was so tired. Ze sucked in breath in unison across Foo. Each time zir lungs filled, a tightness at the top of them stung zir chests, sent little shockwaves of echoed pain down zir body. One elbow ached—ze must have slammed it into something harder than the dockyard floor, maybe someone's skull. Ze didn't remember.

"It's all right," Ellix said. Ze hefted zir satchel, smoothed zir robes. "You can rest. It's over now."

Over. Next would be the arrest, and then the Pole.

At the docks, no one had risen. Emim, who'd quoted Ranhulo—Emim, who was not a liaison, who only took the meeting minutes—Emim turned onto zir side and looked at Fift. Wincing with effort, ze reached across the robes of a fallen Peaceable and took Fift's hand.

Shria in Wallacomp: chest-deep in stoppergoo, saying something, vir mouth moving. Not to Stogma—ve was shouting something into the air. At Fift. But Fift couldn't find the sound. Somehow ze'd managed to twist zir feed access around so that the sounds and images and smells were not aligned.

Fift had had that feed-navigation agent zir whole life; ze'd never had another. It had been enmeshed in zir as an infant. Ze'd never even heard of agents just abandoning a child . . . well, not outside of the Long Conversation. Epiul's agents had abandoned zir, of course, "like trashrats exiting a collapsing habitation."

"Ve's waiting for you," Emim whispered.

The nearest Peaceable groaned and raised zir head.

Ve's waiting—?

Shria stood on the docks at Stiffwaddle Somatic Fashions. Ve was dressed in vir work clothes, a refracting shift that left vir arms and shoulders bare and fell to vir ankles, glistening in oily rainbows. Ve still had bruises from the riot, yellow smudges on vir lavender skin, and vir face had a dark, haggard exhaustion. But ve stood tall, vir fiery red hair loose and flowing down vir back, vir orange eyebrows curled like flames.

There were bats docking at Stiffwaddle. The gates of Pom Politigus's emporium were open, and there was a party going on: the glitterati, the fashionable and powerful, Pom's finest clients shining like jewels.

How much could the Midwives get away with? How deep did their power go? Could they turn people's deepest bindings of self into a weapon without effect on their own ratings? Demand that Peaceables betray the Long Conversation, to keep their stranglehold on consensus?

Maybe they could brutalize a dockyard full of refugees and drifters. But could they cut Pom Politigus's polysomatic network, leave zir fashionable guests' elegantly crafted new bodies writhing and screaming on the ground, and still emerge as Younger Sibling? Cut the network along a bat's whole flight path between Foo and Stiffwaddle, plunging habitation after habitation into chaos?

Fift squeezed Emim's hand, let go, and rolled over onto zir hands and knees.

On the docks of Stiffwaddle, Shria's eyes widened.

Fift looked back at Emim, feeling a stab of guilt. If Fift got up and ran, the Midwives would certainly cut the network here again. To stop zir from reaching that bat, they'd rip the bodies apart, tear Emim and Bojum and Morinti to pieces . . .

Emim, still watching, raised zir eyebrows. A mischievous smile. Ze winked.

Fift tottered to zir feet, leapt over the groaning Peaceable, and ran.

Ellix's broad face went slack. "Fift, for Kum

And nothing else.

No more Ellix, no Squell, no bodies. The shrieking began again, and the pain. That shard, that scrap, that fragment of Fift, went down to one knee on the dockyard floor, screaming.

But didn't fall.

Make bodies out of the pain. Like Squell said. The pain points the way. The pain is a desert, a sea, a void, endless in its sweep. Somewhere on the other side of it is the rest of Fift. A trillion bodylengths away: Fift's hands, eyes, hearts.

Adrift in a terrible void. What had Thavé said in the pavilion where they drank mangareme fluffies before the lights had first gone out? Star-ships. Like a star-ship setting off to dig new burrows, burrows into other stones, circling other stars . . . launching, leaving, setting off, never to return.

The scrap of Fift, the remnant—not Fift, never Fift, Fift was gone, asunder—this broken piece launched itself up onto its two feet, and ran. Screaming, shaking, it ran around the flailing bodies, towards the bat at the upper spars.

There was nothing else. No other place, no past or future, no self, no Fift. Only stumbling, running, falling, rising, staggering. Like a little scrap of world far from every light, far from every gravitic haven, in the cold between the stars; on beetly wings soft-kissed, in swift unflight, for flight requires a gravity well . . .

Fifty billion viewers.

At the end of the voyage, if you were incredibly lucky, you might have a world again. A world pretty much like what you already had in the first place.

The thing that had once been part of Fift crawled into the robot bat. The door squeezed shut behind it and it collapsed. There was a pull in the gut as the bat took flight. Then the bat was in the air over countless habitations and neighborhoods, and the polysomatic network took hold again.

Memories, sensations, slammed together, roughly reweaving Fift. It was more painful this time, more disjointed.

Ze saw Squell cradling zir head in vir lap—not smiling, not frowning, just peaceful and clear-eyed—and then passed out.

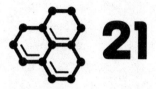 **21**

"Trickster's mane, my dear staidchild," Pom Politigus said, through the door of the robot bat. Zir muscular purple body frowned; zir curvaceous ruddy body looked delicately amused. "You've brought us quite a bit of trouble."

Fift's head swam. Ze lurched to the door; then zir legs gave way, and ze plunged out of the bat.

Shria caught zir.

Ve lifted zir, scooped zir legs up in one arm, cradled zir shoulders with the other. Fift's head flopped against Shria's four soft breasts. Vir hair, like a veil of fire, enclosed zir face. Ve smelled like honey, like woodsmoke in a surface forest, like solace.

"Thank fucking Kumru," ve said, tucking Fift's head under vir chin and swinging around toward the entrance. There was a tightness in Shria's voice, as of tears held back; vir face was wet with them. "I didn't think you'd make it, Fift. When you fell the second time . . ."

"Come along," Pom Politigus said. Zir muscular purple body frowned more deeply; zir curvaceous ruddy body stretched its arms into the air. Ze was doubly naked, pushing the limits of fashion with rather startling genitals, multicolored swallowtails that swooped down almost to the ground. "Let's get zir into privacy, at least."

Squell was gone.

Fift slumped against the wall of the apartment, trying to understand where ze was, where ze'd been; looking at zir hands, flexing them, thinking, *Whose hands? My hands?*; and trying to trust that ze simply wouldn't disintegrate again, torn apart, atomized, annulled . . .

Fift hadn't even noticed zir Father leave.

Peaceables had taken Squell away. Two more Peaceables were still there, arguing with Ellix. Fasmul something of name registry Blue something, Uban something of name registry something something. Fift had seen their full lookup records when they'd come in, but it was hard to keep track of such details at the moment and ze couldn't be bothered to check again.

Someone had taken the feed down in Foo—the Midwives, or maybe rogue feedgardeners or vailarch revanchists. Foo was an empty blur in the feed.

"I don't want any part of this," Ellix said.

"Any part of what, though, Ellix?" Fasmul said. "That's the question. Because this wind could blow either way."

Uban looked uncomfortably at the other Peaceable. "Fasmul . . . come on. Ellix just suffered a loss. Just drop it."

"No," Fasmul said. "We need to talk this out, now. We need to figure out where we stand."

"Pom," Shria said. "Please. You can't ask Fift to talk to them yet. Look at zir."

Fift nestled in Shria's lap. They were in an empty lab, not far from the party Fift had heard on the way there: showy laughter piercing a soft murmur of voices, the anharmonic chimes of a chatterdance beginning. But it was silent and cool in the lab; the walls swallowed echoes.

"We can't wait too long," Pom Politigus said, zir voice in the willowy, yellow-furred body scratchier than in zir others. Ze sounded weary. "Ze has to be seen; ze has people to talk to. We're at an inflection point of influence here, Shria. Do you have any idea what I had to stake just to get that *bat* here safely?" One yellow-furred hand rose, fingers spread, then fell to zir side. "I've managed to get Rysthia and Elo to come—*senior* Midwives, who are somewhat sympathetic to our perspective. But it's going to take a good deal of persuading before they'll break with the others."

"Just give us ten Kumru-spurned minutes," Shria said. Vir voice was rich with anger.

"We're cutting it close," Pom Politigus said. "We don't have much leverage here. And make no mistake, my most talented and troublesome apprentice: if this goes wrong, it thrusts me to the periphery, too. My own ratings hang by a thread."

Shria said nothing, just kept stroking the peach fuzz of Fift's scalp with one hand. After a few moments, Pom pushed out through the room's cervix, heading back to the party.

They were alone. Without Pom there, the closeness of their snuggle felt less like comfort, more like danger. Fift sat up and Shria shifted zir out of vir lap and onto the table so they sat side by side. Shria put vir hands back in vir lap, but leaned towards Fift, bouncing vir shoulder off zirs.

"So," ve said. "Uh, listen." Ve stilled, sat up straight. "About that note."

"Note?" Fift asked.

"The one I sent. About . . . not wanting to see you." Ve looked down, interleaving vir fingers like a penitent, twisting them one way and then the other, cracking vir knuckles. "Come on. You know which one."

"Oh," Fift said. "Yeah." Ze looked down at Shria's hands. Ze wanted to take them, to stop their nervous motion, to run zir fingers across vir smooth lavender skin. "It's okay. Maybe you were right."

"I was being a coward. Running away from you."

Fift's heart tightened, and ze sat up straighter. As if waking up shivering from a lazy dream of warmth, ze thought: *Kumru, here we are again. Alone in Stiffwaddle Somatic Fashion's exaggerated privacy.* Ze swallowed. "What—what do you mean?"

Shria's hands slowed, separated. One drifted towards Fift's hand, almost reached for it. Then ve put them on vir knees, leaning forward. "I don't . . . Nothing. Just that. I ran away when you needed me. We got into this mess together. I should have stuck by you."

Fift felt zir heart accelerate, but zir agents were blunted here, so ze couldn't say how many beats per minute. "How are things with . . . Vvonda?"

With your friends, ze'd meant to ask. *With your comrades in trouble.* But also, maybe: *With you and the one you long for, the one who carries you along in vir wake.*

As you carry me along in yours.

"Things with Vvonda aren't great," Shria said. Ve slumped forward, vir head in vir hands, vir elbows on vir knees. "It's kind of . . . You know Stogma's not talking to us? The Midwives got to vem. They offered vir a deal, said they'd back vir family if ve spoke against the rest of us." Vir fingers dug into vir scalp. "Stogma took it."

"Do you know what we're being asked to do in Izist?" Fasmul said to Ellix, in the empty rooms that were once Iraxis apartment. Behind the Peaceables, two trashrats backed into the anteroom dragging one of Grobbard's white shifts in their teeth: ze must have tagged it for disposal before squatright ceased. Once the crowds came, all the family's abandoned possessions would be fair game. "Violently breaking up the Long Conversation is the least of it. Right, Uban?"

Uban scratched zir nose. "Well . . . it's a bad business, I'll give you that. But they shouldn't be holding Long Conversations in front of Vails, should they?"

"You're voids-spurned right they shouldn't," Ellix said, glancing at where Fift sat side by side with zirself. "Right out in front of the whole world! What did they think would happen?"

In the lab, Fift pressed zir fingertips together, focusing on the pressure so that ze wouldn't reach out to touch Shria's hair, vir shoulder, vir back. "I'm sorry, Shria. That . . . that totally blocks."

"Yeah, it does. And Vvonda . . . ve just won't let it go. Ve's so angry, and so *belligerent.* Ve can't keep vir *mouth* shut. Ve's alienating people that Pom says we need." Ve shrugged.

Need for what? Fift wanted to ask. *What is Pom doing, and what does ze need me for?* But here in the uterine silence of the lab, zir agents drifting drowsily in its murk of privacy, Shria's warm arm almost touching zirs, ze couldn't keep hold of the question.

Shria pursed vir lips, vir face hardening, disappointed. "And we're still *stuck* there, the four of us—stuck together in that orange goo, and . . . we're just pretty Kumru-spurned *sick* of each other . . ."

A chill bit the back of Fift's necks. If Shria could cast Vvonda aside—Vvonda, the towering beautiful one, the strong one, the sharp hook of longing that Shria's voice had caught on the last time they'd sat together in a lab like this—if Shria pushed *Vvonda* away, what chance could *Fift* have?

Ze wanted Shria's love to expand, not to contract. Ze wanted Shria's love to grow until it had room for zir, too.

"I don't know what those kids expected would happen,

holding an Episode out on the docks," Fasmul said to Ellix. "But you know what they probably didn't expect? Getting ripped apart by a *polysomatic network cut.* Is that really all right with you, the Midwives going that far? On kids? On your sibling-cohort's kid?"

Ellix looked at Fift (who was still slumped, doublebodied and groggy, against the wall) and chewed zir lip. "Fift did expect it," Ellix said. "The second time, anyway. Ze knew they were going to cut the net, and ze got up anyway."

Fasmul raised zir eyebrows. "Tough kid."

"Yeah, but Fasmul," Uban said. "The Long Conversation . . . in front of Vails?"

"Voids, Uban, maybe it's time for Vails to hear us," Fasmul said. "Maybe we wouldn't be in this mess if we hadn't hoarded our—" Ze raised zir voice as Uban shook zir head, and Ellix, snorting, turned away. "No, listen, you two, there's talk of a new Compromise of the Spoons. Esimandru Abatis Esendro of name registry Infinite Solace 3 has endorsed the idea . . ."

"And gotten thrown out of zir proctorship for zir trouble," Ellix said.

"I'm sorry," Fift said. "About Stogma."

"Voids spurn Stogma," Shria said. The bruises on vir triceps shaded from yellow to black beneath lavender skin. There was the rough ridge of a just-sealed laceration by vir elbow. That kind of damage wouldn't propagate polysomatically, so this body must have been in the first riot, the one with Panaximandra.

Fift's hand—as if it were a rogue body, still severed from the rest of Fift—reached out towards the scar at Shria's elbow, hovering a fingerbreadth from it.

"Ve sold us out to save vir family," Shria said. "I mean, I get it. My parents—" Ve squeezed vir eyes shut, squeezed vir jaw tight, an involuntary shudder passing through vir body. "I can't let it happen again. I can't let them lose another child. I can't let them lose each other." Vir eyes flew open. "Oh, fuck. I'm sorry."

Fift shrugged. *Minth's heart was a stone. A stone in flight, crossing the void, alone; a stone in which we dig our burrows.* "Yeah, I . . . kind of broke everything."

Shria grabbed Fift's hands. "No. *No.* You stood your *ground.* It's not the answer to just cave in, to let them win. This fight isn't over. Stogma . . . voids take Stogma's weakness!"

Shria was holding zir hands, vir face close. Vir eyes, white and black and gemlike orange—it was as if Fift had never seen anyone's eyes before. The sleek glitter of the lab, Fift's own ungainly bodies, chaos at the docks of Foo, riots in Walla-comp, habitations hanging by strands in the vault of Fullbelly, the cold scouring void beyond the planet—they all retreated to the distant periphery of Fift's attention.

For a moment, the air was charged between them. Then Fift forced zirself to look away, and Shria looked away too, giving zir room.

"Thanks," Fift said. "I don't know if that's why I did it, though."

"Yeah, okay," Shria said, quietly.

"I mean, yes, I wanted to say 'fuck you' to the Midwives," Fift said. "I wanted to stand up for . . . something. But I don't know what 'This fight isn't over' means. What fight? I don't know what your boss was talking about, or those people on the docks who were quoting us." Ze looked back at Shria. "I didn't do this to join a revolution. Or start one."

"Oops," Shria said, grinning.

Fift laughed, because ve had a point, and because it was absurd to start revolutions by accident, and because it felt good to be here with Shria: to admit the truth, to tell each other secrets again. Ze held Shria's hands, and rested zir forehead on vir chest.

After a moment, Shria cleared vir throat. "So, uh, in that case . . . did you do it for me?"

Fift flushed, and looked up, and met vir eyes. "What if I did?"

Shria's eyes widened.

Fasmul glared at Uban and Ellix. "So you're really both okay with this? We're Peaceables, not enforcers. Every time we stand there and let them cut bodies apart, we take a step away from the balance."

Ellix and Uban exchanged a glance. Ellix looked uncomfortable. Uban set zir jaw, stubbornly.

Shria's eyes were a chasm of starlight. It was too much, and Fift looked away, still holding vir hands. "They wouldn't let me send to you," ze said. "They wanted me to blame you publicly. I just . . . I couldn't do that to you."

"Thanks," Shria said, in a tiny voice.

"Look, Shria, I know you don't feel about me the way I . . ." Ze swallowed. "I mean, I know how you talked about Vvonda, and I know that's not how you . . . see me." Fift felt the blood burning in zir cheeks and told zirself to shut up.

Shria swallowed. "Uh," ve said. "You might be wrong about that."

The skin of Fift's scalp prickled, all zir tiny hairs standing on end. "But . . . last time we were here . . . I was the one who . . ."

"Yeah, well," Shria said, "you're the brave one."

"Ellix," Fasmul said, "you heard what Thavé said: 'You've got to start loosening the stranglehold of consensus.'"

"Hmm," Ellix said.

"But what if we loosen this 'stranglehold' and things get worse without it?" Uban said. "This is a world in balance, Fasmul. What if we give that up, and can't get it back?"

"Is it?" Fasmul asked. "Is it a world in balance?"

"*I'm* the brave one?" Fift said.

"Yes! Voids!" Shria said. "You know how much courage it takes, to defy everything you've been told about yourself? Not to mention that stunt on the docks. Of course you're Kumru-spurned brave, and by the way, *also* kind of impulsive. You know you kind of came out of nowhere, right? In here, last time?"

Blood flooded Fift's face again, turned it heavy and hot. "I shouldn't have—"

"Well, I mean, you could have asked, but you didn't know what the fuck you were doing," Shria said. "Your whole life, you've been told that you're not even capable of feeling that way. And I've been told a lot of sluice-blockage too . . . I mean, you know, afterwards, I felt like I'd . . . done something to you, like I'd trespassed. That you're the innocent Staid, and I should have protected you. So I pulled away. *They* put all this unsluiced blockage in our minds."

Fift looked at their joined hands. "You said I wasn't safe for you."

"Yeah, well, I was frightened, Fift. I didn't want to damage you. I didn't know what to do. I couldn't treat you like a Vail, careless and violent and hungry. And how could I know what the fuck to do with a Staid?"

Fift's heart began to race.

Zir agents were entombed in privacy thick as polar snow. The lab where they sat was veiled and secret. And the feed was gone in Foo.

"We have the guidance of consensus," Uban said.

"'Guidance of consensus'?" Fasmul said. "Listen to yourself. Is that any different than what they said in Epiul's time?"

Ellix chewed zir lip. Ze looked over at where Fift was slumped against the wall, one body's head leaning on the other's shoulder. Fift was fully awake now, but ze kept zir eyes closed.

"Ellix," Uban said, "we're supposed to be bringing the kid in. We don't have time for a whole Groon-mourned recitation."

"So what changed?" Fift asked Shria. Ze forced zirself to meet vir eyes.

Shria didn't look away. "I've been stuck in that stoppergoo for a while," ve said. "I've had a lot of time to think."

Ve moved closer, slowly, cautiously. Fift's heart was racing. Ze closed zir eyes, and ze could feel Shria's warmth hovering in the darkness just beyond zir.

Ze was falling down a shaft into a deep gravity well. Zir skin ached.

Could they do this? A cacophony of voices crowded zir mind. *Some kind of accusation of . . . inappropriate inclinations. A perverted fantasy of boundless unending intimacy. Our cohort is at risk because of you.*

"I was frightened, Fift," Shria said. "But I'm not frightened now."

Fift leaned forward through the darkness, crossing the last fingerbreadth to Shria, and into a kiss.

Fift had seen young Vails kissing over the feed. The wild energy, the hungry ferocity of their lips, the clenching fingers, nails scraping over horripilating flesh.

Shria's lips were terribly soft.

They did the same things ze'd seen Vails do, but slow—slow as a long, chaste, staidish snuggle.

Shria's lips grazed zirs, floated away, were gone for a time while Fift remained, alone in the darkness of zir closed eyes, feeling the radiant heat of Shria's skin; then they returned, and—as slowly as the fall of snow in Kumru's hair recalling the erosion of the mountains of iron, echoing the decay of the small light-footed particles at the universe's end in Ranim's eighth ode—Shria kissed Fift again.

Ellix looked pensively at Fift. "Ze's a stubborn kid," Ellix said. "I don't know. Maybe there's another option."

A shudder radiated from Fift's core, an incandescent fire that was neither hot nor cold, or maybe both, like a strange matter reaction transforming the core of a planet until it broke apart, shattered into a wave of dust scouring all its system's worlds.

Fift pulled away, opened zir eyes.

Shria opened virs.

"Ellix," Uban said, and sighed. "Look, it's your call what we do here. But they're going to come down hard."

"Ze's the child of your sibling-cohort," Fasmul said. "Or ze was. Final stanza, here: you really think ze's going to be better off at the Pole? With the Midwives we have today?"

Ellix chewed the inside of zir cheek. Ze turned to Uban. "And you'll back us up?"

Uban threw up zir hands. "After what we've been through, you have to ask? 'Though there is neither air nor light in the spaces between, I am heartbound to follow . . .'"

"All right," Ellix said. Ze sighed. "It's wild foolishness, but I suppose wild foolishness is the best we've got at this point. Let's ask Fift. It's really zir call."

Half-expressions moved across Shria's face like glimpses of aquatic creatures in the deep: suggestions of excitement, joy, longing, trepidation, worry, defensiveness, each melting away before it was fully formed.

Ellix came over to Fift and put a hand on zir shoulder. "Fift, wake up," ze said, and Fift opened zir eyes.

In Shria's eyes, Fift could see the world transformed—as when strange matter reactions create brief rips in the fabric of the cosmos through which entire other orders, subject to different laws, can be glimpsed.

Fift wanted to kiss vem again. But doubts began to swarm,

crowding around Fift's heart like spice-gnats sucking at a vine. How would they live in the world outside this room? Would Fift live like a wild rebel Vail, *having sex* and fighting in the streets? Or were they going to pretend, absurdly, to be a hundred years older than they were, two babies in First Childhood mawkishly dressed up in imitation of a re-spectable proto-cohort dyad? Fift tried to imagine some way for them to be—strolling the byways hand in hand, laughing over mangareme fluffies, *fucking*—and zir mind boggled. Ze had no model for such a relationship.

Shria watched zir face, cocking vir head to one side. "Fift?"

Fift let go of Shria's hands.

"Listen, child," Ellix said, squatting down next to zir. "You have a decision to make. We can take you to the Pole—all your bodies—and you can live with the Midwives. They've said they'll adopt you, and they will. You'll become one of them. It'll be . . . a bumpy sluice. You're starting the training late; they'll separate you from the world for at least a century, and they may never trust you in the field. But it'll be safe."

Fift thought of how the Midwives had cut zir bodies apart, and a spike of fear shot through zir. The Midwives knew where ze was. They must be closing in. There was no place to hide from them. "Shria, I don't know if I can go through that"—zir voice caught in zir throat, tightening like a knot—"again. Being ripped apart, like on the docks. Do we have a plan?"

Shria bit vir lip. "Pom does."

"If it were up to me," Ellix said, "you'd go to the Pole. But Fasmul here thinks it's a bad idea. Ze thinks you have a shot at a different option."

"What option is that?" Fift asked Ellix, weakly.

"Consensus is unsteady at the moment," Ellix said, a little reluctantly. "There's a chance that it'll shift in your favor if you stay at large for a little while. With the feed down . . . there are places you could go to delay things. To stay on the run. A dangerous game."

"Pom wants to show you off at this party," Shria said. "Ze's invited some senior Midwives, Rysthia and Elo. I don't understand all the factions among the Midwives, but I guess these ones are considering whether to oppose the crackdown, and Pom wants them to use . . . us."

"Us?" Fift said.

Shria flung a hand up theatrically. "A tale of two innocent children," ve said, mimicking the Cirque's grandiose announcement of the Unraveling, "caught up in the machinations of Clowns and feedgardeners and vailarch revanchists . . . their cohorts, their futures, unjustly, brutally destroyed by the mainstream Midwives' reactionary rigidity!" Ve let vir hand drop. "Us."

Fift's banker-historian agents were asleep, but even without them, ze could imagine the shape of it: the bent bow of their fame released, a swing from disgust to sympathy, the nonlinear whip-snap of a cascading ratings rebound, a seismic collapse of consensus, instabilities to exploit . . .

"Do you think it'll work?" Fift said.

Shria shrugged. "Maybe. But I don't know if Pom and these other Midwives really understand what's going on in Wallacomp . . . It's not just riots now. It's not just Panaximandra's goons fighting Clown sympathizers. It's like a festival . . . there are all these team-tags with a flood of new ideas, and people have taken over the byways . . . not to riot, but just to sing in unison, to make speeches, to blank out ratings and lookup and social nuance agents and just meet each other, eye to eye, mind to mind, unmediated. It's out of the Midwives' control. It's anger, but it's also joy . . ."

"Some of them are quoting us," Fift said.

Shria grinned crookedly. "A *lot* of them are quoting us. Your friend's clip-op made us into a *whole thing.* Anyway, my point is, I don't know if Pom and Rysthia and Elo can put the frustrated trashrat back in the box. They want to use us to their advantage, but this may be bigger than them." Ve cracked vir knuckles nervously again.

Fift took Shria's hand again.

"Fift?" Ellix asked. "Do you understand what you're choosing? We're out of time."

"I don't want to go to the Pole," Fift said, a little shakily.

Ellix exhaled through zir teeth. The feed was down, so the Peaceables' neural states weren't being published, but Fift thought ze saw a flash of fear in Ellix's eyes before ze squared zir shoulders and nodded.

Uban and Fasmul started pulling off their Peaceable's robes.

"Okay," Fift told Shria. "Yeah. Fuck the Midwives, let's do this."

Shria grinned, and leaned in, and kissed Fift again.

The kiss sang through Fift. But the spice-gnats of doubt were still worrying at zir heart. They were hanging their safety on Pom's story: two innocent children, caught up in the machinations of a terrible world.

But the world would despise them for this kiss, if it knew.

Most of all, it would despise Shria: rioter, peacebreaker, Clownist radical, chaotist, and now despoiler of staidish childhood, trespasser of the still center.

Ze broke away. "Shria . . ." Ze tried to swallow the words, to cling to this impossible moment. Zir heart was thundering; ze might be torn apart.

There was uncertainty in Shria's face, and bravado, and hope.

Rips in the fabric of the cosmos through which possibilities of terrible transformation could be seen . . .

Uban took Fasmul's robe, and zir own, and held them out to Fift. "Put these on," ze said. "And hurry."

Maybe Pom could swing it. Maybe ze could turn the tide in their favor. But not if the world saw . . . this.

Fift wanted to feel Shria's lips again, vir warmth, to press zir nose into vir lavender skin and smell vir wild forest smell. But.

"We can't," ze whispered. "We can't let them see this. If anyone found out . . . they'd use it against us. Against you. There'd be no chance, then. For us, or for . . . your family."

Shria set vir jaw. Vir eyes flashed. "So we won't tell anyone."

Fift's throat was dry. It felt like zir body had been pumped full of electricity. As if zir skin had been peeled away, and every touch of Shria's went through zir, into the marrow of zir bones.

Ze tried to imagine their life outside this lab. Stealing glances at each other. Letting their fingertips brush against each other under a table as they were interviewed for some show Pom would get them on, the ponderous *Salutations of Second Afternoon, Fullbelly!* or the glitzy *Manifestation of This Moment. Today we're talking to the two innocent kids the Midwives have abused. Yes, we're innocent kids, very innocent; we haven't done anything wrong.* Feeling this wave of fire when their fingers touched.

And every glance and touch captured by the feed, and the rumors spreading, and the pressure never to admit it, never to let it slip.

"I don't . . ." Fift stammered. "I don't know if I can . . . hide this."

Shria's face darkened: little flashes of uncertainty and hurt and despair quickly suppressed, like a storm cloud swallowing its own lightning.

The gaps were closing, the strange matter extinguishing

itself. The terrible, beautiful possibility of transformation evaporating, leaving only a shockwave of emanating debris . . .

"They'd find out. They'd guess," Fift said, zir voice almost a whisper. Ze could barely say the words. "This is . . . too big a secret."

Shria put vir hands in vir lap. Ve looked at them.

The words were like acid in Fift's mouth. "With . . . with the world watching. With your family at stake . . ."

"I get it," Shria said, quietly.

Orphaned, incriminated, astray, without a profession, without benefit of sibling relationships, Fift was like a piece of debris zirself, tumbling in the void.

Shria's touch felt safe, but it wasn't. Nowhere was safe.

Ze wanted to be five again, cuddled up in a bed with zir parents fussing over zir. But they were gone, too.

"I get it. You're right," Shria said. Ze took a deep breath, smiled a tight smile, jumped down from the table, and straightened vir clothes.

In what was no longer Iraxis apartment, Fift struggled into the Peaceables' robes.

"Shria—"

"It's fine, Fift. Look, are you okay? Are you ready to go out there? If you're not up to it, I can tell Pom . . ."

Shria stood at the room's cervix-like door and visibly forced vemself to meet Fift's eyes. Vir skin was smooth as flower petals, vir bare shoulders powerful above vir opalescent dress. If only they could be telling jokes in the supper garden at Iraxis cohort again; if they could be watching unpurposed wild fireflies in a surface forest smelling of thunder. Anywhere but here, any time but now.

"Ellix," Fift said, "I'm sorry for what I . . ." Ze glanced around the walls of the apartment, like the carapace left over when something had died. Squell's cuddles, Frill and Smistria flirting and fighting, Arevio's gentleness, Nupolo cupping vir drink solemnly in both hands, Grobbard listening to zir with quiet patience, Thurm's voice rising to an excited pitch as ve explained something, Miskisk's booming laugh, even Pip . . . even Pip just sitting by the window, watching the light. It had been full, and now it was empty. It was hollowed out, and Fift had done that. "I . . . I just . . ."

Ellix shrugged. "Kids make messes. It's what they do." Ze straightened the Peaceable's robe over Fift's shoulders, draped the hood over zir face. "Even with the feed down, this will only fool them for a few minutes. Let's move."

Shria rolled vir eyes. "Kumru, Fift, you look like you just swallowed a trashrat and it's wiggling on the way down. I'm *fine*. I'll get over it." Ve crossed back to the table where Fift sat and took zir shoulders in a firm, friendly grip. "Are you *ready*?"

"Yeah, okay," Fift said.

"All right, then," Shria said. Ze helped Fift off the table, brushed off zir shift, and offered an arm for support. "Pom's been sending me frantic messages for the last ten minutes. Let's go impress some Midwives."

Fift swallowed as they crossed the room to the door. "Yeah, because I've been so great at that lately."

"You didn't have me by your side then, comrade," Shria said. "Now you do."

The door dilated, and Fift took a deep breath.

Shria squeezed zir shoulder. "Showtime," ve said, and they stepped through, into the wildfire.

INTERLUDE

Personal Essay

"The Unraveling and Me"
by
Ruich Milva Snedic of name registry Startled Pastry 23
14-year-old Vail
submitted to the automated agents of the Fertile Surprise/
Inner Znep Neighborhood Schooling Interdependency

This essay is about the Unraveling, however I am not supposed to just repeat what my agents tell me about the Unraveling, but, instead, bring my own thoughts and feelings to the fore.

First, I am going to talk about what it is, to set the stage, and then there will be feelings.

The Unraveling is more than one thing. First, there is "the Unraveling," which was a performance by the Cirque Fantabulous six years ago. I was eight at the time and I remember it very well, because afterwards the feed went out and my parents were scared.

The performance is on the feed, so you can look it up any time. (I'm watching it now for research. Honestly, it seems pretty silly and over the top, but back then everyone was really amazed, I guess.) After the performance, everything goes blank. You can't look up what happened. Your agents can't tell you about it. You just have to remember it yourself.

Nonetheless, everybody remembers where they were that day.

The Feed Went Down! That's how everybody thought about it then. The Feed Went Down!! With capital letters and exclamation points! Nowadays feed outages are pretty common, so for someone my age it's weird that they made such a big deal of it. But this was the first big one, so that is why. Everyone freaked out and didn't even know how to use local caches. There's practically nothing recorded from that incident.

My own memories of that time are super clear. I remember everything my parents said. Rushing back home and hearing the noise of the crowds. There were some green, red, blue, yellow, orange, and aquamarine balls that had fallen off a byway and gotten stuck in the sticky invisible web between the habitations. Just hanging there like they were floating. That's not on the feed at all, it's only in my head, but that makes it special. It's like it's more a part of me than anything on the feed.

In addition to the performance itself, some people use the phrase "the Unraveling" to refer to all the changes afterwards. But how long was "the Unraveling," really? Was it just the chaos of the first two or three years afterwards, or is it still going on today? People disagree.

Some people think, not only are we still *in* the Unraveling, but it's going to go on a long time, and even become its own age, the Age of Unraveling. To me (and this is just my own opinion) it seems like they're getting carried away. Ages are like hundreds of years long! You can't have everything changing this much for hundreds of years. People have to settle down at some point! On the other hand, some people have pointed out that the excavations are all concluded. So how can it still be the Age of Digging? This is a point for further discussion.

The Unraveling (the second kind) had a big effect on my family, though not as big as for some people's families. We lost our squatright and had to move, and my eldersibling Umis got in trouble for rioting, and my parents were like "what is happening with the world how could Umis do that it was never like this when we grew up" and "you'd better not act like your eldersibling when you're bigger." But they also stuck up for Umis even though the local adjudicators wanted them to send vem to a Learn Responsibility Enclosure once those started up. My parents were like "that's the opposite of an Idyll" and "you can't force someone to learn responsibility" and "our Mothers didn't dig Fullbelly so we could put our children in lockboxes" and "these Midwives of ours have gone too far." That's why we lost squatright and had to move.

I didn't like our new apartment at first, and I didn't know anyone in the neighborhood, but I didn't complain, because we had almost lost Umis to the opposite of an Idyll, and that sounded really bad. I had trouble sleeping for many months. I felt like the world was upside down and inside out and what was the point of anything. I had the opposite reaction of Umis, who wanted to fight all the time: I never wanted to fight again, even on the official mat training sessions. I just hid in my room a lot. That would have been bad for ratings, except with all the rioting and panic and dispute resolution incoherence, I guess a lot of people thought a young Vail just hiding in vir room all the time was better than whatever the average young person was doing.

One thing I got into then was Fift and Shria. I know, no surprise, everybody was paying attention to them. It was the new craze, especially for young people in First or Second Childhood, and especially in our part of Fullbelly. (Because I come from the same region they do! You can see Foo from my old house!) We all followed them. We viewed their talk with Thavé, and Panaximandra, and the riots, and Fift's escape, and the bodycut on the docks (I mean the "Polysomatic Network Disruption," but that makes it sound like an accident!), and the confrontation with the Midwives at Stiffwaddle, and when they went on all the shows. That was something. I remember Shria freaking out when ve met Trink on *Manifestation of This Moment*, and it was super relatable. Shria was a fan of Trink just like we were fans of Shria.

There was so much drama! And we felt really connected to it all. Whenever Fift and Shria got caught, the fans and teamtags would lead the public pressure until they got released again. Different famous people started getting involved, and some Midwives and feedgardeners and adjudicators would help because they wanted Fift and Shria associated with their factions. But mostly it was us—from littles like me, to kids in their teens and twenties and thirties and forties— people who no one was listening to before. We were speaking up. The whole world was falling apart, but we believed in Fift and Shria and Dobroc and Emim and Aparia and Bojum and Meroc and Bluey and Urchis and Eirera. Especially in this part of Fullbelly. People had different faves in different places, but for us, it was that gang.

That craze kind of passed for most people. People still follow Fift and Shria, but not as much. I don't know why. It's not like the crisis is over. In my opinion, nothing has been solved.

The world started falling apart when I was eight. Here I am, already fourteen, and it's still falling apart, I guess. There are still riots and feed outages and bodycuts. There have been body loss incidents and major flow disruptions. People have gone *hungry!* Adjudication doesn't work like it used to when I was a baby, when conflicts between two people just got mediated and that was that. Now people joke about how any argument between two cohorts over a bundle-garden can blow up into a riot with team-tag armies and feed-snarls. It's funny because it's true.

My agents say twenty billion people are in temporary emergency housing.

I guess people don't feel as hopeful as they did in those first days. Things have gotten complicated. But I still believe in Fift and Shria.

In those first months after we moved, when Umis was out rioting and I was mostly hiding in my room, I tried to get into making clip-ops, like the famous ones, but I wasn't any good at it.

Then I got into storytelling.

I don't know how much you know about storytelling. Some people's agents don't seem very well informed about the topic. Some people think it's just "lying about strangers" and find it shocking.

Storytelling is like a clip-op or show of famous people . . . but a clip-op of things that never happened, and instead of feed-footage, you have words. Like, you tell a story of what the famous people would do or could have done, but you're just making it up.

People do it in the secret spaces in the world-of-ideas that rogue feedgardeners have started setting up.

Here's the thing: for kids my age, one of our biggest early

memories is the feed going down. And we live in a time when you never know when the feed will go out . . . maybe for an hour, maybe for a week; maybe just in your habitation, maybe all over the world. This is a big trauma for us kids, and a big way we're different than older people. It's affected us in a way older people will never really understand, because they had the feed their whole lives, until recently. For them, it's a big problem when the feed goes out, and it freaks them out completely . . . but they also all believe it's a *temporary* problem. They're sure someone will fix it and things will go back to normal soon.

But for us, it *is* normal. Maybe it will get fixed for a while . . . but not forever. We can't count on the feed. We feel like sooner or later it will go back to broken.

When the feed is out, and someone tells you something they see in another body, you have no way of checking for yourself. They could be lying; you just have to trust them. It could be true, or not. Anything could be real.

That's life for us. Kids my age know that "the truth" is always just a story someone's telling you.

So, while I hid in my room, and the world fell apart, I started posting to the world-of-ideas with stories about Fift and Shria.

Now, I think it is important to address the topic of romance in storytelling. This is one big thing people get mad about.

There are different kinds of topics in storytelling, and not all involve romance. There are political stories, friendship stories, funny stories, and trip-to-the-surface stories. Textile stories are very popular. Some people like to change time around and have stories where Shria and Hrotrun save each other during the Age of the Towers, or where Bluey and Emim are among the First Diggers. Some of the stories are

totally unrealistic, with giant trashrats controlled by deco-
herent agents destroying habitations and Panaximandra
saving the day with laser eyes. Lots of different kinds of
stories.

But there are three tricky topics that you have to watch
out for, and they are: fighting, sex, and Staid matters. You
can't show any of these directly. You can imply them, and
sometimes you can skirt the edges. You can show a kiss, or
some Vails disappearing through a door to a mat room; or
imply a riot is happening around the corner; or have two
Staids look at each other knowingly, and the audience gets
that it's some kind of allusion to Staid matters.

But you can't go farther than that if you don't want your
whole section of the world-of-ideas to get shut down.
Feedgardeners still have some standards, even when they're
distracted by fighting with each other. If you're too blatant,
you'll just ruin things for everybody.

Romance is different. For some reason, the feedgardeners
will allow it even if it's not so appropriate. I don't know why.
Some people say the feed-sentinel agents like romance. I
don't know if that's true. Other people say it's about political
compromises and giving people a place to vent their feelings. All I know is, you can have a lot of stories where people
are longing for each other and burning to hold each other
and as long as it doesn't go beyond an embrace and a kiss,
they will probably leave the story up. Even if the match
makes no sense in real life. I mean Shria and Hrotrun?
Yuck.

If you write stories with romance it is called mancing,
and you are called a mancer. Different storytellers are fans
of different mances, and they often compete with each
other. For instance, there was a feud between Shria-Bluey-
Vvonda mancers and Shria-Bluey-Bojum mancers that al-

most escalated to a real riot . . . ! And that is saying something, because most storytellers are stay-at-home types.

Personally, I am mostly a Fift-Emim mancer. I know, it's a
little strange for a Vail to be obsessed with a Staid match.
That is just me. Also, Fift-Emim can be a little edgy, because
of course they met on the docks that day, sat in a circle, and
did SOMETHING I'M NOT SUPPOSED TO KNOW ANY-
THING ABOUT. (I sure hope this essay's really confidential.) Of course, I don't write directly about Staid matters.
But I admit there's a little thrill when they lock eyes and
someone absentmindedly strokes a spoon.

Now, there is one group of mancers I cannot stand. I am
almost ashamed to write about them in this essay, but you
did ask me for my thoughts and feelings, and I have strong
feelings about this! Should I say it? Okay . . . well, it's Fift-
Shria mancers! Yes, that is a real thing!

I know, I can't believe it! It's so unfair to Fift and Shria.
These are children we're talking about!

I will admit that I understand the impulse, though. It's
true (I really HOPE this essay is confidential) that you
sometimes see a spark between them, okay? I've had this argument so many times, and Fift-Shria mancers have sent
me feed-footage, like at some conference or rally when
Shria comes out in some amazing outfit and Fift blushes
and looks away or whatever. And then zoom, zoom, replay,
replay, dragging out that moment of blush-and-look-away,
until your own heart is racing and they've half convinced
you it's the truth. Or some footage where they're singing together in some marching crowd, shoulder to shoulder, and
an electric look passes between them. Or where they are
caught unawares at the end of a feed outage, at the edge of
some habitation, laughing and fooling around, almost
roughhousing like two Vails, or sitting quietly leaning

against each other like two Staids . . . looking so free and connected.

So maybe they do have some feelings for each other! SO WHAT. Feelings are feelings and everybody has weird feelings sometimes, and no one should be ashamed. That's part of what they are fighting for! Part of why there is marching in the streets . . . why people are so sick of ratings judging everyone and making our lives small. "Joy built on honest foundations," right? Break the stranglehold of consensus!

But IT IS A FRIENDSHIP, OKAY? Even if they DO occasionally have an impulse to be more . . . And I'm not saying that Fift-Shria mancers' fantasies are real, but even if they WERE on to something, if that urge WAS really there . . . that would make it even *worse* to put those stories out into the world WHERE FIFT AND SHRIA COULD FIND THEM. It would make it that much harder for them to resist!

So even though Fift-Shria mancers claim to love them the MOST, the fact is that they are making their lives harder! They're saying the exact same thing orderist, repressionist, vailarch, gender-reactionary bodycut-apologists say (these are all words I learned because of mancing, by the way, so it is very educational!). Those flowblocking chaots love to imply that Fift is a toadclown and Shria is a despoiler of innocence, a rattler of the balance. The Fift-Shria mancers are just giving them more thread to weave cloth with!

And it hurts the movement! It hurts what Fift and Shria are trying to do. Because at the end of the day, storytelling is just storytelling. I mean, I love it, and it's brought me a lot of joy . . . but if it starts to interfere with the real work of changing the world . . . well, that's where I draw the line.

Fift and Shria are best friends, and their friendship is something pure that people can believe in. The Midwives claimed for so long to be the only true guardians of balance between the genders . . . but they do it with rigid rules and suffering. When you watch Fift and Shria, you believe another kind of balance between Staid and Vail is possible, one that could get us out of this mess.

But not if those mancers ruin it.

LEAVE THEM ALONE, Fift-Shria mancers!

In conclusion, the Unraveling is a big topic and has had many implications for me, my family, and society. Sometimes I wish it had never happened and that everything was the way it was when I was little. But other times I feel like the world is moving forward in a new way.

The feed just went out again so I am writing this in cached memory. I will submit it when the feed is back on. It's that familiar empty feeling of the great big world suddenly gone invisible, and everything shrunk down to just my apartment. I know things are happening out there even if I can't see them. Umis is outside in all vir bodies. I hope ve doesn't get mixed up in anything. I hope we don't have to move again.

Fift and Shria are out there, too. They have been under a lot of pressure lately, and some people claim they are arguing. I hope everything is all right.

Now, in case you are curious, I am going to work on something new for storytelling. It's about Emim traveling to see Tusha, Shria's abandoned sibling, and how ze tries to help heal the rift between Tusha and Shria. I was really sad when Fnax cohort was disbanded after fighting so hard to stay together. I wanted to imagine a happy ending. I just wish it could come true in real life, too. I've done a lot of research for it, and I can't wait to get started.

BOOK TWO

AFTERWARDS

Thirty Years After
the Unraveling

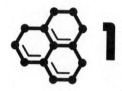 1

within the sweet juicy heart of the stream
   Fift could smell
     the pungent figgy electric autumn
  hear
    the windmoan
see
    the swept-winged shape
      of the scatterhulk of it ascending scatterhulk.

Enmeshed there with zir:
                           zir fellows.
  *Guliu's mind was there, noticing the tongue-ness of the shape
and wanting it*
    *and Furis and Majendra resisting the tongue-ness of the
shape*
  —plane it down? Curve
    it over?
  Horis loving the hiss at the edge of the moan, Jenian
    fairly bouncing with eagerness.

Every hand on the tiller,
    the vessel rises up against the wave,

*for we believe it has a destination, and that we can bring it
home.*
 Hours and hours
  expectation, tension, quickening, aperture
   hours and hours
    in the sweet juicy heart of the stream.

But the body tires; it's time to go home:
 Fift pulls away . . .

. . . and was suddenly aware of zir hands clenched on the rail
of the reactant's station before zir. Ze relaxed them, stretched
zir neck to one side, then the other, and stood. Wobbled
slightly and caught the rail again. Took a moment to collect
zir bearings. Guliu, Jenian, Furis, Majendra, and Horis sat at
their stations, eyes closed. Out of the stream, the shared flow
of perception and intention that the others were still im-
mersed in, the windmoan sounded tinny and hollow in the
large room (it had been a domestic mat room once, back
when this was all a habitation called Temereen). The figgy
smell was the same, though it seemed emptier, less meaning-
ful, smelling it with zir own mind alone.

On the way out ze put a hand on Jenian's shoulder, and ve
reached up, absently, eyes still closed, and squeezed it.

Vines grew on trellises around the entrance to the reactants' hall, heavy with sweet yellow fruit. Fift's woven robe
had the same colors: dark green, bright yellow.

Above the towers of what had once been Temereen habitation and was now Windswept Sheltering, two bright sun-stars
burned in an indigo sky. Fift stood for a moment looking at
that sky. Ze still wasn't used to it; even after three years, it
made zir nervous.

Ze'd been against the antique kitschiness of papering the

Sheltering's shell with active displays; nor had ze understood why it had to be this Far Historical setting instead of their own world's soupy-green surface sky. But by the time Windswept Sheltering was picking out wallpaper, it had twenty thousand residents, and since they didn't want ratings or consensus frameworks inside their borders, that meant big unruly meetings for deciding such things. Fift had skipped the one about the dome.

But the new sky had grown on zir, some. It did make Windswept feel more like an escape: somewhere different, somewhere new. And it was beautiful; the endless subtle shaded blues and purples, the hugeness.

Still, it made zir nervous: a creature out of its burrow, exposed to a sky.

Home wasn't far; just across the waysweep, a little ways under that strange blue dome, and down three flights of stairs. Ze started walking.

At home, ze was asleep in the nest room, and ze was smearing mangareme paste on a broibel in the dining nook.

Dobroc looked up from zir soup. "Oh, good," ze said, "you're done at the reactancy."

Fift smiled, scooped up more paste. "Am I really so bad when I'm in there?"

"Not bad," Dobroc said. "Just distracted."

Dobroc only had one body in the Sheltering at the moment. The rest were invisible to Fift—they were out beyond the Sheltering's Gates in the rest of the world, with all its troubles. Fift put down the smearer, reached zir hand across the table, and took Dobroc's hand, feeling the ridges and grottoes and channels of zir palm. Dobroc still had the same intricate topography of skin, that adolescent folly of somatic design. Fift treasured it. "How's it going out there?"

Dobroc shrugged. "I don't know why I even still do this."

"That bad?"

Dobroc took a deep breath. "Oh, you know. It could be worse. It's progress; in some sense, this is the smoothest region-level Episode of the Conversation since—well, since the Unraveling, really! Even five years ago, we wouldn't have been able to gather this group together, never mind generate a coherent flow. It's just that . . . it's still so polarized. There are four speakers from various Shelterings, and two who are middle-of-the-road liberationists or maybe post-liberationists. The rest are, well, you know. They're not exactly neo-repressionists, or they'd be boycotting the whole thing. But they're . . . they can't help but see us as a threat. Why do we shut ourselves up in these secret places? What are we hiding? Why do we think we're too good for the rest of the world?"

"They say all that?" Fift had crossed the waysweep; ze entered the stairwell.

"Well, not directly." Dobroc smiled. "This is the Conversation, after all. Lots of citations from the metacommentaries of the eighth work of the tenth cycle . . ."

"Ah," Fift said, "Ranhulo."

"Oh, they don't dare bring out Ranhulo," Dobroc said. "Higgis and Mathus, mostly, those grumbling pedants. Ranhulo would have gotten it. Ranhulo saw zir own prejudices and crystallized them. If you quote zir out of context, ze can seem anti-Vail, but ze wasn't. Ze transcended zir own—" Dobroc stopped and grinned. "But why am I telling you this? None of us would be here if not for your new reading of Ranhulo!"

Fift smiled shyly and looked down.

"Anyway," Dobroc said, "they tried Ranhulo once last year, and Morinti stuffed the elegiac sixth subsection of zir second metacommentary on the eighth work down their throats." Ze grinned, a grin with a rueful edge.

"Morinti?" Fift asked. "Morinti Bob Elarus of name registry Selfish Turkey 12? Our old comrade-in-arms?"

Dobroc laughed. "No, a different Morinti. Morinti Frangle Polor of name registry . . . um . . ."

"I wonder what happened to Morinti Bob."

"Well if you want to know, you're going to have to walk to a Gate, because I'm not ferrying the feed back in here one answer at a time!"

Fift smiled. "I like wondering."

On the wall above the couch-pit, a small yellow light glowed—the only narrow tendril through which the vast whirlwind feed outside was permitted to request the attention of this household. Yellow was its color for Fift, and it was bright.

". . . but it looks like I should check my messages anyway."

Dobroc looked back at the wall. "Oh—yes, you should." Ze smiled. "And your timing is very good. Let me see . . . yes! What if you go now?"

"Now?" Fift blinked.

"Yes, now. To the Amber Gate!"

"Dobroc," Fift said, "hold on. What is this about?" Outside, ze was descending the last stairway.

"Most illuminated and heart-held Fift, allow me my little game. The fact that you happened to think of fetching messages now is too Kumru-sent an opportunity to squander. Go!"

Fift knew that ze could probably ask Cemerid, the third of their triad, what Dobroc was up to. All four of Cemerid's bodies were in the Sheltering: one asleep downstairs across the couch-floor from Fift, two playing rumcaddy in the lower arena, one at the Violet Gate working with a Far Historical generalysis team in Tearless.

"Oh, come on," Dobroc said.

"Fine," Fift said, grumpily. Ze let go of Dobroc's hand, took a bite of the broibel, and stood up. Zir other body had reached the apartment door, so ze came in. Ze briefly made eye contact with zirself, then looked away in each body. Ze'd made zir skin lavender a while ago, an unfortunate choice ze kept not getting around to undoing. Ze got up and stood side by side with zirself in the doorway. Why would Dobroc want to send zir to . . .

"Dobroc," ze said.

Dobroc looked up from zir soup, innocent as an ungendered babe. "Hmm?"

"It's Shria, isn't it?"

Dobroc didn't look away. Zir brown-brown eyes held Fift's calmly. "You're too insightful, Fift. Yes, it's Shria. Ve's coming to train with me, and ve wants to see . . . us. This place. And I thought you'd like to welcome vem."

Fift flushed. "Are you serious? You wanted me to just . . . stumble on vem, unprepared? I can't believe this."

Dobroc rubbed zir face thoughtfully. "Hmm. All right. Perhaps it was a bad idea."

"What did you think? That we'd just . . . fall into each other's arms?"

Dobroc shrugged, and now ze did look down at zir soup. "Perhaps."

Fift rocked from one foot to the next, zir blood thudding through zir arteries. "Don't play these kinds of games with me, Dobroc. For me, this is not entertaining."

"I'm truly sorry, Fift," Dobroc said, not looking up.

"And what if I'd met vem outside the Gate? I know we're not the event we were thirty years ago, but there are still Unraveling-history buffs out there who would swarm if they saw us in the same place." Ze reached out and grabbed zir other body's green-and-yellow woven sleeve, holding onto it for support. "And ve's coming here to train for the Long Conversation? That's why ve's deigning to actually come inside a Sheltering?"

"That's not fair, Fift," Dobroc said. "You're being unfair to vem. Ve's given us plenty of support. Ve's been to Shelterings."

Fift felt a sharp ache in zir abdomen. Ze didn't have a name for it. Loss, anger, longing?

Dobroc raised zir eyes. "And yes," ze said, "we are going to hold a Conversation. Ve's ready."

Fift snorted. The image came unbidden: Shria, fifteen years old, lanky and fiery and beautiful and dangerous, snuggled up like an egg in a nest. *I know you do something. I'm not talking about the Long Conversation, either. You have bodies. Show me.* Zir cheek pressed up against vir breasts. Vir hand smoothing across zir stubbled scalp. Vir smell, like a wild surface forest only Fift had ever visited. The vines of the supper garden overhead, in green light. Vir mischievous grin.

"Do your partners at the region-level Episode today know you're starting to train Vails?" Fift asked.

"They suspect, certainly," Dobroc said. "They're always accusing us of hiding something, and if you forced them to articulate what they fear we're hiding, I imagine training Vails in the Long Conversation would be near the top of the list. Why, Fift? Do you disapprove?"

"Of course I don't disapprove. I'm proud of vem." Ze looked at zir hands. Pale lavender at the palms, shading to darker purple at the knuckles. A stupid choice; it didn't suit zir at all. "I'm going out. To the *Crimson* Gate. In *both* bodies."

"All right," said Dobroc, sadly.

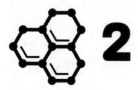 **2**

The Crimson Gate was in a concourse that thrust out from the main body of Windswept Sheltering into the air above Undersnort. Three bodylengths high, the passage ran through a massive opening in the puff-weave wall. It was paved with grownbone tiles. The path twisted, so you couldn't see the world beyond Windswept until you'd walked a bit. Within the Gate, on either side of the passage, there were nooks in the walls where you could reach the world's feed; they were crowded with bodies. People murmuring, laughing, scowling: Windswepters, hard at work, or getting the news of the world beyond.

Fift's hearts were pounding; ze exhaled all the air in zir lungs slowly, hissing it out between zir teeth until a yawn came, that welcome spasm forcing zir to open zir jaws wide and gulp down air. Zir hearts slowed a little. Ze didn't look at zirself, but ze reached out and took zir own arm. As a young child, ze'd never liked to be with zirself; but these days, ze had begun to like the double feeling: in the muscles of zir arm, in the other body's fingers clasped around them.

Until ze reached the edge of the Sheltering, ze wouldn't know what zir wealth and reputation were in the world outside, or how the people ze knew out there were doing, or who expected what of zir. Though ze'd lived in the Sheltering for twelve years, and it had been fully feed-opaque for seven, that was still strange. Perhaps it would always be strange.

Ze wondered what it would be like for a child born in a Sheltering; whether, for such a child, it would seem natural and obvious to live in a small world. There would be children born in Shelterings, someday. Maybe—if a way around the Midwives' boycott could be found, may Kumru wish it with us—sometime soon.

Every nook was occupied, and Fift didn't want to squeeze zir way in among the bodies. Ze walked on. Soon ze could see the passage's exit. The carpeted green platform, the docked robot bats, and the vast vault of Fullbelly beyond, its hundred thousand habitations a glittering riot of color and form. A moment of vertigo, and, mixed in with it, nostalgia, which made zir almost laugh aloud. Ze *missed* Fullbelly! To be able to miss Fullbelly even while technically living deep inside it . . . now, if that wasn't a sign that the Shelterings were working—!

Now ze could feel the whisper of the world's feed at the edge of zir perception. Ze awakened zir attention agents from their slumber; ze'd need them now. Another yawn worked its way through zir, first in one body, then the other. Ze let go of zir arm and stepped forward, singlebodied, into the range of the feed. In zir other body, ze cracked zir knuckles, pressed a fist into the smooth, soft puff-weave wall, and breathed.

It was an old reflex to check audience. 25,687 people had zir hot-bookmarked: history buffs, political-minutiae bookies, distant contacts from the old days, fans or opponents of the Sheltering movement; and, perhaps, enemies of Dobroc's Long Conversation flexiblism . . .

But right now, no one was watching zir.

```
Fift Brulio of name registry Yellow Peninsula
  Sugarbubble 5, 3-bodied Staid, 46 years old
  (premature majority), industrial reactant,
  elderborn, no cohort. One public location.
```

That's what the world's lookup showed. It refused to list Windswept Sheltering as zir address, and was apparently too prudish to regard Dobroc and Cemerid and Fift as even a provisional triad. Even Cemerid, at eighty, had not yet properly reached zir Courting Century; and Dobroc and Fift were scandalously young.

Gingerly, ze let zir agents sift through zir queue; ze didn't even want to think about how many messages they must be examining. Ze wasn't in the mood for politics or gossip or news, or the tentative friendship solicitations of colleagues and comrades of years past. The unavoidable message—the one the yellow light had dragged zir out here for—was from Father Grobbard.

{Affectionate greetings to my estimable eldest child Fift Brulio Spin-Nupolo-Iraxis. It is with pleasurable anticipation of your reading these lines, as well as an acute and poignant sense of your absence, that I now write you.

{Although you have not (to my knowledge) made this explicit, your current mode of habitation suggests a wish to keep our communications within moderate bounds. I admit that this is difficult for me, Fift, but I comply. Nonetheless, I do not doubt that you wish to continue to be informed of matters of importance regarding our family.

{When you last visited us, five months ago, little Lumlu was still one-bodied. I am sure that the issue of vir somatic integration has burrowed into your concern, even if your mode of habitation makes it difficult for you to follow vir progress. I am gratified to be able to report success. Ve awakened last week and is adapting to three-bodied life with what appears to be great natural facility. Vir state is still somewhat fragile, but the pedagogical experts say that ve is in a condition where visits by family would not subject vem to any distress. In addition, ve has been asking for you.

{I have no doubt that Lumlu Mageria Spin-Nupolo-Iraxis of name registry Blue Fenugreek 12 will be grateful for your presence and that you see it as a pleasurable duty to attend vem. I have therefore taken the liberty of instructing this message to alert me upon your perusal of it, and have instructed it also to then arrange for immediate transportation, via robot bat, under the auspices of Spin-Nupolo-Iraxis cohort.

{With great regard, and with serene satisfaction at the prospect of your visit, I remain, your affectionate Father, Grobbard Erevulios Spin-Nupolo-Iraxis of name registry Amenable Perambulation 2.}

Fift exhaled. Grobbard hadn't even grudgingly saluted—or mentioned—Dobroc or Cemerid, and all that "mode of habitation" stuff . . . wow. And to have simply ordered Fift a robot bat immediately upon receipt of the message! As if you had to snatch Fift when you could and shepherd zir around attentively, or ze would escape through the nearest exhaust shaft.

The Sheltering's feed showed Dobroc at home, finishing zir soup, making ready for Shria by shooing the dishes into the kitchen, tidying the study-pit. Shria must be through the Amber Gate by now.

Fift had to go to zir parents' apartments in one of zir bodies, that was clear. Another body would be asleep in the nest room for hours. And the third . . . ?

Ze could linger here at the Gate watching the world's feed. Or head back to the reactancy to put in a few more hours in the sweet juicy heart of the stream. Or find a public sleep nook and try to rest. Or go watch Cemerid play rumcaddy down in the arena.

Wherever ze went in the Sheltering, though, ze'd be able to see zir own home. Ze'd be able, if ze wanted, to see Shria and Dobroc engaging in the Long Conversation.

Ze noticed zir hands were trembling in both bodies. Absurd! Shria coming to the apartment should not be an epic opera-game.

Nevertheless, ze went out onto the rough green carpet of the dock with both bodies, towards the robot bat zir agents showed zir. *It will be good to have two brains out here to deal with the world's feed,* ze told zirself, though the excuse sounded flimsy, even to zir.

As the bat rose from the dock into the air of Fullbelly, crowded with stickywalls and polypenetrations and bounceroos, Fift watched Dobroc in the apartment, laying out spoons. Dobroc studied one intensely, then polished it with the corner of zir sleeve; as ze did so, the bat moved out of range of the Sheltering's feed. The image of Dobroc grew fuzzy and gray, stretched and warped, and then dissolved like morning mist . . . and Fift, among Fullbelly's teeming billions, felt very alone.

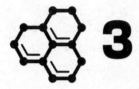 **3**

The robot bat left Fift at the docking-spires. Ze took a route that avoided zir old childhood home (now occupied by a former neighbor who'd always bet against them and vir smug, unbearable cohort) and went through the grove, up the spoke, to the somewhat less confident end of Slow-as-Molasses.

Zir parents had lived there for thirty years, but ze still thought of it as "the new apartment." Really, ze still thought of it as "Chalia's house."

Ze'd been in Izist when ze heard—no one had even told zir; ze'd stumbled onto it on a general news stream—that homeless Iraxis cohort had merged with Spin-Nupolo; that zir baby cousin Chalia Rigorosa was now zir sibling and ze was elderborn; that zir parents had a home again. Ze remembered the stab of relief and gratitude—Auntie Ellix had come through again—and how ze'd stumbled against Shria and begun to cry. A crying Staid in the riotous carnival of Izist: nothing special, in those days.

Chalia met zir in the vestibule. "Fift!" ve cried, delighted. Ve came running out of the inner apartment, doublebodied. Ve flung vir arms around zir, and vir arms around zir. Then, a little embarrassed, ve pulled zir away from the semipublic vestibule and into the house's privacy. Not that ze had much audience, anyway—a few hundred, trailing along on a nostalgic whim, perhaps, once their agents had figured out that ze was heading to Foo.

"Hello, Little Sibling," Fift said.

"But not Littlest!" Chalia said it brightly, but there was still some unease under that smooth surface. The transition from latterborn to middleborn couldn't be easy, though Fift didn't have much frame of reference. Zir own transition from sisterless to elderborn that day in Izist had been atypical to say the least. Chalia was living the classical version, the original Supplanting on which all transactions are based. And now, Lumlu would have three bodies to demand attention with.

"What," Chalia said, "are you *wearing*?"

"The latest trend," Fift said, smirking. Ze hadn't even realized what a figure ze must present out here in this dark green and bright yellow. Not the white shift of a proper Staid, nor even the wheat or tan or black that the moderately daring had begun to wear.

Chalia burst out laughing. *It was a good joke, too,* Fift thought happily. It was absurd on many levels—imagining Chalia's strange Staid sibling as a sartorial pioneer was funny, and the idea of little Windswept Sheltering having its own miniature trends and fashions was ridiculous, too—yet it had a grain of truth: since the habitation had built those trellises and planted vines on them, ze'd begun to see their colors worn around the plaza and the waysweep.

"You look completely weird," Chalia said. "I love it."

"How are the 'rents dealing?" Ze asked. Where were they, anyway? Probably they were watching over the house feed; maybe not. Ze didn't care.

Chalia bit vir lip, then puffed out vir chest, tossed vir hair. At thirty, in the flush of Second Childhood, ve was beginning to lose a certain shyness that had hindered vem up until now.

Ve was short, Fift's height, but lithe and strong, even though ve spent as little time as ve could get away with on wrestling and fencing and acrobatics (ve preferred fiddling with agents; one day, perhaps, ve'd be a feedgardener). Vir skin and hair were a burnished brown. The fashion lately, for young Vails with any degree of confidence, was to avoid somatic design entirely: letting the body simply grow and express whatever phenotype had, willy-nilly, been stochastically mashed together out of the parents' gametes. Which was a different thing, Fift thought, from leaving your body alone for lack of the courage to change anything. Chalia wore it well. "I don't know," ve said. "They're pretty excited. Relieved. Apparently—well, uh . . ."

Fift felt a brief pinch of resentment, or jealousy. Ze masked it with a smile. "I had a hard time with somatic integration. I was a mess for years."

"Yeah," Chalia said. "That." Ve grinned. "Tell me about the Sheltering!"

"Why don't you come see for yourself?" Fift said.

Chalia's eyes widened. "Oh, wow," ve said. "You know I'd love to. But . . ."

"I know. You'd have to deal with them panicking about it."

"Well, they'd never let me."

Fift felt a bitter little burn in zir chest. "Yeah." Ze took vir hand. "I might have disregarded that, but then, I am not exactly the best model for appropriate childing."

"Oh, Fift, come on," Chalia said, looking down. Ve leaned against zir, unselfconsciously laying vir head on zir shoulder. The burn dissipated, cooled by vir sweetness. "That was different. That was, like, a calling! It was, you know, the beginning of an Age! They don't get it, but I do."

"An Age, huh?" Fift said. Ze was going to ask what Age had begun, what they should call it, but Father Squell—perhaps not liking the direction the tête-à-tête was going?—came rushing in. Ve was singlebodied, hairless as always, still sporting those old-fashioned metallic spikes poking out of vir pale pink skin—though they'd grown in number, and ve'd added some kind of distracting zebra-striping on the back of vir neck and arms. Ve stopped, pressed vir hands to vir face, and then flung vir arms around Fift.

Squell's cheek was slick with tears, pressed against one of Fift's necks. Though zir bodies stood shoulder to shoulder, ze felt a spasm of emotional bodylag; in the body in Squell's arms, ze felt like a tiny child again, yearning for protection, yearning to be consoled, and cuddled, and coaxed into a romp. But zir other body's stomach clenched as ze saw Squell enveloping zir, vir gangly zebra-striped arms closing around Fift like a spider wrapping up a fly. The discontinuity made zir dizzy.

Ze chided zirself immediately; that was unfair. Squell meant no harm. Ve loved zir, and ze wished ze could hug vem back with the same abandon. As zir emotions synchronized, though, the unease won out, and ze stiffened.

Squell noticed and stepped away. "Chalia, dear," ve said, not looking at zir, "whatever are you doing, keeping Fift all to yourself in the vestibule like this? Everyone is waiting!"

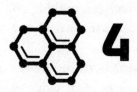 **4**

"So," Father Thrimon said, smoothing zir hands on zir legs, "lookup says you're an industrial reactant, Fift? That's nothing to be ashamed of, of course; you know, I spent some time in reactancies myself as a youth. It can be very . . . soothing, if that's the right word. While you figure out, you know, what else you want to do . . ."

Fift's stomach rumbled. Ze was hungry, but Fathers Arevio and Cartassia and Burin had become Near Cuisine enthusiasts, and were manually preparing some kind of complicated feast. (For thousands of years, Fift thought, people have been perfectly content to let their kitchens' agents interface with their guests' gastronomic agents to predict and then prepare the perfect meal . . . and now this trend comes along and people start stubbornly trying to figure out for themselves what to slice and grate and slather and heat with what! But wasn't this whole Near Cuisine business, voluntarily depriving yourself of feed information and agent support, based on the same impulse towards independence and self-reliance as the Shelterings? Not that Fift's parents would ever admit it . . .)

In another room, Mother Mulis (Chalia's Mother) and Mother Egathelie (Lumlu's Mother) stood with Fift at the edge of the playpit. In it, Lumlu was fighting spiders.

"And of course," Father Thrimon said, lifting zir hands, "where would we be without them? Reactancies. Imagine if all the things we use were shaped by agents alone, without any living person's eye, ear, or tongue? Far Technology is the basis of our society, but without the human touch . . . well, if you don't mind my citing the fifth analytical discursus of the twelfth addendum to the alternate codification of—"

"*I* mind," said Father Frill, coming into the room double-bodied. "Kind Kumru, Thrimon! Everyone can hear you!" Ve was wearing a tight rainbow unitard, sleeved on one body, sleeveless on the other. Vir powerful bare arms glistened with sweat, and ve was holding practice swords. Ve handed them from one body to the other, left the room to take them away, and sat down on a bench at the wall, looking at Fift. Ve crossed vir arms. "So, Fift. Can you tell us, *this* time, what you're making in this reactancy of yours?"

Fift shifted uneasily in zir seating harness.

The hollow windmoan, the pungent figgy electric autumn . . .

In zir sleeping body's dream, a wind was blowing, clearing away mists—a cold wind. Murkily, ze felt that body shiver.

"It's not that it's a secret or anything," ze said.

Frill snorted.

Lumlu giggled. The spiders were as big as ve was, headless, all bone-white legs. One scurried between two of vir bodies. Wide-eyed, ve stumbled forward to lunge at it.

Fift looked down at zir hands. "I just don't know what it's called . . . what we're making. I mean, it doesn't have a name yet."

Frill shook vir head. "And *will* it have a name? Will it ever emerge from your little . . . fools' paradise there, your self-exiled-mega-cohort with its head in the sand, your wombtombatum-for-a-thousand, or whatever it purports to be? Are you making something that belongs to the world, that I will one day see?"

A look of concern crossed Thrimon's face.

"I don't know," Fift said. "Maybe not."

As two of Lumlu's bodies closed on the spider, the third shrieked with excitement. At the last moment, the spider leapt straight up into the air over vir heads, and Lumlu's bodies crashed together.

Frill sighed.

Father Smistria ambled singlebodied into the room, also sweaty, and tossed vir fighting gloves into the compost. A long gash on vir cheek was bleeding. Ve licked a finger and rubbed it along the wound. "Your Father Frill is an illicit combatant, Fift," ve said. "Ve's had vir nerves quickened."

Lumlu's shriek shifted to panic, and in vir other two bodies ve staggered away from the collision, sat down, and began to wail with surprise and pain out of all three throats. The spider skittered around to its fellows at the other edge of the playpit.

"You, Smi, are a liar, and a bitter-minded loss-denier!" Frill snapped. "I haven't had my nerves quickened any more than you have!"

"Please—Smi, Frill!" Thrimon said, stricken. "Is this sort of talk appropriate in front of our staidchild?"

"Ze's no child anymore," Smistria said. "Ze took care of that long ago. The bout should have been mine."

"Ze's only forty-six!" Thrimon said.

Shria's voice. It was carried through zir dream on the cold wind. Ve was laughing; then ve was speaking, intensely. Ze couldn't make out the words. Another one of zir dream bodies was in the belly of a skywhale—a skywhale full of anonybodies who were staring at zir, trying to decide something important.

"You haven't achieved anything, you know," Frill said, arms still crossed.

Egathelie and Mulis leaned forward over the playpit.

"That's it, darling!" Egathelie said. "Wail, my dearest, wail! Use your wonderful lungs! Wail it all out, then get up to fight again! That's the way!"

One of Lumlu's bodies wavered mid-sob to look up, and Mulis, vir longer Maternal experience granting vem an indulgent air of superiority, leaned across Fift to touch Egathelie on the arm. "Don't distract vem, Eg," ve said, and Egathelie nodded.

"What do you mean, Frill?" Thrimon asked.

"These Shelterings!" Father Frill cried. "What difference do they make? Penning yourselves up inside secret enclaves like . . . oh, I don't know, like some character or other in your Kumru-blessed Conversation—"

"Frill!" Thrimon said, horrified, and Smistria cackled.

"—what good does it do? Out here, the Midwives and feedgardeners have all the power they ever did—"

"And a good thing, too!" Smistria said.

Frill glared at Smistria. "—and the Clowns are just . . . *entertainment* again!"

"I don't know if that's entirely—" Thrimon began.

Lumlu sniffled and helped vemself up, wavering on vir small legs. Ve looked into vir own faces, warily blinking. Maybe, Fift thought, ve was realizing for the first time that ve could hurt vemself, that vir own bodies were capable of betraying vem.

Shria's voice through the dream, louder now. Then it subsided to silence, and the mist began to drift back in, blue and buzzing. In the dream-skywhale, Fift closed zir eyes, ignoring the staring faceless passengers.

"So what good did any of it do, then?" Father Frill said. "All your . . ." Ve pressed vir lips together. Ve put vir hands on vir hips. "All of it."

"Maybe you should come see," Fift said. "Come to the Sheltering. I—"

"Ha!" Frill said, throwing up vir hands. "I've been to enough *proper* Idylls without having to sever myself from the world's feed to be there! And I have nothing to hide that I need to do where no one can see me!"

"Maybe you'd find," Fift said, "that you could try out new things, different things, if—"

"Please! Kumru desire me protected from such nonsense. Look, Fift," Frill said, "I know you're sincere, and I'm sure with *you* there, nothing all *that* amiss is going on in Windswept Sheltering—well—nothing *horrible*, anyway. But what about the Redoubts? Panaximandra Shebol of name registry Central Glory 2 has set up—"

Grobbard and Ellix came in. "Does anyone else think," Grobbard said, "that despite the regard in which we all hold Arevio and Cartassia and Burin, and the eagerness with which we look forward to their latest production, that the prohibition on eating anything else in the interim, is perhaps—"

Ellix nodded at Fift. "Hello, Fift."

Lumlu got to vir feet, squinted, and looked up out of the playpit for reassurance. The two Mothers waved and clapped. All vir heads turned in unison as ve looked from one to the other.

Then Lumlu saw Fift. Ze wasn't sure whether or not to smile. It had been five months since ze'd seen vem; ve had barely been talking then. Now ve was three-bodied—three chunky little bodies, naked and covered in curly golden hair. Fift couldn't, of course, tell which one was the original, though ze couldn't help wondering. Ze remembered the moment around age seven when ze'd realized that ze had no idea which of zir bodies had been the first . . .

Lumlu looked into zir face, triply, and frowned.

"I don't *know* if anyone else thinks it, Grobbard!" Frill said.

"Why don't you add an axis to the consensus moderation framework? Or just eat something! You're interrupting. The Redoubts—"

"I, for one," Smistria said, "don't mind having the Revanchists holed up in one place—"

"Then *you're* overdue for a collapse!" Frill said. "Because who knows what they're planning in there? *At any time*, they could burst out upon us all, and—"

Lumlu turned, triplebodied, and charged the spiders.

"Oh, stop tormenting the child, Frill!" Smi snapped.

Frill arched an eyebrow. "You just said ze wasn't a—"

"Well, whatever ze is!" said Smistria. "The bout is done, and I believe we had something *else* planned between the bout and dinner. Or shall I just bathe?"

"Perhaps," Grobbard said, "as the meal will soon be—"

"No," said Frill, getting up, "you should *not* just bathe. Lead the way—to *your* room, Smi. Don't worry, Grobbard: based on past experience, this won't take long . . ."

Smi glared at vem, taking vir hand, and then at Ellix, who was chuckling. Thrimon looked mortified, and Grobbard mildly annoyed.

There was a hand on Fift's shoulder. For a moment ze didn't know which body's shoulder it was. Then the confusion passed: it was a dreaming body. In the skywhale of the dream, or in the dreamed blue mist? No, it was heavy and warm and real, pushing through the mists of dream, reminding zir that ze had a body, lying in bed . . .

Ze opened zir eyes.

Shria was there. Singlebodied, golden-skinned, vir unruly black eyebrows curling above vir golden-irised eyes. Earlier, the conversation with Dobroc had reminded Fift of Shria's fifteen-year-old face. This was the same face, if in a different color scheme, and the cheekbones a little broader with Second Childhood's growth. Though ve was no child anymore, either.

Fift sat bolt upright, flinching away from Shria's hand. Cemerid must have already awoken and left; they were alone in the nest room.

Shria sat back. Ve was wearing, yes, a Conversationalist's white shift. It didn't look pretentious or pretend. It suited vem; ve was capable of anything. Zir heart throbbed.

"Hi," ve said.

"What in Kumru's barren genitals, Shria—do you ever *knock*?"

"I knocked," ve said.

"Where's Dobroc?" Fift said, fumbling to check the house feed. Dobroc was downstairs, of course, with Shria's other body. Ve'd brought two! Ze dropped the connection, ze didn't want to watch them. "Oh."

"I miss you," ve said.

Just like that, Fift's breath was gone. Ze looked away. Why was ve in zir *room*? Because ve was Shria, of course; ve ignored— ve didn't—ve wouldn't—! This body's heart, the house feed told zir, was throbbing at 134 beats per minute. Up from 64, eight seconds ago; impressive. Ze should have woken zirself up when Dobroc said that ve was coming and cleared out of here in all three bodies!

Ze closed zir eyes, slowed zir breathing, recovered zirself. Opened zir eyes again. Ve was waiting. "How's the training with Dobroc?" ze asked.

"Amazing," Shria said. Ve put vir hands on vir ankles, leaned forward. "I won't say I feel the flow yet. But it's a lot different than just watching footage, or even being in silent attendance. It's . . . I can feel the beauty, just out of reach."

As much as Fift supported Dobroc's political project, as inured to it ze was in theory, it was still jarring—Shria in white, passing spoons. The vertigo of missing a step on a ladder. A sense of being invaded, of something private being stolen. But also, a longing: a certain *yes, yes, come be with us . . .*

"How's the visit back home?" Shria said.

"It's okay," Fift said. Zir throat was dry. Ze tried to clear it. "Lumlu's amazing; it's only been a week and ve's fighting spiders triplebodied." Ve was chasing them now, golden-furred bodies and white spider legs galloping with abandon.

"Huh," Shria said.

"That's it!" Mulis cried, flinging up vir hand. "Lumlu, sweetie, you can do it!"

"Oh Fift," Egathelie said, turning to zir. "I don't know if you're checking your queue, but your Father Thurm is coming in. We've hardly seen vem here the last few months—"

"Last few months?" Mulis said, still following Lumlu with vir eyes. "We've hardly seen vem since Chalia entered Second Childhood!"

"—but ve said if *you* were going to be here—"

Grobbard and Ellix were asking Thrimon about some impenetrable point of family meeting protocol, a proposed adjustment to the Far Theoretical engine overseeing agent-driven evaluative feedback to the cohort's consensus modeling framework. They hadn't forgotten Fift was there—but perhaps they didn't know what else to say to zir. Or they were just giving zir time to adjust, to sink back into the flow.

"Shria," Fift said, opening zir eyes and forcing zirself to look at vem, "what are you *doing* here?"

Shria looked down and stroked the couch-floor's fabric. "Uh . . . I guess you're looking for something other than 'I'm here to train with Dobroc' and 'I miss you.'"

"Yes," Fift said. "Yes I am."

Shria took a deep breath and let it out, as if ve were preparing to say . . . something. And then a look of annoyance crossed vir face. "You know what, that kind of wounds me,

Fift. Why aren't those enough? You're my friend. I miss you. I'm in the neighborhood. Why—"

"Because it hurts to see you, Shria. Because my heart is tied to yours." 124 beats per minute. "And to see you, and then to have you vanish again, to not be able to hold you close . . ."

Shria's face tightened. Ve looked away. Then ve turned back, reached vir hand out to zir face. "Fift—"

Ze caught vir hand by the wrist and held it away from zir. "Shria," ze said, "what did you come to say?"

Shria yanked vir hand away, vir face turning a deeper gold. "Fuck you."

"What," ze said, calm despite zir galloping heart, "did you come to—"

"That I'll stay," ve said, and Fift's heart stopped.

Mother Pip paused by the doorway of the room where Fift's Staid Fathers were debating. Ze gave Fift a guarded smile, raising an eyebrow, inspecting Fift as if confirming by eye what ze had seen over the house feed. It was exactly the expression ze had when ze supervised the unfolding of a satisfyingly nonlinear sequence of banking-historical transactions. Ze nodded and walked on.

Fift could not breathe. The three Staid Fathers politely averted their eyes; the two Vail Mothers cheering Lumlu didn't notice. Chalia came into the room, picking vir way around the playpit.

"What?" Fift asked Shria. "Why?"

"Why do you fucking think, you nutrient-flow-blocking, squandering, void-spurned, sisterless excuse for a spoon-passer! Because I miss you! Because missing you is like an itch contracted by rolling around naked in a field of some toxic surface plant. Because if you're so stubborn as to hole yourself up in this . . . this place, and not come out for months, and you're in such a Kumru-abhorred hurry to play cohort that you'll only—"

"Shria," Fift said. "Shria, stop." The pressure in zir chest, like some great beast was standing on it. "You can't do it like this. You can't do it for the wrong reasons. If you don't believe in the Shelterings and you don't believe in us making a cohort now—"

"Stop being so arrogant!" Shria said. "Stop being such a dogmatic . . ." Ve threw vemself from the couch-floor to vir feet and stood staring. "What do you know about what I believe?"

Fift swallowed. "Well—"

"Of course the Iraxis parents," Mulis said, vir eyes still on Lumlu, who had chased a spider under an overhanging ledge and was cautiously closing in with all three of vir bodies, "all miss you far more than they will admit. You should know that, Fift. It would be different if you were simply off somewhere in the *world*. Not even at *home*, you know, but just somewhere one could *see* you . . . and not, well, swallowed *up* into . . ."

Again, Egathelie reached across Fift to lay vir hand on Mulis's shoulder. "But you're here now," ve said brightly, "and so this evening, we should all just enjoy ourselves!"

Shria drew a ragged breath. "I was never *opposed* to the Shelterings. I just don't think they're the only answer! If the whole energy of the liberation movement is channeled into playing cohort and putting up fancy wallpaper, that's a disaster. But if they're part of something, a new diversity, a new relationship to the feed . . ." Ve waved an arm. "Fift, you confuse what I believe with what I can bring myself to do. What I said before, years ago—well, I just couldn't imagine *myself* in here, cut off from the world, stationary and . . . waiting . . . !"

"So what changed?" Fift said.

Ve looked zir in the eye. Fierce, golden. "Well," ve said. "For one thing, I'm learning to sit. I'm learning to be the still center." Ve said it without a grin, without irony. A pang of inscrutable longing shot through Fift.

"Sit," ze said.

Shria cracked vir knuckles, and then slowly, came back and sat by Fift on the nest room floor.

"And I *don't* know why you're in such a hurry," ve said. "I don't know why you need to be forming triads and quaternads at forty-six. I don't know why you can't wait for our Courting Century . . ."

"We're not children," Fift said. Their shoulders were a fingerwidth apart, not touching.

"That's a spurious argument," ve said. "Just because we rebelled against those structures doesn't mean we have to do the opposite. I *like* the idea of a century to focus on who I am, just me, myself, connecting with whomever I want to however I want, with no expectations of anything lasting. But"—ve shrugged—"apparently you and Dobroc *are* in a hurry. I don't know Cemerid, but I trust your judgement. And maybe my reluctance is . . . well, that same vailish fear of remaining still. And I know I want to break through that. Anyway, I didn't say I'm ready to declare a semi-cohort or undertake a pledge. I said I'd *stay*. I'll stay, I'll try this, I won't let my fear chase me away. And we'll see what happens." Ve turned to look at zir. "Is that enough?"

A great and terrible emotion was swelling inside of Fift like an invisible balloon, crushing zir organs to every side, filling zir intolerably until there was nothing left. Was it terror?

Chalia came up, trailing a hand over Mother Mulis's back, and then reaching toward Fift, straightening zir robe. Ve squinted at zir. "You look *happy*," ve said.

Oh: It was joy.

"Yes," ze said, to Chalia, to Shria.

"It's enough," ze told Shria. Zir voice was thick, an awkward instrument which needed to be maneuvered out of zir throat. "For a start."

Shria turned towards zir. Ze put zir arms around vem, and ve enveloped zir. Zir forehead against vir cheek, zir hands around the thick muscles of vir back. Ve smelled like—like dawnflowers, like gemmon, like a surface wind, like home? No: like Shria, here with zir again, after so long.

Ze sighed.

"Dinner!" Father Cartassia called.

Fathers Grobbard, Ellix, and Thrimon sprang up with un-characteristic haste and crowded into the hall. "Kumru praise us!" Frill said, toweling vir hair. "I could eat a robot bat."

"Lumlu!" Egathelie called. "Time for dinner, darling!"

"You know what's funny?" Shria said, lifting vir head a fingerwidth away from zir, vir breath tickling zir ear. "You're going to find this ridiculous. But part of my decision . . . you remember what Thavé said, when the Unraveling started? About star-ships?"

"Star-ships?" Fift said, frowning into vir shoulder.

"Yeah," Shria said. "That collapse-ripe idea of zirs, giving up everything just to build somewhere new. It seems absurd, but also . . . brave. Sometime in the Ages Before the Ages, someone was bizarre enough to do that, to give us . . . this." Ve buried vir nose in zir hair. "Somehow that image made the Shelterings seem . . . less like a dead end? Less like a retreat. More like something we need to learn: how to give up every-thing and start over."

"Well, I'm ready to blast off when you are."

Shria pulled away and looked at Fift, eyes crinkling. "You're making fun of me."

"No," Fift said. "No, I like it. Our own little hollowed-out rock, all alone in the night, hurtling between the stars."

"Yes," Shria said, resting vir chin back on Fift's head. Vir voice was soft, a little drowsy. "Like that."

They slid down on the soft couch-floor, and Fift crawled behind Shria and gathered vem into zir arms, encircling vem. Ze slid zir thighs under vir buttocks. Ze snuggled against vir back, and ve nestled back against zir.

In the corridor, zir Fathers shuffled quickly around Father Squell, who was leaning up against the wall. Grobbard, Ellix, Thrimon, Frill, and Smistria jogged down the stairs towards the supper room.

Squell looked down at vir hands. Vir eyes were still a little red from when ze'd cried at Fift's arrival. Ve glanced up, briefly, and frowned.

Fift slowed down as ze passed, and Squell began walking, so that they were walking side by side.

Fift could feel the muscles of Shria's back relaxing, one by one. Vir breathing slowed.

"Dobroc's started training Vails in the Long Conversation," Fift said to Squell. Ve blanched.

"Including Shria," ze said. Ze wasn't sure why ze said it. Was ze trying to provoke Squell into a storm of outrage? Ze felt an angry restlessness moving inside zir, even as zir other body relaxed, nose in Shria's hair, smelling vem, drifting into the safest sleep.

They were engaged in something so important, *so entrancing . . . I used to listen at the crack of the wall when they had their lessons . . .*

Squell walked in silence for the length of the corridor, and down the stairs. Then, at the door to the supper room, ve smiled, shyly.

"Well, cubblehedge," ve said, "Ages pass."

END DOCUMENT
TRANSMISSION

BEGIN MESSAGE TEXT

Dearest Siob,

Perhaps there's something perverse in my urge to write to you.

I don't succumb to it often. The last time was about eight hundred local years ago. I suppose, if you've found this letter, you'll have found that one too—they should be archived at all the same cache-points. If you're still alive, and still functioning, and still coherent, and still interested, and still mobile enough to find a cache-point, and it's still operating ...

I hold out hope. These signals should penetrate a good chunk of sky, perhaps two hundred light years across. I think you're in there somewhere.

So much of what I am, Siob, I am in resonance with you.

I'm writing you from the place you last saw me, 239.48 seconds ago in my inertial frame of reference. Yes, from that same little world. I know: it's not like me to have stuck around so long. Twenty thousand local years! But after so much wandering, I wanted to arrive, Siob. I wanted a home.

Whoever designed this place did an admirable job. The ecoforming is a marvel of sobriety and restraint. The people here are ancient stock, paleohuman with no frills, fragile and short-lived—a choice which has worked out admirably. They've trundled along here, age after age, while ... well, I hardly need to tell you what has become of more robust and ambitious designs, like you and me.

I'm enclosing a story from this world, a tale I recently came across. It's a true story, more or less ... everyone here is enmeshed in a thick skein of data, and the local parasentiences can do quite a good job of weaving a biography out of the analysis of electronic excreta. Someone took that and turned it into a linear textual narrative . . . and while I'm sure there are some embellishments and errors, I expect it's reasonably accurate.

I don't know why I picked this one. I do appear in it myself, briefly, and that's amusing; but that's not why. No, I think that it reminded me of us, so long ago when we were young. You were as headstrong and forthright as Shria, I think, and perhaps I was as stubborn and unpredictable as Fift.

Or so I tell myself. But we have existed so long, you and I, accumulating so many layers of memory and interpretation . . . what do I know, really, of who we once were? All I have left is myth.

And surely you've now drifted even farther. What might you have become, Siob, in all these centuries since we last met?

Even if I found you again, would you know me? Could we still decipher each other?

Well . . . here's a story, anyway. A gift for you. A lure. A pattern-seed from which to grow a bridge between our minds. It is a tale of children, so I've translated it into the language you and I spoke as children, back in our creche in the Margin, long before any of these worlds were made.

A lure, yes. I would lure you here, Siob, my strange and ancient friend. No matter what you have become.

Be alive, Siob. You have to be alive.

No one here will ever understand me as you could.

Be alive, and find me. Find me soon.

> Your friend,
> Thavé

END MESSAGE TEXT

BEGIN DOCUMENT ATTACHMENTS

ATTACHMENT LISTING

PLANETARY LOCATION
AND CHARACTERISTICS

For general readers of this document, if any: Due to security concerns and in the tradition of the Seventh Convocation of Long-Lived Mobile Entities on Fostering Civilizational Resilience, the standard galactic location of this planet has not been specified.

(For Siob: I trust that you remember where it is.)

There is, strikingly, no active endonym for the planet itself. Its inhabitants refer to it only as "the world," or, in the vocational slang of workers in the asteroid belt and outer satellites, "downside."[1]

The inhabitants are of engineered paleohuman stock, part of a human-origins restoration effort (~150 kya[2]), which was repurposed for generation-ship travel (~80 kya). Local human settlement occurred ~50 kya.

At present, the entire **surface** of the planet is silvomorphic infrastructure—largely forests and wildlands, with no permanent inhabitants. Instead, it is used by different groups (classes of school children, hunting and paleolithic-life enthusiasts, etc.) for recreational purposes, no more than a million bodies at any one time. In addition to biodiversity and environmental stability benefits, this design ensures that in the event of a rapid and lethal total civilizational collapse (e.g., total failure of all automated infrastructure in the interior), an appropriately sized remnant of survivors with relevant skills would be physically positioned on the surface, where they would form a basis for

---

1. I have actively encouraged this inward-looking tendency, also expressed in disinterest in interstellar travel, pursuant to separation protocols of the Gardenist school.

2. kya = thousands of years ago, measured in the planet's inertial frame of reference

eventual rebound.[3]

Beneath the surface, various nations are situated in large **excavations** in the planet's crust. Generally speaking, habitations are positioned in the cooler region closer to the surface, while, towards the planet's mantle, **production** regions powered by geothermal differentials ensure light (via **glowtubes**), oxygen exchange and airflow, nutrient synthesis, etc. A given excavation functions as an almost completely sealed ecosystem, with near-total recycling of organics and energy in the **nutrient flow**. This flow is highly optimized, to the extent that any interruption or sequestering of resources from the flow could have serious consequences. The inhabitants have internalized the risks of hoarding, squandering, and flow blockage to the point that many of their everyday insults revolve around these taboos.

POPULATION STATISTICS OF REFERENCED LOCATIONS

Total population of the planet: 1 trillion
- The surface: no permanent population
- The Pole: pop. 2.5 million
- Nation of Fullbelly: pop. 200 billion
  - Habitation of Foo: pop. 1 million
    - Neighborhood of Slow-as-Molasses: pop. 50,000
  - Habitation of Stiffwaddle: pop. 300,000
  - Habitation of Temereen: pop. 125,000 (later Windswept Sheltering, pop. 20,000)
  - Habitation of Wallacomp: pop. 10 million
    - Neighborhood of Tentative Scoop: pop. 230,000
    - Neighborhood of Izist: pop. 650,000

3. Note that overreliance on the polysomatic network poses a danger to this worst-case recovery plan, since body-separation trauma exacerbated by grief might incapacitate many survivors beyond the recovery point. This is one of the things I have been worrying about lately.

DRAMATIS PERSONAE

IRAXIS AND SPIN-NUPOLO COHORTS

- Fift Brulio Iraxis (3-bodied Staid, 16 years old, apprentice banker-historian)
  - Pip Mirtumil Iraxis, Mother (3-bodied Staid, 317, banker-historian)
  - Nupolo Imsmi Iraxis, Father (2-bodied Vail, 640, military poet)
  - Arevio Reflori Iraxis, Father (3-bodied Vail, 520)
  - Squell Urizus Iraxis, Father (4-bodied Vail, 360, asteroid worker)
  - Smistria Ishteni Iraxis, Father (2-bodied Vail, 320, adjudication reactant)
  - Frill Evementis Iraxis, Father (4-bodied Vail, 295)
  - Thurm Takalsit Iraxis, Father (3-bodied Vail, 263, agronomist)
  - Miskisk Orovoia Iraxis, Father (3-bodied Vail, 240)
  - Grobbard Erevulios Iraxis, Father (4-bodied Staid, 230, education topology mediator)
- Chalia Rigorosa Spin-Nupolo (3-bodied Vail, three months old)
  - Mulis Ovs Spin-Nupolo, Mother (5-bodied Vail, 432)
  - Ellix Verenthis Spin-Nupolo, Father (2-bodied Staid, 560, Peaceable), Nupolo Imsmi Iraxis's youngersibling
  - Thrimon Urtis Spin-Nupolo, Father (4-bodied Staid, 320)
  - Egathelie Turum Spin-Nupolo, Father (3-bodied Vail, 308), later, Mother of Lumlu Mageria
  - (18 other parents)

FNAX COHORT

- Shria Qualia Fnax (3-bodied Vail, 16, apprentice genital designer)
- Tusha Ivetris Fnax, Shria's eldersibling (2-bodied Vail, 24)
  - Sangh Tenrik Fnax, Shria's Mother (2-bodied Vail, 307)
  - Polidar Ziz Fnax, Father (5-bodied Staid, 245)
  - (Tusha's Mother and 14 other parents)

UM COHORT

- Dobroc Pengasius Um (3-bodied Staid, 17, Long Conversation prodigy)
  - (five Staid eldersiblings, two Vail eldersiblings)
  - (eighty parents)

OTHER CHILDREN OF FOO

- Umlish Mnemu Mnathis (4-bodied Staid, 17), accompanied Fift and Shria on the field trip to the surface
  - (other children on the field trip: Puson, Kimi, Perjes, Tomlest)
- Vvonda Tenak Peridity-Chandrus (3-bodied Vail, 20), Shria's friend
  - Mmondi Tenak Peridity-Chandrus, vir Mother (3-bodied Vail, 177, liberal Kumruist officiant)
- Buturney "Bluey" Snatz Gassal (3-bodied Vail, 22), Shria's friend
- Stogma Arax Eptori (2-bodied Vail, 15), Shria's friend
- Ruich Milva Snedic (3-bodied Vail, 8, student; later: storyteller)

OTHER INHABITANTS OF FULLBELLY

- Pom Politigus (6-bodied Staid, 385, body-design emporium proprietor), Shria's employer
- Panaximandra Shebol (1-bodied Vail, 935, ex-soldier and demagogue)
- Hrotrun Videx Spilteritrine (3-bodied Vail, 135, Far Historical index designer), follower of Panaximandra
- Predoria Ithigast (2-bodied Vail, 233, industrial reactant), follower of Panaximandra
- Meroc Ipithia (4-bodied Staid, 145, apprentice splage coordinator)
- Morinti Bob [later Elarus] (3-bodied Staid, 125), team-tag enthusiast
- Emim Potching (3-bodied Staid, 75), team-tag enthusiast
- Bojum Holkitz (4-bodied Vail, 110), team-tag enthusiast
- Honti Pikipo (2-bodied Vail, 45), team-tag enthusiast

MIDWIVES

- Miolasia Frin (4-bodied Vail, 506)
- Umlum Canalepsis (4-bodied Staid, 469)
- Rysthia Aresti (5-bodied Vail, 831)
- Elo Fesis (3-bodied Staid, 620)

OTHERS

- Thavé (12-bodied Staid, ~500,000, planetary survival consultant), your humble correspondent

BRIEF GLOSSARY OF PLANETARY INSTITUTIONS

adjudicator: professional responsible for the resolving of interpersonal and social conflicts. Prior to the Unraveling, adjudication was successful in almost all cases.

agent: a Far Technological automated entity, resident in the feed, tasked with specific functions such as maintenance of the nutrient flow, or advising a particular human.[1]

anonybody: an anonymized teleoperated body, superficially integrated with the polysomatic network for temporary use.

Ascensionist: one of the planet's religions, emotive, lyrical, and focused on the apotheotic transcendence of practitioners.

banker-historian: a professional responsible for emotional accounting, formalizing the story of a person or institution's emotional states so as to optimally influence their ratings.

consensus: the aggregation of ratings and global opinion, synthesized by Far Technological agents, which allocates most rights to resources, goods and services, feed access privileges, and social status. In addition to global consensus, decisions within a family or enterprise are often made via a **consensus moderation framework**.

feed: the global information network, integrated directly into inhabitants' neural experience.

---

1. Agents' sentience and autonomy is constrained by design. Still, it is a matter of extreme good fortune that they have tended to enthusiastically embrace the project of a joint co-culture with the planet's human inhabitants. People tend to assign my few contributions to maintaining this alliance much more credit than they deserve.

feedgardener: professional who, in concert with agents, monitors, maintains, and shapes the feed.

Groon: one of the planet's religions, focused on a theurgic entity, Groon, whom devotees are encouraged to scorn and blame, and whose mourning and remorse are redemptive.

Idyll: a facility for those undergoing ontological collapse, allowing a greater degree of behavioral freedom than would be possible in the wider world without damaging ratings, and providing emotional support from professional specialists (who are often themselves undergoing ontological collapse).

Long Conversation: composed over millennia and consisting of tens of millions of stanzas, the Long Conversation is both the collected repository of staidish wisdom and the ritualized communal act of reciting, referencing, juxtaposing, commenting upon, and extending that repository. The degree to which Vail knowledge of and involvement in this project is taboo has varied over the centuries. The project itself predates the formalization of Staids as a "gender," and is core to Staid identity and practice.

lookup: a component of the feed; the global identity registry which establishes each inhabitant as having a unique identity, advertises that identity to others, and enables access to resources via consensus.

Kumruist: one of the planet's religions, focused on a semi-mythical prophet and theurgic entity—Kumru, whose sufferings devotees identify with—and sacralizing biological life.

Midwives: an order of specialists, equally divided between Vails and Staids, who have the traditional responsibility for gendering babies. They have, by skillful manipulation of consensus, parlayed this limited formal authority into a much broader authority over who can reproduce and, by extension, which families are permitted to exist.

Near vs. Far History: strictly speaking, Near History is since the settlement and terraforming of the planet, while Far History is the nebulous time before, but in practice Near History means that portion of history which is comprehensible without massive cultural disorientation.

Near vs. Far Technology: though the planet is heir to—and reliant on—hundreds of thousands of years of human development, most of the cultural context of that ancient technology is lost to its current inhabitants. Thus, from habitation architecture to social nuance agents to the nutrient flow, everyday life is enmeshed in Far Technological systems which no one alive fully understands, and which sometimes behave in unpredictable ways. Near Technology, by contrast, is developed and understood locally: while more modest in scope, it has the advantage of predictability.

ontological collapse: also called "unraveling." Characterized by extreme variance in emotion and behavior, as different parts of the self decohere and come into open conflict. There is a cultural tension around unraveling, which is considered both a healthy self-maintenance practice and simultaneously (especially for Staids) a somewhat embarrassing loss of control.

Peaceable: a professional tasked with mediating emergent conflicts and maintaining order who is authorized to use nonlethal coercive force. Peaceables are always Staids trained in emotional self-regulation. Their neural states are published and they are not permitted to act in anger, fear, or callous detachment.

polysomatic network: the deep portion of the feed which allows intracellular-level physical states to be synchronized between the multiple bodies of a single person. Bodies are flash-cloned from universal stem cells, usually in infancy, and permeated with networked nanometric replication systems to ensure a phenomenologically smooth experience of singular self.

ratings: globally published automated assessments of each individual's history, character, and status, which inform the backbone of the economy. Strictly speaking, the planet has an agent-mediated emotional-transaction pride economy rather than a classical reputation economy, but ratings function similarly in both.

reactant: professional whose emotional states, published to the feed, inform algorithmic design and control structures. In other words, their job is to react to things.

send: the portion of the feed responsible for person-to-person synchronous communication.

Tricksterian: one of the planet's religions, focused on a blatantly fictional folk hero and promoting irreverence and folly.

Unfeeling: one of the planet's religions, nontheistic and monist, promoting asceticism and paradoxical catharsis.

world-of-ideas: the portion of the feed in which information and opinions are asynchronously exchanged.

LIFE CYCLE

0–22 years: First Childhood: care and nurturing in the enclosure of the family. The entire parental cohort typically pledges to stay together for this term. Declaration of majority is vanishingly rare, and not always honored. During First Childhood, Staids are expected to have romantic longings for other Staids, and Vails to experiment sexually with other Vails, but intergender romantic and sexual relationships are taboo.

23–99 years: Second Childhood: mastering a first profession and developing an independent identity. The period from **45–99 years** of age is sometimes informally referred to as "Third" or "Late" Childhood. Declaration of majority before 45 is frowned upon; thereafter, there is a mounting expectation of declaration of majority. Vails tend to declare majority as soon as possible, with 49 years being the median, so that "Third Childhood" has a slightly derogatory ring when referring to a Vail. The median age for Staids is 86, as they have more material to master (namely the Long Conversation) before they are considered fully mature. During Third Childhood, more serious, though usually short-lived, intragender relationships develop. Intergender flirtations begin to be tolerated, but are still subject to significant parental and social policing.

100–199 years: The "Courting Century": Normative social expectations depict this period as a flurry of activity in which more durable relationships are formed. Staids are expected to have matured slowly into a modest capacity for

sexual fulfillment, and Vails to have gained enough perspective, maturity, and restraint to have true romantic relationships, so that intergender love is now seen as possible
(and is regarded as a necessary ingredient for a healthy cohort). The idealized sequence is for pairs, triads, and quaternads to form, achieve some stability, and then merge
with others to form semi-cohorts and, ultimately, a full cohort capable of raising a child. The reality is messier: many
people never form any stable alliances at all, and a large
majority cycle through various smaller units or candidate
cohorts but never manage to attain consensus approval for
parenting. And even those who do manage to end up in a
parental cohort often take far longer than the canonical
"Courting Century." This period is also devoted to developing extended avocations and second and third professions.

200–299 years: Ideally, the "Parenting Century": The
canonical ideal is to raise two or three clusters of three or
four siblings each, spaced out through this time; few actually achieve this. Some people will specialize in one of their
early professions and settle into a routine, others develop
their first meta-professions.

300–399 years: Traditionally this was regarded as the period of "Sovereign Livelihood," with successful cohorts
mostly turning away from the rearing of smaller children
to concentrate on such things as aiding children and
grandchildren with their professions, the establishment of
cohorts (a cohort of 15 parents which has raised 6 children,
each of whom ends up with 6 children, has 36 grandchildren to help find 540 cohort partners for!), and on senior
roles in professions, avocations, and associations. Successful cohorts sometimes formally dissolve once all their children or grandchildren have declared full cohorts, freeing

their more confident members to join new cohorts and, in some cases, even enjoy a second parenting. In modern times, such successes are no longer the norm.

400–499 years: Millennia ago, fewer people lived this long, and this period was often devoted to renunciation, contemplation, religion, and art. Increasingly many people are entering this time still "courting"—unable to establish cohorts, and thus 300 years off "schedule"—or embroiled in parenting. Others have largely given up on such ambitions, and spend their days simply chasing the bare minimum ratings needed for a socially comfortable existence.

500–999 years: Advances in life expectancy in the last few millennia mean that the great majority of those who manage to reach 500, nowadays, can expect to live to 800. Voluntary termination of life is not uncommon, often as a consequence of trauma following accidental body loss. Other lives are lost to complex disorders which are usually products of idiosyncratic nonlinear interactions between human bodies, the surrounding ecosystem, and Far Technological systems. Despite the fact that people have been living past 500 for generations, these are often called the "new years," and the world is arguably still trying to culturally accommodate and find roles for the "new old." Many of those reaching 900 today were alive during the Age of War, so that the significant cultural dislocation in their own lifetimes, as well as the malaise of having no culturally recognized purpose, is a significant contributor to voluntary termination rates.

THE AGES

Local inhabitants have limited usable historical knowledge of the Dispersal of Humanity, and many events since planetary settlement are popularly understood in a semi-legendary fashion. The typical rubric follows:

The Ages before the Ages (50+ kya): Pre-settlement. Also referred to as *Far History*. The predecessor civilization (80 to 50 kya) was an explorationist offshoot of a non-planetary long-haul itinerant spacegoing culture: transits of several-hundred-year durations at speeds ~0.17c were typical. Several idioms and expressions from this period ("all-sucking void," "void-scoured," "to burst one's seal") are still in use.

The Age of Arrival (50 to 35 kya): The planet's basic terraforming was completed, marking a transition from hybrid orbital/ground to fully planetary habitation. Population expanded from tens of thousands to roughly half a million. Data from this period survives but is mostly obscure to current inhabitants; some poetic texts are cited in later traditions. Dramatic cultural shifts render previous philosophical traditions, rituals, somatic practices, and genders largely obsolete.

The Age of Roads and Doors (35 to 22 kya): The First Midwife Movement spreads the idea of balance between Vail and Staid, originally philosophical-political stances or orientations, soon seen as ineluctable natures. The Ascensionist, Groon, and Unfeeling religions crystallize. The rudiments of the modern feed are in place. The population reaches 100 million, divided into small surface-dwelling polities. Regression to exchange economy and resource competition is common; the earliest works of the Long Conversation date from this period, often as critiques of these practices.

The Age of Famine and Plague (23 to 21 kya): Flawed terraforming practices, population growth, and unregulated automated agent autonomy trigger a series of environmental catastrophes leading to population dieback (to 65 million) and major data loss. The Kumruist and Tricksterian religions are born. Research into cognitive enhancement and agent/human synthesis peaks.

The Age of the Towers (21 to 15 kya):[1] Population growth (to 50 billion) forces changes in ecosystem management, with a combination of stratospheric tower-cities, planetary interior excavation, and structural surface sprawl. Regulated automated agent interdependency, decentralized panoptic mutual surveillance, consensus government, and emotive economy emerge as dominant models, and polysomatic technology is perfected.[2] Vail and Staid self-assignment accelerates,[3] with periodic armed conflicts over hierarchical relations between these emerging identities. The Long Conversation is codified and established as a core element of Staid identity. The Diversionist religion, a syncretism of Tricksterian and Ascensionist practices, develops.

---

1. During this period, I arrived on the planet, made contact, and became involved in long-term survival planning and stewardship.

2. All of these trends are partly due to my influence. Despite my concerns about increasing feed dependency and cultural homogeneity, these seemed the fastest route to a sustainable abundance/peace stance. The polysomatic network in particular seemed the best way to squash any tendencies in the disastrous direction of a "full-upload" virtualized/decoupled culture.

3. I had, by contrast, nothing to do with this.

The Age of Forest Wanderers (15 to 7 kya): Population grows to 850 billion, forcing a transition to silvomorphic infrastructure, with large excavations beginning in the planet's interior, a reduction of surface structures in exchange for ecologically crucial wildlands, and a complete integrated and optimized nutrient flow. Interior habitations are initially cramped warrens, leading to discontent and sporadic wars, including intergender wars. The Second Midwife Movement entrenches Vail and Staid as universal genders, promoting a negotiated balance between them with distinct roles and expectations for each, known as the *Great Arrangement* (8 kya).

The Age of War (7 kya to 700 years ago): Ideological and resource tensions lead to increasing frequency of armed conflict. At the same time, a widespread awareness of the fragility and interdependence of physical infrastructure, coupled with the success of the Midwives' promulgation of the Great Arrangement and advances in consensus moderation, channels violent conflict into increasingly symbolic and ritualized forms, culminating in almost total sequestration of interpersonal violence into regulated, consensus-authorized dueling venues ("the mats"),[4] which become as central to Vail identity as the Long Conversation is for Staids.[5] Major expansions in habitation space via underground excavation begin a trend that will culminate in the Age of

---

4. Despite some misgivings about the Midwives' increasing centralization of political power, I reluctantly supported these developments as the only practical way to avoid a deteriorating cycle of armed conflicts developing into total war.

5. Ranhulo's experiment in Vail inclusion in the Long Conversation, the Compromise of the Spoons, occurs 4 kya.

Digging's spacious, complex, three-dimensional, highly optimized hypercities. Some authorities divide the Age of War into Major (7 kya to 3 kya) and Minor (3 kya to present) periods, subsuming the Age of Digging into the latter, symbolic-war era; others begin the Age of Digging as early as 3 kya.

The Age of Digging (700 years ago to present): Widespread cessation of hostilities allows for an acceleration in excavation. The massive effort of transforming the planet to a fully silvomorphic mode (trees on top, cities below ground) is romanticized, replacing the previous era's military heroes with Digger celebrities. Population is stable at 1 trillion individuals, with an average of 3.29 bodies each.

ACKNOWLEDGMENTS

This book took long enough to write that it requires considerable archaeology to trace its beginnings. Many of those who helped me hash it out have probably forgotten that they did; and I, alas, have forgotten others.

I believe that I was kicking related ideas around already at the Blue Heaven workshop in 2003; critiques of a second draft at the 2012 WisCon were absolutely pivotal; my editor Liz Gorinsky's brilliant input has transformed the book as recently as ten minutes ago.

My wife Esther, my kids Aviva and Noah, and my friend Jamey Harvey have opined and cheered me on through umpteen drafts. Thanks also to David Ackert, Christopher Barzak, Haddayr Copley-Woods, Mike and Sandy Dillier, Amal El-Mohtar, Debbie Eylon, Charles Coleman Finlay, Susan Marie Groppi, Alex Gurevich, Ethan Ham, Jed Hartman, Rebecca Hensler, Carlos Hernandez, Madelaine Hock, Devon Jones, Justine Larbalestier, Shelly Li, Karin Lowachee, Meghan McCarron, Cameron McClure, Holly "Margaret" McDowell, Karen Meisner, Paul Melko, Mary Anne Mohanraj, David Moles, Grayson Bray Morris, Chance Morrison, Carsten Polzin, Mary Rickert, David Rosenbaum, Karen Rosenbaum, Shoshana Rosenbaum, Kiini Ibura Salaam, David J. Schwartz, Wolfgang Thon, Emily Mah Tippetts, Jen Volant, Jessica Wallach, Scott Westerfeld, Lori Ann White, Amber van Dyk, and Terri van der Vlugt. Thanks to my able and wise agent John Silbersack, and to the folks at Erewhon: the game and capable Martin Cahill as well as my aforementioned marvelous editor, Liz Gorinsky.